LOST SOULS OF LENINGRAD

A Novel

Suzanne Parry

SHE WRITES PRESS

Published 2022
Printed in the United States of America
Print ISBN: 978-1-64742-267-7
E-ISBN: 978-1-64742-268-4
Library of Congress Control Number: 2022906046

For information, address:
She Writes Press
1569 Solano Ave #546
Berkeley, CA 94707

She Writes Press is a division of SparkPoint Studio, LLC.

To my parents, Loraine Lefrançois Baxter and
E.R. Baxter III.

And for Leningrad's *blokadniki*.

AUTHOR'S NOTE

A LOT HAS BEEN written about World War II, but comparatively little about the Soviet Union and its wartime ordeals. When I was in high school and university, a rather narrow perspective of the Second World War was taught. In general, the Eastern Front did not get much emphasis. Decades later, my children learned a somewhat broader history. If there is any one reason why I have written this book, it is to illuminate the Soviet experience.

My semester as a college student in Moscow during the Cold War (perhaps now considered the First Cold War), and my subsequent work for the US Department of Defense as an arms control negotiator in the 1980s, allowed me to interact with Soviet citizens, Soviet diplomats, and Soviet military personnel. This story has its foundation in those experiences.

The protagonists of this novel are fictional characters wrapped around actual events. A few historical figures appear briefly in the story: Commissar of the Navy, Nikolai G. Kuznetsov; head of the NKVD, Lavrenti P. Beria; Leningrad Philharmonic Orchestra conductor, Yevgeny A. Mravinsky; Radio Committee Orchestra director, Karl I. Eliasberg; and journalist/poet, Olga F. Berggolts. Their words and actions sometimes adhere closely to the historical record, but I have taken plenty of liberties to further the story.

The main events in the novel are a matter of historical fact. Nazi Germany attacked the Soviet Union in the early morning of June 22, 1941. In eleven weeks, Leningrad was surrounded and cut off from the rest of the country. There were close to three million civilians in the city when the Germans pulled the noose tight.

The bombings of the Badayev food warehouses, Gostiny Dvor, and Finland Station are all a matter of record as is the evacuation disaster in Lychkovo.

The naval retreat from Tallinn in late August 1941 was calamitous for the Soviet Baltic Fleet with over 13,000 casualties. By contrast, in the better-known Dunkirk evacuation of 1940, 3,500 British forces lost their lives (although much larger numbers were captured).

During the winter of 1941–42, almost no food was available to average citizens in Leningrad. The daily bread ration fell to 125 grams for dependents, under four and a half ounces.

The Ice Road—the Road of Life—was the Soviet Government's attempt to save the city once all land routes were blockaded.

In the spring of 1942, the authorities cajoled thousands of emaciated citizens, mostly women, to clean the city.

Composer Dimitri Shostakovich's Seventh Symphony, the Leningrad Symphony, was performed in Leningrad on August 9, 1942, by the Radio Committee Orchestra to significant acclaim.

The Siege of Leningrad lasted from September 8, 1941 until January 27, 1944. The precise number of civilian deaths will never be known. Estimates range from the original official Soviet number (632,253) to the more accurate but still approximate figure of one million. The vast majority of deaths occurred during the first year, in what is often referred to as the starvation winter of 1941–42. After that time, resupply efforts proved sufficient for the remaining, much diminished, population.

Leningrad was just one corner of the Soviet Union devastated by World War II, the Great Patriotic War as it is known in Russia. The statistics defy comprehension: nine million Soviet soldiers and nineteen million Soviet civilians died. This novel is my earnest and heartfelt effort to draw attention to the Soviet experience and to honor the story of Leningrad and her citizens.

Although it is not a story of Stalin, the brutality, lack of regard for life, and absence of human rights that characterized his years in power demand our revulsion and opposition. The ongoing fight by the Russian leadership against values we hold dear—truth, freedom, justice, and human rights—should remind us all that however imperfect our pursuit of those values, it is far better than the authoritarian alternative.

March 2022, Washington, DC

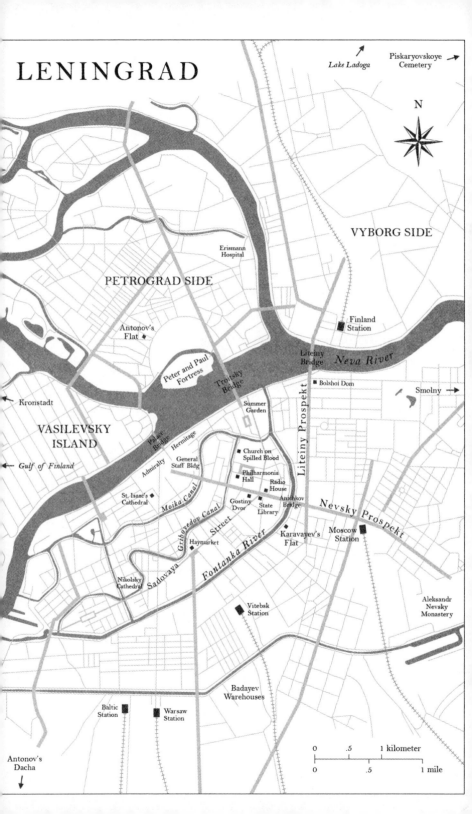

THE KNOCK AT THE DOOR
January 1941

A LONG THE BROAD, late-night avenues of central Leningrad, the last of the concert-goers hurried home ahead of curfew. They hastened down side streets and darted into courtyards, while Sofya leaned against the wall of the artists' entrance inside Philharmonia Hall. She pulled on her boots as her comrades finished sharing a cigarette and some gossip with the guard.

By the time the three musicians made their way up Nevsky Prospekt to Sadovaya Street, the roads and sidewalks were deserted. Indistinct halos around the streetlights cast a reluctant glow. Collars up against the snow, her much younger colleagues turned off together, leaving Sofya to walk alone through the once elegant city. She touched a pocket, checking for her *propusk*, the pass which allowed her to be out after curfew.

Every shadow and every breath of wind reminded her that the city was a playground for the secret police. When he was alive, Andrei often met her after evening performances. Carrying her violin case in one hand and holding her arm with the other, he made her feel safe, even as the city turned on itself. When the arrests started, no one thought it would happen to them. They'd done nothing wrong. But then friends and acquaintances disappeared, people who also hadn't done anything wrong. Stalin and his subordinates found fault with all manner of innocent citizens and benign circumstances. Soon old grudges and petty darknesses oozed out of apartments and work-places. Neighbors spoke against neighbors. Once defined by music, literature, and majestic architecture, a vibrant city where people thought, and thought out loud, Leningrad had become a drab version of its former self—little more than a tarnished tomb holding a body without a breath. Not unlike its namesake on eternal display in Moscow's Red Square.

Two shadowy figures loomed ahead on the Anichkov Bridge. As she drew closer the burly policemen blocked the sidewalk, bears stalking a defenseless elk calf.

"What are you doing out at such an hour? It's past curfew. Where are your papers?"

A gust of wind whistled as they snarled and snapped. Sofya's heart raced even though her paperwork was in order and she'd done nothing wrong. Why, it wasn't even past curfew. Still, doing everything by the book didn't mean she couldn't be arrested. She tried to hide the trembling in her hand as she extended the pass which allowed her to be out between midnight and five in the morning. "I'm with the Leningrad Philharmonic. We just finished a performance and I'm on my way home."

A third officer wandered up and Sofya recognized him from the neighborhood around the concert hall. She struggled to recall his name, certain they'd spoken before.

"What's going on here? Why are you delaying Comrade Karavayeva? Can't you see she's a musician?" He pointed to her violin case. "Her papers are in order. She walks this route all the time. She lives right there." He gestured at the street running along the Fontanka River.

Desperate to retrieve the officer's name, Sofya searched for the memory of their introduction. On the way to rehearsal? After a concert?

He stepped toward her. "How was the performance tonight, Comrade Karavayeva?"

"Thank you, Comrade, Comrade Volkov," she replied, his name

popping forth. "The audience especially enjoyed the Romeo and Juliet Overture."

"*Konechno*. Of course." His face softened. "Everyone likes Tchaikovsky."

"*Pravilno*. That's right. Always a favorite." She smiled. He appreciated music. She thanked Officer Volkov as he returned her papers, wished him a good night and turned for home.

With her first steps away from the bridge, Sofya heard the men exchange a few words followed by laughter. She hugged the violin case to her chest and walked with restraint, not wanting to draw more attention. What good were rules if there was no protection in obeying them?

Sofya shivered, her heart still racing, as she slipped through the street entrance of Fontanka Embankment 54. They should be ashamed—badgering a woman my age. Even the secret police must have better things to do than bother a hard-working, law-abiding *babushka*. She shuddered again from the chill reminder that life in the Soviet Union could always get worse.

The courtyard's archways and angles loomed, familiar but unsettling. The Karavayevs had moved into the building decades earlier when it was new, captivated by its architecture and lured by the convenient location on the edge of central St. Petersburg. After the revolution, when the Communists were eager to equalize living standards, most city apartments were consolidated. Complete strangers soon shared single-family dwellings. Communal living meant curtained corners, sleeping mats in hallways, and a single bathroom for a dozen or more people. At first, Sofya guessed her brother's unique history protected them from the indignities of shared housing, but after he died and her professional status grew, she wondered if their apartment was perhaps an unspoken privilege, a reward for her years with the Philharmonic. Regardless, she lived in constant fear of the municipal housing authorities.

Creeping into the apartment so as not to disturb her son and daughter-in-law, she hung her coat and tucked her violin into a corner, then followed the hall to the bedroom she shared with her granddaughter. Just enough light filtered through the two windows to cast a faint glow on Yelena's sleeping form, buried under blankets. Sofya tip-toed about the room, more out of habit than any real concern about waking the sound asleep teenager. She slipped on nightclothes, picked up a book, and padded into the tidy kitchen.

The small samovar stood alone on the table. Every time she had a late performance, her son made sure it was hot before he went to bed. After drawing her tea, she settled in the living room, snuggling into the sofa's familiar contours. Sofya savored this hour before bed, reading or reviewing the evening's performance, surrounded by intense quiet with everyone asleep.

She opened Pushkin's *Dubrovsky,* a tale of injustice and lost love. Quickly engrossed, the unexpected sound of heavy footfalls and loud male voices startled her. Sofya knew who it was, what it was. Plenty of people had already vanished over the last several years. Intellectuals, artists, life-long Bolsheviks, even military officers by the thousands. After the incident on the way home, she guessed they were coming for her, a suspicion that knotted her insides.

The book slipped from her lap as she stood. A desperate whispered prayer, "God protect us," escaped her lips as she pulled the belt on her dressing gown tight. Her pulse quickened and she slid toward the entry, ears alert.

The booming steps grew louder as the men thudded down the hall toward her. For a moment there was nothing but silence. Sofya held her breath. Heart hammering, she inched toward the door and strained to listen.

A fist banged hard and repeatedly. Sofya jumped, even though she was expecting it. She hesitated, but when the fist roared again, she leaned forward and reached for the doorknob.

They filled the entryway, pushing past her, smelling of stale cigarette smoke and alcohol. The frightened apartment manager followed, clutching her keys in case no one opened the door. She did double-duty as the civilian witness. A despicable role in this circus. Sofya pitied her.

"We're here for Major Aleksandr Karavayev. Where is he?" Without waiting for her answer, two of the agents thundered toward the back of the apartment.

At her son's name, Sofya froze. There had to be a mistake. Unable to make sense of what she'd heard, she willed herself after the intruders.

Squinting in the light, Aleksandr appeared in the hallway as the agents approached.

"I'm Major Karavayev."

The two thickset men flanked him. A third, smallish officer, narrow-faced and sharp-nosed with eyes like dark pinholes, approached the trio.

"Aleksandr Andreiivich Karavayev. You are under arrest. Get dressed and bring your identification papers."

Fear and confusion rose in Aleksandr's countenance. He and his wife, Katya, exchanged a look and she shrank into the shadows. He disappeared down the hall, escorted by the two thugs. A moment later Yelena stumbled out of the bedroom.

"Papa? Mama?"

Sofya stepped forward and pulled her close, shielding her, while silent Katya clutched the neck of her nightgown and edged toward them.

The rat-faced man walked from room to room like the master of the house. He pulled the drawers out of the mahogany secretary, dumping the contents on the floor but not examining what was there. Out of the corner of her eye Sofya watched him finger Lenin's *What Is To Be Done?* then carefully return the book to its place of esteem.

Next, he went into her bedroom. She heard the fearful thumps of volumes hitting the floor and steadied herself, wondering if he would find what was behind the bookcase. Instead, he came out as quickly as he went in. It was all part of the routine, frightening people, conducting arrests when families were asleep and vulnerable.

"What's happening, *Babusya*?"

She held her granddaughter, but couldn't form a reply. Aleksandr came out in his uniform, buttoning the jacket. Service medals and campaign ribbons flashed across the left chest. He handed his papers to the rat-faced man. Yelena latched onto her father. He kissed the top of her head whispering "I love you" as he pried her arms away. Sofya pulled Yelena close as she cried out, "No! Not Papa." Aleksandr grabbed his heavy military greatcoat off the hook as they propelled him out the door. There were no explanations, no last words, only a stunned and desperate look on her dear Sasha's face. One moment Sofya had a son; the next, he was gone. It was over in the space of a few hundred heartbeats.

BETRAYAL

February 1941

THE *BOLSHOI DOM*, the Big House, as the headquarters of the secret police was known to locals, could have been any other government building except for the line of women winding down the street and around the block. That symbol of suffering lengthened as the arrests grew, stretching like a gigantic, slow-moving centipede.

Sofya now joined the queue. As much as her schedule allowed, she waited in the cold, hoping for news of Aleksandr. Sweet Yelena wanted to help, arguing she could hold a place in line, but Sofya wouldn't allow her granddaughter anywhere near the prison. Meanwhile, Katya was her typical enigmatic self.

"You know I can't do that," Katya said. "My position is precarious now."

"But what about Sasha?" Sofya tried to avoid the issue of loyalty to the State.

"Aleksandr is important, of course," Katya said. "But nothing will come of waiting at the Big House. We won't see him unless he's released. So why risk aggravating the authorities? Why risk ourselves and Yelena?"

It was true that supporting Aleksandr could make things worse, but Katya's fatalism frustrated Sofya. There were more important things than always protecting oneself. Like standing up for family. Standing up for what was right. Besides, no matter what Katya might think, no matter how special she might believe she was, no one was beyond Stalin's reach. Plenty of Party faithful had disappeared.

❧

On a day that began like any other in the late winter of Sasha's arrest, Sofya reached the front of the line at the *Bolshoi Dom*. After so many days of waiting she'd almost given up hope. Her heart pounded as she climbed the steps and approached reception.

"Karavayeva, Sofya Nikolayevna. I'm here to inquire about my son, Major Aleksandr Andreiivich Karavayev." She forced her voice to remain neutral, almost pleasant, like she was asking for two hundred grams of cheese at the store.

The officer seated behind the desk looked right through her. "No one here by that name."

"I was told he's been here since his arrest in January." She'd done her homework, already taken risks by petitioning certain authorities. Careful to stay respectful, she reached inside her bag and pulled out a small bundle wrapped in newspaper. As she set it on the desk, the paper fell open to reveal a pair of socks and a small, homemade loaf of dark bread. A piece of string held the socks on top like a sad, floppy bow.

"May I leave this for him?"

The officer shrugged, his lack of emotion adding to the bleakness of the place.

She started to ask if she could see Aleksandr, but lost her nerve when another officer picked up the package and put his nose to the bread, sniffing appreciatively. She stiffened, but before she said something she'd regret, a third agent approached with a handful of papers. The senior officer scanned the documents, pulled one out and slid it across the desk to Sofya.

"According to this, former person Karavayev is no longer a guest of the NKVD." Sofya saw disgust in his eyes. To him she had no rights, deserved nothing. "And you no longer have any reason to be here," he added, dismissing her with the flick of a hand.

She glanced at the paper then stuffed it in a pocket. A "tenner."

Ten years in a labor camp. A common enough sentence for someone who wasn't guilty of anything. As she clutched at the rail and stumbled down the steps, she knew their lives had taken a terrible turn. Should Aleksandr even survive, he would never again hold a decent job. His army career was over. He'd probably never live in Leningrad again, but be forced to move to some far-flung community after serving out his sentence.

Once out of sight of the prison, she read the paper carefully and her heart jumped. Stamped at the bottom were the golden words, "Right to correspondence." Everyone knew that "Without the right to correspondence" almost certainly meant your loved one had been shot. The camp number and address was far from Leningrad, but not far like Kolyma, at the other end of the world. The gold mining camps there were rumored to be the worst. Still, they could just as well work him to death in a lumber camp.

As her legs carried her through the city, she brushed away a few tears. No sense in letting self-pity take control; life was hard for everyone. She wasn't the first to have a son taken by the secret police. In many ways she was fortunate. Raised in a privileged family and gifted in music, she'd been blessed with parents who sacrificed to make her career a reality. When the Revolution came, her brother had protected them. And even though she hadn't been lucky in love, she'd built a good marriage. No, she couldn't complain. She detested what her country had become, but she'd been luckier than most.

That evening, she searched for an appropriate moment to tell Yelena that the faint hope of her papa's release had vanished. As the minutes ticked past, she knew there would never be a good time to share such awful news. Her dear Lenochka missed him so much. The way he'd help with difficult school assignments. His gentle reminders that it was more important to be hard-working and smart than beautiful, even though Yelena was all three.

After dinner, Sofya scooted her chair close as her granddaughter did homework. Yelena had become even more diligent with her papa gone.

"Lenochka, there was news today." Sofya kept her voice from trembling, but her eyes filled and she blinked to bring her granddaughter back into focus.

"Not Papa?" The teen suddenly straightened and looked up. "What's happened?"

"It's not that," Sofya patted her granddaughter's arm. "Papa's alive, but they've sent him away," she continued, wiping her tears and sniffing. "A labor camp—ten years."

Yelena put her arms and head down on the table, hair cascading over her shoulders. Sofya stroked the yellow strands and leaned against her.

Yelena's muffled voice came up out of the tangle of arms and hair. "Are you and Mama going to be arrested too?" She lifted her head, chin quivering, face pallid.

Everyone knew it worked that way. Family members were often next. Katya—now the spouse of an 'enemy of the people'—would probably be first. But Sofya was at risk too, despite her family history. Oh, God, they could even take Yelena. Fifteen wasn't too young to disappear into the maws of the *Bolshoi Dom*. Fear started to crush her and she stifled a cry. There were hideous rumors about what happened to beautiful young women at the hands of the secret police.

Sofya pushed the thought away and tried to act self-assured. "It was an anonymous accusation. And remember, your great-uncle was part of the cause." Sofya didn't want to think her brother's years with Lenin might not matter anymore. A flood of stalwart Bolsheviks had been swallowed by the system—Bukharin, Tukhachevsky, even Leningrad's own Sergei Kirov.

"I miss Papa so much. It already seems like he's been gone forever. Ten years? I'll be grown in half that time."

The harsh reality, the permanence of Sasha's absence, gripped Sofya. Would she even live long enough to see him again?

She handed her granddaughter a hanky. "Just think about how much you love him and how much he loves you. No one can take that away. Your papa wants us to remain strong and hopeful. No matter what."

The apartment door opened and Katya came into the kitchen looking for dinner. After Aleksandr's arrest, she increased her time on the radio crew, believing hours translated to devotion. Her job with the Radio Committee had her going door to door, confiscating private radios and installing receivers so the Party could control what the people heard. Radio Leningrad and government newspapers were the only sources of information. The ubiquitous *tarelka*, a plate-like radio receiver, sat in the corner of their living room.

Katya poked around for dinner, looking in the pots Sofya had kept warm. She stopped and turned, examining their tear-stained faces and subdued expressions.

"What's going on?" Katya asked. "Did something happen?"

"Sasha has been sent to a labor camp," Sofya said. "Ten years."

"He was found guilty then." Katya uttered the unthinkable.

Yelena narrowed her eyes at her mother. Sofya bristled.

"Innocent people are found guilty every day," Sofya snapped. "Why can't you admit the truth? Sasha is no more an 'enemy of the people' than you or I. He's innocent. You know that."

"I understand," said Katya. "But do any of us really know the truth? Innocence to one may be guilt to another." Her arrogant tone grated.

"The truth is the truth. And you know Aleksandr. You know your family."

"Yes, but I know the Party too." Katya hurried out of the kitchen. Sofya followed and pushed her way into the bedroom, cornering her retreating daughter-in-law.

"What did you do?" Sofya hissed. "Maybe you've fooled Yelena. Not me."

Katya didn't respond. She twisted her plain wedding band round and round.

"He loves you. You destroyed our family, *your* family." Sofya's chest tightened.

"I didn't mean for this to happen." Katya spluttered and sank onto the bed. "He became distant." Her words burbled out between sobs. "The war with Finland last winter changed him somehow. I made a comment in front of colleagues."

All the air in the room rushed out. Sofya steadied herself against a wall. The Winter War had been hard on Aleksandr. A military embarrassment. Since then, he had kept to himself more, maybe been a bit withdrawn. But that had nothing to do with loyalty.

"His whole life has been devotion," she said. "Loving his family, serving his country, supporting the Party. How could you suggest such a thing?"

"I'm sorry." Katya made a pitiful, wounded sound. "It was an accident. Please don't tell Yelena."

Sofya wanted to lash out, to punish her. Instead, without a word, she reached for the doorknob. Gulping the cool air in the hall, she slipped into the bathroom and filled the sink with water. She splashed it on her cheeks, then held her hair back and plunged her face in. After drying off she glared at herself in the mirror.

The first time she met her soon-to-be daughter-in-law, Katya greeted her as *Tovarishch*. Comrade. The revolutionary term had become commonplace, spreading with the Bolshevik push for a classless society that Sofya thought was genuine, at least in the beginning. But neither the word, nor the equality it sought to encourage, was ever personal. Rather than make everyone equal, it kept everyone at arm's length. The Karavayevs never used the term with family or close friends.

That first evening, tall, golden-haired Katya strolled about the apartment with the imperious air of one secure in belief. Aleksandr, captivated and adoring, didn't recognize her unhealthy devotion to the new socialist system and the Communist Party. He pulled Katya close while she hovered over the family's few treasures displayed in the dark, polished secretary. Sofya and Andrei both noticed her flash of excitement when Aleksandr showed her the personalized copy of *What Is To Be Done?*

Katya turned and looked out a window, quoting Lenin, *"This is the road to a World Revolution."* She sounded like a schoolgirl reciting lessons. *"When there is a state there can be no freedom, but when there is freedom there will be no state."* Sofya held her tongue, recalling another Lenin assertion. *"A lie told often enough becomes the truth."*

In those days, there were varying degrees of support for the new communist experiment. The Karavayevs believed in the Bolsheviks—Andrei had fought for the Reds—but that belief was colored by history and tempered by reality.

Some citizens possessed devotion so blind that they overlooked the new leadership's cruelty. Others seemed unwilling to think for themselves. And yet another group was motivated by greed and ambition. Their support for the Communists was a ladder to the top, or at least an insurance policy. Sofya had never quite figured out to which group Katya belonged.

In the early years of Aleksandr and Katya's marriage, this didn't matter. Nor did the fact that Sofya wasn't fond of her daughter-in-law. The young couple lived across town with Katya's parents and the distance bred contentment, if not affection. Everything changed one winter when Katya's parents fell victim to a virulent influenza. Before the shock wore off, the Party took away their apartment, and Aleksandr and Katya moved in with Sofya and Andrei. At first Andrei provided a calm balance to the combined household, but since his death Katya's behavior had gone increasingly unchecked and unchallenged.

Now, with Sasha in prison, there was no control over the steady drip, drip, drip of Katya's criticism. Sofya's books were a favorite target. Katya liked to say that books were an indulgence for the intelligentsia and personal collections shouldn't exist in a classless society. She didn't even know about Sofya's hidden volumes.

Long before Katya entered their lives, when Sofya's books outgrew their shelves of raw wood and bricks, Andrei constructed an elaborate bookcase. Floor to ceiling, slightly recessed, it filled an interior wall in the large bedroom. The dark, polished wood held Sofya's escape from the ever-tightening constraints of reality. Andrei hadn't built the library just for his wife. A private man, not a trusting one, he constructed the bookcase with a phony back that gave access to storage within the wall. When two removable shelves were taken out and the spring hinge pressed, the false back panel would pop open. He lined the space with cedar to keep bugs and rodents away, and over the years they'd used it to store everything from valuables to woolens.

No one but he and Sofya, not even Aleksandr, knew of the hiding place and shortly after the Revolution, Sofya began concealing those of her books deemed unacceptable by the new Soviet government. By the time Katya and Aleksandr moved in, there were no controversial volumes displayed. Still, that didn't stop her daughter-in-law from harping on Sofya's passions and predilections—music and literature—as symbols of the intelligentsia.

Sofya smoothed her hair before leaving the bathroom. She didn't understand Katya any better now than when she first entered their lives. Katya worked for the Party and knew what was going on: neighbors informing on neighbors, betrayals just to pay back some perceived slight or small offense. She had always been self-centered and naive.

A dark thought appeared. What if the betrayal was intentional? Sofya shook the idea free.

Katya might be reckless, but she wasn't evil.

When Sofya entered the kitchen, Yelena turned from the sink. "You and Mama arguing again?" Sofya knew their sharp words were difficult for the teen. Yelena loved them both. As much as Sofya wanted to defend herself and tell Yelena the truth about what her mother had done, she couldn't bear to hurt her granddaughter that way.

Instead, chastened by the look on Yelena's face, she said, "I'm sorry we don't get along."

"I know Mama's different," Yelena shrugged. "She says lots of things that don't make sense. I mean, how could the Party possibly know more about Papa than we do?" She returned to the last of the dishes. "Mama sees the world differently. Doesn't mean she's right, but it seems like she never lives up to your expectations." Yelena sniffed and added. "You always say family is everything.

THE PHILHARMONIC
March 1941

AT PHILHARMONIA HALL, the last of the applause faded and Sofya gathered her music. The muted sounds of people exiting the auditorium blended with the murmuring of her colleagues. Other post-performance noises began to swirl: stagehands moving chairs and equipment, workers on the catwalks above. When she looked up, Yevgeny Mravinsky, the conductor of the Leningrad Philharmonic Orchestra, loomed over her.

"Comrade, come to my office when you've finished."

She nodded. "Of course. I'll be right there."

She gripped her music so tightly the pages began to tremble. Ever since Katya lost her job and Party membership, Sofya feared she would be next. And although she didn't value her Party card and its privileges the way her daughter-in-law did, she might also end up with an obscure factory job. Or worse.

Walking to Mravinsky's office, she clutched her violin and bow, her life. She knocked and entered at his invitation. He avoided her eyes, gazing at the ground between them. A handsome man, despite the receding hairline that aged him. His sober demeanor also made him seem older than thirty-seven. The same age as her Sasha.

"There's no easy way to say this," he began, finally looking at her. "Today was your last performance with the Philharmonic. Tomorrow you are to report to the Radio Committee Orchestra. Director Eliasberg is expecting you."

Sofya stared at Mravinsky, a bit unsure of what she'd heard. The

RadioCom was Leningrad's second-tier orchestra. Could it be she still had a profession and a livelihood?

The conductor lowered his voice. "And I imagine he's thrilled to be getting you, a musician of your caliber."

One of the most accomplished members of the Philharmonic, Sofya had held a first violin chair for many years, the lone woman in such an elevated position. She had no dreams of promotion beyond that; music was emphatically a man's world. Instead, she developed a talent for suppressing the resentment that flared whenever less-experienced male colleagues were promoted.

Now however, to be able to play was all she wanted. She nodded at Mravinsky, stunned and grateful, controlling the impulse to thank him even though he'd just let her go.

As she turned to leave, he added, "You've served the city and this orchestra well."

"Thank you." She took a breath and collected herself. "I'll do my best to maintain a tradition of excellence."

A smile played at the corners of his mouth and he raised his chin. "I have no doubt."

Sofya closed the door and leaned against the wall, letting out a huge sigh. A simple demotion. Her dear brother had reached out from the grave after all. Even if he couldn't save Aleksandr, he'd protected her. Awash with relief, she threaded her way to the dressing room, the knot in her stomach loosening with every step.

Quiet enveloped the hallways now, but a few people still wandered about the wardrobe rooms and equipment storage areas. At the far end of the hall, the percussionists wrestled with their ungainly instruments. When she turned the corner to the women's dressing room, she bumped into a man standing by the door.

"*Izvinite pozhaluysta.* Pardon me, please." She stepped back.

"Sofya. Sofya Nikolayevna."

She froze at the familiar voice, then let it fill her like the intoxicating notes of a favorite symphony. She looked past the gold braid on his sleeves to study his face, aged in a way that suited him. His eyes held hers as if there had been no years of separation.

"Vasili." Her voice caught. "What a pleasant surprise. Is Anna here?" She looked around the hallway for his wife.

He shook his head. "She's doing poorly and can't be alone. Doctor says it's early senility. But her sister is visiting so I was able to have a few hours to myself."

Neither of them seemed to notice the bouquet in his hand.

"I'm so sorry. How terrible for you and the family." Her voice was warm and her words heartfelt. It was the only way she knew how to be with him. "Let me put these down." She nodded at her full hands and disappeared into the dressing room. They hadn't seen each other for ages—not since Andrei's funeral six years ago. And before that? So long she couldn't remember. She glanced in a mirror. Disheveled and sweating from the effort of the performance and her conversation with Mravinsky, she patted the beads of moisture on her face and smoothed the errant strands of hair before returning to the man who'd once meant everything to her.

"Terrible about Anna." She touched his arm in sympathy.

"Thank you," he said, covering her hand with his. Warmth radiated up her arm.

"It's been difficult. She's worsened rapidly. Doctor says only a few more months." He looked down and began to whisper. "I didn't come to talk about Anna though, but about Aleksandr. A horrible thing. When I heard, I swear I felt your grief."

So he knew Sasha had been arrested. She glimpsed her pain reflected in his doleful eyes.

He looked around and pulled her into a corner. "So many officers gone. There's an invisible net hanging over everyone, catching everything. Casual conversations, glances, even our thoughts seem to be overheard." His eyes darted down the hall again.

Overwhelmed by his concern, she pressed her lips together in a futile effort to maintain her composure. He drew out his handkerchief and wiped her tears with it—a gesture at once so intimate and so natural that more tears fell.

"If there's any comfort or support I can offer, you must call," he said, putting the piece of linen in her hand. "I can only imagine how difficult it is, bearing this alone, without Andrei."

She doubted he could imagine what it was like to see your son taken away, to have no help facing the bleak reality. Self-conscious about soiling the crisp square of fine cloth, she sniffed hard to stop her nose from running. Dabbing at her face, she inhaled his scent. Earthy, like leaves in autumn. She inched closer, letting her guard down as the past reared up. Did he suspect he was Sasha's father? Was that why he'd come?

The urge to confess welled up inside, a growing tightness in her chest. But instead of allowing the truth out, she swallowed repeatedly to keep it down and searched Vasili's face for any sign that he might know Aleksandr was his son. His expression showed nothing more than the friendly concern of an old friend.

"It's been . . . difficult," she said. "Unimaginable really. Yes, it would be easier if Andrei were here, but mostly I'm glad he's gone. Sasha's arrest would have destroyed him."

She paused a moment, but then continued. "And, if things weren't bad enough, I just came from Mravinsky's office." Confiding in Vasili felt so natural. "I've been demoted," she blurted out. "To the Radio Committee Orchestra."

"Oh, no. Sofi."

Her heart cracked open. Only family called her Sofi.

"There's nothing to be done," she said. "In fact, crazy as it seems, I'm grateful. To be able to play at all." She knew he understood how tenuous things were. She could be in prison herself right now. "And you being here is such a kindness. I've been discouraged, alone."

She had few friends, almost none since the arrests gained momentum. And even before Stalin took friendships and neighborliness away, her secret made her a loner. Afraid of getting too close lest someone notice Aleksandr bore little resemblance to Andrei, she kept to herself, devoted exclusively to her violin and her family.

"You aren't alone," he said, and his gaze assured her he meant it. "I'm sorry I can't stay longer. I must get back to Anna." He moved to go before remembering the flowers. "These are for you. It was wonderful to see you play, you're as brilliant as ever." One side of his mouth pulled up in a charming crooked grin she recalled.

"*Prekrasniye.* They're lovely. Thank you."

As Vasili disappeared, she clutched the flowers to her chest. It had been ages since someone had done something nice for her.

CONDOLENCES
April 1941

VASILI ANTONOV BURIED his wife on a Tuesday.
When Anna's mind first began its slow slide into oblivion, he pressed the doctors for help and consulted specialists, determined to find another outcome. Although good at generating solutions, in this he was helpless. Anna slipped away, bit by bit, month upon month, year after year. The senility diagnosis became a death sentence fulfilled.

Today he felt less sad than he expected. The doctor told him death can be a relief when someone you love is in a terrible way. Anna was no longer hurting, lost and in distress, but, despite the doctor's words, there was guilt too.

An hour before guests were scheduled to arrive, Vasili stood in the parlor, gazing at the portrait of Anna above the mantel. Gorgeous in a rich royal blue dress, she looked strangely commanding, not at all like her true self: a predictable, reserved woman who didn't ruffle easily or react strongly without serious provocation. She'd say the most obvious things about the most ordinary topics. Conversation for Anna consisted of simple observations—the rain was dreary or a friend's new dress lovely. Worst of all, she didn't read books.

Early on, Vasili tried to hide his disappointment at her lack of engagement. He winced, remembering the time he bought her a fine German Leica. She never used the camera, claiming it was too difficult to get the settings correct. Perhaps it was complicated, or perhaps her confusion was an early manifestation of what would eventually bury her mind. In any case, why had her gentle nature bothered him so? There were many good things. She was an excellent cook and an exemplary hostess. She was devoted to him and adored being a mother. When he was on deployment, especially during Maksim's childhood, she managed the household without him, often for months at a time. Why did it matter so much that they didn't share the same interests or temperament? She was capable in many ways that mattered.

On top of all that, she was striking: tall, with heavy auburn hair framing her flawless face. He was intensely attracted to her when they first met. Sparkling green eyes flecked with gold entranced. Full lips seduced. A body that begged for the pleasures of the bedroom. But when they were alone, the spark was just that. Not a flame, not a bonfire, certainly not a conflagration. Just a spark. Several years after Maksim, with no success at conceiving a second child, her disinterested nature extended to physical pleasures as well, and they stopped trying. Life became simpler and smaller with each passing year and Vasili found the calm and narrowness suffocating.

Forty years ago, she was the exquisite daughter of well-connected family friends. He was starting his naval career. It was the right time for marriage. His parents thought her elegance, manner, and good family a perfect fit. Of course, it was the idea of her that attracted both his parents and himself. The fact was Vasili had little idea what he wanted in a spouse back then.

The first time he saw petite, raven-haired Sofya was at a dinner party some months after he and Anna were married. From across the room he watched her in a friendly but animated discussion with three men, her dark eyes flashing. The group ended up laughing and agreeing to disagree in the genteel way of dinner party conversation. She had a deep, throaty laugh, full of life, and seemed a different sort of woman—charming, but also smart and engaged. Vasili stared.

The opportunity to speak with her finally presented itself when he glimpsed her alone in the library. Her back was to him as she examined the books, touching the spines with a single finger, tracing the titles with reverence and sensuality. Her touch hovered over a particular volume.

He cleared his throat so as not to surprise her, but she jumped anyway.

"Oh, Vasili Maksimovich, I didn't hear you."

"I'm sorry to have startled you, Sofya Nikolayevna. Please excuse me for interrupting your privacy."

"The interruption is quite welcome. I hope you don't mind that I was looking at your library. The door was open and I can't resist books." Her smile was entirely genuine and her manner so free that he felt as if she was confiding in him.

"I'm flattered, please feel at home. Books are also my escape."

She regarded him intently, her voice soft, as if her words were for him alone.

"A kindred spirit. Everything in the human experience can be found in books, don't you think? I have just a tiny collection myself and am always looking for things I haven't read. This Dumas, for instance. The State Library has a French copy, but my French isn't good enough."

"Mine either." He laughed and grinned. "But you know French?"

"A bit. Two years at university and then last year my parents and I spent three months in Paris for my music studies. My conversational French is passable. But to read French literature? That's beyond my grasp."

"Paris, you're lucky," he said. "A city that captures the imagination. And the home of the great Victor Hugo."

"My favorite writer." Her eyes flashed. "Don't tell anyone—" she looked around conspiratorially "—but I think *Les Miserables* is better than *War and Peace*."

"Blasphemy!" he teased. "Don't worry. Your secret's safe with me."

She colored, then waved a hand along the shelves. "Have you read most of these?"

Vasili chuckled. "Not even close." He reached over her shoulder for the Dumas, mesmerized by the eagerness in her eyes, an energy he recognized in himself. Then, unsteadied by the nearness of her, he stepped back. "But I have read *The Count of Monte Cristo.*" He held it out. "Would you like to borrow it?"

She hesitated, dropping her gaze for an instant before meeting his eyes. "Very much, but are you sure it wouldn't be an inconvenience?"

"Of course not. You must take it." He handed it to her. "When we next see each other you can tell me what you think. It's a favorite. A brilliant plot with some unexpected twists."

Suddenly they were no longer alone. "There you are, Sofya," said Andrei. "I should have known you'd be in the library." He seemed bemused. "I see you've discovered Vasili's secret. He pretends to be a military man, but in truth he's a closet intellectual." They smiled at Andrei's good-natured teasing.

"Andrei, I hope you don't mind that I've been showing your fiancée my library."

"Not at all. But it's time we joined the others for coffee. Sofya, I'd like to introduce you to another of my colleagues."

"And I must return to my lovely wife," said Vasili with a slight bow.

Sofya thanked him for the book. He watched her turn, wondering if there had been something there, or if he'd just imagined that she held his gaze for a heartbeat longer than customary.

That moment loomed large in his memory. Her finger caressing the books like a lover might her beloved, the animation in her eyes, her self-confidence, the way she knew herself made him want to be known by her. For several glorious months they hid their love from the world, certain that their marriages were mistakes. Indeed, there was no other possible conclusion. All else faded in comparison to Sofya. Then, everything was upended. Anna's pregnancy shattered their plans for a future together. They sacrificed love and personal happiness on the altar of duty and honor.

Now both their spouses were gone. God, he hoped she'd come this afternoon. She was full of life, the good and the bad of it, when they spoke at the concert hall after her son's arrest.

The doorbell brought him back to the present. Startled but pleased, he found an old friend behind the door. Admiral Nikolai Kuznetsov, now Commissar of the Navy, the highest-ranking naval officer in the nation, took his hand and pulled him close.

"Vasili. I'm deeply sorry about Anna. A gracious, charming woman."

"Thank you, sir. She was indeed." Still shaking hands, they moved inside. "It's kind of you to call. I can imagine how pressed you are these days." Rumors about the Germans had been circulating among senior military staff. The Commissar must be working long hours.

"Nonsense. We've been friends a long time. I can't imagine not paying my respects."

They'd known each other since Vasili commanded the cruiser *Krasnyi Kavkas* and a young Nikolai Gerasimovich Kuznetsov was his executive officer.

"Besides," continued the Commissar, "it's no exaggeration to say serving under you taught me more than anything else in my career." He gripped Vasili's shoulder. "That was a good year. You showed me how to command a ship. And remember all the nights we spent drinking?" Kuznetsov smiled, then his face turned dark and his voice became a whisper. "One can't talk like we did back then." He looked around, changing the subject. "Truth is, I came early to see you about another matter. Is there someplace private?"

They slipped into the library.

"You've probably heard the rumors," Kuznetsov said. "Seems the non-aggression treaty was just a way for Hitler to bide his time in the East while focusing on Western Europe. Their divisions are on the move. Not entirely clear what they're up to, but it can't be good. We need to prepare. Once the ice clears next month, you'll take the *Leningrad* into the Baltic. Check on our ports and airfields. Identify the most critical weaknesses and report back to me."

"Yes, sir. I'll be glad to be on a ship again." He'd been teaching naval cadets for several years. A favor from Kuznetsov, allowing him to care for Anna as she worsened.

As the Commissar left, Vasili's spirits rose at the idea of a naval command. He'd been in the city too long. He wanted a change. Yet, there was Sofya. This might finally be their chance. He had a month before the ice would melt. A month to discover if she cared for him.

Other guests began to arrive. Friends came to pay their respects and share condolences. Some tried to remind him of all the good in his life, and perhaps he needed reminding. Beaten down by years without love and desire, even if filled with loyalty and devotion, Vasili wanted more than to reflect on the good in his past. He wanted to believe there was life yet to be had.

A couple of hours later, feeling the strain, he sat and closed his eyes. When he opened them, Sofya was standing in front of him. He jumped to his feet, and took her hands. Even in her ordinary, almost shabby black coat, she sparkled with the same iridescent aura as in his memory. They brushed cheeks. He sensed she understood his loss and maybe even his complex emotions.

"I am so sorry, Vasili. I know how difficult it is. Such an empty space."

He saw her remembering Andrei and paused, allowing room for the memory. She always said exactly what she thought. No skirting emotions. He admired the almost uncomfortable honesty which came naturally to her. It took a certain skill to be both forthright and agreeable.

"Seems our lives are little more than a series of losses," he said. She'd lost so much. First him. Later, her brother, a revolutionary, died in tragic circumstances. She revered her brother. So did her parents, who quickly succumbed to their grief. Then, six years ago, Andrei's heart gave out. Now, she might not see her son again. Only her granddaughter remained.

"Yes," she said, "but there's been love and joy too."

"Even in that," he whispered.

He gazed at her as she stared at the floor, silent. She seemed more self-controlled than he recalled, less open than when he comforted her about Aleksandr's arrest. But something in the shifting of her feet gave her away. Perhaps the hard shell she wore—a grim determination to continue forward in an ever more cruel and capricious world—did this. The years of revolution, war, and famine. Stalin with his five-year plans and purges had crushed stronger people than Sofya. Or maybe he'd simply made her uncomfortable, alluding to their past. Did she think of him much? It had taken him years to subdue his feelings, and thoughts of her were always there, just beneath the surface. Flustered and uncomfortable with the niceties required by the occasion, Vasili wanted to tell her the simple truth. He'd missed her. Profoundly.

He stepped forward, but just as quickly, Sofya retreated.

"I'd like to greet Maksim and his family," she said.

"Of course. They're in the dining room. Let me introduce you."

They navigated around a few small groups of people. "I'll get you a cup of tea, while you find something to eat," he said pointing to the food.

The table was laden with fresh bread, butter and cheese, a large platter of sliced ham and a smaller one nearly empty but for a few fragments of eggs and caviar. An assortment of small sandwiches and cookies formed a chessboard of alternating shapes and colors. He watched her select a sandwich like she was making a chess move. They'd played chess long ago at the *dacha*, in between all their love-making. The wooden pieces were an ornate set of imperial Russia with enchanting carved and painted figures—a tsar and tsarina, an orthodox priest, a cavalry officer on horseback, imperial guards as pawns.

The large, ornate samovar rested on the sideboard against the wall. Tea cups and glasses adorned spaces to the right and left, themselves an interesting collection of patterns. Vasili held her tea while she fixed a small plate of food. Then he guided her over and reintroduced her to his son and daughter-in-law, whom she hadn't seen for many years. Vasili stayed in the background as Sofya gave her condolences. He didn't want to intrude, yet he wanted to hear her voice. It soothed him, like a happy memory. He watched her reminisce with Maksim and Yulia, telling a couple of lovely stories about Anna. Listening to her, gazing at her, he felt transformed. Even in his grief, Sofya had such an effect on him.

Other guests arrived, and Vasili forced himself across the room to greet them. Sofya sipped her tea and took a few bites from her plate. He watched her chat with an acquaintance and noticed her energy and emotion, that old spark. Then he caught her glancing at him.

He cut one conversation short, only to be cornered by someone else. He escorted those guests to the dining room and waited until she looked over again, then locked his eyes on hers. She flushed, and hurriedly placed her plate and cup down and slipped out of the dining room. Vasili cut off her escape by getting her coat.

At the door, he thanked her and held her hand too long, willing his charm to work on her.

"Let's have tea sometime soon, Sofya. We hardly had a chance to talk."

She hesitated, and his heart dropped. Doubt crept in. Perhaps she'd let go of the memories. Then her eyes warmed and she said, "*Mnye nravitsya*. I'd like that."

Holding the door, Vasili watched her step into the hallway. She glanced at him over one shoulder. The slight smile on her lips and intensity in her eyes sent sparks across the small space.

THE PAST RETURNS
April 1941

RAIN PELTED SOFYA as she left the Antonov's. She clutched her umbrella and hoped the long walk home would calm her. The rush of memories and emotions had taken her by surprise. All these years she'd told herself her feelings were gone. Instead, it seemed she'd simply learned how to live with the quakes of desire, pushing them down over and over.

She should have been warmer toward Vasili. When Andrei died, he had been there for her, holding her hand briefly amidst the low-murmuring crowd of friends and colleagues. His kindness had been a tremendous comfort. Now, when he needed support, she'd been distant. She was afraid, and fear made her do what she always did: withdraw.

By the time she crossed the Neva, the rain had moved westward. She gazed at the Admiralty and its striking gold spire. Vasili taught naval cadets there. To her left, the majestic Winter Palace, Leningrad's masterpiece, sprawled along the river embankment. Decorated with columns and elaborate statues, the prominent symbol of imperial power now held the Hermitage, the nation's preeminent museum. She and Vasili had once spent an afternoon strolling past the astounding Rembrandts and Repins but seeing only each other. Her yearning was so strong she nearly threw herself on him in a deserted corner of the museum. Today, she again felt that intoxicating combination of desire and admiration.

At the Griboyedov canal, she turned to the silent, forlorn Church on Spilled Blood. The riot of colors and wild beauty of its onion domes had grown dull from enforced neglect. Abused and shuttered, it bore the heavy cloak of official disapproval reserved for anything related to the Romanovs. Every time Sofya heard the latest rumor of its impending destruction, she grieved a bit. The kaleidoscope of glowing golden mosaics within the Russian Orthodox exterior was spectacular. How ironic that in a city filled with architectural marvels, the most uniquely Russian edifice of all was doomed.

As she continued through the city, other memories of Vasili rose. The late summer weekend at his *dacha* where they conceived Aleksandr: the colors changing, the air still warm, the smells of leaves and grass and earth all around. Vasili stood on the porch waiting for her. He crossed the lawn, swept her into his arms and carried her inside the cozy two-bedroom cottage. They got no further than the sofa in the living room—her small bag still on the front lawn where she dropped it.

It was the only time in her life she'd had sex more than once in the same day. They'd ended up in every room, and Vasili had teased her that he wished the *dacha* were larger. She smiled thinking of it. The next day they took a picnic to his favorite spot by the creek, where they made love again, their bodies caressed by the breeze and each other. Afterwards, lying on the blanket in his arms, she noticed even the creek seemed to gurgle in pleasure.

Back in the city, they planned their life together. They'd annul their marriages by bribing the church authorities. Perhaps move to another city to escape the stigma, or even leave Russia. Sofya convinced herself it would work. Love does that sometimes. Makes you believe things that aren't possible.

Was she doing that again? If she and Vasili did care for each other—if their love could be rekindled—then she'd have to tell him the truth. She desperately wanted to believe he'd still love her once he knew about Aleksandr. But that might not happen. And deep down, that was why she hadn't been open or genuine. The idea of sharing her secret unmoored her because she was afraid of losing him a second time.

It was true that it had lost some of its power now that both Anna and Andrei were gone. Telling Sasha would be most difficult of all, but he wouldn't be released for years and it certainly wasn't something she could put in a letter. In time, Yelena would also need to know. But first, she must tell Vasili. Regardless of how he might take the news.

Perhaps he'd known all along, putting two and two together when Aleksandr was born nine months after their passionate weekend. Or perhaps he'd guessed much later, like at Andrei's funeral when he and Aleksandr stood together, two military men engaged in conversation. Two men with similar builds and the same eyes.

True, it was possible he didn't have a clue. There were plenty of men like that, men who didn't think about how much time had passed between when they'd had relations with their lover and her giving birth. But she liked to think Vasili was more discerning. The few times they'd crossed paths over the years there seemed more to the way he would squeeze her hand and say how well she looked or how pleased he was that her career was successful. His intimate gaze in those moments said, "I know about Sasha. I know how difficult it's been."

Whether he knew or not, suspected or not, surely he'd understand her need for secrecy. In the early years, she was afraid of hurting Andrei, and also of what he might do. He could leave her. She didn't yet have a career, and a scandal would prevent her from getting one. Even worse, Andrei might challenge Vasili. Although formal duels were rare, it wasn't unheard of for two men, especially military officers like Andrei and Vasili, to go into the woods with pistols and their seconds.

As the years passed the idea of disrupting their families seemed increasingly cruel. The secret stayed buried but controlled her life, turning her inward. She became cool and wary, losing the passion and unbridled enthusiasm of her youth. She kept people at arms-length and avoided friendships, fearful that if someone learned about Aleksandr's parentage, they'd use it against her.

Now though, with their spouses gone, it was time. He so obviously had feelings for her and she wanted to be honest. How would he react? It upset her to imagine herself in his shoes, realizing how hurt she would be if roles were reversed. Perhaps she shouldn't be in such a hurry to tell him.

She felt herself at an impasse. She needed to tell him, she wanted to tell him, but not just yet. It would be best if they were closer before she revealed the news. And after all, Anna had just passed away. Even if she and Vasili were drawn to each other, there had to be a respectable interval of grieving. They could recapture their love and look toward the future before having the difficult conversation about Aleksandr. In this, time was on her side. A few months would make everything easier.

A SECOND CHANCE
April 1941

VASILI WOKE THE morning after the gathering for Anna with a dry mouth, stiff neck, and pounding head. Rays from the low, bright sun attacked him through the library window and his arm lay across his face, blocking the unwelcome light. He was on the sofa, fully clothed.

Pushing himself to a sitting position, his foot clipped the empty vodka bottle. It rattled and rolled before coming to rest against a table leg, an unpleasant reminder of his attempted escape from reality. He clutched his head. Shame had driven him to vodka. Anna was barely in the ground and all he could think about was Sofi. What kind of man did that? The kind who had spent his entire life in love with someone other than his wife. Sometimes he hated himself.

To be fair, Anna hadn't been herself for many years and he'd been loyal. He'd nursed her and cared for her. But the truth was his feelings for Anna never compared with his yearning for Sofi. He'd always been kind to his wife, but there had been little emotional connection. Still, he felt like a cad. Sixty years old and grasping at a chance to live for love rather than duty.

He stood at the bathroom sink, splashing icy water on his face and rinsing his mouth, trying to get rid of the toxic combination of vodka, cigarettes, and shame. Two strong coffees, a hunk of dark bread, and a brisk walk to the Admiralty cleared his head but didn't banish Sofya from his thoughts. Teaching that day was a torment. He couldn't focus on anything but her. When his last class concluded, he took the streetcar up the Nevsky.

At the Karavayev's building he tucked his cap under one arm, climbed the stairs and knocked. A willowy teenager opened the door.

"*Dobriy vecher.* Good evening. May I help you?" she said, her eyes bright blue disks.

"G-good evening," he stammered. "I'm Admiral Antonov, Vasili Maksimovich. An old friend of Sofya Nikolayevna's. Is she at home?"

"Pleased to make your acquaintance, Admiral Antonov. I'm Yelena Karavayeva, her granddaughter. Do come in."

"Yes. We met some years ago at your grandfather's funeral."

Her eyebrows came together. "I'm sorry."

He could tell she had no idea who he was. "You wouldn't recall, it was but a moment."

"My grandmother isn't home. She has a performance this evening."

"Of course. Please tell her I came by." He looked down, then glanced at his watch. "Perhaps I'll see if I can get a ticket." He moved to the door then turned back. "Do you know where the RadioCom is playing this evening?"

"I'm not certain, but she mentioned that it's an important performance so perhaps Philharmonia Hall." She smiled. "Very nice to meet you, Admiral. I'll tell her you stopped by."

As the door closed, an unexpected surge of affection came over him. Yelena seemed so familiar. She reminded him of his own grandchildren. He hurried to the concert hall where a seat on the right side of the dress circle allowed him to watch Sofya. Her face looked young as she played. Even from a distance, Vasili could see she was relaxed but focused, no pinching between her eyebrows, and he recalled her saying that facial tension made playing more difficult.

He drifted away with the music. His mind emptied of concerns and filled with the notes vibrating through the auditorium. It was the strange magic of both classical music and great literature to take him out of the present to a place of beauty.

When the final curtain fell, he moved with the appreciative audience down the wide staircase, then stepped out of the crowd to find the backstage door. Wandering the halls, he caught up with Sofya at the artists' entrance, where her new colleagues were congratulating her. She'd had a spectacular violin solo, one of Paganini's Caprices. The bow and her fingers had sprung off the violin, like it was a living thing. The other musicians must be overwhelmed by her talent, but it seemed a different group, more relaxed than the Leningrad Philharmonic. Maybe the demotion to the Radio Committee wasn't such a bad thing. He stood against the wall for a few minutes and when the group dwindled, stepped forward.

"Comrade Karavayeva, a captivating performance," Vasili said with artificial formality. "Especially that Paganini. I could tell you enjoyed yourself."

She beamed at him. "Thank you. I'm glad you're here."

"May I walk you home?" Vasili whispered.

Twilight was ending, and the sky grew dim. He carried her violin, and relief flooded him when she took his free arm. At her apartment, she invited him in.

"You're not too tired to talk?" he asked.

"Not at all, and I'm starving. Have you eaten?"

"I didn't get a chance. I came straight from the Admiralty to see you. Yelena told me you were performing. What a poised young woman."

Sofya nodded. "You can imagine how difficult it's been with her papa gone, but she's muddling through. Some tears, of course, but she's strong."

"Like her grandmother," he said, and Sofya smiled at the compliment.

She hung their coats and put a finger to her lips. In the kitchen she whispered. "We should keep our voices low so we don't wake Yelena or Katya."

She prepared a large omelette as they chatted. When they sat to eat, he reached for her hand, unable to hold back any longer.

"Sofi, I know this will seem inappropriate, what with Anna so recently passed. Please forgive me. She and I didn't have a real marriage for many years. And I leave in less than a month for a command in the Baltic. I'm determined not to miss the chance to tell you how I feel. The years have sped, but not my feelings. They have always been there, just beneath the surface. I've spent decades trying to forget you, what we had, what might have been."

He gazed beyond her, into the past, hoping she felt the same, and took an audible breath. "Is there any chance you might still care for me? We aren't so old, you know. We could have some years together."

Sofya took his hand and pressed it to her cheek. Her eyes sparkled and then filled. "I never stopped thinking of you. After Andrei died, I sometimes wondered if we'd get another chance."

"Let me love you, Sofi."

In reply, she put out her other hand. He stood, pulled her to him and they kissed. Gently at first, letting their mouths remember, then deeper as their passion rose and melted the years of loneliness and separation.

They sat again and ate, almost shy with each other after the sudden expression of their feelings. Voices still low, they chatted about Sofya's transition to the RadioCom and moved to the living room where the old sofa welcomed them.

"It may be shabby, but it's the most comfortable piece of furniture here," she said, patting it fondly, after setting two small glasses of vodka on the side table. Barely velvet and barely burgundy anymore, the armrests were so worn it was impossible to discern the original fabric.

"Function over style," he teased. "What a good communist you are."

They smiled at his humor. Of course, she had no choice but to keep her sofa. No one but the most senior Party members had the connections necessary to replace such an item.

"A toast," he said, lifting his glass. "First, to Comrade Stalin." She chuckled and he whispered, "We don't want anyone thinking we aren't patriotic." Then he went still for a moment and his voice filled with emotion. "But most importantly, here's to us. To second chances."

"To us." Sofya touched her glass to his and sealed the toast with a kiss.

They sat close, enjoying the nearness of each other, feeling young and unencumbered by the press of either personal or national history. They slipped into a companionable ease; talking freely, like lifelong friends, or like husband and wife meeting after a long separation. Leaning against each other, the struggles of life in Leningrad diminished. The story of their city was one of loss, wars and rebellions, oppression of one sort or another. Understanding the tangle of tyranny and strife had become difficult indeed. At least now they would navigate that maze together.

SPRINGTIME UNDER STALIN
May 1941

L ENA GAZED OUT the windows of her classroom at a tree, plump with buds. Trees made her think of her father, how they used to walk about Leningrad together, comparing and identifying different species. He'd always been fascinated by the way nature leapt forward every spring in a rush of buds and blossoms and leaves. New life. She tried to blink back her tears, hoping no one would notice and only half-listening as the teacher droned on.

The bell rang and Lena's best friend, Tatiana, or Tanya for short, jumped up and stood in front of her, giving her time to compose herself. The two girls linked arms and went straight to the courtyard to escape the crowd. A bit of gossip and boy-watching would be a good distraction. There was one boy in particular they had their eyes on lately. Pavel Chernov studied violin with Lena's grandmother, and he and his friends often played chess after school.

The boys arrived right after Lena and Tanya and set up their chessboard not far from where the girls sat on a low cement wall. Lena tried to maintain an air of casual disinterest, but she took in everything about Pavel: every laugh, tilt of the head, and glimpse in their direction.

"He's always looking at you," Tanya said. "It's obvious he likes you."

They'd had this conversation before. Tanya saw "evidence" of Pavel's interest in the smallest things whereas Lena thought Pavel's casual attention showed nothing more than his genial nature. He was nice to everyone, but still, maybe he was interested.

"You know," Lena said, "yesterday he was rehearsing at our apartment and when I walked in, he looked right at me, smiled, and didn't miss a note. And then he came into the kitchen before he left, looking for me I think, but then—"

"What happened?" Tanya squealed.

"Nothing. I was so nervous I couldn't think of anything to say. My mind went blank."

"Oh, Lena." Tanya's excitement hissed out like air from a balloon.

"I know, I know. A perfect opportunity and I froze. Pavel's face went all red. I still don't know what to think. Maybe he was just being polite. But, why would he have come looking for me if he didn't like me at least a little?" She stared into the distance. "His smile was so—"

"So gorgeous? And what about those eyes?"

Lena flushed and poked her friend.

"I can see you two together." Tanya used her hands as she described them. "You, with your perfect figure, dazzling white smile, and gorgeous blond hair flowing in the breeze. And Pavel next to you, tall and dashing, with those piercing eyes."

Lena ran her fingers through her long locks. "I don't know." She didn't want to admit that there were moments she had much the same daydream, she and Pavel, hand in hand.

Tanya elbowed her. "You need to quit thinking about him and do something about it."

Lena wound strands of her hair around her fingers. "Maybe you're right. I could have sworn he wanted to talk, but it was so awkward."

"Pavel's really shy," Tanya said. "I'm sure he's thinking right now about how he'd like to be with you." The two girls looked across and caught Pavel looking at them.

A moment later, the boys erupted into laughter. Pavel had check-mated Dimitri in a handful of moves and Dimitri stood abruptly, accidentally knocking over the chessboard. Pieces scattered about the courtyard and the boys laughed at his clumsiness. Pavel waved them off, and gave his friend's shoulder an amiable shake. As they collected the chess pieces, Pavel turned toward Lena. He smiled and waved. She smiled back and gave him a tentative wave in return.

"See! I told you," Tanya whispered. "He's not afraid to pay attention to you in front of his friends."

Lena said nothing, afraid of sharing her feelings. She trusted Tanya, but still, she didn't want anyone to know how she really felt. Not unless Pavel felt the same. Excitement bubbled inside her.

The girls parted ways for their respective homes. The afternoon sun peeked out from behind the clouds, somehow making Lena feel hopeful. Maybe Tanya was right and Pavel did like her. The trick was to find a way to talk to him alone, away from school. She'd overheard her grandmother telling him about a Saturday session at the Radio House. Today was Thursday. Suddenly, she knew just what to do.

❧ ❧

Pavel bounded down the stone steps of the Radio House. Despite the years of lessons and encouragement from Sofya Nikolayevna, he never thought of himself as a musician, not a real musician anyway. Lately though, playing felt more natural. He was learning difficult pieces with greater ease. He'd already decided to study engineering at university, but maybe he didn't have to give up the violin to do that.

He turned left on the Nevsky, dodging crowds of people. The entire city was enjoying a break from the depressing weeks of rain. Families strolled along the city's main boulevard, *babushki* in their drab headscarves carried shopping bags, and couples walked hand-in-hand.

A half-block down he saw Lena. Ambushed by the sight of her, his heart skipped a beat or two. Her perfect face scanned the crowd and then she spotted him, raised up on tiptoes, and waved. Scarcely believing his good luck, Pavel smiled across the sea of people. He went toward her, wondering what to say and how to appear as relaxed and confident as she looked.

"Lena. Hi." His voice cracked and he cringed inside while trying to maintain a cool exterior. "Funny seeing you here."

She flashed a brilliant smile, blue eyes bright, and said nothing about his nerve-induced voice-crack. "Well, I knew you were rehearsing and I guessed you'd come this way." Her cheeks flushed at the admission. It made her even more beautiful. She fidgeted, her feet scuffing along the sidewalk. "I thought maybe we could do something." Her voice, soft. "If you have time, that is. We could go to the Haymarket." She looked up.

"Sure. That sounds great." The thunder in his chest drowned out everything around him. Afraid she could hear the pounding, he stepped back.

"My grandmother doesn't like it if I go there alone," Lena continued with a slight roll of her eyes. "But sometimes there are good bargains."

"My mother doesn't like it either. She says there are too many 'unsavory' elements." Pavel raised his eyebrows and chuckled.

Leningrad's big, open-air market at Sennaya Square had a bit of everything. Dozens of stalls held the usual array of fruits and vegetables, packaged grains, cheese and kefir, but also dried goods, small appliances, and clothing. For decades the market had operated at the fringes of normal commerce. Bargains could be had, but it was also frequented by pick-pockets, petty criminals, and worse.

"I'm game." Pavel took hold of her arm just above the elbow, trying to maneuver them to the outside of the sidewalk where it was less crowded. They stepped up into the streetcar at the intersection of Nevsky and Sadovaya.

Standing close to her as the streetcar rattled along, he noticed the fresh, slightly medicinal fragrance of her shampoo. Balsam? Lena slid her arm through his and after they got off, he reached for her hand. He couldn't believe they were together. He glanced at her and she tightened her grip, smiling. Oh, God, she was beautiful.

Pavel had been admiring Yelena Karavayeva for months. Last week he had a lesson at her apartment instead of the Radio House, a rare and wonderful circumstance. He got up the nerve to talk to her afterwards, but when he walked into the Karavayev's kitchen he became completely tongue-tied. She stood at the sink doing dishes, her back to him with a dish towel slung over one shoulder. All he saw was her curvy behind, snuggled into a pair of work pants. He'd cleared his throat, but when she turned and smiled, he was so rattled that all he squeaked out was a quick, "See you in school."

Now, here he was. Alone with her.

"So, what kind of criminal activity should we look for?" Lena said with a laugh. When she closed her mouth, her wide lips formed the most tempting bow-shape. Pavel got lost, entranced, thinking of kissing her, wondering how soft and delicious her lips would feel on his. Aroused by that single part of her, he turned away, thankful for loose-fitting trousers.

"You can't fool me," Pavel said smiling. "You're not a trouble-maker."

"True enough," Lena said, raising her eyebrows. "But we all have secrets." She cast him a flirtatious sideways glance and he wondered what secrets she kept. For his part, Pavel couldn't think of anything. Well, except touching himself when he thought about Lena in that way. He puzzled over her mysterious private side. Did she want to kiss him, touch him? Damn. He needed to think about something boring.

"Maybe you aren't the only one with secrets," Pavel teased.

"Well, I'll tell you one of mine if you'll tell me one of yours." Lena paused. "Let me guess. You, Kolya, and Dimitri sneak vodka from your parents."

"We've definitely done that. It's only a secret from our parents."

He smiled, relieved that he didn't have to reveal how he felt about her. "Now, your turn. A secret about you and Tanya."

"You're going to be disappointed." She shook her head. "Tanya is the straightest arrow in school. Worst thing we've ever done is snitch cigarettes from her dad. We tried to smoke them, but it was pouring rain. When we finally got one lit, Tanya inhaled so deeply that she had a coughing fit. After we stopped laughing, we took a few drags, but it tasted nasty. In the end it wasn't very exciting." She shrugged her shoulders. "Do you smoke?"

"Once in a while, but I don't really like it either."

The two dodged crowded kiosks, while Pavel wondered if sex would be the same as smoking and other forbidden things—a bit of a let-down. What a depressing thought.

Lena moved toward a stall selling oranges, a rare find. "Look at these," she said, tugging his arm. "Expensive, but we haven't had any for months. Even my mother will appreciate them."

Pavel watched her buy three and then suggested they walk over to the Yusupov Gardens. The old Yusupov Palace, not to be confused with the Yusupov Palace on the Moika Canal where Rasputin met a gruesome end, sat far back from the street like a castle in some fairy tale. The ornate, wrought iron entrance gate added to its allure. Popular with families and couples, its gardens covered several acres in front of the old residence and included a picturesque lake, several stunning tree-lined paths, and a surprising amount of privacy.

"That's a great idea," Lena said. "The lilacs will be starting to bloom."

What Pavel heard was, "I want to be alone with you."

He carried their bags, and when they came to a somewhat secluded bench, they sat. A group of lilac trees across the path cast an enchanting spell on the afternoon. The purple clusters were poised to bloom and gave off just a hint of perfume. The teens held hands and talked about school, their friends, and plans for the summer.

Adjusting her coat against the gusty breeze, Lena scooted closer to Pavel until her leg rested against his. He thought again about kissing her when the bells of Nikolsky Cathedral startled them both.

"Drat! Six o'clock already. Seems like we just got here. I wish I didn't have to go." Pavel looked at her hand as he held it in his.

"Me too," Lena said. "But my grandmother will be wondering where I am by now."

They hurried toward Sadovaya and caught a streetcar in the direction of Lena's home.

"I'll walk you as far as the canal," he said when they stepped off. "But I've got to hurry."

"You don't have to walk me that far. Thanks for going shopping. It was fun."

Pavel let go of her hand when they reached the bridge. "I had a lot of fun too." He looked into her breathtaking eyes. "See you soon?"

"Yes, see you at school." Her eyes danced as she turned away.

Pavel wished he'd been braver. As he crossed the street, he realized he still held her shopping. He sprinted after her. "Your oranges," he said, breathing hard and handing her the bag.

"Oh, I completely forgot!" She laughed and took it from him. "Thanks for remembering." Her smile was a jolt of electricity to Pavel's heart.

He leaned down and pecked her on the cheek, surprising them both, then ran back across the bridge and down the street toward home.

PREPARING FOR THE INEVITABLE
June 1941

VASILI SPED THROUGH the labyrinth of marble floors and stairwells in the General Staff Building, his footsteps echoing in the nearly empty corridors of power. With a goliath so close, headquarters should be a hive of activity. Instead, it was oppressively quiet. Silence rather than directives. The status quo instead of preparations.

His briefing with Commissar Kuznetsov was short and difficult. The four-week inspection tour of ports and airfields in the Baltic region had been disheartening. Even the large Soviet naval facility on Kronstadt was not war ready. And if the Soviet military couldn't prepare its most essential northern naval base, what could it do? Meanwhile, the Germans were about to attack. According to the Commissar—one of the few men he'd trust with his life—enemy divisions were massing along the border and Comrade Stalin seemed paralyzed. Without preparatory steps, it could be a bloodbath. The only good thing to come from the meeting was his new command—the *Kirov,* a fast, agile ship with the best guns in the Baltic fleet. And even that was mixed news. It meant he was leaving tomorrow morning and had only until then to spend with Sofya.

The weeks before he'd left in May had been the best of his life. He and Sofya had a powerful connection. And the years of separation had made them more appreciative and gentle with each other. They both knew the value of what they shared.

He'd wanted to marry Sofya from the moment they were reunited, but they agreed to wait a reasonable interval after Anna's death out of respect for Maksim's feelings. Now war was coming. A hollowed-out sensation filled his gut as he approached the building. At best they faced months of separation. Perhaps he had no right to dream of personal happiness at a time like this, but he was no longer willing to deny the desires of his heart.

His long legs took the steps two at a time. When he phoned yesterday to tell Sofya he was coming, she'd suggested meeting at his home, rather than hers. She must have intuited from his voice that they needed privacy. Their connection astonished him. Even from afar, she understood things, understood him.

He yanked open the apartment door and called out, then heard her, the clunk of something set down in a hurry. In a moment she scurried into his arms. The flurry of endearments and kisses slowed as he enfolded her, as if she were part of him.

"My love, I've missed you."

After a moment, she wriggled out of his grasp and stood on her tiptoes, beaming at him.

"I missed you too. Life has been entirely dull without you."

He put his hand under her chin and leaned down to kiss her again. He wanted to give her the joy of a simple reunion. He wanted to ask what she'd been reading and what music she'd been working on. He wanted to plan walks in the park and weekends in the country. Instead, he was filled with the urgent news that their world was about to change.

"Are you all right, Vasya? You don't look well." Sofya's brows knitted together. She reached up to touch his cheek and he took her hand and kissed the palm.

"I'm fine, as well as possible under the circumstances. But the nation is facing a grave threat. I have much to tell you."

He pulled her into the kitchen where she turned to start the coffee. Anxious, Vasili tugged at her again. "*Sidet*, sit," he said, urging her to the wooden cook's table. It was spartan and small, comfortable in its simplicity. An east-facing window looked out over old Petrograd. They'd started many days here during their first weeks together in April.

"I've just come from briefing Commissar Kuznetsov. The situation is grave. German divisions on our border."

Sofya hesitated. An eyebrow rose. "I thought we had a treaty with Germany?"

He nodded. "All the more startling because of that. But it turns out the treaty was just some sleight of hand, a cheap magician's trick to distract us while Hitler was busy in western Europe. Now that he's made progress there, it seems he wants everything back, and perhaps the rest of the Soviet Union as well." He struggled with how much to tell her. Stalin's distrust of the military was common knowledge. She knew thousands of officers had disappeared. Her son was an example of a good Red Army soldier sent to Siberia for some idiotic, manufactured reason. No, he couldn't tell her that the military was in far worse shape now than it had been just a half-dozen years ago. It was too depressing.

Sofya leaned in. "But Germany's already at war with most of Europe."

"It does seem incredible, and it may be short-sighted for the Nazis to spread themselves so thin, but they've devoted the last decade to building their capabilities. Hitler's not crazy, he wouldn't start a war unless he thought he could win."

Vasili knew German technology and military production had changed the face of war. Soviet factories, resources and manpower could eventually surpass Germany's, but it would take time. If Stalin didn't implement immediate steps to raise readiness, the Soviet military would fall even further behind.

"They're poised along the entire length of the border, including the northern frontier," Vasili continued. "Depending on how many divisions, and how things go, they could reach Leningrad in a matter of months." Vasili rested his hand on hers. "I know that you won't like this idea, but you and Katya and Yelena may need to leave."

"It's hard to imagine things getting that bad." Her eyes narrowed.

"I'm not suggesting you get on the first train after the war begins, but, if the Germans drive hard toward Leningrad, evacuation may be the only reasonable course of action."

"If the worst does happen," she said, "and the Germans are some-day at the Narva gate, especially then, we'll need citizens to stay and fight."

"Fight how, Sofi? With what? We don't even have enough weap-ons for the army. The Nazis will slaughter everything in their path. They won't treat civilians any better than soldiers."

Sofya was a Leningrader through and through. A staunch defender of its traditions in art, music, science and literature, she would see leaving as betrayal. She called it "the city," as if there was only one metropolis in all the world magnificent enough to warrant that title. Her devotion didn't mean she was unaware of its many con-tradictions. The opulence and excess of the monarchy still evidenced in the many Rastrelli-designed palaces stood in sharp contrast to the pockets of poor, destitute dwellings straight out of Dostoyevsky or Gogol. Of course, those contradictions were not much remedied under the Communists. Rather it was as if the classes of people had simply switched places.

Sofya's face screwed up. "All the able-bodied people can't simply leave if we go to war. Isn't that what the Germans would want? For us to run away. For us to hand over our treasures and industries."

"I know how you feel." Voice grave, he paused and took her hands. "But if Leningrad is their objective and they get the upper hand, evacuation may be the only choice." She returned his serious look. "Don't confuse foolishness for bravery. Leaving may take cour-age; staying may be foolish. Remember, I'll be unable to protect you."

Sofya raised her chin just a fraction. "You mustn't worry," she said. "I'll pay attention. I won't be stubborn or anything. Yelena's too important."

"And you are too." He leaned forward and kissed her over the tiny table. Sober thoughts filled the silence while he rubbed her wiry hands, bare of jewelry as always. The ends of the fingers on her left hand were worn smooth and square from playing the violin; the nails cut short.

"Everything else seems unimportant, but how are things? Yelena? Katya?"

"Better with Katya." She stood to pour their coffee. "We'll never see eye-to-eye, but I'm beginning to believe it was just carelessness on her part. I don't think she really intended for Sasha to be arrested. What's hardest is that she won't defend him. Always focused on the Party. Although since she lost her job and Party card, she's less enthusiastic about that too, or less vocal. I wouldn't say she's repentant, but perhaps humbled. She doesn't criticize. And we don't argue, which is good for Yelena."

"You sound sympathetic. Has she apologized? Written Aleksandr?"

"I don't think she's written, but I know she's sorry. She pays more attention to Yelena." Sofya sighed. "I haven't told her what her mother did, even though there have been moments when my spiteful side takes over and I want to." She winced at the admission. "No good would come of that."

"You're right. Yelena doesn't need more pain on top of losing her papa." He patted her hand. "Such a smart, steady girl. I miss her, you know."

"And she misses you. I'm definitely not a challenging chess partner." Her look was self-deprecating.

Vasili disappeared to organize his return to Kronstadt and arrange a car to transport things to her apartment. Less than an hour later, Sofya had sorted the pantry contents. He came up from behind and wrapped both arms around her. She leaned back into his embrace.

"Now's my only chance to get to the bank," he said. "You know how important cash will be, there'll be shortages everywhere, and prices will skyrocket. Come with me. The weather's cleared and we can walk a bit."

After stopping at the bank, they strolled hand-in-hand, pockets full of money. The sun struggled behind the persistent clouds of a cold, wet spring, yet pedestrians filled the park inside the Peter and Paul Fortress. It was a Sunday, and city-dwellers would not be kept indoors by the blustery rain. The trees wore their dazzling array of green like a new wardrobe and lilacs perfumed the air.

Soon they found themselves back at the apartment, drawn by the inevitable press of preparations. When Sofya began dinner, he went into the parlor. He sprawled on the small mahogany sofa, his head bent at an uncomfortable angle on an arm rest, one leg hanging off, foot on the floor as if ready to jump up.

He woke to Sofya against him. She'd wedged herself into the tiny space at his waist, and lay on his chest. He put his arms around her. "Waking to you is better than any dream."

She kissed him and smiled. "Let's have dinner and then you can finish getting organized. I'm ravenous."

As they ate, they discussed what Sofya should take to her apartment.

"I'd like some of your books."

Vasili nodded. "Why don't you do that while I get my papers together. And I need to give Maksim a call. Can't tell him much, but I want him to know that I'm taking a command."

He stepped away, then turned back. "The *dacha*." He and his father had built the country house when he was a teenager. It had been the family's escape from the pressures of city life ever since. "You should go. Maybe make a day trip with Yelena. There are some personal items I'd like to keep safe. Books, the only decent photo-graph of my parents, a coverlet my grandmother made. Might be other things. The caretaker butchered a hog last fall like every year. A hindquarter will be cured and in the root cellar by now. Would be nice for you to have that."

"Don't stress, Darling. We'll make a trip."

He gazed at her as she stood at the sink. "Sofi, there's a gun at the *dacha*. Top shelf of the bedroom closet."

She sighed and nodded.

Less than an hour later, he stuck his head in the library where Sofya had made several piles of books. "I left a message with Yulia—Maksim wasn't home. Might be for the best. Would've been hard not to say anything about what's coming." His eyes fell over the stacks she'd arranged and he raised an eyebrow and grinned. "I hope the car is large enough."

He left her still perched on the library ladder and went down the hall to the bathroom. He began to fill the tub and removed his clothes, carefully hanging his uniform.

A moment later she called to him through the door. "Taking a bath?" Her voice carried a hint of desire.

"Hoping to," he called out and opened the door, facing her in a provocative state of undress. "Join me?" He arched his eyebrows and grinned beguilingly, his own longing obvious.

"You should be so lucky," she replied out of the corner of her mouth while playfully pushing him back in and pulling the door shut.

"I *am* lucky," he shouted.

He slid into the hot water and scrubbed himself with a bar of soap. Soap had been one of the hardest items to find after the Revolution. Even twenty years later, it was a small miracle he still appreciated. He reached for a towel and wedged it behind his neck so that his head rested on the high-backed edge of the porcelain tub. He reclined and closed his eyes, enjoying the luxury of hot water and thick air. Only a few things felt better than this.

The door opened.

"My love." He lifted his eyes to her.

Steam filled the room, gathering at the ceiling and making everything appear slightly indistinct. She leaned over, kissed his head, then his lips.

"Did you change your mind?"

"Maybe." Her eyes flashed with the promise of sex. "First, let me wash your hair." She knelt next to the tub and lathered soap, then ran her fingers through his short hair. After rinsing, she massaged his temples. He sighed and she kissed him again, longer this time, and reached for him under the water.

He groaned. "See how much I've missed you."

She stepped out of her dressing gown and into the tub, water splashing over the sides.

For a brief spell, Vasili forgot everything but Sofya. Her touch, her caresses emptied his mind. It was just the two of them. Afterwards, reluctant to break the spell even as the water cooled, he cradled her along the length of him, sharing the heat of his body and memorizing the curves of hers.

"You know, I've never done that in a bathtub before," she said.

"Me either." He flashed a sly grin. "I guess what they say about old dogs isn't true."

She smiled and kissed his stubbly cheek, her fears bubbling up.

"How long do you think it will be before we see each other again?"

"I don't know. I could be in the Baltic a while. At Kronstadt eventually." He paused. "I promise to write, and your letters will mean so much."

"I like to write," she said. "I'm telling myself that we've been apart for many years, so what's a few months, or even longer. The uncertainty will be hard—not knowing when it will start or how long it will last—but I'll be here when you return."

That assurance pushed aside some of his fear. "That's all I need to know. And promise you'll prepare—as much food as you can hide and your savings from the bank."

"I will." Her voice rasped. "And please Vasya, protect yourself. Be careful." He kissed her softly and she whispered. "Come back to me."

THE FIRST DAY
June 1941

IN THE EARLY morning quiet of the next day, Sofya waited outside with Vasili. She breathed in the freshly washed smell of the air, rinsed of pollen by the night's rain. They stood in silence under the shroud of low clouds, having already said everything that needed saying. His arm tight around her shoulder, Sofya leaned against him. The simple black trousers and navy jacket of his everyday military attire suited him. Even the gold braid along the sleeves indicating rank seemed a modest adornment. She reached up, touching the almost invisible flashes of silver at his temples. The bags under his eyes were dark and the lines on his face like canyons.

As the car pulled up to take him away, Vasili bent down and kissed her in slow motion on the forehead, like she was something precious. He hugged her a last time and whispered "I love you." She stood on tiptoe to kiss his cheek and whisper the same.

The driver took the overnight bag and his other hand held the rear door open. Sliding his briefcase across the seat, Vasili clambered in. He looked at Sofya as the driver closed the door. His direct, unfaltering gaze and the almost imperceptible raise of his chin told her he'd be back. She put two fingers to her lips, sending him a last kiss.

The slight whooshing sound of tires on wet pavement faded as the car grew smaller and disappeared around a corner. Sofya shivered and wrapped her arms around herself against the sudden chill, offering an earnest plea to the sullen sky.

On top of her fears, she hadn't told him about Sasha. The entire four weeks he was gone she'd planned and rehearsed what she would say. But when he rushed in with the terrible news of German divisions threatening the Soviet Union, she couldn't talk about Aleksandr. It was too weighty on top of the grim news of impending war. How she wished she'd told him in April. Right after Anna died and they confessed their feelings for each other. If she'd told him then that Aleksandr was his son, there would've been time enough to repair any damage. Instead, dreadful circumstances trapped her into keeping something so important from him. The guilt ate at her.

Climbing the steps back to the apartment, a bit lightheaded, she was glad for the press of things demanding her attention. Anything to avoid worrying about Vasili. She set the apartment keys with those to the *dacha*. The small satchel stuffed full of paper currency rested on a chair. A fine, silk carpet, not too large, lay rolled up on the floor.

She walked through the rooms, making mental notes of the remaining furniture, the bedding, the clothes still hanging in closets. Maksim and Yulia had taken some things back to Moscow. Vasili gladly let them ship several pieces of furniture. The once grand apartment felt forlorn, almost austere, as if it too were preparing for war.

Her car arrived at ten, the driver, surly and brusque, sported a chin so weak it disappeared into his fleshy neck. At first, he sat in the vehicle ignoring Sofya as she carried boxes and bags down to the street. Chain-smoking, he watched her make three trips, after which she stood next to the bundles, hands on her hips, catching her breath. Using her kindest voice, she suggested how appreciative she and Admiral Antonov would be for his help. And there it was. The glimmer of understanding that he could get something in return for a little bit of effort. He carried the carpet down, and then made several trips for the books. When they arrived at her apartment across town, he jumped out of the car, insisting she do nothing but direct him. Afterwards she slipped him a fifty ruble note and pulled an unopened bottle from the shelf. He tipped his head down before thanking her, eagerly accepting the money and the vodka.

Neither Katya nor Yelena questioned the things Sofya brought from Vasili's. He was on a long deployment. He didn't want things to spoil. He wanted her to have some of his books. They'd be curious though, suspicious even, if they saw her filling the house with additional food and supplies. Preparing for war when there was no war was the kind of thing that could get her thrown in prison. She'd have to be careful.

The following day, after her morning rehearsal, she took a bus to the large grocery store on Liteiny Prospekt near secret police headquarters. All the stores in the city were state-run, but they weren't identical. This store's large selection had caught her eye on one of those trips to the *Bolshoi Dom*. Sofya chose numerous commonplace items: oatmeal, canned beets, tea, but also some harder to find things like tinned beef and fish. She spied shelves full of kasha—they must have gotten a huge delivery. The rows of cereal compressed into paper-wrapped rectangles sat like books on a library shelf. She'd always been fond of the simple grain, served with a nice dollop of butter. Lightweight and easy to store, she'd slip them onto her closet shelf behind the heavy blankets she just put away. She wanted to take a dozen, but put four back, afraid of drawing attention. Maybe she'd return later.

Methodical, intent on following Vasili's urging, Sofya squeezed in visits to all her favorite stores, focused on essentials like flour, sugar, and canned goods. Everywhere she went, she paid close attention to how people looked and acted. Did others know war was coming? Nothing in the city seemed out of the ordinary and the urgency with which she'd approached her preparations on Monday faded as the calm days passed.

Toward the end of the week, she went to the Haymarket. The sprawling expanse of semipermanent stalls filled one side of Sennaya

Square. It teemed with people struggling to make a living, striving, pressing, insisting, convincing shoppers to buy, determined to make a kopek at any cost. Normally kept away by the urgency of their business and the disparity between their condition and hers, to say nothing of the black marketeers, today the mood in the market was almost upbeat and Sofya felt invisible as she examined the wares. The white nights of summer had arrived, and people had more energy. The long days were always celebrated, everyone and everything lighter in the pleasant weather.

Memories of sporadic electrical service, especially during the Revolution, drove her to the household section. She stocked up on candles and matches, then bought a new flashlight with extra batteries. Winter was far off, but that didn't stop her from thinking ahead. She hunted for warm boots for Yelena, but there wasn't much selection in June. Before leaving the Haymarket with her rucksack on her back, she bought a five-liter metal container and had it filled with kerosene. On her way home, she stopped with her cumbersome load to read the newspaper posted outside Gostiny Dvor, the largest shopping arcade in Leningrad. No mention of Hitler bearing down on the Soviet Union. Sofya felt as if she had weeks to prepare. Maybe Vasili was wrong.

Buoyed by her successes, she spent the next morning at the *banya,* the public bath. After a quick cleansing scrub and rinse, her skin rosy, she skipped the sauna and tiptoed across cool tiles to the main bath. Of all the city's *banyas,* this was her favorite. It had the same shabby communal shower, the same wood-lined sauna with thick, hot air smelling of cedar, the same fire with its grate of stones on top, buckets of water and birch branches alongside. But its soaking pool set it apart. Sofya found a spot where she could rest on the underwater ledge and lowered herself gingerly into the hot water. She closed her eyes and listened as the conversation swirled.

It was the usual gossip and gripe session, short supplies of this and that, the poor quality of bread, the absence of fresh meat from city stores altogether. One woman talked about how much better it was in the countryside. "You can raise a few chickens, grow your own vegetables, maybe have a hog in the backyard." The comment reminded Sofya about the *dacha*, about Vasili. Everything reminded her of Vasili. She saw him in her mind, aboard a naval vessel, in the dark waters of the Baltic, squinting into the sun.

Still no hint of war.

On Sunday, June 22nd, a week after Vasili's departure, Sofya headed to a morning rehearsal without her usual enthusiasm. Leningrad's notoriously short summer had arrived and she could think of several things she'd rather be doing outdoors. It was a perfect day to walk along the Neva, or through the Summer Garden. Plus, she still hadn't gone to the bank. Vasili had given her most of his savings, but they both knew that only vast sums of cash had any power in wartime. She vowed to make the bank her next priority.

Her simple wooden chair was more uncomfortable than usual and the music insufficiently challenging to demand her entire focus. From the orchestra's general lack of concentration, she knew she wasn't the only one anxious to be finished. When the conductor dismissed them early with an exasperated flick of the baton and sharp turn of his back, Sofya felt a twinge of guilt. Poor Eliasberg, always wanting them to be better than they were. What envy he must harbor. The best musicians in the city were with the Leningrad Philharmonic, getting all the accolades, making recordings. The Radio Orchestra would never compare or compete.

Many of her colleagues made their way to the stark basement canteen. It was just past noon, and Sofya followed the crowd for the *pelmeni*, tiny, delicious dumplings that were worth a few more minutes indoors, even on a beautiful day. The cafeteria line quickly wound down the hall, and Sofya asked the man behind her to hold her place while she claimed a seat. He grumbled, but she took it as a sign of assent and set her coat and violin on a chair at a long, narrow wooden table. Returning to the brisk-moving line, Sofya soon sat down with a small plate of the prized *pelmeni* and a warm cup of mushroom soup nestled against a thick slice of dark bread.

The first mouthfuls of soup were comforting and she speared a tasty dumpling while nodding at her friend, Gennadi Romanovich, an oboist, to join her. As he sat, a voice came over the loudspeaker announcing a broadcast. "*Vnimaniye, vnimaniye.* Attention, attention." The kitchen clatter quieted, but people continued to murmur and move through the line. When Deputy Premier and Foreign Commissar Molotov began speaking, conversations halted and servers put down their utensils. Everyone watched the loudspeaker as if it were Molotov himself rather than a gray box mounted in the corner.

> *Citizens of the Soviet Union, the Soviet Government and its head, Comrade Stalin, have instructed me to make the following announcement: Today, at four o'clock in the morning, without declaration of war and without any claims being made on the Soviet Union, German troops attacked our country. . . despite the fact that there was a nonaggression pact between the Soviet Union and Germany, a pact the terms of which were scrupulously observed by the Soviet Union. . . .*
>
> *The government calls upon you, men and women citizens of the Soviet Union, to rally even more closely around the glorious Bolshevik Party, around the Soviet Government and our great leader, Comrade Stalin. Our cause is just. The enemy will be crushed. Victory will be ours.*

Molotov's concluding phrase echoed in the plain, cavernous room and silence settled over the stunned musicians. Still holding her empty fork, Sofya regarded her tray, examining the bits of butter starting to congeal on the dumplings.

A single metal chair grated against the floor. An elderly veteran from the instrument room stood and addressed the gray loudspeaker. "Fascist dogs. Who do they think they are?" His gruff, deep voice filled the room. "The Nazis want war, well, they've got one now. They'll choke on their ambition, just like all the others." Murmurs of support swirled and claims of Soviet superiority spread out from the old man like ripples on a pond.

Sofya said nothing. Her eyes caught Gennadi's and she saw fear. They were of a generation experienced with hardship. Revolution, war, famine, oppression. She quickly drained her soup bowl and put the dark bread into her pocket. She swallowed the remaining dumplings without tasting them, dropped her tray with the dishwashing crew, and rushed for the exit.

On the street, Sofya paused to examine the contents of her purse. All week she'd carried more cash than usual. Crossing Nevsky Prospekt, she entered the large grocery store in Gostiny Dvor. She bought as much food as she could carry and then waddled the long blocks home, bags and violin case bumping against her legs.

Sofya was struggling with the apartment door when Yelena pulled it open.

"Lenochka." She let out a heavy breath. "Thank you."

Wordlessly, her granddaughter took the cumbersome bags and set them on the kitchen floor, then stepped back into the hall, looking frightened and much younger than fifteen. Sofya studied her red-rimmed eyes and quivering chin, then hugged her fiercely.

"Quite a shock." Sofya pulled her over to the kitchen table.

Yelena's eyes glistened. "I keep thinking about Papa."

"Me too, Sweetheart. Admiral Vasili said if war comes, some will be released to fight."

"Maybe he'd be safer in the camp." Yelena said, her face pinched with the effort of trying not to cry. "I shouldn't have said that. It's just . . ." She stopped, her eyes wet and full again.

Sofya hugged her, rocking slightly, working hard to hold the fear at arms-length. "It's going to be okay, Lenochka. You're worried, we all are. If it helps, think about what your papa would want." She pulled back to look at her granddaughter.

"He'd want to come home." Yelena sniffed. "He'd want to fight for his country."

"Yes." Sofya's voice was sad and soft. "I'm sure that's right, even after everything, that's exactly what he'd want." Sofya sat heavily at the table. "But he'd also want us to be safe, to be prepared. And that's what we should focus on now."

Yelena poured her grandmother a small glass of lukewarm tea.

"You know, struggling with those bags, a memory of your great-grandmother popped into my head. I must have been six or seven, and I opened the apartment door to let her in. She was weighed down by bags of food, just like I was now. It was during the typhus epidemic and my parents stocked up on everything. For weeks your great-uncle Aleksandr and I never went outside. Mamochka was so afraid we'd get sick." She looked down for a moment before continuing. "But it worked. We stayed healthy. Anyway, the point is, we have to take things into our own hands. We can't expect a steady and plentiful food supply during war."

"Should we go to the store again?" The color had returned to Yelena's face.

"Yes, but first I need to go to the State Savings Bank. We need cash. Even though food may not become scarce right away, we'll see price increases tomorrow or the next day."

Outwardly calm, inwardly Sofya cursed herself for not following Vasili's urging to withdraw her savings right away. She'd been complacent, putting it off all week while she hoarded food, thinking she had more time and feeling flush with the cash he'd given her, plus the several envelopes of money she always kept hidden behind the bookcase. Now, hoping it wasn't too late, she grabbed her bank book from the top drawer of the mahogany secretary.

Arm in arm, Sofya and Yelena struggled through the crowded streets. The entire city had rushed out after the news. At the bank, they found a disorderly crowd, rather than a line. The initial murmuring of the throng became a steady rumble. Sofya feared the bank might simply shut its doors if the crowd grew too large or too impatient. Surveying the swelling number of police, she knew there were even worse outcomes.

She pulled Yelena so close she could smell the apple she'd just eaten. "Go to the store on Lomonosov Street," she whispered. "Get canned goods, flour, sugar, things that won't spoil. A much as you can carry. I'll meet you at home." She pressed some rubles into Yelena's hand.

The teen nodded, biting her bottom lip. Stuffing the cash into a pocket, she stepped into the mob behind them. Shifting imperceptibly, the crowd opened a tiny space and swallowed her.

Small and slight, Sofya edged through gaps in the crowd and made her way toward the bank entrance. When someone exited, the guards allowed the next person outside to join the privileged interior queue. Soon she was through the doors of the bank. Unlike the chaos outside, the lines inside were disciplined and orderly, the atmosphere subdued. Under the watchful eyes of the bank manager and several armed guards, separate lines of five or six customers radiated from each of the three open teller windows. The lines moved slower than usual as everyone was withdrawing large sums.

Sofya fingered her simple gold necklace as she waited, rubbing the gift from her mother over and over like worry beads. An ornate gold crucifix adorned it for many years, but Sofya removed the cross after religion became risky. Still, she always wore the chain.

As she moved up in line, a change in mood filtered from behind the teller windows. The bank manager, seated at a desk talking on the phone, now paced between the tellers, whispering instructions and then speaking to the guards. Sofya crossed her arms against her chest.

Finally, the teller motioned Sofya forward. Producing her worn, gray passbook, she said, "I'd like to withdraw my savings." Trying to hide her racing heart, she stood back from the window. The woman took the passbook without reacting. Since Molotov's announcement everyone was requesting huge withdrawals. The manager interrupted, calling all three tellers to his desk where they huddled out of earshot. Their expressions grew dark. One gestured at the lines.

They returned to their positions after the brief conference. Sofya refused to look the woman in the eye and fixed instead on the teller's hands, watching her pull the remaining cash from her drawer and begin counting. It didn't look like much. Suddenly, a loud rattle and bang came from another teller's station. The manager had pulled down the wooden shutter.

Out of the corner of her eye, Sofya watched the next window also slam shut. Her heart sank. The last teller, her teller, seemed poised to write something in her passbook, but paused and wrote on a scrap of paper. Sofya's skin prickled with each sharp scratching of the pen. The manager approached, his eyes shifting about the room as the guards herded people out of the bank. The teller whispered to him and he glanced at the piece of paper. He shook his head. The teller pushed the passbook through the window and put the remaining cash back in her drawer. Sofya squeaked out a few words. "*Nichevo*? Nothing? Couldn't you give me some of my savings?" The shutter rattled and banged closed just like the others. A guard grabbed her upper arm, forcing her to the door with the other disgruntled customers. A chorus of complaint rose, but the guards pushed everyone outside into the large, angry throng.

Under heavy protection, the manager announced that banks in the city would be closed until Tuesday and there would be a new withdrawal limit of two hundred rubles per month. The irate buzz of protest swarmed all around as Sofya slipped along the edge of the building.

Two hundred rubles? In a wartime black market that wouldn't buy much. Damn, damn. How could she have been so stupid? Her heart hammered as she threaded her way around the back of Gostiny Dvor, anxious to get home, away from the crush of people.

"How was the bank?" Yelena asked, as Sofya shuffled into the kitchen, head down.

"Frantic," Sofya said. "I didn't get anything. I was right there, with the teller, and they ran out of money. Hundreds still waiting." She shook her head.

Yelena's face fell. "The store on Lomonosov was in a panic too. I couldn't believe the crowd of people trying to get inside. I managed to push in, but the shelves were stripped bare, as if a swarm of locusts had been through. I found four jars of preserves by digging around the back of some shelves on my hands and knees."

"Better than nothing." Sofya examined the identical jars, flashing garnet in the light. "Just wait. Even when they restock, they'll never keep up with demand. And prices will climb." Sofya didn't voice her fear that without her savings they weren't prepared for war. She had only two tasks: hoard food and get to the bank. What would happen if the war was difficult and long? When Vasili's cash was gone?

They emptied the bags from Sofya's earlier trip in silence. Yelena hopped down after putting the last few things on top of a cupboard. "Have you heard from Admiral Vasili?"

It was too soon, but still a tightness welled up in Sofya's throat and she shook her head.

"Might sound strange," Yelena continued, "but I miss him."

Still distracted and upset by the bank fiasco, Sofya couldn't even force a smile. "I'll tell him in my next letter. It'll make him happy." She wasn't surprised that Yelena developed an attachment to Vasili. He spent many evenings at their apartment before he deployed in May, talking to Yelena about school and playing chess. Sofya could see the two of them at the kitchen table, hunched over the chess-board. The way he encouraged her and made light of his own skills reminded her of Aleksandr.

"You'll beat me soon enough." He said one evening shortly before his deployment. "Good thing I'll be away for a while." He laughed out loud.

No wonder Yelena was so comfortable with him. He laughed like her father too.

How Sofya wished Vasili were here now. He would hold her, tell her they had enough cash, and remind her how successful she'd been with the food. Turning to outrun her tears, she stumbled, grabbing the table with one hand and the doorframe with the other. Yelena was at her side in an instant, an arm holding her in a half-hug.

"You're tired," Yelena said. "Such a day. I'll fix supper. You should rest."

Sofya nodded weakly. She left the kitchen and went to the entryway, picked up her violin case and wiped her tears roughly on a sleeve. In the living room, she lifted the instrument, touching its curves with her fingertips, then set it under her chin and put the bow to the strings. The enchanting but melancholic strains of Mahler's Adagietto rose like an offering. The wistful, lyrical notes filled her with longing, filled her heart with Vasili.

THE PEOPLE'S VOLUNTEER CORPS
June–July 1941

T HE PUNGENT STENCH of summertime sweat and unwashed bodies filled the streetcar where Pavel gripped an overhead strap and strained to keep his balance. His best friends, Kolya and Dimitri, chatted excitedly about the stunning announcement of war while Pavel gazed out a window. He'd been planning on spending lots of time with Lena Karavayeva this summer. But now, everything had changed.

Like most in Leningrad, the three teenagers rode the wave of patriotism sweeping the city. Propelled by loyalty, a sense of adventure, and bravado, they tried to join the Red Army. At seventeen they were almost of enlistment age, and they'd heard enough tales of underage youths fighting in previous conflicts to believe it possible now.

The streetcar slowed as it neared the recruitment center. The conductor rang the bell in a half-hearted attempt to clear the congested street. Men jumped down even before it came to a complete halt. Scattered and jostled like marbles, the boys fought their way to the sidewalk where Pavel backed up against a building to watch the crowd.

"You all right?" Kolya turned toward Pavel. "You don't seem like yourself."

Pavel, or Pavlik to his friends and relatives, looked around to make sure they were out of the crowd and away from prying eyes and ears. "Just the age requirement."

"What's the worst that can happen?" Dimitri shrugged. "Maybe they'll yell at us, maybe they'll throw us out, but it's war. They're not going to put us in prison for trying to enlist."

"You aren't afraid, are you?" Kolya narrowed his eyes.

"Hold on." Pavel drew himself up to his full height. "I'm not afraid. But we have to show our papers." He looked down. "Besides, my parents will kill me."

Pavel hadn't said anything about his father's view that war was something to be avoided at all cost. His papa had fought in the last conflict against Germany. It was something he refused to talk about, always saying it was best forgotten. When the three teens cut short their week of hunting and fishing at Kolya's *dacha* and rushed back to the city after Sunday's stunning news, the first thing his papa said was that under no circumstances should Pavel enlist before he was old enough, and even then only if there was no other choice. "There are plenty of ways to serve your country," his father had said.

"My parents don't want me enlisting either." Kolya shrugged. "But we have to do something. We can't sit around waiting to turn eighteen. Our country needs us."

"It's a chance to be part of something," said Dimitri. "We'll get to fight the filthy Nazis."

As Pavel led his friends down a side street, looking for a short-cut to enlistment and glory, he cast another glance at the dense, fit throng moving up the street. Despite his father's concerns, it was hard for Pavel to imagine anything other than a rapid victory over the Germans.

The disorganized line crept along, hours passing before the three friends glimpsed the registration tables. Finally at the head of the line, they found a rigid set of requirements and a humorless, stern interviewer who told them "not to waste the Red Army's time again," and to "come back when you're old enough to fight." Humiliated, the boys hurried out.

"I don't understand." Kolya said. "We won't be bigger or stronger in six months."

"*Soglasno.* Agreed," said Pavel. "But don't worry. We'll get our chance."

"Wait a minute!" Dimitri said. "I don't turn eighteen for a year. The war will be over by then. We need to do something now."

A couple of days later their enthusiasm revived after a city-wide call went out for civilian volunteers. A militia was being created and those too old, too young, or otherwise unable to enlist in the military were encouraged to mobilize with this new corps: the People's Volunteers.

Again, the line spilled down the street. It was more orderly this time and a much broader cross-section of citizens showed up. Elbow to elbow, there seemed to be thousands of ordinary people surging toward the recruitment building: men and women as old as their parents, plus plenty of older teens and college students. Pavel noticed more than a few grizzled veterans, some in their ancient uniforms complete with service ribbons and medals.

Party administrators and office workers in their white shirts buttoned at the collar walked together in small groups. Laborers in work boots and grease-stained overalls strode alongside doctors in white hospital jackets and nurses with sturdy shoes, pale blue dresses and matching caps. The crowd gave off a charged intensity and the hair on Pavel's arms stood on end.

When finally motioned forward, he approached a table covered with stacks of papers. A commanding, surly woman rested her hands on an enormous ledger. She wielded a sharp pencil like a weapon.

"Name?"

"Chernov, Pavel Ivanovich."

"Date of birth?"

"15 December 1923."

"Address?"

"Pugachev 9."

"Any skills?"

"Skills?"

"Yes. Abilities, experience."

He glanced at the large pictures of Lenin and Stalin on the wall behind her. "I'm a good violinist," he said, looking back at the woman who held his fate in her hands.

"Anything practical?" she said, eyebrows raised and an edge to her voice.

Pavel saw exasperation in her wide eyes and pursed lips. Or perhaps, he thought kindly, it was just exhaustion.

He hesitated for a moment. "I'm good with machines. I can drive and repair just about anything. Trucks, farm vehicles, things like that."

The woman's face was a question mark, her eyebrows still raised.

"I worked on a collective farm last year," he explained.

"Very well," she said, scribbling notes and dismissing him with a flick of her hand as she called, "Next!"

Working on a collective wasn't unusual and Pavel's months with his uncle's family had exposed him to all sorts of equipment and machinery. Some nascent mechanical abilities awakened. He'd started by tinkering, and the tinkering became repairing, and the repairing grew into modifying engines and replacing parts in creative ways. The entire collective hated to see him return to Leningrad.

The day after he registered with the Volunteers, Pavel learned he was assigned to a transportation unit handling logistics for the Leningrad Front—a different path from his friends. He tried to convince himself it was important work. The Red Army needed all sorts of things to fight a war: weapons, machinery, food. He'd help provide those things. But still, working in Leningrad seemed far from the war effort. All the volunteers he knew, especially his friends, were assigned to construction battalions that would head toward the front lines to dig trenches and tank traps in an effort to slow the enemy. Their work was urgent: building defenses, stopping the Nazis. He'd be stuck loading and unloading freight cars, or driving trucks with supplies.

Pavel's discouragement didn't last long—he wasn't one to feel sorry for himself. Instead, he organized a picnic along the Neva River by the Peter and Paul Fortress before his friends scattered. He invited everyone he knew, including Lena and her best friend, Tanya.

The three boys got there early to claim a large grassy area for fútball. A narrow swath of sand ran along the river's edge. Lena and Tanya arrived before the game got underway. Pavel approached the girls and pointed out where he was sitting. Distracted by Lena's short skirt and long, bare legs, he left Dimitri in charge of his team.

"Hi Lena, Tanya. Put your things here," he said, pointing to an old cotton blanket he'd arranged on the sand. Of course they came together. They were best friends. And Tanya was plenty nice, but Pavel really wanted to be alone with Lena.

"Thanks for inviting me," she said, smiling as she set her bag down.

"Yes," said Tanya. "And such a nice day." The two girls exchanged a look and Tanya added, "Well, I'm going to watch the game. See you two later."

Lena waved as her friend walked away and Pavel sighed in relief.

"I'm glad you could come." Pavel's eyes fixed on her. "Isn't it crazy how fast everything has happened? One minute we were looking forward to summer and now we're at war." He shook his head. "Did I tell you we tried to enlist? Dimitri, Kolya and me."

"Are you kidding?" Her eyes grew wide.

"We thought they might take us, but they were strict about being eighteen."

Yelena shifted about, crossing and uncrossing her ankles. "Were your parents upset?"

Pavel colored and winced. "I didn't tell them. They'd already told me not to try."

"Well, there's nothing to be embarrassed about. I think it was brave." Lena had her hair pulled back in a low ponytail behind one ear and she wrapped her hands around the length of it repeatedly, turning it into a single large curl.

"Maybe, but stupid too. The whole thing is wild. Two weeks ago, I was thinking about an engineering program."

"Well, the war won't last long, and when it's over you can still study engineering."

"That's the plan," Pavel said. "According to Radio Leningrad, the Germans are on the run."

"Nothing but good news so far," she agreed. "Speaking of news, Tanya and I signed up for a youth brigade."

"You did?" Pavel imagined Lena standing at the Komsomol meeting, her red neckerchief tied neatly under the collar of her white blouse. In his mind, the blouse was snug in all the right places and her legs were bare under her skirt, just like today.

"It was exciting," she said. "I was beginning to think we'd be left behind while everyone else in the city gets to help. Now we report to the Summer Garden in three days." Her face glowed. "They told us to bring shovels." She brushed an ant off her foot and lowered her voice. "My grandmother heard they're packing the Hermitage, crating everything to send east by train."

"Probably smart to plan for bombing raids," Pavel said. "The Nazis may try to repeat what they did to London." The German bombing campaign against London had made the news often during the previous fall and winter. It was hard not to admire the tenacity of the English.

"The British must be made of tough stuff," Lena said.

"My dad says the Germans underestimated them." He began to whisper. "His factory is moving to Kuibyshev. Makes me worried for my mother and sister. I hope they can join him."

"Your father's factory leaving already?" Lena whispered too. "My grandmother mentioned there's talk of evacuating the Leningrad Philharmonic and the Kirov Ballet."

"Even more shocking than my father's factory."

She nodded. "Makes me wonder what's happening at the front."

They both gazed at the Neva River, watching the sun sparkle on the water. It dominated the city from where they sat near the edge. The Winter Palace and the spire atop the Admiralty looked small on the far side of the broad expanse of water. A gray warship cruised upriver.

"Well, I'm glad there's a way for me to contribute," she said. "It won't be glamorous, but I don't mind, even if it's boring work."

"Lots of us will be doing ordinary jobs. Look at me—supplies," Pavel said, unable to hide his disappointment.

"I don't know, working on the Leningrad Front could be important."

"Still, it's not like Dimitri and Kolya. You know, they leave day after tomorrow."

"Really? My mother too. She also joined." Lena scooped cold, gritty sand over her bare feet and wriggled her toes.

"You don't think they could be going to the same place?"

Lena's brow furrowed. "It would be a crazy coincidence. My mother says there are thousands of volunteers." She hesitated. "When do you leave?"

"Not for five more days."

Pavel watched her play with the sand. He snuck a glance at the perfect skin below her neck, his gaze moving to her breasts. She would look fantastic in a bathing suit. When she moved her hand close, he slipped his fingers between hers. "Do you think we could go to the movies before I leave? I'd really like to see you again."

"I'd like that." She leaned into him. And then she added, "I'm going to miss you."

She moved her face closer and his eyes lingered on her mouth. He leaned over and kissed her. The soft pressure of her lips lasted several seconds, long enough for Pavel to tingle from someplace deep. A little current of electricity started in his groin. Lena rested her head against his shoulder. The sounds of the match reminded him they weren't alone, but he looked around and it seemed no one was watching. Anyway, he wouldn't have many more chances to show her how he felt. He kissed her again.

❧ ❧

Lena accompanied her mother to the train, hoping to be a support. They'd spent more time together the last few months. Sometimes they did the shopping or went for a walk. Mama almost never mentioned Papa, but when she got a certain look on her face, a faraway distracted look, Lena could tell she was thinking about him. During one of those quiet moments, Lena told her about Pavel. Not about them kissing, of course. But she described all his good traits, especially how smart and kind he was. Mama seemed happy for her.

Hundreds of citizens—women, older teens and college students, workers, professionals and Party functionaries—crowded the packed train station. They were headed south and southwest to build defensive works to stop any Nazis that might make it past the Red Army. The Volunteer Corps was high on morale, although if her mother was an example, low on equipment. Lena assumed the volunteers would be back soon. After all, Radio Leningrad was already proclaiming military successes at the front. As they stood on the platform, she watched her mother, unsure what she was thinking and wondering what to say.

"You're very brave, Mama. Have you gotten any information about where you'll be working, or for how long?" The destination on the departure board was listed as Luga, a town south of Leningrad in the direction of Pskov.

"Nothing but the orders to report here today," her mother replied.

"The only thing they told us was to bring a change of clothes." She held up her small rucksack. "And implements for digging too, but you need the shovel. I'm sure there'll be something else for me to do."

Lena smiled a tight smile. Her mother had a talent for making things go her way.

She faced her mama to say goodbye and saw a softening in her usual remote countenance. A shadow hovered over her face, love perhaps, or regret. A few tears dampened her cheeks. Lena hoped they were for her and reached out for an embrace.

Her mama buried her face in Lena's hair as she held her. "Try not to worry. I know it's a lot to have both of us gone. But you have your grandmother and she's so good at everything. You two can look out for each other. And it'll only be a few weeks. I'll be back before you know it. I need to do my duty just like everyone else. Especially with your father unable to serve."

Lena was puzzled by her mama's words. What did her decision have to do with Papa?

Her mother stepped back and smoothed her hair. "This way, I'll regain the Party's trust."

The train whistle sounded and the conductor called out the imminent departure. All around them passengers said their final farewells and jumped aboard. The train began to rumble and her mama grabbed her rucksack and raced up the steps.

Lena's farewell, "Take care of yourself, Mama. I love you," was drowned out by the roar of the engine. As she turned away, Lena stumbled on the crowded platform. When she regained her balance, she spied Pavel's friends in a crowded train window. Kolya caught her eye, a look of surprise and recognition passing over his face. Lena waved and called out, "Good luck."

FREEDOM, OF A SORT
July 1941

SOFYA'S BLOUSE CLUNG to her and a particularly large rivulet of sweat ran down her back. She strained under the weight of two heavy bags and her violin case. Since the war began, she was never empty-handed. And usually in a hurry too.

The entire city moved at a frantic pace. Everyone had a job and everyone did their part. Sofya focused on two things: music and food. As the only orchestra left in the city, the RadioCom was in tremendous demand. They performed dozens of concerts and made numerous recordings, the latter of which often played on Radio Leningrad. Sofya loved her full schedule, even if the outsized popularity of the 1812 Overture made her tire of Tchaikovsky.

Food prices rose as she said they would. Still, after a lifetime in Leningrad she knew the city's stores and often managed to be in the right place at the right time. She'd memorized the delivery schedule for the local basement specialty shops, and she heard by word of mouth when the larger, modern grocery stores had surpluses of any sort. She knew where to get meat and the location of the freshest vegetables. It was knowledge she put to good use.

Like today. She carried a half kilo of butter in one of her bags, and didn't care that she'd paid ten times the pre-war cost. Lots of people balked at the exorbitant prices—she heard the complaints everywhere—but this was why Vasili had given her so much money. In addition, she'd gotten her withdrawals for June and July and would go to the bank every month. Two hundred rubles wasn't a huge sum, but it would help if the war was long.

As she started up the stairs, bags throwing her off balance, the single, shared phone in the entryway rang. She sighed and hesitated, not wanting to set everything down. Perhaps one of the neighbors will come. The Karavayevs rarely got phone calls, but after the fourth ring, she dropped her bags on the landing and scurried down the steps to grab the phone.

"*Slushayu.* I'm listening," she said, catching her breath and wiping the sweat from her face with a sleeve.

"Mama? It's me. Aleksandr," the voice said. "I'm in Moscow. I've been released."

Stunned, she said nothing. Then, unbelief gave way to the reality of her dear Sasha's voice. Her throat burned and she began to cry.

"Mama? Are you there? It's me."

The tears became a flood and she sobbed in relief. "Sashenka."

"I only have a few minutes. It's now *Captain* Karavayev, and I'm at Red Army headquarters about to join my battalion. I've been assigned to a motorized unit. I'm not sure where I'll be. I'll write soon, but you can reach me with the 16th Army." He paused. "I'm fine. Wish I could see you, all of you. Is my Lenochka there?"

His words rushed over the line. He would be thinner now, in his new uniform, leaning against a wall in the headquarters building. Her son—released to fight. She wiped her face and took a deep breath.

"Sasha, I can't believe it's you. We're well. Yelena and me, that is. But Katya left with the People's Volunteers two weeks ago. We've heard nothing."

"I was wrong about Katya," he said.

"Let's not talk about that now, Sasha, I'm just so thankful to hear your voice, to know you're, you're . . ." Alive. She was overjoyed he'd survived his first months in the camp. But she didn't want to weigh him down with her fears. "Yelena's not here. She'll be so disappointed to have missed you." Every word caught in her throat and she swallowed hard, trying not to cry during their precious minutes.

"Hug her for me. Tell her how much I miss her. I miss you too," he said.

She heard the gravel of emotion in his words. "I'll kiss her for you." Her own voice cracked. There was so much to say and she was desperate to keep talking. Was he okay?

"I need to go, Mama. Please take care of yourself. Be safe."

At that moment, the door to the apartment building opened and Sofya exclaimed into the phone, "Wait a moment. Yelena's here." Sofya trembled as she handed her stunned granddaughter the receiver, hardly able to speak. "It's your papa."

Yelena took the phone in both hands and exclaimed, "Papa, is it really you?"

A glorious cascade of bells vibrated over the line.

"It's really me, *malenka maya*, my little one. I've been released. I'm in Moscow. I report in a few minutes. Just sad that I can't see you. Are you well?"

"Oh yes, Papa. Working hard in the war effort. Building defenses for the city. And studying hard in school before that."

Sofya leaned close to the earpiece, listening to her son.

"I'm proud of you, Lenochka." He sniffed.

"I miss you so much, Papa. You must come back to us. I love you."

"I love you too. Don't worry about me, my sweet. I'll be back when the war is over—maybe before that if I get leave. It's wonderful to hear your voice. Take care of yourself, and your grandmother. I have to go."

Sofya leaned ever closer, straining to hear her Sasha while Yelena choked out the words, "You can count on me, Papa."

"Goodbye, *malenka*."

Sofya called into the receiver, "Goodbye, Sasha," before the line went dead. She imagined him clasping the phone as he regained his composure. Tears ran down Yelena's face, her eyes squeezed shut, the phone still cradled in her hands. Sofya replaced the receiver and put her arms around her granddaughter. They both shook with sobs, holding each other, then Yelena croaked, "Papa's out!" They smiled and laughed through their tears, the two of them talking at the same time in a jumble of words and interruptions and emotions. "Can you believe it? How did he get released?" "They must need more officers." "And he sounded so good." "It's like a dream." "How was he able to call?" They held each other's hands and hugged over and over before finally collecting Sofya's bags and making their way upstairs.

THE DACHA

August 1941

YELENA YAWNED a second time as they walked in the bright, early morning light to catch a *tramvai*, a streetcar. "Sorry," she said, covering her mouth.

Sofya took her granddaughter's hand, tracing the strange network of rough edges and patches of new pink skin on her palm. The blisters had healed, but Sofya hated how Yelena's hands had gotten torn up during the first long days of digging with her work brigade.

"I'm the one who's sorry. You have to spend your day off with me," Sofya said.

Yelena linked arms with her grandmother. "Don't be silly. What else would I be doing? And besides, I'm not letting you travel alone. It might be dangerous."

"Not with this," Sofya said, patting her pocket.

Travel into and out of Leningrad had been restricted for weeks, but when Sofya received an official transit document in Vasili's last letter, it meant they could go to the *dacha* and get his things. With Commissar Kuznetsov's signature and raised seal, it allowed her and Yelena to come and go from Leningrad at will. It was a powerful piece of paper. Vasili must have gone to a lot of trouble to get it. Perhaps the situation was more urgent than it seemed. No one really knew what was happening in the war. At least none of the average citizens. Radio Leningrad broadcast positive, encouraging news. But Sofya knew it wasn't the whole truth. It could be a tactic by the authorities to keep the people calm. The furious preparations in Leningrad had an urgency that was hard to square with the optimistic news reports. And now the transit letter.

Sofya and Yelena hurried across jagged pavement, big sections broken up by tanks and other heavy equipment. Since Molotov's announcement, every day had a new intensity: citizens mobilizing, industries moving east, munitions factories in overdrive. Volunteers dug enormous trenches on Leningrad's outskirts. Things of value were camouflaged, buried, or transported hundreds of kilometers away. The city was changing, spinning faster and faster like a giant centrifuge spitting out machinery, people, entire enterprises. Even the youth brigades worked long hours burying sculptures from the Hermitage, digging bomb shelters, and building scaffolding to protect city monuments.

Defenses appeared everywhere. Anti-aircraft guns ringed the Winter Palace and St Isaac's, pointing accusingly at the heavens. Zeppelin-shaped barrage balloons floated above the city, pulling at their winches, part of the developing nightmare. The gold spires of the Admiralty and the Peter and Paul Cathedral had disappeared under gray paint.

The *tramvai* rumbled up behind them. Boarding with factory workers headed for a long day, Sofya saw only women. Three months earlier it would have been a crowd of mostly men in overalls and flat cloth caps.

At the train station, the throngs of people gave off a low, throaty hum. Anxiety swirled thick among the groups of women and children fleeing Leningrad. Their unease was contagious. Sofya grew tense as she heard snatches of their anxious conversations. "Mama, I don't want to go. Please, let me stay." "Now, now hush. Your grandmother can't go alone. Papa and I need you to take care of her. I'll join you as soon as I can."

Announcements came in a constant stream from the loudspeakers. Although they were taking a simple day trip, Sofya gripped the transit letter and examined the list of destinations. They could go far from the war: Kuibyshev on the Volga, Novosibirsk, or all the way to exotic Tashkent, the new wartime home of the Leningrad Philharmonic. Was that why Vasili had sent the document?

Evacuation still seemed an extreme step. Although getting food was time-consuming, with long, unavoidable lines, the rations were generous. Prices rose nearly every day, but there was still food in the stores. Most importantly, there'd been no bombings, just a couple of air raid drills. Sofya paid little attention to the endless positive reports from Radio Leningrad, but it seemed possible the Red Army was holding back the Nazis.

Now, they were surrounded by crowds trying to evacuate. Uncertainty buzzed in her head. It made sense that children were leaving Leningrad. But her and Yelena? She brushed away the nagging thought.

As the outskirts of the city ran past their window, both women gaped at the barricades, the tanks, and miles of newly-dug trenches. The more defensive measures she saw, the less secure Sofya felt. The idea of evacuation buzzed back like a pesky fly.

They disembarked at the village of Alexandrovskaya to find the tiny hamlet thrumming with energy. People crowded the ticket window. Strange to see a long queue in a small town.

The main square consisted of a handful of buildings in addition to the train station. A large cluster of birches surrounded by grass and edged with bricks occupied the center of the square. Numerous small groups of ragged people sprawled on the grass. Others sat with their backs against buildings. Curious.

They pulled out the simple bread and cheese they'd packed that morning and walked out of the village toward Tsarskoye Selo, eight or nine kilometers away. It was a nice day, and Sofya hoped they could get a ride from a local. Sure enough, just past the last houses and rough side-streets, a cart slowed and the driver offered a lift. In the countryside, everyone knew everyone else, so their presence was a welcome novelty. When Sofya mentioned they had just come from the city the man raised his eyebrows. "What for? Aren't you safer in the city? Wife and I are leaving soon. We've got family in Kazan."

Sofya explained that they were there to check on Admiral Antonov's *dacha*. Mentioning the Antonovs distracted the driver and he chatted at length about notable summer residents. By the time he ran out of stories, the turn to the *dacha* came into view. Sofya pressed a few coins into his hand, thanking him for his trouble.

A huge oak tree marked the narrow lane and at the end of the lane, Sofya stopped. Some of her sweetest, most powerful memories were from here. But now, the cottage looked small, lost in a sea of neglect. Tall grass and shrubs grew wild and broken branches were scattered about. Thick with moss, the roof and beams holding the porch seemed worn and unsteady. The romantic retreat of her youth had become little more than a shabby two-bedroom cottage without running water or a toilet. When she unlocked the door and stepped inside, they heard the scurrying of rodents in retreat.

Yelena shrank away, her nose wrinkled in disgust.

"Don't worry." Sofya patted her arm. "It's just field mice. Nothing like the city rats we sometimes see. The pantry cupboard is to the left of the kitchen sink." She pointed the way. "Why don't you start there?"

Yelena sighed. "I hate mice."

"Don't be so squeamish," Sofya said. "They're more afraid of you."

As Yelena tiptoed into the kitchen, Sofya heard her mutter. "Not very reassuring."

Sofya gave the curtains a tug, sending dust swirling through sunbeams. She surveyed the living area, not certain what to look for. The bookshelves held a small collection, and she flipped through the volumes. A copy of *War and Peace* inscribed to Vasili by his father caught her attention, and she put it aside. The entire country was reading Tolstoy. Turning to the mantle, she noticed a single large book, the very same volume of *Les Miserables* which Vasili had read from all those years ago during their weekend together. She held it for a moment and put it with the Tolstoy. At the other end of the mantle, in a similar place of esteem, was the photograph of Vasili's parents. Standing side-by-side, they looked unnaturally stern. Sofya recognized Vasili in the strong set of his father's shoulders. She looked closer, thinking of her parents, filled with a flash of nostalgia for that long-ago life which seemed so simple compared to recent decades.

Next to the fireplace, on a small table in the corner was the chessboard she remembered. It hinted at the controversial nature of the pieces, although it was not a celebration of the monarchy. It was a piece of art, edged with finely carved panoramas of St. Petersburg under the tsars. The Winter Palace along one side, Peterhof with its gorgeous gardens along a second, the Catherine Palace in the town of Tsarskoye Selo on the third edge, and lastly the Peter and Paul Fortress. Sofya wondered if the ornate imperial Russian figures were close by, but their absence made her think Vasili had gotten rid of them. Maybe he'd burned or buried them after the Revolution. Sofya set the chessboard on the sofa with the books and photograph.

She heard her granddaughter moving noisily, banging cupboards to keep the rodents at bay. She poked her head into the kitchen to check on her progress.

"Flour and sugar." The teen pointed to three large identical jars on the counter.

"Mmmm," Sofya muttered. "Glass jars. The rodents have been trouble for a while."

Yelena nodded at several bottles of vodka and champagne. "And plenty of alcohol."

"While you finish in here, I'm going to check the vegetable garden," Sofya said.

As Vasili had described, the garden lay next to the fenced pigpen, which was not too close to the house because of the smell in summer. The caretaker put in a garden every year and got a young pig or two to fatten up and slaughter in the fall. He'd salt and smoke the meat. Some for the Antonovs and some for the himself; a good arrangement for everyone.

Of course, this year was different. The pigpen was empty and the caretaker had probably volunteered. Overrun with weeds, the garden still showed evidence of tilling and planting under the green and brown chaos. An image from childhood flashed—her grandmother squatting next to a garden plot in a village outside the city. Sofya smiled and knelt by the mounded rows of leafy plants. She dug into the side of one, uncovering a small potato, and then another and another. She rushed back to the house.

"Good news in the garden," Sofya said, a bit breathless. "Potatoes."

"That's a relief. Not much here." Yelena gestured at the meager supplies she found: the alcohol, flour, and some kasha, plus several jars of pickled vegetables. Vasili loved pickled cucumbers and green beans.

"I guess I'm not surprised. Looks like the caretaker had just started stocking the cupboards for the summer season. Still, there should be pork in the root cellar."

"Hope so," Yelena said. "That would make the trip worthwhile." She moved toward the back door. "How about I get the potatoes?"

Sofya smiled and nodded and went into the dim second bedroom. Twin beds covered with matching light brown blankets dominated the room. An ancient candle sagged in a dish on the nightstand.

In the larger bedroom she folded the handmade coverlet Vasili mentioned, then opened the nearly empty closet. Balancing on a chair to reach the high shelf, she ran her hand back and forth until it bumped into a box.

"*Babusya?*" Yelena called out as she came in. "I've got quite a pile of potatoes. And I found some radishes too. Do we have a bag or something?"

"I'm back here," Sofya answered. Sitting on the bed, she cradled the handgun.

"Is that what I think it is?" Yelena's eyes were saucers.

"A Tokarev," Sofya said. "Like your *dedya* used to carry. Your papa too, for that matter."

Yelena came close. "Can I hold it?"

Sofya slid the magazine out and checked the chamber before handing it to her.

"*Dedya* used to say it was easy to use, but not all that accurate." She smiled. "I'm not really sure about the accuracy part. Your papa said Grandpa wasn't a particularly good shot."

"Are we taking it with us?" Yelena examined it, aiming at nothing in particular.

"Of course. You never know, we might need it."

Grim-faced, Yelena handed the gun back. "I should probably know how to use it."

"As soon as we're home." Sofya turned. "On second thought, maybe you should try it now—where no one will hear."

Sofya took the box and Yelena followed her outside to the back of the cottage.

"It's quite simple. The cartridge holds the bullets. You slide it into the magazine well," she said, pushing a cartridge into the bottom of the pistol grip until it clicked. "Then you pull the safety back and ease it to the half-notch position. Like this."

Yelena took the gun and practiced loading it.

"Now, aim at that tree," Sofya said, pointing to a large spruce perhaps thirty feet away. "If you're using this, your target will likely be close."

Yelena gripped the gun and held it at arm's length.

"Support your right hand with your left, for balance," Sofya said, as her granddaughter aimed at the tree.

"That's it. Now fire."

The retort was accompanied by a small kick which threw Yelena's hands into the air. At the tree, they found the bullet hole above their heads.

"Perfect shot," Yelena smirked. "If I'd been aiming at a giant."

Sofya chuckled. "Good for the first time. Now you know how it works. Just in case."

After loading the vegetables into one of the many string bags Sofya always carried in her pockets, they packed their rucksacks and started for the root cellar. The undergrowth was thick and damp between the *dacha* and the creek. A bit of the old path appeared, opening into a small clearing by the stream. Beyond that, the bank got steeper. The large rocks Vasili described came into view, and behind some ferns they found the small wooden entrance. Yelena put her shoulder to the door and it creaked and scraped open. Sofya ducked inside with her flashlight. Maybe four meters deep, it had a rough dirt floor with wood beams along the ceiling. Sofya smelled the rich, damp earth and imagined the worms at work beneath her feet creating the life-giving soil. Even in the middle of summer it was cold. Funny how such a place would protect its contents from both the heat of summer and the cold of winter. One wall was covered with empty shelves on bricks. A wooden barrel with a small crowbar on top stood in a corner.

Yelena held the flashlight while Sofya used the crowbar to pop the lid, then plunged a hand into the sawdust. She struggled to lift out the heavy pork leg.

"Oh my," Yelena exclaimed, as Sofya brushed off the sawdust clinging to the meat. The aroma of smoked pork filled the cellar. They both leaned close and sniffed.

"I've never seen meat like this." Yelena said.

"It's been years since we had a whole ham. Decades, maybe."

Sofya put her nose against the meat and inhaled again. "My goodness. Does anything anywhere smell so good?"

Yelena sniffed too. "Now I see why Admiral Vasili wanted us to
make the trip."

They reorganized the rucksacks, and Sofya placed the gun at the
very bottom of hers. She'd say it was the Admiral's if it was discovered. Private weapons had already been confiscated by the authorities. The chessboard went in next. Then the coverlet and other things.

"Are you going to be able to carry that? Here." Her granddaughter lifted it up and Sofya slipped her arms through the straps. Then
Yelena swung the other, much heavier, pack up onto her own back.

Balancing their loads, they struggled through the dense foliage,
sweat dripping down their faces and collecting in their armpits.
Sofya strained to keep up with Yelena. Once on the road, the footing
improved. And they weren't alone. A steady stream of people was
headed toward the village. Mostly women and children. All carried
belongings. Sometimes several generations were together, an elderly
family member pushed along in a cart. From snatches of conversations, Sofya and Yelena learned these were villagers fleeing ahead of
the advancing Germans.

"Are the Germans really so close to Leningrad?" Yelena said in a
fearful whisper.

"Let's not talk about it here," said Sofya. "Maybe we can learn
more in town." Glancing around, she was stunned at the exodus.
Suddenly everything came into focus. The frenetic preparations in
Leningrad, the transit document from Vasili, and now a flood of
people fleeing eastward. The war was going badly. The Germans were
coming.

Sick to her stomach, Sofya reached into her pocket to touch
the paper from Vasili. He had sent it so they'd escape Leningrad.
Instead, they were collecting ham and potatoes. Still, they could use
the transit letter again. It wasn't a one-time pass. She'd figure out an

evacuation plan as soon as they returned. At the very least, she had to get Yelena to safety. Across the Volga. Somewhere the Germans could never reach.

In the village, hundreds of people filled the train station, all clamoring to get away from the approaching enemy. Sofya checked their return tickets as they worked their way through the station and onto the platform. She began to fear the small suburban train, just four or five cars long, wouldn't be able to handle so many passengers, especially if other stops were equally crowded.

"Our best chance will be to get on this first train. More people are coming into the station all the time, and others will be trying to get on in other towns as well."

"Don't worry," Yelena said. "I'll find a way. Stay close."

As soon as the crowd heard the rumble of the approaching loco-motive, chaos erupted. Children cried and mothers shouted instruc-tions. "Hold my hand!" "Stay with me!" "Don't let go of your brother!" People pushed and anxiety swirled thick and heavy. An elderly couple stumbled, and in that instant they were separated. Sofya could see the man's frantic face, his words drowned out by the twin roars of the crowd and the train. Yelena inched her way to the front of the platform while Sofya, jostled and unbalanced, struggled to stay close. Long, steady blasts of the whistle sounded, signaling the train wasn't going to stop. The engineer looked panicked. He leaned out, eyes wild, scanning the crowd as the train crawled into the station.

When the first car passed, people leaning out windows, Sofya sensed Yelena knew what was happening. Agile even with her heavy pack, the teen caught the handle of the second car and scrambled up the steps of the slow-moving train. Sofya ran a bit to keep up, push-ing, grabbing the handle and fighting to climb the steps at the same time. She stumbled, and in a decisive fraction of a second her grand-daughter leaned out and grasped her rucksack, lifting Sofya into the air as her foot found a step. They sprawled into the vestibule, out of breath and stunned.

After scrambling into a corner, Yelena took off her pack and peered through the door into the car. People jammed every seat and filled the floor.

"What's going on?" said Yelena. "This is crazy. The train didn't even stop."

A woman, curled opposite with a young child, spoke. "Don't you know?" She looked around to see if anyone could hear. "Horrible things are happening. Luga was bombed."

"Luga?" Yelena repeated, her voice high and eyes wide. Her mother was in Luga. "Were you there?" Sofya frowned to discourage the conversation.

The woman whispered. "We caught the last train out as the Germans attacked." The woman's whisper was so faint it seemed she herself didn't believe they'd escaped.

Sofya leaned close to Yelena and whispered. "Shhhh." It was risky to talk about the war. Someone might overhear. The two of them sat there, huddled against their packs.

When the woman took her child to the bathroom, Sofya turned to her granddaughter, taking her hand. "I know you're worried. But it's dangerous to talk." Yelena wiped her face on a sleeve. "It's shocking news, but remember, we don't know much. Not even where your mama was when the Germans attacked. I'll try to get some information about the volunteers from the District Committee. In the meantime, try not to think the worst. Hang onto hope."

Yelena nodded and stared blankly at the countryside as the train crept toward Leningrad.

They arrived mid-afternoon. Occasional whistle blasts rose above the thrum of voices in the packed station. Announcements came over loudspeakers, temporarily drawing the attention of the anxious, but orderly crowd. Caught in the sea of refugees, Sofya gripped Yelena's hand as they inched along, bent under the weight of their rucksacks. Nearing the end of the platform, she saw the reason for the delay. The secret police had set up a checkpoint, processing refugees, interrogating everyone, inspecting suitcases and bundles, scattering personal items, making arrests.

Sofya whispered to Yelena, "Don't say anything. Let me talk. If they ask, you were helping your grandmother. That's all you know."

Two young agents approached. They wore the intimidating flat blue hats of the secret police.

"Where are you coming from?" one growled.

"We're Leningrad residents. We were in Alexandrovskaya."

"No one's allowed out of Leningrad. Where are your papers? Open these!" The other gestured at their bulging packs.

Sofya nodded to Yelena and they set them down. Rumors abounded about spies and provocateurs infiltrating the city. The NKVD suspected everyone. Sofya produced their documents, the powerful transit letter as well as their ordinary residence permits. The first agent's brow furrowed as he studied the papers while the other rifled through their rucksacks. "What's all this?" He scattered jars and books. Sofya faced the agent holding their papers when suddenly the precious smell of their pork reached her nose. They could take the hindquarter, or anything else. Worse, in another minute they'd find the gun and she might be arrested. Sofya forced herself to project calm even though her heart pounded like a jackhammer. An older agent approached as she pointed to her documents.

"Admiral Antonov sent us, on Commissar Kuznetsov's orders, to retrieve these goods from his *dacha*." Sofya gripped her hands together so they wouldn't tremble. "He's planning to hold a victory party when we defeat the fascists and wants these supplies on hand to celebrate the very moment we've conquered the German dogs. No doubt that will be in a matter of weeks."

Sofya's mention of the Commissar—as well as the sanctioned

Party position regarding a quick victory—got the attention of the senior agent. He motioned the others to move to the next passengers and examined the papers. Squinting at the signature and seal, he returned their documents and wordlessly waved the two women through.

EVACUATION

August 1941

LENA RETURNED to her Komsomol brigade the day after the trip to the *dacha*. Exhausted from a poor night's sleep and agitated about her mother and the war news, she stared at the front of the room and waited for her assignment. If only her mother hadn't joined the Volunteer Corps. She could be building tanks at the gigantic Kirov works. Instead, she was in Luga. Under attack. An official rapped the wooden podium and Lena jerked to attention.

Volunteers were needed to support an upcoming evacuation. This would be no ordinary exodus of women and children. Instead, thousands of unaccompanied youngsters were being sent away from Leningrad. Their parents had critical jobs and would remain in the city. Teachers and Party officials would lead the evacuation, but dozens of older youths were needed to help.

On her way home that afternoon, Lena felt guilty about not wanting to volunteer. She still belonged to the Komsomol, even though she'd expected her membership to be revoked after her papa's arrest. Mama lost her job and Party card, her grandmother was demoted, but Lena was obligated to the Communist Party. Moreover, she had experience working with children after school. In fact, now that she and Pavel were a couple, she thought of their future, building a family. Their children would be tall, but would they have Pavel's dark eyes or would they be blue-eyed and fair? Not that those things mattered. They'd certainly be smart, maybe musical like Pavel and her grandmother.

Helping with the evacuation meant leaving Leningrad. Her grandmother would be alone and that didn't seem right. Yesterday's trip proved they needed each other. Duty to country was important, of course, but what about family? Abandoning her *babushka* with the Germans getting close seemed unthinkable. She stepped off the streetcar, almost colliding with the head of school in the process.

"Yelena! I'm glad to see you. You heard the announcement this morning." Comrade Pavlova was a tall, imperious woman, a 'force of nature,' Lena's friend Tanya liked to say. She grabbed Lena's arm and pulled her onto the sidewalk. "Be sure to request an assignment in our sector of the city. You're so good with the young ones. The evacuation could be difficult for some." Her brow knitted. "Of course, it can't be helped. They have to go without their parents. You'll be such a comfort, a real calming presence."

"But I'm already doing valuable work."

The head of school clucked her tongue. "Of course you are. You have many gifts. But this is far more important than working in a youth brigade. Excuse me for being so blunt, but it's a desperate situation. We cannot send these children away without support and supervision. Many of them are very young. I won't take no for an answer."

The woman stood close. Lena struggled to keep eye contact. "Yes, Comrade, I understand, but I have family obligations as well. My grandmother will be alone if I go."

"Family obligations are secondary. You are a Komsomol member. Have you forgotten your duty?" Comrade Pavlova's eyebrows rose sharply. "Do I need to pay your grandmother a visit? Sofya Nikolayevna is a capable woman and can manage well enough on her own. Much better than hundreds of unsupervised tots."

The woman was relentless. Lena knew she was beaten and forced a resigned smile. "Yes, Comrade. I'll request our sector. Maybe I'll know a few children."

"Bravo, Yelena. That's the spirit! You're a courageous girl, and the city is grateful."

Comrade Pavlova turned away and the wind swirled her open coat about her, magnifying her imposing presence as she boarded another tram.

Lena hung her head and turned for home. What rotten luck. Cornered by the head of school. Entering the apartment, she slammed the door and started complaining.

"Calm down, Lenochka." Her grandmother made room on the sofa and they sat close. "Shhh. Not so fast. Start at the beginning."

Lena's words tumbled out: the announcement, her reluctance, the consideration of duty and loyalty, then the unfortunate run-in with Comrade Pavlova. Lena wanted to be here in Leningrad with her grandmother. They were a team. They needed each other. She couldn't leave. What would happen if things got worse?

"I understand how you're feeling, Sweetheart. Of course, it would be best if we could stay together, but you can't ignore your duty." She paused and sighed. "I think you must go. I'll manage. I have my work colleagues. If things get bad, I can stay at the Radio House."

Lena was puzzled by her grandmother's calm. Being together was clearly the best thing. Besides, everyone else she cared about was here, especially Pavel. Already on the verge of tears, Lena slipped down off the sofa to sit on the floor so she wouldn't have to look her *babushka* in the eye. With the sofa as a backrest, her fingers traced the stitches in the rug.

"I don't want to be far from Pavel or the Petrovs either. Right now, he's somewhere on the outskirts of the city. Even though we don't see each other, I feel close to him."

Her grandmother ran her fingers through Lena's hair, absent-mindedly braiding it as they talked. "You mustn't worry about Pavel. Trust me, distance won't destroy your feelings for each other. There's no doubt of his affection." She smoothed and divided the long blond strands and gently twisted them. "Nearly everything is out of our control these days. All we can do is focus on helping our country in whatever way we can. This is your way. You'll be protecting the next generation while their parents work for the nation's defense. It's important. Plus, you'll get out of the city. Far from the war."

"What about you? I'll be worried sick. Maybe you should evacuate too." Lena's voice filled with concern. "This changes things. How will you get your rations if you become ill?"

A weighty silence filled the apartment.

"I haven't had time to think about what your evacuation means for me," her *babushka* said. "Maybe it does change things. Perhaps after you're far from Leningrad, somewhere safe, I can use the transit paper to join you. We'll see what happens—how close the Germans get. You'll need to write as soon as you can, so I know where you are."

A week later, rucksack on her back, Lena walked to Moscow Station. She'd written Pavel, confiding her deepening affection and asking him to check on her grandmother if he ever came into Leningrad. She said a tearful goodbye to Tanya and her family, wanting her best friend to come with her, but understanding that with Mrs. Petrov working long hours in the war effort, Tanya needed to care for her younger siblings. And then there was her grandmother. Just thinking about her alone in Leningrad as the Nazis drew near made Lena weep. She tried to be strong, but they'd sobbed, hugging each other, promising to take care of themselves, promising they'd be together again when the war was over.

The scheduled departure was an hour away, yet children and their parents already congregated in the station. Lena checked in with the other chaperones and received basic instructions. She carried her clipboard to her assigned train, scanning the names. There was just one she recognized: little Talya was in her group.

Although early in the morning, sweat clung to her as she stood at the steps to the correct car and greeted the freshly scrubbed youngsters and grim parents, checking the children's names off her list. Each child had a handwritten number pinned to their clothing identifying their group and carried a small bag of food and a few extra clothes. Lena was in charge of eighteen four- to six-year-olds. So young. She watched the parents trying to soothe their frightened, crying children. "Just like going to the *dacha* for a few weeks." "It'll be an adventure." "We'll join you soon, but right now we have to stay with the factory." How hard it must be for them to pretend every-thing would be all right. Everyone knew the war was going poorly.

Comrade Filina materialized out of the crowd as her daughter ran up and hugged Lena.

"Oh, Yelena. *Slava bogu.* Thank god. Seeing you here is the only good thing about this mess. Now at least Talya will be happy. You know, last year, whenever you helped with her class she'd come home saying 'Yelena this,' or 'Yelena that.' She adores you."

"And I adore her. I'm so glad she's in my group." Lena hugged the tiny five-year-old. "Go find a seat, Talya, I'll be right in." She added in a soft voice, "Say goodbye to your mama."

Talya started up the stairs with her mother, just as an official happened by. "No parents on the train. You'll have to wave goodbye from here."

Talya's mother stepped down and walked along the outside of the car, shouting as Talya made her way on the inside. "Obey Yelena, *malenka*! Follow instructions and pay attention. I love you!" So many children on the train were crying and calling to their parents that Lena couldn't tell if little Talya was all right.

She rushed to board the remaining children, giving parents what little assurance she could, then climbed up herself and greeted the other chaperone. The children who filled the opposite side were older, eight or ten perhaps, and they were a rambunctious lot. Lena's group

was calm by comparison, probably in a state of shock at being separated from their parents.

Some sniffed and cried, some tried to be brave, but Lena knew
they had little grasp of the nature of war and why they had to leave
their homes and families. Lucky for Lena, the little ones calmed soon
after they departed. A train trip was special. She encouraged the novelty of the experience. They sang and played, spirits rising as the train
travelled south of Leningrad to the town of Demyansk.

Waiting for housing arrangements outside the station, there
was a sudden flurry of activity. Word sped among the adults—the
Germans were closing in. The evacuees had been delivered not to
safety, but straight into the path of the enemy. A Red Army detach-
ment appeared with military vehicles and the children were ferried to
another station, Lychkovo, about forty kilometers north, where other
trains waited. Lena kept the children holding hands in their own
small group during the urgent changes. She distracted them with the
whisper game. Even the simplest phrase, "A dog barked," or "A goose
was loose," ended in fits of laughter when the last child repeated what
she'd heard.

After they settled into the second train, Lena again led the children in some songs. Clean and neat, the girls in cotton dresses and
boys in short pants were a tired, subdued lot. Sturdy Ivan, a pudgy
six-year-old with a serious countenance, insisted on sitting with
his younger sister. "My papa told me I'm in charge now." He carried a small suitcase containing everything for the two of them. She
watched him open it with the care of a much older child and hand his
younger sibling a small square of bread with a piece of cheese.

Lena walked up and down the aisle, looking out windows, anxious and wishing the trains would get started. Little Talya huddled
by a window. Along the opposite side of the carriage sat children
from other groups, shuffled around in the rush to get away from
Demyansk. Where was their chaperone? Lena got them started on an

alphabet guessing game. "I see something that starts with the letter *a*," said a girl wearing a blue dress with a white pinafore. Her blond hair was braided tightly, both braids adorned with bright blue ribbons matching her dress. The rest of the group began to guess what it was she spied. As they shouted out possible answers, Lena heard a low, distant hum. The girl with braids leaned out a window, pointing at the object beginning with *a*. In the same instant, the hum became a rumble, and Lena realized they were under attack.

She ordered the children to crawl under the seats and cover their heads. The sound of the planes grew so loud that she couldn't hear herself yelling as she crawled in after them, pushing their little bodies together and against the wall. Explosions thundered as bombs struck the train. They lifted into the air and crashed down. The clinking of shattered glass surrounded them. For several moments, the only sounds were those of destruction. Then, thick black smoke filled the carriage. Her ears rang from the explosions, but she soon heard the high-pitched, heart-rending cries and screams of the children. Coughing and crawling, Lena reached for them, cajoling the stunned and injured to follow her. They inched out into what remained of the car on their bellies and hands and knees, shards of glass inflicting more damage to tender skin. Lena pushed and lifted debris to create a passage of sorts. Two chubby legs, one without a shoe, stuck out into her path. She squatted there, amidst the smoke and broken glass, the cries and carnage, and pulled little Ivan from under a collapsed seat, other lifeless bodies tangled there. His right hand still clutched the handle of the suitcase. His sister had vanished. She pressed her fingers to his limp neck, hoping, but there was no pulse. Lena held him to her chest for a moment and rocked him, then kissed his still perfect cheek through her tears and placed him gently on a twisted seat.

Spotting daylight through the smoke, she coaxed and carried the living toward a gaping opening in the train. She half-slid, half-jumped down the train's metal side, and turned to help each child out of the wreckage. Her persuasive coos and steady hands had them sliding and jumping into her arms. She inspected them, looking for injuries, dabbing at cuts, and giving out hugs. She counted fifteen, and realized three were older children she didn't recognize which meant she'd lost much of her group. And where was Talya? Lena spun around, looking for the little elfin blonde. Even in the chaos and smoke, Lena had to find her. As she started to climb back into the wreckage, a man in a railway uniform ran toward them.

"Get those children out of here, Miss! The planes are circling back. You only have a couple of minutes."

"There are others inside. I can't leave them!" Her voice grew shrill and unnatural.

"You have no choice. Save these," he said, pointing at the tattered group. "Across that field to the woods. Go back in the train and you'll all die. Quickly now, Comrade. Run!"

His words drove her. Even with the smoke and cries of the injured swirling all around, she organized the children into pairs and explained they must run as fast as they could across the field to the safety of the forest. No stopping, no looking back. She pointed to their destination. The group began running away from the train. She scooped up the youngest child and, after a couple of steps, stumbled over something. Looking down, she saw a head with no body. Looking down again, she recognized the blond braids with those bright blue ribbons, now covered with red. A cry gurgled from her throat and she hesitated, then rushed away from the gruesome sight.

Adrenaline, along with the insistent murmur of planes in the distance, propelled her forward, urging the children to move as fast as possible. Helter-skelter, they raced away from the wreckage and cries and blood. Faces filled with fear, legs churning, the older children leapt through unplowed rows in the rock-strewn field. Lena raced ahead carrying the toddler. Reaching the wood, she set the youngster down and looked back at the field dotted with children. The planes were coming now, she could see them, dark birds of prey. Fear froze her, but oh, the children. They weren't going to make it. As the oldest ones tumbled in, she told them to help others to safety while she went back. The remaining children were scattered, some trying to run, a couple on the ground, sobbing. Lena raced back into the field, brushed the battered knees of a boy who'd fallen on rocks, his short pants no protection. Squatting down, she encouraged him and then glanced up and saw the black and white crosses on the wings of the planes, modern day crusaders bent on destruction. The explosions and sounds of the machine guns ripping through the trains a second time drowned out everything.

In the middle of the field, she and the last few youngsters were easy targets and she expected to die at any moment. Running, stumbling, crying, she gathered the stragglers and they somehow made it to the cover of the trees. The children collapsed, sobbing and whimpering, some staring at the disaster they'd just escaped. Lena counted them. Fifteen. Yet, out in the field, not far from the train, one tiny child remained. Crouched on the ground, she had her hands pressed against her ears. From the safety of the forest, Lena stared at the last child. Talya. She yelled to her, begging her to get up and run. Petrified, still Lena raced across the open field, each second an eternity, and swept the paralyzed youngster into her arms. When she reached the cover of the trees, she gasped for air, unable to understand how she and Talya and the others were alive. Had the German pilots been merciful, or had they simply not bothered to fire at them?

Over and over, she hugged the children, wiped their tears, mud, and blood, all the while speaking calmly. "You are the bravest children in the entire country. I am so proud of you for following my directions. And see, here we are, safe in this wood where the Germans can't find us." A lie to be sure, but one that reassured her as well as the youngsters.

They had no food or water, and it was already late afternoon.

Lena's breathing calmed, but her heart still raced. Standing at the edge of the forest, she watched flames devour what remained of the station. Billows of dark smoke rolled off the wreckage. She stared, willing other survivors to materialize, safe, unharmed, but there were few signs of life.

Lena leaned against a tree, little Talya wrapped around one leg. What now? It was too dangerous to go south, toward the center of Lychkovo. German soldiers wouldn't be far behind. In the opposite direction, beyond the trees, she spied a barn. Even though they were exhausted, she gathered the children again and explained they were going to a nearby barn to find food, water and a place to sleep. They set off again, not racing for their lives, but still moving as quickly as their little legs could go, tripping, falling, picking themselves up, the older ones helping the little ones, encouraged and coaxed along by Lena.

The barn was deserted, but hay made it a comfortable spot for them to rest. Several of the children fell asleep within minutes, and she told the others that they must stay where they were and remain quiet while she looked for water. There might be a well nearby, but she found nothing and afraid to venture far with dusk arriving, returned empty-handed.

That night, fitful, hungry, thirsty, and scared, the children slept huddled together. Lena drifted in and out of a shallow, troubled sleep, waking repeatedly to fear and unfamiliar noises. At first light, they set out on foot.

Everything urged her north, out of the path of the Nazis. After tramping through fields and forests to remain hidden, they rejoined the railroad tracks. The children were too young, too hungry and thirsty to walk very far, but eventually they'd reach another town. She decided they should take their chances with no water or food rather than risk facing the enemy, and really, what else could she do?

They walked, taking turns holding hands. Sometimes they sang a song or Lena told them a story, but most of the time they were quiet.

They stopped every twenty minutes or so to rest, or when one of them had to pee. After six hours, Lena began to despair. They sat on the tracks, the children whimpering with thirst, hunger, and exhaustion.

She felt it before she heard it, jumped up and hurried the children out of the way as the train came into view, already slowing, leaving a small trail of black smoke fading into the blue sky. Lena stepped close to the tracks, waving as the red star on the engine grew larger. Several soldiers jumped down and ran to where she stood with the children behind her.

"It's all right, Comrade. We're here to take you back to Leningrad," a young soldier said.

She nodded, using a bit of her shirt to wipe her eyes. "We're desperately thirsty. And some of the children have nasty cuts and bruises."

"We'll take care of the injuries. You and the children were at Lychkovo?"

Lena nodded, looking down, seeing the blond braids again. "We ran into the woods after the first attack. They were so brave." She turned and knelt down, gathering the youngsters close. "Children, these are our soldiers. They're here to take us home."

The children relaxed. Some were happy to be lifted into the train. Others wanted to climb up the steps themselves. A few needed encouragement. She gathered each reluctant soul and explained again how this train was going to Leningrad. Home. To their parents and families. Once the children were aboard, Lena stood at the bottom of the steps gazing up at the train. She started shaking violently. A young officer jumped down.

"Comrade, I'm sorry for what happened in Lychkovo."

Still trembling, she stuttered. "The t-t-train. I c-can't."

The officer continued. "There's no other choice. The nearest road is miles away and the Germans are closing in. You must get on. I'll help."

He moved slowly but decisively, his kind, firm demeanor encouraging Lena as he put a strong arm around her and propelled her up the steps of the train, ignoring the tears that streamed down her cheeks. As soon as she sat, he brought water and she drained the cup, then handed it back for another, murmuring, "*Spasibo.* Thank you."

"Little Ivan," she drew in a sharp breath, and wept anew, burying her face while the soldier kept an arm around her.

"You're safe now. We'll get you home. Everything's going to be all right."

What did that mean? The Germans swept down from the sky and killed hundreds of children. Nothing could make that all right.

The train lurched forward, and for the first time since the ordeal began, Lena cried out. She put her head down and closed her eyes, trying to convince herself she was not on a train, not about to be bombed. But with her eyes shut, the worst images and sounds took over: the bloody, blonde braids, the fearsome *bra-ta-tat* of the guns, the lifeless bodies, the screams and cries. She opened her eyes to escape reliving the horror, staring forward, shaking with fear, clutching the arm rests until her hands ached.

News of the attack spread through the city, and by the time the train arrived, the railway station was crowded with frantic parents. Word of the grim statistics sped like wildfire. Grief-filled cries and desperate pleas filled the massive station, a thunder of pain, each voice its own but also indistinguishable in the community of suffering.

Exhausted and numb, Lena stood on the platform listening to the sound of sorrow. Medical workers rushed about, pushing people aside to get to the injured. At first, she didn't know what to do or say. Desperate parents prodded, grasped, and yelled, trying to find their children. When a Party official approached, accompanied by a second adult, she turned to her charges, hugging each one and assuring them they would be reunited with their parents very soon.

She tried to hand the youngsters to the unfamiliar adults, but the children wouldn't have it. Frightened and frozen by the crowd and the noise, they reattached themselves to Lena's hands and legs. A few grasped fistfuls of her clothing.

⌖ ⌖

When Sofya queued for bread after a long, morning rehearsal, she overheard the shocking news. "Did you hear?" "Yesterday's children's evacuation. The trains were bombed in Lychkovo." Another stricken bystander said, "Bombing children? Fiends."

A wave of nausea overcame Sofya. Yelena. Talk of the disaster rumbled through the line like a gathering storm, but Sofya was already running to Moscow Station. Spare my grandchild. Please God. She stumbled along the sidewalks.

Images from years past—Yelena as a blond-headed toddler, then Aleksandr as a baby—rose in her mind. From the moment her Sasha was born, she'd been overwhelmed by love. There were times she was certain no one could feel what she felt for her son. Of course, that wasn't true. All mothers, or most mothers anyway, felt the extreme power of maternal love. Sofya tripped, falling to one knee before righting herself. Oh God, the poor mothers.

A huge crowd jammed the entrance of the railway station. Fighting her way up the steps, she pushed strangers aside, clutching at flimsy hope like flotsam in rough seas. Sobbing alone amidst the frantic throng, Sofya cried. Lenochka, my Lenochka.

Pitiful moans of grief, the death throes of a beast, led her to the platform. At the nearest end, so close she could touch it, the train engine still steamed and clanked. Sofya craned her neck to see through the crowd of hysterical parents. A woman screamed at a Party official, gripping his lapel, "Why? Why? You took her away! To die alone. No matter what happens in Leningrad, we would have been together. Better to die here, with family. My poor, Anya. Alone, afraid. How could you do this to us?"

Sofya shed fresh tears for the woman, for everyone gathered on that platform. Gazing up and down the throng, she saw medical personnel attending survivors on stretchers. Other children were herded along by various officials. Nowhere was her tall, striking granddaughter.

As her panic and fear rose, Sofya glimpsed a flash of blonde hair on a tall figure in the middle of the platform. Enveloped by a crush of people, Yelena emerged. Sofya's legs gave way at the sight of her granddaughter. A stranger helped her back to her feet as she focused on the peculiar group moving her way. Yelena, pale as a wraith, trailed by a dozen or more bedraggled tykes. The two women locked eyes. Sofya let out a cry of relief as her granddaughter collapsed in her arms.

BADAYEV BOMBED
September 1941

IT HAD BEEN two weeks since Lychkovo, and Yelena had mostly stopped crying out at night. Sofya woke to soothe her granddaughter when she did have a bad dream, and kept a close eye as the teen threw herself back into her brigade's projects. For the last week she'd been filling sandbags—preparation for the expected bombs. Every morning Yelena got up extra early so she'd have time to walk to work. No matter how far, she refused to get on a streetcar.

Sofya's schedule grew more rigorous too. Since the Leningrad Philharmonic and the Kirov Ballet had been evacuated, the demand for lesser companies such as the Radio Orchestra and the Musical Comedy Theater increased. Like an ingenue with a full dance card, Sofya moved from rehearsal to performance and back again. It was easy to push aside thoughts of evacuation. Lychkovo had traumatized them both.

One evening as they relaxed with their books, the unfamiliar, frightening wail of air raid sirens pierced the quiet. Yelena flinched. There'd been practice drills earlier in the summer, but now the hair on Sofya's arms prickled.

She rose and reached for a heavy sweater. Yelena grabbed her coat off the hook by the door. They locked the apartment and scurried down the stairs, their movements staccato-like. The insistent repetitive whine of the sirens spurred them through the courtyard. Sofya heard a menacing rumble behind the shrill alarm and gripped her granddaughter. They held onto each other in the darkness and dodged small groups of people, all scrambling for cover in the frightened, blacked-out city.

Both women had located their assigned shelter weeks earlier. Out the south entrance, a quick right turn, one block down and across Rubinstein Street. As they started down the shelter steps, Sofya saw it was nothing more than a basement—larger than the tiny furnace room in their own building, but probably no safer.

Dozens of people squeezed into the soon cramped space with two long benches and a single candle for light. Everyone hung on the startling sounds of war, the distant thunder of explosions and the sharp *ack-ack* of anti-aircraft fire. The two women huddled together on the floor, Sofya's arm tight around her granddaughter. Yelena twitched with every boom and sinister sound. Poor thing. Sofya kept up a one-way conversation, trying to make the experience easier. Why hadn't she thought to grab something for distraction? Next time she'd bring a chessboard, a flashlight, a deck of cards. She'd also wear something heavier, maybe grab a blanket. From that evening on, Sofya kept a bag with essentials by the apartment door.

After only an hour or so the all-clear sounded. When they dragged themselves out, the streets were like pitch, except for the flicker of the occasional flashlight. Sofya peered up and down the street, then southwestward, for evidence of the attack.

"What do you think happened?" Yelena gripped Sofya's hand, unease in the soft timber of her voice.

"I don't know. But it must have been far from here. There's no smoke, no fire, no rescue vehicles." She squeezed her granddaughter's hand. "Let's go home."

The next morning, the city hummed with speculation about the raid. In the long bread line, conversations no longer focused on the strength of the Soviet military. Gone were the comments about stopping the Germans in their tracks and tanks rolling out of the Kirov factory.

All summer Radio Leningrad told the citizens only what the Party wanted them to know, a sanitized version of events that made people less anxious. Propaganda was an easily digested meal, but now the reality of war couldn't be denied. Military units and vehicles moved through the city every day, some headed to train stations for deployment, others to defensive positions on the city's perimeter. Factories had been evacuated. Those producing munitions were operating round-the-clock. Workers took on long shifts so others could enlist. Schools were turned into hospitals. The frantic energy that filled everyone with purpose in June and July was replaced by fear. German bombs had found Leningrad.

At the head of the bread line, Sofya kept an exacting eye as the attendant cut and weighed her ration. After the most recent reduction, she and Yelena together received three-quarters of a kilo of bread per day. It wasn't a precipitous decline, but the supply of other food, plentiful but expensive in July and early August, had plummeted. Stores were nearly empty. It helped that Sofya could still get a bowl of soup that didn't count against her ration coupons at the Radio House canteen. She didn't want to use their hidden supplies any sooner than necessary.

On the way home, she stopped to examine the Party newspaper, *Leningradskaya Pravda*. It was posted in dozens of places and Sofya scanned the paper often, wondering when there'd be some actual news of the war. The front-page screamed for attention.

The enemy is at the gates of Leningrad! Grave danger hangs over the city. The forces of the Red Army are fighting in the immediate vicinity of Leningrad, holding in check and overcoming the assault of the insolent enemy, who with his last strength tries to break through the valiant city.

Sofya leaned against the wall. The situation must be dire. Over the next days she waited, fearful and on edge, for the Nazis to enter Leningrad. Instead, the skies opened and fire rained down.

On September 8, Sofya wasn't supposed to be performing, but the Musical Comedy Theatre had lost some of its musicians and she stepped in. At the end of Act One of *The Bat,* the sirens sounded. As the whine of planes thrummed in the distance and the chatter of anti-aircraft guns began, the director of the theater stood on the edge of the stage. "There is no shelter in the theater," he said, squinting in the spotlight. "Everyone must sit or stand close to the walls, where it is safest." The dutiful theatergoers scurried from their seats, murmuring and pressing against the walls. Explosions shook the building while the patrons gasped and huddled close together.

When the booms and blasts moved off, Sofya and the others finished the performance. The moment the curtain fell, she grabbed her things, Yelena her only thought. Mesmerized by the crimson southern sky, she raced through the streets, heart thudding from exertion and fear. Flames scampered up the billows of smoke, a raging inferno illuminating the city.

"Thank goodness you're home!" Yelena leapt up from the kitchen table.

Sofya gasped for air, leaning on her granddaughter until the pounding in her chest subsided.

"Where were you during the attack?" Sofya asked.

"Our shelter," Yelena said. "The bombs were close. So many explosions. When I got home, I saw the sky."

Sofya clung to her. "I ran all the way. The city is on fire. Good Lord, what a sight!"

They stood at the window a bit longer, transfixed by the ghastly view.

࿇

An acrid stench woke Sofya well before dawn. After getting dressed, she sat with a cloth over her nose while having tea. Yelena soon joined her in the kitchen.

"Smell woke you too?" Sofya said.

Yelena nodded. "It's awful."

"The fires. I've been holding my nose or using a hanky."

"Does it work?" Yelena pinched her nose closed. She raised her eyebrows.

"Except you can't do much of anything with one hand holding your nose," Sofya said.

Yelena laughed and Sofya smiled at the honking sound.

"Come on, you silly thing, we might as well get our rations early." Sofya checked her watch. "Grab a couple of scarves."

Leaving the building, they nearly collided with someone blackened with soot.

"Hello, Sofya Nikolayevna. Lena."

It was their downstairs neighbor, Vladimir Radchenko, who lived with his mother and little brother. His father had joined the Red Army.

"Vladik! Is that you?" Lena said. "What happened? Are you all right?"

"The Germans bombed Badayev last night. I was working late when the alert sounded. I didn't even make it to a shelter, the bombs fell so fast. Explosions all over the freight yards. When I realized the warehouses had been hit, I ran back. Most of the buildings were already done for, all that wood. Like dropping a match on a haystack." He shook his head. "There were two people with hoses trying to save a storehouse, so I helped." He shrugged and turned his black palms up.

"Oh my, are you sure you're okay?" said Yelena.

"I think so, I didn't get burned. We tied wet rags over our faces, and kept dousing ourselves with water. The only thing that hurts is my chest," he rubbed it with one sooty hand.

"How brave," Sofya said. "You must be exhausted. Hurry now. Your mother will be frantic." Sofya knew how close the Radchenkos were. She often saw Vladik running errands for his mother or bringing his little brother home from school.

He nodded, looking down, hunched over like an old man. "I just wish we could have saved more. Can't imagine what's going to happen to the city now."

He dragged himself up the stairs. In the dim light, Sofya saw the shock in Yelena's wide eyes and then heard the fear in her question. "You think all the food supplies are gone?"

Sofya spoke softly. "Sounds serious, but I want to believe our leaders were smarter than to store everything at Badayev."

Arm in arm, they hurried toward the bread store.

"Probably means rations will fall," Sofya continued to whisper. "It'll be even more important that we manage our food." She'd been planning to itemize everything and get an idea of how long their supplies would last.

"Don't worry," Yelena said. "I won't say anything—even to Tanya."

The rumor mill ground on while they stood in the early morning queue. "How could such a thing happen?" "Leaving the city's supplies in such a vulnerable spot." "Badayev is lost, well, that's the end for us. It'll be famine for sure." More than the usual resignation in the voices, Sofya heard consternation, anger, and a powerful undercurrent of fear.

Alarm spread through the population, fed by the next devastating piece of news—the last railway linking Leningrad to the rest of the country had been taken by the Germans. Sofya's beloved city, its food supplies burned to the ground, was now encircled by the enemy.

SEARCH FOR A SCAPEGOAT

September 1941

ADMIRAL VASILI ANTONOV sat at a long conference table with the commander of the Baltic Fleet and a dozen other senior officers. He saw his own shock and despair in their faces. After the fleet's desperate nighttime retreat from Tallinn to the Kronstadt naval base, they gathered to review the losses. Attacked by torpedoes, mines, and the Luftwaffe, nearly one-third of the two hundred ship flotilla sank during the disastrous journey. Over thirteen thousand dead. The deadliest event of Vasili's career.

The door swung open and Naval Commissar Kuznetsov entered, stunning the group by joining their post-mortem. The mere sight of him changed the energy in the room. The assembled naval brass sat straighter and spoke with greater conviction. Kuznetsov gave them courage. The Commissar remained mostly silent amidst the disheartening reports, but his presence alone was enough to restore the men's faith in themselves. It was just what they needed, especially in light of what was to come.

At the end of the dismal discussion, Vasili made his way over to Kuznetsov.

"It's clear I made the right decision," the Commissar said as they shook hands. "You on the *Kirov.* Your leadership and the ship's firepower was key to the fleet holding out in Tallinn."

"Thank you, Comrade Commissar," Vasili said. "She's quite a ship."

"Come on." Kuznetsov nodded at the exit. "Let's get some air."

The two men made their way out of the building to the privacy of the outdoors. Vasili offered him a cigarette and then took one for himself. He inhaled deeply, blowing the smoke out slowly so it gathered above them—their own personal cloud.

"It's been a while since I commanded a vessel like that. Agile and powerful, fine crew."

"Well, the crew's to your credit," Kuznetsov said. "You prepared them."

When Vasili first took command there were some jokes about the "old man" up on the bridge, but no more. He spent hours reviewing tactics manuals, devising navigation problems for the crew to solve, putting them through a variety of evasive maneuvers. His attention to detail, his unflagging energy, fairness, and steady demeanor endeared him to his men.

"We had time on our hands," Vasili said. "Becalmed like a sailboat in Tallinn harbor most of the summer, paralyzed while the Germans mined the route to Kronstadt, waiting for directives, waiting for someone from headquarters with balls enough to order the retreat."

Kuznetsov enjoyed the insult. "That's asking too much. Someone in charge with balls."

"Present company excluded, sir," Vasili said.

A grin appeared on the Kuznetsov's face. "Believe me, my courage has been tested."

They walked around the staff building facing the harbor and up a short steep path. At the top of the rise, they faced an engineering marvel: the nearly two-hundred-year-old and still fully functional dry dock of Peter the Great. A ship damaged in the retreat was already under repair below them.

Vasili took another drag on his cigarette. "The ones who really went beyond the call of duty were the brave lads of the cadet corps. They bought us the time we needed. Our future naval leadership, slaughtered in hand-to-hand combat on the Narva highway." More than anything else, Vasili hated giving that order. Hardly more than boys, many of those fresh-cheeked lads had sat in his classroom at the Admiralty. What a waste.

"It won't be the last group of young men slaughtered," Kuznetsov said. He took a final pull on his cigarette and carefully ground it into the dirt at his feet.

Both men stood in silence, staring at the vessel under repair. Out of the water, the destroyer appeared massive.

"I didn't say much in there on purpose," the Commissar began again, "but, the responsibility lies at the top. The order to retreat should have come through weeks ago."

"In private, you won't find an officer who disagrees with you," Vasili said.

"Even Pantaleyev? He made quite an argument for the importance of defending Tallinn to the last so as to draw German strength off Leningrad."

"Yes, sir, he did, but that wasn't a private conversation, and perhaps he's a bit more fearful than most of contradicting the leadership. I'm not defending him, but every man in that room would rather die in battle than in the *Bolshoi Dom*."

The Commissar nodded. "Well, I'm not going to offer any of you up to those wolves."

Just what Vasili had been hoping to hear. At least Kuznetsov had their backs. He wouldn't sacrifice the fleet leadership for a disaster that wasn't their fault.

Workers clambered about the destroyer under repair, a strange ballet with ropes. They climbed across patches of raw steel welded here and there along the hull like so many band-aids. The metallic smell of a welder's blowtorch drifted up as silver-blue sparks flashed below. Vasili passed Kuznetsov a second cigarette.

"Personally, sir, I think your view is the only reasonable one. If we

had evacuated ten days earlier, with minimal loss of men and mate-
riel, wouldn't Leningrad be in a stronger position right now?" He let
his rhetorical question hang in the air. "I don't think the Germans
ever cared much about Tallinn. They never committed many forces
to its capture and its greatest value was always as a means of inflicting serious damage on the fleet." Vasili inhaled long and hard on his
cigarette. "Which they did."

"Agreed. But that's not really the point anymore," Kuznetsov
said. "The point is, how do we deal with the backlash that's coming?
The losses are too disastrous to ignore, and they're saying someone, somewhere is to blame. They're looking for a scapegoat and
despite their own culpability, it won't be anyone in the Smolny." The
Commissar started back down the path. "NKVD and Party officials
will be snooping around, looking for little inconsistencies, some way
to assign blame."

"A grim thought," said Vasili.

"Maybe not as bad as it sounds. Admiral Tributs did a thorough
job covering his ass, and the rest of yours as well. A good man and a
smart one too. He left a solid paper trail. They won't be able to ignore
his many requests for help, for orders to retreat."

They approached the building, their voices lowered in an instinct
for self-preservation.

"Officials will be here soon," Kuznetsov said. "You'll all be interviewed. The question is whether or not they listen to what you have
to say, or have already made up their minds."

A deep depression engulfed the fleet. Every naval man on Kronstadt
had lost a friend or known someone who died in the Tallinn disaster. The sounds of those hours still filled Vasili's head: the buzzing
planes, whistling bombs, chattering anti-aircraft, and the thud
and roar of the ship's massive guns. The sea had been aglow for
hours, the Soviet Navy's burning hulks as watery bonfires. When a

torpedo or mine found its target, blinding flashes lit the night sky. Every time another ship was hit, Vasili pictured the bodies. Now, when he walked the streets of the town adjacent to the naval base, he saw grief. Widows, fatherless children, the entire town wept for its loved ones.

With time, Vasili knew both morale and damaged vessels would be repaired. He supported his crew by reinforcing their valiant performance. He couldn't tell them the truth, that the military leadership had hung them out to dry, so he used Pantalayev's reasoning—the fleet had to stay in Tallinn until the last moment to draw the Germans off Leningrad.

Still, it was difficult keeping so much to himself, and he was desperate to hear Sofya's voice. He tried to call, but discovered the phone in her building was disconnected. That evening, despondent, missing her, he retired to his quarters. There, on the desk, he found an official envelope containing orders to report to the Smolny Institute—headquarters for both the Communist Party and Leningrad Military Command.

He gripped the paper in sweaty hands. Shit. They were still looking for blood. Despite Kuznetsov's assurances, Vasili imagined a dark, dank cell. Weeks of isolation with little food and lots of time to brood on what might come. Interrogations, beatings, torture. Whatever it took to break him and extract a confession. After that, the firing squad.

The meeting took place a few days later. A small group of naval brass, Vasili included, disembarked at Smolny pier. He eyed the elaborate camouflage draped above the buildings as they walked up the incline from the river. Sunlight struggled through the netting which looked like trees and other greenery from the air. The vise in his gut tightened.

Like so much else in the last fifteen years, this was a lose–lose situation. When things went right, Stalin and the Party received the credit. When things went wrong, someone else was to blame. Today he and his colleagues were that someone else.

Solicitous and wary, Vasili and the other flag officers were escorted to a windowless basement room. Senior Party leaders sat along the far side of a table, smoking and chatting under large pictures of Lenin and Stalin. Vasili shuddered when he recognized Lavrenti Beria in the center, the infamous head of the secret police. A short, balding man with rimless glasses, he was unassuming enough, but every bit as cruel as Stalin, another small, ordinary-looking man.

The questions were the same as in the earlier interviews. He suspected the interrogators were just waiting for them to slip up and provide a reason for arrest. Vasili had decided that if he was going to die, it would be after speaking the truth, integrity intact.

"The men performed brilliantly, both leading up to and during the retreat itself," he began when it was his turn. "Starting with the young cadets of the Academy who fought fiercely in hand-to-hand combat to provide time to load the ships, all the way up the chain to the officers, who employed every tactic possible to escape minefields, torpedo boats, bombers." Vasili's gaze flashed between Beria and the table between them. It was hard to look into the man's eyes for more than a second or two. The rumors about him, the stories about what he did to young girls were disgusting. He was a ruthless, barbaric man. "We did not have sufficient support, Comrade." Vasili tried to explain. "A handful of minesweepers could not do a job meant for a hundred. There were no Soviet planes to beat back the Luftwaffe. Without support, the retreat was doomed from the start."

Leaning forward, palms on the table and eyebrows drawn together, Beria raised his voice. "What do you mean *doomed from the start*?" His mouth twisted into a sneer. "What kind of attitude is that? If all our senior officers have that attitude, we might as well just give up now."

Beria's knife-edged criticism echoed and the room fell silent.

Vasili felt sweat under his arms and a trickle down his back, where it collected in the waistband of his trousers.

"I think you misunderstand me, Comrade." Vasili said.

Expressionless, the NKVD chief leaned back in his chair. "Enlighten me then."

Vasili pushed aside thoughts of what this creature could do to him, to those he loved. "We were pinned down in Tallinn without land or air support. The Eighth Army was supposed to defend Tallinn, but it was damaged and scattered. Most of what remained of the Eighth had, in fact, retreated too far east of Tallinn to be of any help, and the Soviet air force in the region had experienced massive losses in the first days. As I understand it, there were almost no Soviet planes left in the Baltic region. Those are the circumstances that made the retreat so costly. And given those facts, I believe the entire fleet, officers down to the newest recruit, conducted themselves admirably and fought bravely." Vasili felt a flash of pride at defending his men.

"Ahh, yes. Circumstances. Facts." Beria's disparaging tone grated. "Precisely what the Commissar told me. Still, did the fleet do all it could?" He turned back to Admiral Pantalayev, who had already been grilled. "Tell me Comrade, why didn't our fleet fight harder? Why were the Fascists so successful?"

Pantalayev hesitated. Beads of sweat appeared on his forehead. The air in the room grew thicker. He started to explain the complicated situation once again.

"No, no," Beria cut him off. "The fleet is not supposed to concern itself with its limitations. It must work out active operations and fight, attack with everything it has."

What else could any of them say? The situation they'd faced was obvious, and there was no sense repeating themselves. How else could they respond to the accusation that they hadn't fought hard enough or well enough or smart enough? Best to let Beria have the last word.

"Well, Comrades, we'll put this ugly incident behind us."

Grim-faced, the NKVD chief abruptly stood. "One can hope that the fleet will perform better in the future." He turned his back on the stifled naval brass and strode out of the room with his subordinates scurrying behind.

And that was it. The inquisition was over, or perhaps the leadership was simply distracted by the next emergency. Regardless, it seemed that Beria, and by extension, Stalin, wanted to go on record as blaming the fleet officers. Vasili was certain that behind the scenes, Commissar Kuznetsov must have convinced them that fleet command was not to blame.

A Party official stood and announced, "These proceedings are closed." Relieved, repelled, and desperate to escape, Vasili nevertheless let the Party powerful exit first. Disgust roiled over him as he walked from underneath the Smolny's camouflage into a brilliant September afternoon. Even in wartime, even while defending the nation, the knock on the door could reach anywhere.

THE NOOSE TIGHTENS
September 1941

VASILI RAPPED ON Sofya's door and waited. He knocked again, then dug in his pocket for the spare key she'd given him. Perhaps the silence meant she and Yelena had left Leningrad.

As he stepped into the entry, she came around the corner from the bedrooms.

"Sofi, you're here." His voice was hoarse, like he had a cold. He pulled her slight frame close. "I thought maybe you'd left."

She looked up at him. "I'm afraid we've missed our chance, but what's wrong? Why are you here?" The concern on her face confirmed that he must look like hell. He certainly didn't feel anything close to normal.

"Are you hurt?" she asked.

"I'm all right. But the fleet's in disarray. We escaped the Nazis last week only to face a tribunal today. I've just come from the Smolny."

"*Bozhe moi.* My God."

"They're looking for someone to blame." He followed her into the kitchen and sat heavily in a chair. "I don't have much time. I have to get back to Kronstadt tonight."

"Let me make some coffee," Sofya said. "And something to eat?"

"That would be wonderful. I'm ravenous."

She sliced and buttered some bread, then added a leftover chicken cutlet to the plate.

"Eat first," she urged, "then you can tell me what's going on."

He inhaled four or five mouthfuls, hardly pausing to chew. "I haven't had a decent meal in days." After another minute, shoveling the last of the cold chicken into his mouth, he began telling her of the disastrous retreat. The coffee percolated. Sofya poured two cups and led him into the living room.

Energized, he began to pace. "The leadership's in chaos, it's no way to fight a war. Admiral Tributs did everything he could, tried to get orders, warned them we needed minesweepers and air support to get to Kronstadt. They gave us no help at all, and then blamed us. Twenty-five troop transports—sunk. Thousands, dead. It could hardly have been worse." He took off his uniform jacket as he strode back and forth, then hung it on a chair.

"Eight weeks in Tallinn harbor, waiting for the order to retreat. Day after day ships arrived, wounded soldiers and refugees poured in. Over two hundred vessels. It was obvious all along we'd have to retreat, but instead of doing it when it could have been successful, Moscow let the Nazis fill the Gulf with mines.

When we finally left Tallinn, the sky was lit like a fireworks display. The *Virona* sank before my eyes, filled with support personnel, spouses of fleet officers, journalists too, most drowned. One of the officers on trial with me lost his wife—shameful what he went through."

He gazed at Sofya, wide-eyed and perched on the sofa edge. She slipped into the kitchen and poured several fingers of vodka into one plain glass and no more than a splash in another. "I have an evening performance," she said, by way of explaining her tiny serving. "How horrible," she continued. "Watching so many ships go down, having so little support from the top."

He gulped half the contents and continued to pace and talk. "It's been a series of inquisitions, perfect horse shit. And this morning, a session with Beria himself. Can you imagine?"

At Beria's name, Sofya's hand flew to her mouth. Stalin's chief executioner had a well-deserved reputation for cruelty.

"Oh, Sofi, I'm sorry to distress you."

"It's shocking. Of all the things that might happen during war, I wouldn't expect you to have to defend yourself to the head of the secret police."

"I thought it was the end, a firing squad or the camps. The Party blames us, but it seems Kuznetsov defended us behind the scenes, clarifying that we'd been asking for help, for permission to retreat. No doubt he saved us." His hand shook as he took another drink. "Now, with the Baltic full of mines, the remaining ships are grounded." The first tiny smile crossed his face. "I suppose that's one positive thing, I'll be fighting the war from Kronstadt, close to you."

He stopped pacing and looked at her pale, troubled face. "*Prosti menya*, forgive me." He sat and kissed her gently. "You're upset. But all's well. I'm here. Now tell me what's happening? The city looks different. And why didn't you and Yelena evacuate?"

She sat up straight, facing him. "Yes, yes, I'll get to that, but the most important thing is Aleksandr." Her eyes flashed. "You'll never believe it. He was released. Telephoned from Moscow. He's assigned to the 16th Army."

"He's alive and out? That's extraordinary news. I heard some officers were released, but hardly dared to hope." Vasili beamed. "The 16th means he's involved in the defense of Moscow. That's a coincidence. I had a letter from my daughter-in-law saying Maksim had joined up. He's also on the Moscow Front."

Sofya had been looking up at him, smiling and nodding. Now her lips pressed together, as if holding back an avalanche of emotion. The instant he pulled her into his arms, it swept forth. After wiping her face, she took a couple of breaths and recounted the details of the phone call—especially how good Aleksandr sounded. "I can't help but be optimistic. I'm certain he'll return, he's smart and strong."

"I think so too." He raised his glass. "To Aleksandr." Sofya clinked hers against his, but after a sip she took a deep breath. She seemed distracted or upset—not herself.

"What's bothering you, *dorogaya maya*, my darling?" Vasili said.

Sofya looked at him, about to speak, then shook her head. "Nothing."

He took her hand, thinking she was just emotional about Aleksandr being released and they sat in silence for a moment or two until he changed the subject.

"So, now tell me what happened with the transit letter," he said. "I hoped you'd get as far from here as possible. But after I sent it, well, the Germans moved rapidly."

"I didn't realize the situation was so dire until after we went to the *dacha*," she said.

He poured himself another vodka as she described the trip, the chaos in the train station, the two of them with huge packs and Yelena pulling her into the moving train where they learned about the situation in Luga.

"Standing in the Alexandrovskaya station, surrounded by all those poor people fleeing the Germans, the situation became clear. I finally understood that we should go east, to the Volga or beyond." Her eyes locked on his. "That's when I knew why you sent the paper. The Germans weren't far and were coming our way. But after the disaster in Lychkovo, evacuation is out of the question."

"Lychkovo? What happened there?"

"You haven't heard, of course," Sofya said. "Such a catastrophe, I thought I'd lost Yelena." She stared past him. "She was part of an effort to evacuate two thousand children from the city, children whose parents have critical jobs and must stay. The trains were accidentally sent to the front and the Nazis bombed them as they sat in Lychkovo station. Only a few hundred children survived. Yelena and sixteen youngsters escaped on foot, running away as the planes attacked. They hid overnight without food or water, finally picked up by a Red

Army train the next day. She saw children dead, mutilated." Sofya shook her head. "I don't know if she'll ever get on a train again. She walks everywhere. Avoids streetcars. Air raids are a trial. She trembles uncontrollably whenever we're in a shelter. It's been so difficult for her. The horrible news about the volunteers and then Lychkovo."

"Poor Yelena." Vasili shook his head and pulled Sofya's hand into his own. "How could they make such a mistake? It's harder and harder to have faith in our leaders. Don't lose hope about Katya though. The military report on Luga is grim, but there is word from Gatchina and Chudovo of volunteers reaching those towns. It could be a very long time before you know what happened to Katya." He rubbed Sofya's hand and sighed. "I'm sorry there's such uncertainty."

"It's so hard for Yelena," Sofya said. "Both her parents. No news."

Neither spoke the horrible truth. Things were going to get worse.

"Sofi, you should consider evacuating by boat. Across Ladoga. With the city surrounded and land routes closed, it's the only option left."

Sofya nodded as he spoke. "Do you think they'll take ordinary civilians across?"

"You aren't ordinary," Vasili said. "Your transit papers should put you at the top of the list. It's worth checking with the District Committee."

"Still, how would we get to Ladoga? A train is out of the question." She fiddled with her vodka glass. "I was so relieved when she was assigned to the children's evacuation, thinking she was going to get far away, somewhere safe. Then it all went wrong." She looked down. The grave reality silenced them both.

After a long moment, she continued. "I have other bad news. I didn't make it to the bank in time. After you left, I was so focused on food that I put it off." She looked down. "Now there's a two hundred ruble per month withdrawal limit. I'm so disappointed in myself."

"You haven't used all of my savings, have you?"

She shook her head. "No, there's plenty left, but I should have made it a priority. It just seemed like food was more important."

"That's understandable." He went into the kitchen and one by one, opened the cupboards. "Look at these."

She smiled back at him. "And that's not all. I have more stored in the bedroom. We really do have enough food for months, if we're careful. And if we get some rations." She took his hand. "Vasya, there's something I need to tell you."

The sound of the apartment door interrupted them, and Vasili went into the hall as Yelena called out. "I'm home." Bedraggled and dirty, her mouth dropped open.

"Oh, Admiral Vasili, it's so good to see you. What a relief!" She flushed, and took a step back, composing herself. "I'm so glad you're here."

He beamed. "And I'm delighted to see you, young lady. I think of you often. It's been a difficult time, especially for you." He gripped her shoulders. "You're very brave," he said in a low voice. "What presence of mind, what courage you showed, saving those children." When he was certain she wasn't going to cry, he relaxed his grip. "And the uncertainty about your mother. Don't lose hope. We know a number of volunteers escaped from Luga. They won't be able to return to Leningrad. Be patient for news."

She nodded and at the sink began to scrub the grime from her face and hands.

"You two entertain yourselves," Sofya said. "I'm going to change."

He turned again to Yelena. "How's the brigade?" Her eyes were duller than he remembered, and her countenance flat. The trauma was all over her face.

"Fine. A bit tedious these days. We're filling sandbags," she said. "Nothing as dramatic as burying the Anichkov stallions in the Summer Garden."

"I noticed the bridge. Looks naked without those massive statues."

There was a long pause. Where was that fresh-faced, exuberant teen? "I'm sorry I can't stay for a longer visit," he continued. "I must return to Kronstadt tonight. After I walk your grandmother to Philharmonia Hall." He waited again. "So, tell me about Pavel. Any news?"

"I guess my grandmother tells you everything." She brightened and one corner of her mouth turned up.

"Well, perhaps not everything." He grinned.

"Pavel's well. Handling supplies for the Leningrad Front right now, but he keeps hoping for something more exciting."

Sofya returned, concert-ready. He hugged Yelena and kissed her cheek. "I'm so glad to see you, Yelena. And remind Pavel that his job is more important than ever with the blockade."

"I will. And don't worry about us." She eyed her grandmother. "We're a great team."

He put the thought into his tiny stash of hope as he and Sofya walked down the Fontanka embankment to the Nevsky. Vasili felt the weight of this separation sitting on his chest like a stone. The Nazis had surrounded Leningrad, the railways had been cut, and he was leaving. Bombs would shriek down on the city. The food supplies would run out. Millions of civilians and no way to feed them. And then the Nazis would march into Leningrad.

He had to convince her to leave. "Sofi, the situation is beyond grave. Rail lines cut. The city surrounded. The bombing of Badayev the other night was just a taste of what the Germans have planned. They will bomb and bomb. Incessantly. Until the city is a crumbling ruin. Then they will enter Leningrad and kill or imprison anyone still alive. At best you'll be slaves. You know what they'll do to Yelena . . . to both of you. You must leave. You must get to Ladoga and find a way across. If Yelena won't take the train then walk to Ladoga if you must. Pack your rucksacks with a change of clothes and a winter coat. All your money, your documents, and enough food for ten days. Your violin. Nothing more. It's forty kilometers to Ladoga. You can make it." He paused, agitated and out of breath. Finally, he saw some fear in her eyes. "I'm sorry to frighten you, but you cannot stay here."

"Vasya, I promise to explain the situation to Yelena. And, I'll go to the authorities and ask. But, I . . . even if we walked to Ladoga, even if there are barges and I could convince her to take one, we'd still have to travel by train after crossing the lake. She's so fragile right now. She's not herself. All those children, her mother, her father. I fear there's no way to convince her. And I must take care of her. She's the most important thing."

They were both right. He'd always admired Sofya's self-reliance. But now, it made him sick at heart.

"Sofi, I don't want to spend these few minutes arguing. Of course, you must protect Yelena. But you must use the strength of your personality, your wisdom and experience, to convince her. The Red Army is in retreat and what's left will be directed toward protecting Moscow. Do your best to get out. Perhaps in another week Yelena will be stronger."

At the stage entrance to the concert hall, he held her in his arms. Filled with dread, he knew it might be months before he'd see her again. If he'd see her again.

"Vasya, remember we have plenty of supplies. And I promise you, at the first sign of German troops coming into the city, we will go. Somehow. Like you said, we'll walk to Ladoga if we must. I understand what's coming if the Nazis enter Leningrad."

He felt a flicker of relief. "Thank you, Sofi. Please try to convince her."

"I will." She touched his cheek as confirmation.

He stepped back and she reached behind her neck and undid the clasp on her gold necklace. She kissed it and pressed it into his hand. "This way I'll always be with you."

His throat tightened and all he could do was nod.

"I love you," she whispered.

Vasili kissed her quickly and watched her disappear into the concert hall.

GOSTINY DVOR

September 1941

ONE MORNING a couple of weeks later, Lena stumbled out of bed to the bathroom, her head thick and fuzzy. The strong light from the window meant it was late. Eyes still closed, she sat on the toilet and peed, then staggered back to the bedroom. Her head throbbed. She squinted at the bedside clock. Ten o'clock. Darn. It'd take all day to get bread now.

Already at the kitchen table, her grandmother barely moved when Lena shuffled in.

"Morning, *Babusya.*"

"Hello, Sweetheart."

Her grandmother looked exhausted, holding her head in one hand and a glass of tea in the other. Lena toasted the remaining dense, stale bread and poured her own tea. She wasn't even fully awake and the entire day had gone awry. She chewed the unpleasant tasting bread. Even jam couldn't disguise the harsh texture and woody taste. Sipping her tea helped it go down.

"Last night was awful," Lena said. "How many times did we go to the shelter?"

"I lost count," her *babushka* said. "Sorry I can't do rations today. Early rehearsal."

Rations had been reduced twice since the Badayev fire. Almost overnight it seemed, food had become everything. Stores were empty. Technically, each person could get two days' bread at a time, but usually customers weren't allowed more than a single day's ration because supplies were so low. It didn't really matter what the ration cards said or what the rules were if there wasn't enough food to go around. To make things worse, from the moment the Germans encircled the city, the quality of bread coming out of the State-owned bakeries deteriorated. Rumor had it that ground sawdust was being added to stretch the flour supply.

Her grandmother had been right about other things too. There were air raids several times a day, sometimes all night long like last night—just as she said would happen. Terrifying bombing attacks that sometimes started as the faint buzz of a horsefly only to become a swarm of bees and then finally a thunderous rumble as the planes dipped to drop their payloads. Heart pounding, racing to a shelter, she felt like she was trying to outrun them. Just like in Lychkovo.

The raids were so frequent they slept in their clothes. At the shrill, urgent whine of sirens, she and her grandmother would stumble out of bed, bleary-eyed, grab their coats and the bag by the door and head to the shelter. There were always dozens of people there—a press of tired, cranky adults and fussing children with their smells, noises, and complaints. Spending so much time in the crowded shelter was a strain, but it was the exhaustion and permanent, dull headache that wore her down. What she wouldn't give for some sleep, glorious sleep.

Her grandmother had tried to convince her they needed to leave Leningrad, that the bombing raids would be nonstop and the Nazis might fight their way into the city. But she couldn't do it. It was hard enough in the air raid shelter. She'd gotten better with the smaller explosions—ones you could hear, but not feel. She and her grand-mother would keep right on reading or playing chess. Then there were louder ones that caused the shelter to tremble. People clutched each other and whimpered. Her grandmother always reached for her hand. Lena would close her eyes until it passed. Sometimes a few chess pieces skittered off the board and they'd have to start over. But when the bombs were truly close, bits of dirt and masonry fell from the ceiling and the walls, you could hear glass and other things breaking as if an enormous freight train was thundering through the building. All around her people cried and mumbled long-forgotten prayers. She would pull her coat up over her head then and try to disappear.

She would never get on a train again. Not now. Not ever.

"I better get going." Lena said. She refilled her grandmother's tea and kissed her cheek.

"Be careful. Pay attention," her *babushka* said.

As Lena made her way to the largest of the several bread shops in their neighborhood, she thought about her grandmother's words. Not so long ago, Baba Sofya would send her out the door in the morning with a hug and a kiss and the imperative, "Learn something." School was an opportunity, learning a gift, something that made life better. Maybe someday she'd hear those encouraging words again, instead of the harsh reminder that everything was dangerous.

The end of the line was blocks away. As the minutes dragged, she fidgeted, unnerved about how quickly the situation in Leningrad had changed. Her brigade was filling several streetcars with sand. The vehicles had been positioned on main southern arteries as part of the system of barricades. She could hear her Komsomol leader exhorting them to work harder, faster. "The Germans are at the gates! There's not a moment to spare." Each day was more urgent than the last. The Nazis, just a handful of kilometers away, really were at the gates. She and her grandmother had talked about what they would do if a ground attack came—escape to the woods north of the city and try to make it to Ladoga. There were plenty of empty *dachas*, and lots of Red Army troops on the Finnish border. At any cost, they would avoid being taken prisoner. The rumors of what the Nazis did to women were too horrible.

She daydreamed about Pavel to distract herself. Before he left, they talked about everything: school, their families, even their hopes and dreams. When she was with him her stomach felt empty and her heart speeded up. He could have any girl in school, but she was the one he kissed, the one he confided in, the one he asked to write.

Someone snapped at her. "Close the gap. What's the matter with you?" Lena sighed and glared back at the woman, but moved up in the line so there wouldn't be any empty space. Everyone was irritable. The morose, disdainful expressions which Russians typically wore had become agitated, angry, and intolerant.

Just over two long hours passed, and Lena finally turned the corner. Not far now, she could see the entrance less than half a block ahead. She edged closer to the woman in front of her, willing the line to move faster. Lena was almost at the shop, less than a dozen people to go, when the maddening sirens started. As the crowd scattered like buckshot, she hesitated, hating to abandon her place near the front of the line. The sirens cranked up to a wail. With the swelling hum of aircraft, rumbling, buzzing like a plague of metal insects, Lena finally bolted. Yet, instead of diving for the nearest apartment building basement, she ran. There was a real shelter not far and she hated taking cover in basements. Common sense told her they were death traps. If the building was hit, they'd all be buried by the falling rubble.

The first explosion rolled the earth and an invisible fist slammed her to the ground. Dust and grit rose. Her ears rang, as if the bomb's whine had lodged in her head. Pushing herself up on hands and knees, she cried out from the searing pain in her left arm. The shelter. It was close. Rising to a crouch, unsteady, holding her arm, she stumbled forward, coughing, eyes stinging. Tumbling inside, she scrambled down the steps as someone banged the door shut behind her.

Below ground, she felt secure. The bass rumble of the bombers, the terrifying explosions, and the sharp *ack-ack* of Soviet anti-aircraft guns were muffled. Lena sat on the bottom step to examine her bleeding arm, scraped knees and torn pants. Someone scooted over to make room, while another stranger found the first aid kit, then cleaned and bandaged her cuts.

"I'm all right. Thank you." Lena said.

"Are you sure? That elbow is nasty." The young woman in factory overalls snapped the kit closed. "You should have it looked at when we get out of here," she said.

"Thanks for the help. To tell the truth, I'm more worried about my ears. There's this horrible buzzing and everything sounds far away."

An older man sitting nearby looked up. Lena was taken by his thick, wavy shock of white hair, disheveled but dashing. Like Pavel's. He had the same intense dark eyes too, and for a moment Lena imagined her sweetheart as an old man.

"Explosion caught you," he said. "It'll go away. The ringing in your ears."

She nodded. He made room so she could lean against the wall. She cradled her left arm. After two or three more sets of explosions, the buzzing in her ears did start to diminish. They waited for the all-clear signal. People dozed. How long had it been? An hour? Two?

When she finally climbed out into daylight, her knees were stiff and her arm throbbed. Toward central Leningrad she could see smoke. Worried about her grandmother, she crossed the street in front of the park and hustled toward home, holding her arm against her side.

Passing the bread shop, Lena slowed and noticed the line reforming. She knew what her grandma would do. Nothing was as important as rations and she joined the queue. The Radio House had a good, deep basement. Baba Sofya was probably fine. Most likely still rehearsing.

With one eye on the smoke in the distance, she watched the attendant snip the little squares with today's date off both ration cards, then measure, cut, and weigh the bread. At the same time, she heard a few voices down the line. "I heard that Gostiny Dvor was hit." "Probably full of people too." "Filthy Germans! Bombing civilians. Just wait. They'll get theirs."

She bit her bottom lip to keep it from trembling. The Radio House stood across Nevsky Prospekt from Gostiny Dvor. She stuffed the bread into her bag and rushed outside.

Gostiny Dvor was the main shopping center in Leningrad. The two-story structure held dozens of shops. It fronted the Nevsky on one large city block and then ran even longer down Sadovaya. The oddly shaped building was a popular landmark. Everyone shopped there.

As she hurried toward the center of town, the sounds of emergency vehicles grew louder. Stopping at home to make sure her grandmother wasn't there, she raced up the three flights, holding her elbow tightly against her side. Part way up, she heard her best friend's frantic voice.

"Lena. Lena. Help me! Are you there?" Tanya was pounding on the Karavayev's door.

"Tanya, what's wrong?" Lena crested the stairs, bending over to catch her breath.

"Lena, you've got to help me." Her eyes were huge, her hair wild. Tanya grabbed Lena's arm, and she cried out in pain.

"What's the matter?" Tanya let go and stepped back.

"I fell getting to a shelter," Lena said. "I'll be all right, just my arm. What's going on?"

"It's Mama, the children. They went shopping. Mama said they were going to Gostiny Dvor." Sputtering through her tears, Tanya put her face in her hands and slumped to the floor. "They left the house while I was doing chores. After the all-clear, I heard people saying Gostiny Dvor had been hit. They haven't come home." Her shrill words grew louder and louder, echoing in the hall. "I have to find them. I don't know what to do."

Lena squatted next to her friend and took her hand.

"Stay calm. We'll find them, Tanya." Lena stood and opened the apartment door to toss her bag inside. "Let's hurry."

The girls zipped down the stairs and out to the Fontanka Canal. Plumes of dark smoke rose in the direction of the shopping center. Lena squeezed Tanya's hand and kept them going. After crossing the canal, the Nevsky grew thicker and thicker with people and vehicles. The girls slowed to a walk. Clouds of smoke and dust made it difficult to breathe. Something terrible had happened. The buildings on the opposite side of the Nevsky, the side where her grandmother worked, seemed untouched. The Radio House and their favorite cafeteria were right there. She recognized the distinctive Singer Building further along the street. Even through the dust and smoke, the far side of the Nevsky looked intact. Lena stared, just to be sure.

Mesmerized by the turmoil, Tanya's eyes were wide and glassy. Shouts and commands flew along the street, blaring sirens drowned out some of the cries for help. Debris littered the ground. Gritty, smoky air burned their eyes. A narrow path for emergency workers had been cleared in the almost impassable street.

The two girls picked their way through the wreckage along the edge of the State Library. From there, they had a clear view. The front of the shopping center was a huge, gaping crater. Much of the rest was in flames. The dead and injured lay in the street. Rescue workers, firefighters and ambulances raced everywhere.

"No. No. NO! NO!" Tanya screamed.

Lena pulled her against the library.

"Look at me, Tanya!" Lena shook her friend. "I know you're scared. I'm scared too, but it doesn't help to be frantic. We can't find them unless you stay focused. Let's go to the back where there's less damage. Did your mama have a favorite store?"

Tanya cradled her face in her hands. Wiping tears and snot on a sleeve, she nodded. "On the far side, near the news kiosk next to where we used to get our dance clothes."

The girls hurried to the rear of the shopping center. There, the building appeared undamaged, a shocking contrast to the front. Lena felt a surge of hope. Bystanders helped the injured. She looked away, imagining Lychkovo, the head with blond braids and little Ivan, chubby and lifeless. Unsteady, she took a couple of breaths. She had to be strong for Tanya.

Past the back perimeter they heard a familiar voice over the din, shrill and teary.

"Mama. Where's Mama?"

Irina! Tanya ran to scoop her up. Lena looked around and saw Sergei sitting on the steps of a building across the narrow street. She rushed to him and knelt down. His eyes were blank. Then his tears, little trails of dirt down his cheeks, signaled recognition. Lena hugged him.

"Are you hurt?" she asked.

He looked down. Tattered remnants of his socks still clung to his bare, bloody feet.

"Oh, Sergei."

He sobbed into her shoulder for a few minutes, and she held him.

"The sirens came when we found my boots," he said. "Mama tried to find the shelter but bombs fell right away. I don't know what happened. It was so loud. Everything fell apart."

"Do you know where Mama is?"

He shook his head. "We were all together. Mama had Irina's hand and she told me to follow, but something knocked me down. When I got up, I couldn't see, it was all smoky. People were crying and screaming. I tried to get out, somebody brought me here, then Irina. My feet."

"You are so brave." Lena hugged him again. "Don't worry, we'll take care of your feet."

Behind her, Tanya came to comfort her brother. "You should stay here," Lena said. "Sergei needs you. I'll go inside and see if I can find Mama."

Stunned and pale, Tanya nodded.

Lena began to pick her way through the wreckage. Arm throbbing, she hooked her thumb into her belt to support the injured limb and with her good hand, pressed a used hanky over her nose and mouth to stop the poisonous smoke that burned her throat and stung her eyes. Glancing at rescue workers as they cleared debris from a body, she looked again. There was so much dirt, it took her a few moments to be sure. Mrs. Petrov's face was gray and her eyes and lips closed. She didn't seem to be breathing. Lena began to cry.

"Please," she sniffed. "I know this woman. Her children are outside. Is she . . . ?"

Dust rose around the filthy rescue worker.

"She has a pulse. No idea about her injuries. She's on the next ambulance."

Lena grabbed a crumbling wall. "Do you know where she'll be taken?"

"Couldn't tell you, we've almost got her clear." He nodded in the direction of the exit. "Wait outside until we get her loaded. You can ask the ambulance driver."

She nodded and returned to Tanya and her siblings. She pulled her friend aside.

"I found Mama." She tried to be brave, but a sob squeaked out of her throat. "She's alive, but they don't know how badly she's hurt. She's unconscious. They're taking her to a hospital."

Tanya's body shook as Lena squeezed her with her good arm. Cheek to cheek, their tears intermingled.

"Be strong, Tanya," Lena whispered. "Remember, you aren't alone. Why don't I stay here—the children shouldn't see her like this.

You go to the ambulance. It's right around the corner. Find out where they're taking her."

When Tanya returned, her face was steely and bloodless. Clutching Irina close and holding Sergei's hand, she told them that Mama was going to the hospital. "I don't know what's wrong with her yet. I'll find out later," she said.

Tanya's voice was unsteady. Lena watched her siblings, but they seemed too stunned and shocked by what they'd been through to notice Tanya's fear.

"We're together, it's going to be okay," Tanya said. "First things first, let's go home."

Tanya lifted Sergei onto her back and looped her arms through his legs, careful not to brush his feet. Irina wanted to be carried as well, but hampered by her injured arm, Lena coaxed the youngster into walking with a promise of chocolate. At home, the girls cleaned and bandaged Sergei's feet as best they could, picking out bits of glass with a tweezer and scrubbing gently while Sergei whimpered. They bathed both children and gave them each a small cup of soup. Lena cuddled with Irina and Sergei on the sofa, reading to them, while Tanya took a streetcar to her aunt's apartment across town. An hour later she returned, dismayed.

"They're gone," Tanya said, waving a piece of paper. "She left this letter, explaining how they got approved for evacuation and had less than twenty-four hours to prepare. They crossed Ladoga yesterday. What'll we do?" Crestfallen, Tanya looked down at the crumpled paper.

Lena's mouth fell open. "Had your aunt talked about leaving?"

Tanya nodded. "I overheard her and Mama. Mama wanted to wait until she got Papa's opinion, I think she felt guilty about leaving the factory. Auntie Marina took my *babushka* and my cousins." A flicker of hope crossed her face. "At least they're safe."

"Well, don't worry. Even without your aunt, we're here. We can get your rations, watch the little ones, whatever you need."

Lena tried hard not to look too grave, but poor Tanya. Mama in the hospital, two young siblings, her father far away with his factory. Other relatives evacuated. How would she manage?

"Listen, I'm sorry, but I need to go." Lena took Tanya's hand. "My grandmother will be worried, it's past six." Lena hugged her friend. "Be brave. The little ones need you to be strong." They looked at the two youngsters asleep on the sofa. Tanya sniffed and nodded.

"I'll be back," Lena said. She grimaced at her swollen, discolored arm. "Probably tomorrow. Looks like I need to get to a clinic tonight. But, don't worry, my grandmother can help and I'll go with you to check on Mama." She pulled her still stunned friend into a tight one-armed embrace and hurried out the door.

EVACUATION REDUX
October 1941

L ENA HAD BEEN to funerals before, but none so bleak and unnatural as this. There was no family to support Tanya and her siblings while the simple wooden casket was lowered into the ground. The priest intoned important words, mostly unfamiliar, but the ritual was comforting. Since the war began, the Party frowned upon religion less and Tanya said it was what her mama would have wanted.

In place of relatives, Lena and her grandmother flanked the three Petrov children, two pillars trying to hold up the collapsing threesome: little four-year-old Irina, wailing, inconsolable and uncomprehending, Sergei, rigid and face forward, with silent tears dampening his cheeks, and Tanya, struggling to be strong, yet devastated in the way of one just beginning to understand that life will never be the same.

After the funeral, Lena and Sofya led them home, the sad, small group still disoriented. By the time they arrived at the Petrov's apartment, the sky was spitting tiny, icy raindrops. That afternoon, they sat huddled together, wondering if any of the Petrov's neighbors and friends, those still in Leningrad, would stop by to offer their condolences. Before the war the apartment would have been jammed with people. Tanya's school friends would have crowded around her, bringing her tea, holding her hands, whispering caring comments. Mr. Petrov would have stood in a corner, smoking cigarette after cigarette while friends nodded and gripped his shoulders, sharing his grief. Relatives would be on the sofa entertaining Irina and Sergei, while Lena and her grandmother served plates and plates of food: huge dishes of dumplings, pots of soup, plates of *zakuski*, snacks. The war took away all that. Already most people remaining in the city were holed up in their apartments, increasingly focused on nothing more than the next morsel of food.

At least the cemetery—behind Trinity Cathedral in the Alexander Nevsky Monastery—was beautiful. Like most religious institutions, the monastery was shuttered after the Revolution. Closing it didn't change the fact that Great Prince Alexander was the most heroic figure in Russian history. Every schoolchild learned how he defeated the Teutonic knights and became ruler of Russia. While the priest chanted, Lena's thoughts drifted to a class trip when they'd seen Eisenstein's film, *Alexander Nevsky*. She and Tanya left the theater reciting Nevsky's words: "*Whoever will come to us with a sword, by a sword will perish.*"

After the funeral, Lena spent every day with Tanya and the children. She played chess with Sergei, dolls with Irina, and read them books. On cloudy, rainy days when bombs were less likely to fall, she took them to the school playground or for short walks while Tanya waited in line for bread. Lena couldn't go back to brigade work until her arm healed. In the meantime, she showered Tanya and her siblings with love.

The four of them went to the cemetery every third or fourth day. It had a lovely stream running through the green expanse dotted with granite and marble markers, crosses and tombs. Tanya seemed calmer standing there, in front of the gravestone with her mother's name. Lena liked going along. Her presence was a support, or at least a welcome distraction, and the monastery stirred memories of her father. She had walked the same paths with him, visiting the well-known, older, small cemeteries flanking the monastery entrance. One of them, the Lazarevskoye, was the oldest cemetery in the city. Picking their way through the tight labyrinth of decaying tombstones, voices soft out of respect, her papa would tell her about the military leaders, famous architects, scientists, and other important historical figures buried there.

Opposite was the Tikhvinskoye, a less crowded cemetery where the artistic greats of the city rested. As a child, she'd been drawn to Tchaikovsky's grave, with its two angels and cross surrounding a bust of the composer, carved out of gorgeous dark marble. While Tanya and the children sat on the grass at their mother's grave, Lena would disappear into the smaller cemeteries, listening for her father's voice.

On the walk to the bus stop after one visit, Tanya seemed especially distracted. The children skipped ahead.

"I know it's hard," Lena squeezed Tanya's hand. "I wish I could help."

"You already do so much." Tanya glanced at Lena. "It's just . . . I can't believe she's gone. Seems like we'll walk through the door and she'll be there, standing in the kitchen with her apron on, smiling at us."

"She was the best mother, a kind and wonderful person." Lena pulled Tanya close with her good arm as they walked. Sometimes it felt like they'd both lost their mothers. Her mama had been gone three months with no news. Still, better than having buried your mother. The information that trickled through the city about the People's Volunteers was not good. Lena clung to a fraying thread of hope.

Wiping away tears, eyes on the ground, Tanya spoke. "I've been thinking. More than thinking. Rations have gotten so small, we're hungry all the time. Even with your help we hardly have any food. Look how thin the children are and it's only been a month. I'm scared." Tanya's voice caught. "Even though I haven't heard from Papa, I've decided we should leave. My whole family is gone. Auntie Marina, my grandma and cousins evacuated. Uncle Ivan fighting. Papa with the factory." She took a deep breath. "They're still taking citizens by barge. If we're going to go, now's the time, before things get worse, before the ice comes and the barges stop."

Stomach churning, Lena drew her coat tighter. Evacuation meant danger, perhaps death, but so did staying in Leningrad. She glanced ahead at Sergei and Irina. "I think you're right."

"You do?" Tanya turned to Lena, eyes eager. "I'm so relieved. I've been questioning myself all week. Should we try to leave or should we stay? I didn't talk to you about it right away because I know how you feel about evacuating."

"You've got to do what's best for them," Lena said, nodding toward the children. "People are hungry, it's getting worse. You need to be with your papa."

"Exactly what I think." Tanya grabbed Lena's good hand. "So, the first thing I have to do is apply to the District Executive Committee for travel documents. With no parent in the city and two young siblings, I think they'll approve."

"Of course, they will." Lena fumbled in her pocket for a hanky.

"I'll miss you so much," Tanya whispered.

"You'll come back when this is over."

The girls stood behind Sergei and Irina at the bus stop. Lena pulled her shoulders back.

"So, when shall we go to the district office?"

Tanya smiled and hugged her. "I couldn't do any of this without you."

Two days later the teens went for travel documents. They left the children with Lena's grandmother, departing before first light, hoping to be near the front of the line. An arctic cold had struck the city. Silent, the girls kept their heads down, braced against the bitter wind.

A woman behind the desk interviewed Tanya, and gave her several papers to complete. The girls had brought everything that might be necessary: identification papers, residence permits, birth records, her parents' marriage record, her mother's death certificate, their school enrollment forms, and papers from her father's work.

Tanya finished the forms and handed everything to the official. Lena fidgeted, bouncing her knee up and down during the long wait. The apparatchik pulled out another form which she completed herself before passing it to Tanya for her signature. Then the official stamped it with three enthusiastic and loud thumps. She stamped the other completed forms as well. Lena raised her eyebrows and elbowed Tanya. The multiple stamps meant the Petrovs were approved.

"You'll leave Leningrad the day after tomorrow," announced the official. "You will meet the train at Finland Station. It departs at seven in the morning. Bring your identification papers, of course, and that document." She pointed to the paper Tanya signed.

"You're each allowed one suitcase or bundle. If your siblings aren't able to carry theirs, you'll have to do it for them. Anything you can't carry will be left behind. And don't forget food. Once you get to Finland Station, there's nothing until you reach the other side of Ladoga. Under the best of circumstances, the trip is ten hours. When the weather is severe the barges can be delayed. Be prepared. It can take several days."

Tanya paid close attention and nodded, her eyes growing big as the woman spoke.

"In addition, you understand it's a dangerous and difficult trip. The Germans have been attacking the barges and the trains. There are many risks and you are taking full responsibility for the peril involved." The woman's eyes narrowed. She seemed to be relishing her little speech.

"My goodness!" Lena interjected. "Is it necessary to frighten her, Comrade? Her mother was killed. She has to do what's best for her brother and sister. Please have some compassion."

The woman rolled her eyes and waved her hand to dismiss them, muttering something about how compassion wasn't part of the job. The girls rose as one.

In the hallway outside the office, Tanya said, "I can't believe it. We got approved. Just think, by this time next week we'll be with Papa. I wonder if he's gotten my letter?"

"Don't worry," Lena said, "you'll find him through his factory." Thinking of her own father, wondering where he was, what kind of battles he was fighting, Lena turned away. Even having grown up in a military family, war was hard to imagine. Men killing other men, machine guns, grenades, tanks. Images from Lychkovo rushed in and she changed the subject.

"I hope you don't mind. I had to say something," Lena whispered. "I know it wasn't my place, but that woman was mean, lecturing you about how awful the trip will be."

"Of course. Why are apparatchiks like that?" Tanya's face screwed up. "They act like doing their job is a big favor, always reminding you that they're in charge." She grabbed Lena's good arm and smiled. "Of course, I'm glad you didn't say anything until after I got the papers."

As they emerged from the building into the wind and snow, Tanya continued. "Oh my God! And did you see how fat she was?"

Lena smirked. "I guess she hasn't been lucky enough to be on the Leningrad diet."

The girls giggled as they held on to each other, disappearing into the whiteness of the swirling snow.

THE LIBRARY
October 1941

A TINKLE OF LAUGHTER filtered into the apartment and Sofya stepped out of the kitchen. The Petrov children looked up from their game.

"Good news!" Tanya said as she and Yelena burst in. She rushed to Irina and Sergei. "We're going to join Papa. Day after tomorrow we start for Kuibyshev."

The children jumped up and threw their arms around their sister.

"Is it far?" Irina asked. "I need my dolly." Tanya kissed the top of her head.

"Can we take my chess set?" Sergei looked at his sister shyly.

It was the first time Sofya had seen the three of them smiling and happy since the Gostiny Dvor bombing. They were getting out. Thank God. Tanya and her siblings would soon be with their father. Far from the war. Far from food shortages and fear. It felt like the Petrovs were leaving in the nick of time. Before winter closed the last door out of the city. Sofya's relief was tinged with something else. Envy, perhaps.

After the Petrovs left, bubbling over with plans for what they needed to pack, talking excitedly about seeing their papa, Sofya tried again to convince her granddaughter to evacuate. "All we have to do is take the transit document to the district office."

"I'm doing better," Yelena said, face downcast. "I've managed to ride the bus a few times, but Ladoga?" She looked up, bright blue eyes pleading. "Please stop trying to convince me. I already feel terrible.

Besides, you and I can do this. We have each other, that's how we're going to manage. And anyway, the Nazis haven't come any closer."

Yelena's optimism was a powerful thing. She had such faith in the two of them. As if they were somehow a greater force together than they were individually. And it was true that the Germans seemed to have dug in. Maybe Vasili was wrong about a ground attack.

Two days later, well before dawn, Sofya and Yelena helped the Petrovs to Finland Station, where a trickle of the millions still in Leningrad were trying to escape. Tanya carried most of their belongings in a heavy ruck-sack, while the children gripped smaller bags. Yelena hugged Irina and Sergei and then clutched Tanya amidst tears and promises to remain safe and write and to see each other when the war was over.

After the train pulled away, Sofya and Yelena stood outside the station doors, hearts heavy. Two soldiers smoked and talked in low tones nearby. "Thank God our boys on the Moscow Front are giving the Nazis hell." "I heard they had to move units away from Leningrad."

Eyes wide, Sofya hurried out of earshot. "Did you hear?"

Yelena whispered. "Maybe that's why there's been no attack."

As they walked along the building, Sofya eyed the dozens of bits of paper taped or glued to the wall. The handwritten entreaties for help had begun to appear all over the city, fluttering in the wind like little white flags of surrender. The sad for sale notices offered furni-ture, an Oriental carpet, clothing, furs, books, jewelry, dishes, silver, everything and anything in exchange for food or cash. Tears filled her eyes when she read the ad for an Amati violin, "any offer con-sidered." She imagined the starving owner exchanging the valuable instrument for a kilo or two of bread. People were that desperate.

They took a streetcar across Liteiny Bridge and then split up close to home. Yelena would get their bread ration while Sofya went to the much-diminished Haymarket. The first stall Sofya passed offered some gray, ground lumps labeled as cat. A slimy sheen on the meat, reminiscent of something long spoiled, turned her stomach. She stared anyway, fascinated by what now passed for fresh meat. Alongside were several small bird carcasses. Two hollow-eyed boys not yet Yelena's age, guarded the display and eyed the people shuffling past. Their gazes shifted about as if looking for an easy mark. Sofya pulled her coat tight and turned away.

Past several vendors with household goods and clothing she paused at a pile of blackened, shriveled potatoes and some sad, wilted cabbages. There'd been rumors about people digging vegetables in fields close to the front lines, risking their lives. They'd hide in the woods, waiting for dusk when they'd crawl on their bellies through the dirt, pulling half-frozen vegetables out of the ground. Sofya imagined the Nazis, feeling safe in their trenches, shooting at anything that moved. She hoped the filthy bastards would freeze to death in those earthen coffins.

Sofya looked around to check that no one was watching and dug in her pocket for the right number of bills. The vegetable seller snatched the cash from her in exchange for two miserable-looking cabbage heads that not long ago would've been considered animal feed. The woman's hollow eyes and angular cheekbones were what six weeks of deprivation looked like.

Riding the streetcar home, Sofya gazed at the oak grove as they rumbled past. It was a lovely shady spot to read a book or have a picnic on a hot summer day. A place she frequented when she wanted to escape the press of apartment living. Most trees in the city were bare by October, but not the oaks. They clung stubbornly to their canopy of dull, dried leaves. She noticed people underneath the majestic arbors, scrabbling in the dirt and snow. Acorns were edible, as long as they were well-soaked before cooking. People had gathered acorns after the Revolution. What else would the citizens soon be eating if the blockade wasn't broken?

She got off one stop before the shattered remains of Gostiny Dvor to make her monthly stop at the bank. The stores were now entirely empty and if the black market was the only way to find food, she'd need her monthly two hundred rubles more than ever.

Turning off Sadovaya, she approached the bank. There were no lights inside. She climbed the steps to the main entrance where she found a huge padlock on the door and a sign that read, "*Zakryto.*" No explanation, no information, just "Closed."

Disheartened, she walked toward the Nevsky to get a lunch of warm broth at the Radio House canteen. The soup had become little more than hot water with a few potato peelings, but she ate a meal there every day as it didn't count against her rations. Big institutions and factories in the city had canteens and workers got to supplement their food that way.

At the corner of Sadovaya and Nevsky, Sofya paused, staring at the State Library. A row of small, white columns interspersed with windows ran the length of the building. Although she admired the pastel palaces and ornate bridges that gave Leningrad its distinctive European character, there was something modest and appealing about the library. She was fond of its understated style, especially compared to the baroque buildings grandstanding along the city's waterways. As she stared, someone exited the main entrance. Sofya picked her way toward the door.

Once a regular, she couldn't remember the last time she'd visited the library. The Communist Party controlled all aspects of culture. New art, new literature, new music, and new drama had been found for the new world where workers ruled. Everything had to support Soviet norms. Books that didn't conform to the ideals of socialist society or promote communist values were not allowed. Anything that showed the Soviet Union in a poor light was eliminated. The steady disappearance of important literary works became impossible to stomach. It reminded her of everything else that was constricted and controlled. During the last twenty years, the library had become a soul-crushing place. She went less and less.

The door gave way with a familiar whoosh, like the breaking of a vacuum seal. The building itself seemed to exhale and warm air embraced her.

At the main desk, the formidable librarian pushed up her glasses. Her scowl softened as Sofya approached.

"The library is open?" Sofya asked.

"As you see, every day." The woman waved a hand over her domain. "We have no plans to close, life must go on." Her pride carried a sureness that was comforting.

Sofya thanked her, encouraged somehow. Extreme circumstances brought out the best in some people.

In the main reading room, rows of dark, polished tables beckoned. Sofya breathed deeply, hungry for the scent of varnish, pencil shavings, and ancient paper. The windows were boarded up for protection, but she recalled how natural light used to fill the room with a soft glow. Beyond the tables, the back wall hid behind deep rows of books while a narrow circular staircase in one corner led to the second level. To her left, a maze of bookshelves obscured a group of smaller tables. There, hidden from most of the main reading room, Sofya and Vasili met during those long-ago golden months, hiding their passion behind walls of books.

Feeling Vasili with her, she walked down the aisle, enveloped by the musty, comforting smell of learning until she reached the table where he first confessed his love.

Sofya sat. She forgot about the bank, the daily struggle for food, the city's fight for survival, the heartbreak and tyranny of the empty spaces on the library shelves. She rested her hands on the polished wood, inhaling the sweet smell of books, absorbing the power of love and the nourishment of stories. Eyes closed she was transported to a place beyond the war.

EVERYMAN'S WAR

October 1941

IN AN UNDERUTILIZED factory canteen deep in the enormous Kirov works, Pavel sat on the edge of his chair. He picked at the chunks of tasteless boiled meat, alert for the sounds of incoming artillery. A whine usually meant it was close, but not too close. If it started to sizzle or hiss, he dove for cover. Much of the industrial complex had been moved east before the Nazis surrounded the city, yet there were still plenty of valuable targets and enemy artillery pounded the area, already pock-marked with craters like a moonscape. While he ate, Pavel never got too comfortable.

His company had settled into this no man's land along Leningrad's southern perimeter. They constructed all kinds of defensive works—iron tank barricades, cement pillboxes, artillery and machine gun positions—to defend the Stachek, the artery running south. The Germans were only a few kilometers away and it was nerve-wracking being so close.

Captain Lagunov appeared between the tables and the room quieted.

"Men, looks like we're saying *do svidaniya,* goodbye to the Stachek."

A rumble of approval rolled across the tables. Lagunov raised a hand for quiet.

"New orders. At fifteen hundred today, we depart on foot for the freight yards, several kilometers east. Those of you with family in south and central Leningrad have time to check-in, if you hurry. Whatever you do, be at the freight yards before eighteen hundred."

The captain didn't need to remind them that tardiness would be considered desertion. Ever since Stalin's Order No. 270 directed deserters be shot, everyone knew disobedience of any kind, even accidental, would not be tolerated. Pavel couldn't really imagine the captain shooting one of his men for being late, but it was war. Crazier things had already happened.

The captain nodded once and left. An immediate clamor broke out.

"Well, I'll be damned. Captain's gone soft," said the regular army man next to Pavel.

Another soldier chuckled. "Yeah, sounds like he actually cares about us."

"He knows what's good for morale, that's for sure," a third added. He stood and gave Pavel a friendly push as he went past. "Hey, Pavlik, if you're going to check on your family, or that girl you're always mooning over, you better get going."

Mouth full, Pavel lifted his head in reply. He sat with soldiers much older than himself most of the time rather than other volunteers. Their experience made him feel safe. Some had fought in the civil war and there was a steadiness about them that reminded him of his father.

Grabbing his still untouched bread, he stacked his tray for the overwhelmed kitchen crew and joined the crowd moving for the exit, swept into the wave rushing back to the building where they were billeted. He threw everything into his duffel and in twenty minutes was aboard a streetcar running north. He had five hours, plenty of time.

Pavel hadn't seen Lena since early July, but she wrote often. Her letters were funny and engaging, and she had a way of making everyday things interesting. Trips for rations were a never-ending source of entertainment. Pavel heard about how much they'd fallen after the Badayev fire, but in his mind Lena wasn't struggling. She gave news of their friends: those who evacuated, volunteered, and the few still in Leningrad. She used first names and generalities to avoid drawing the censors' attention. Her most recent letter was sad and short, sharing the news that Mrs. Petrov died. He got a couple notes from his mother too, but it was the envelopes from Lena that made his heart leap.

Pavel spent twenty minutes of his precious time waiting at a bus stop until someone told him there was no fuel for the city's buses. Further up the street, he hopped a tram that deposited him a ten-minute walk from home. Winter arrived early and a few inches of packed snow already covered the streets. His breath hung like fog off the Baltic, dense and damp, something he could touch. As he walked, the silent snow accumulated on his shoulders and pack. He'd anticipated the smashed buildings and piles of rubble, but not the quiet. The streets were deserted, ghostly.

He turned the corner for home, then stopped. Two apartment buildings should have been on his left. Instead, jagged bits of masonry stuck up through a mountain of rubble like rotting teeth. The pile of pulverized concrete, scattered with bits of furniture and possessions, was frosted with fresh snow. A third structure had lost an entire wall, separated with almost surgical precision. The opening revealed apartment contents to the world and reminded him of a precarious dollhouse. Through the veil of white a baby crib tilted at an uncertain angle, a bed seemed about to slid out the opening, and a kitchen table and chairs waited for their occupants. Pavel looked away, uncomfortable seeing something so private, and then his legs buckled. He dropped his bag to the sidewalk and sat on it. Mama. Raisa. His grandmother. They couldn't be buried under that. His eyes stung and he stared down the empty street. The office of the District Soviet could give him answers, but he didn't have time. Perhaps Lena and Sofya Nikolayevna could help. Lightheaded, he stood, lifted his duffel and set off for the Karavayev's.

Pavel rang their apartment from the entryway door and glanced around the silent courtyard while he waited. The door opened, a woman exited and he lunged past her. The silence inside was even more oppressive and out-of-place. He heard no conversations behind the closed doors. There were no smells of soup bubbling or meat frying, no grandparents calling to their grandchildren, no laughter, no life. He raced up the three flights and pounded on their door. "Lena? Sofya Nikolayevna? Are you home? It's Pavel."

Nobody answered. Sick to his stomach with fear for his family, Pavel sat on the top step. Now what was he going to do? His only option was to leave a note. He'd ask Lena to check with the District Committee. She'd get word to him about his family.

Opening his bag, he rummaged for a scrap of paper and a pen. As he started to write, he heard the entryway door. Cold air and women's voices floated up. He flew down the steps two or three at a time. Lena and her grandmother stood at the bottom, stamping their boots and brushing snow off their coats. Their mouths fell open at the sight of him, and all three exclaimed at once.

Upstairs, his words tumbled out. "Our commanding officer gave us time to check on our families. We're getting new orders and I have to be at the freight yards before six. I went straight home to see everyone, but our apartment building is gone, destroyed—"

"Pavel, wait," Lena said. "They evacuated before that happened. You didn't get my letter?" She squeezed his hand. "How awful that you didn't know."

"Really? I thought, I thought . . ." He turned away and sniffed.

"I'm sure they're safe," Lena said, taking his coat with hers.

Pavel saw the cast on her arm. He touched it gently. "What happened?"

"Oh, I'm fine. I fell getting to a shelter last month. It's nothing."

A broken arm wasn't nothing, although her response made sense. She faced difficulty every day—bombs, artillery, the city surrounded, the stores empty. What was a broken arm compared to all that? When she told him about the attack on Luga and the lack of contact with her mother, he pulled her close, trying to soothe away the pain. He didn't yet know how, but he had to help Lena and her grandmother.

Sofya came over and squeezed Pavel's shoulder. "Tea's ready, but first I want to show you your things." They followed her to a corner of the living room. "Your mother came to tell us they were leaving and she brought your belongings for safekeeping." Empty apartments were already a target. People searching for valuables to trade for food. She pointed to a corner and then slipped back to the kitchen.

Pavel and Lena inspected the clothes, books, his violin. He stooped over the small pile. His life, such as it was. "Not much, is it?"

"It must be a shock—your home," Lena said.

He nodded. "I mean, I'm relieved to know they evacuated. Hopefully they're with Papa. But, now I'm the only one still in Leningrad."

"I'm here too, Pavel." She squeezed his hand.

He hugged her, and she leaned up to kiss him. She was here. For him.

Lena led him into the kitchen. "And you still have a home, right here with us, until the war's over and your family returns."

Sofya nodded. "Oh, Pavel, it's a lot at once, isn't it?"

"I knew about the bombings." He hung his head. "We've been under attack just like everyone, but I didn't expect to find my home gone. I'm so happy my family is safe."

Sofya placed the samovar on the table while Pavel went to the door to retrieve his duffel. He reached inside, pulled out the small loaf of bread from his lunch, and handed it to Lena.

"No, Pavel, I can't take this."

"My rations are many times yours, plus, I get meat, potatoes, and a hot meal most days. I won't starve." He smiled. "Besides, if you're family now, you must take it."

"Well, we're not going to starve either. We worked all summer and have lots of food to supplement our rations," Lena said.

"I'm not surprised." He grinned. Sofya Nikolayevna was always focused and organized. Lena had a reputation at school as someone who got things done. Together they must be invincible. "Still—" he set the bread on the table "—this is for you."

Then he pulled out a half bar of chocolate. The women hadn't had any since the one they shared with the Petrov children after Gostiny Dvor. The sweetness and creamy texture of chocolate melted in their mouths, delicious.

"What a treat," Sofya said. "Thank you."

Pavel asked Sofya about her playing.

"We're still busy rehearsing and performing. I've been glad for the distraction. The Leningrad Philharmonic left for Tashkent months ago, so the RadioCom is in demand. Our numbers have diminished of course, some enlisted or volunteered."

He'd always liked his music teacher's amiable nature, how she never made him feel awkward or looked down on him even though she was one of the best violinists in the city. Today he was especially grateful for her warm, steady demeanor.

"So, Pavel, you've really gone to some lengths to avoid practicing, haven't you?" Sofya Nikolayevna teased him with a grin.

"The next time I come for a visit we'll play a duet," suggested Pavel. "Now that my violin is here, I have no excuse."

"That would be wonderful. I'll be sure to keep practicing so you don't show me up." Pavel watched her disappear into the kitchen. "Your grandma is really something."

"You know she likes you, she told me so."

Pavel blushed and took her hand. "And what about you? How do you feel about me?"

"Isn't it obvious?" Her eyes dazzled and her pink lips beckoned.

He reached over and tucked a bit of hair behind her ear and they kissed.

"It means everything to know that you're here and thinking about me, waiting for me," he said. "Your letters help so much."

She stroked his hand. "Writing makes me feel close to you, as if we're going through this together, even though we're apart."

Pavel checked the time again, and then stood. He had his arm around Lena as he said good-bye to her grandmother, happy he didn't have to hide how he felt.

Holding hands as they walked down to the entry, Pavel felt Lena lean into him. They hugged, a long embrace, and when he stepped back, he pulled her away from the door and into the alcove under the stairs, hidden from view. There, he kissed her with abandon. The first tentative kisses became longer and deeper, with open mouths and tongues exploring. Pavel hadn't done up his coat and his arousal was intense. Lena's every curve pressed against him and all he wanted was the pleasure of her body on his. His hand drifted down to her behind to pull her into him. He moaned and said her name.

"I wish I didn't have to go," he said, looking into her eyes, memorizing every detail.

She returned his intense gaze and responded in a husky voice. "I think of you all the time. I miss you so much." Her voice cracked a tiny bit. She held his hand against her cheek.

He slipped his other hand behind her neck and pulled her lips to his one last time. The words slipped out. "I love you, Lena." The look on her face told him she thought it was the most natural thing in the world to say. In reply, she rose on tiptoe and brushed her lips against his. "I love you too, Pavel."

Her eyes sparkled icy blue, like a clear winter sky.

FINLAND STATION

November 1941

P AVEL GOT OFF the streetcar with time to spare. If only he'd spent another few minutes with Lena. Everything about the war disappeared when he held her under the stairs. The pressure of her lips and the way her body moved against his had sent pleasure from his groin to his chest and all the way to his limbs. As he left her in the doorway, even his feet were warm.

He loitered on the fringes of the freight yards, not wanting to share his happiness and not wanting to heighten the disappointment of those who hadn't seen family. A few soldiers drifted toward him, grumbling about the captain not yet revealing their destination.

"Shit. You know what this means don't you?" Bogdan, a middle-aged soldier, gray hairs scattered through the stubble of his beard, muttered under his breath.

"Can it be worse than being on the Stachek? At least we won't be artillery practice for the Nazis anymore," another said.

"Damn right it can be worse," said Bogdan. "If we're going east to shore up Shlisselburg, it'll be much fucking worse than dodging German artillery shells. It's a blood bath there, hand-to-hand combat, rifles at close range, bayonets. Kill or be killed."

They'd all heard stories from the previous generation, but only a couple of the soldiers in Pavel's unit were old enough to have seen combat.

"Have you ever killed a man?" Bogdan continued, addressing no one in particular. "Stabbed him and seen the light go out of his eyes?

Wiped his blood off your hands? Well, I have, and it's fucking ugly business."

Back in June and July Pavel was desperate to fight the Germans. But that was before he saw artillery shells pulverize men, sending body parts and flesh flying. And since then, Kolya and Dimitri and hundreds of other volunteers had been killed in Luga. Now his stomach turned at the thought of combat.

After waiting in the cold for several hours, the captain's voice finally rang out.

"Fall out! Get on the train."

At the command, several hundred men clambered into the unheated cars. They smoked, played cards, and slept. It was the middle of the night before the train staggered forward, lurching and crawling to its destination.

Slumped in his seat, Pavel woke when the train shuddered to a final stop. He rubbed his stiff neck and peered outside. Even in the dim light, he recognized the blackness just beyond the makeshift train station. He sniffed at a fishy smell. They were on the shore of Lake Ladoga, the largest lake in Europe. Pavel had been here on holiday with his family. When calm, it was paradise; when stormy, a monster.

As his unit left the station on foot, Pavel noted new development all around the sleepy lakeside hamlet. Warehouses in various stages of construction stood a short distance from the train depot. On the lakeshore, he glimpsed new docks for the barges taking civilians across the lake. His mother and sister had been here, carrying their bags, helping his frail grandmother walk down to the pier and climb aboard. His mother hated boats. The motion made her sick. Looking out on the rough, dark lake he knew it must have been a difficult crossing.

Pavel's unit walked a distance to several small barracks in a large pine grove. After getting their assignments and stowing their gear, word spread that once the lake froze, they'd be bringing food into Leningrad from Kobona, a nothing spot some thirty-five kilometers across the narrow part of the lake in Soviet-held territory. A way to get around the German blockade.

That evening in the mess hall, striding back and forth, his rich baritone resonating through the long, low-ceilinged room, Captain Lagunov told his men of their critical work. As soon as the ice was thick enough, they would resupply the city across the frozen lake. Should they succeed, the citizens of Leningrad would survive. They would be heroes. Should they fail, the city would starve. They would starve too. Rations were critically low, and without a supply line in the next weeks, there was no hope. It was their duty to protect and serve the people, and now they had the honor and responsibility of being the most important link in the chain to save the city.

The captain's words made the back of Pavel's neck prickle. When Lagunov stopped pacing, the reality of the difficult task settled like a chill over the unit.

"On the ice road," he continued, "you'll face the Luftwaffe and Mother Nature. Neither will show you mercy. Remember, even when the ice is thick enough, even in the coldest winter, it's unpredictable. Fissures and crevasses will appear, water will break through unexpectedly. Without a doubt, as soon as the Nazis realize what we're doing, the screechers will come hunting, and you'll be sitting ducks on a massive field of white with nowhere to run, nowhere to hide."

Walking back to the barracks, heart still pounding, Pavel turned to Bogdan. "I don't know whether to be afraid or excited."

"Sounds like we're being thrown to the wolves," Bogdan said. "A death wish."

"Yeah." Another soldier joined the conversation. "We'll be easy to see, crossing a frozen lake, and the Nazi flyers will use us for target practice. I'd rather stick to repairing railroads."

"But they need us," said Pavel. "You heard the captain, the city's going to starve."

"Better you than me, kid," said Bogdan.

The ice on Lake Ladoga was weeks away from being thick enough to support vehicles. Pavel had plenty of time to dwell on the coming dangers while he worked on the old railroad from Leningrad, a simple, little-used excursion line for vacationers. Now it needed to support the heavy rail traffic essential to supplying a large city. Laying sections of new track and regrading parts of the rail bed was dirty, exhausting work, but Pavel was the first man attacking repairs each morning and the last one to stow his tools every afternoon.

"Hey, Chernov. What's the matter with you?" One of the volunteers grabbed him by the shoulder on their fourth or fifth day. "I told you to stop working so hard," he snarled, looking around to make sure the lieutenant in charge was still in the woods taking a dump.

Pavel stumbled, pushed again. A second man tripped him. On his knees, he tried to stand but the first thug put his boot hard in the small of his back.

"It seems you need a lesson, little Pavlik." He took Pavel by the neck and shoulder and ground his face into a pile of snow-covered gravel.

The lieutenant's voice rang out. "What's going on over there?"

"Nothing, Comrade Lieutenant. Chernov fell, that's all."

Pavel wiped the blood and grit from his face. The small, angry gash on his cheek served as an unpleasant reminder of what could happen if you stood out.

On the morning of November 7, the captain called Pavel into his tiny office near the barracks. He must have done something wrong, made a mistake. Maybe his zealous work ethic was frowned upon higher up the chain of command. Shit. He knocked on the office door and took a deep breath.

"Come in," said the captain through the door.

Pavel entered, saluted, and stood at attention. "Chernov reporting, Comrade Captain."

"Close the door, I have a job for you." He pointed at a package the size of a large briefcase, wrapped in brown paper and tied with twine. "This parcel needs to be delivered to this address." He handed Pavel a slip of paper.

"Yes, sir." Pavel stood a bit taller.

"Take the afternoon train. If all goes well, you can stay overnight with your family. Of course, who knows if things will go smoothly. You need to return by tomorrow evening latest."

"Yes, Captain. Thank you for the assignment, sir."

"You did some fine work on the railway. As soon as the ice thickens, there'll be no opportunity for leave. Right now, everything's ready for the Ice Road except the ice."

"Yes, sir." Pavel nodded. "Anything else, sir?"

"Be sure to report when you return. And be careful, we're expecting an attack."

Pavel nodded. Today was the anniversary of the Bolshevik Revolution. A huge holiday in the Soviet Union. Normally there would be a parade, with everyone off work and lots of eating and drinking. There wouldn't be much celebrating this year. Not in Leningrad anyway. Maybe not in Moscow either. He'd heard the Germans were closing in on the capital too. Pavel tucked the package under one arm, banished the negative thoughts, and raced down the slight incline from the office. He was going to see Lena.

The train's scheduled departure was delayed. Darkness had long fallen when it pulled out of the village and chugged toward the city. There were a few soldiers on the train, but its real cargo was freight— the last supplies brought across the lake by barge. With scattered ice forming, the barges were grounded. There'd be no more supplies until the Ice Road was up and running.

After a couple of hours moving at a pace not much faster than a brisk walk, they jerked to a halt. Pavel could hear the battle raging over the city. Waves of German bombers made repeated runs while anti-aircraft batteries barked back. In between the attacks, there was the near constant exchange of artillery fire, the distant thud-booms with the frightening, shrill whine of incoming shells. Although broken by flashes of the howling battle, the darkness made it impossible for Pavel to tell how close they were to the city. Fires popped and flashed on the black canvas, casting an unsettling light.

He fidgeted, trying to guess the train's location. Eventually, desperate for information, he stumbled through the dark cars, feeling his way until he reached the engine.

"Who's there?" said a gruff, unfriendly voice.

"I'm Chernov, Comrade. A passenger." He smelled cigarette smoke.

"Engine's off-limits. What do you want?"

"Yes, sir, I was just hoping for some information. I have orders to get to Vasilevsky."

"Yeah, yeah, we all have orders." Visible now from the glow of his cigarette, face smudged with dirt and grease, the trainman exhaled smoke toward Pavel. "Seems the Nazis have some of their own. Finland Station's been bombed. We're stuck here until daylight."

"Do you know how far we are?"

"Thinking about walking?" The dubious trainman continued. "Fifteen kilometers, give or take. Up to you, of course. Dark and dangerous out there but feel free to hop off anytime."

The shadowy figure disappeared up the ladder and Pavel made his way back to his seat.

Hours later, the air battle over, he woke to the lurch and roll of the train. As they crawled along, the sky lightened and soon Pavel made out several sets of tracks converging, but by the time the train stopped, smoke filled the air, making it impossible to see much of anything. One of the engineers came through the car, announcing the train would go no further and passengers would have to proceed on foot. Finland Station, or what was left of it, the trainman added softly, was less than a kilometer away.

At first, Pavel followed the tracks. Soon, the broken outlines of the station and surrounding buildings emerged through the veil of smoke. As he got close, the tracks disappeared altogether. Clambering through craters and wreckage, he saw train cars flung like toys and a section of track ripped apart like a giant zipper. The detritus of people's lives, their meager belongings, were mixed with huge chunks of steel and cement. Broken bodies were scattered, some blackened by fire, others coated with gray dust. He averted his eyes, ignoring the voice in his head that said, "That's someone's arm."

The main platform had taken a direct hit. Tracks on both sides had vanished, buried under debris or blown apart, and Pavel found himself in a hole, gazing up to where the platform should have been. He tried not to look too closely at what he was climbing through. Unfamiliar sharp metallic smells assaulted him, and his eyes and throat burned from the dense, acrid smoke. The powerful stench of what he guessed was burning flesh made him hold his breath, and he paused to tie a scarf over his face leaving only his eyes uncovered.

He clambered on his hands and knees, as one might climb a steep sand dune or narrow, rocky trail, looking for safe footholds and things to grab onto. Once he reached what remained of the platform, his eyes swept the cavernous space, roof gone, not a single track or train untouched. He watched groups of firefighters and rescue workers dotting the disaster. They searched for survivors and stacked the dead. The pile of corpses was a small mountain and even from a distance Pavel recognized the smaller bodies of children. Evacuees, headed for Lake Ladoga, had been waiting to escape when the Nazis struck.

Dizzied by the magnitude of what had happened and desperate to get away, he turned for the front of the station when a human sound caught his attention. He looked toward the far side, searching for movement, when he heard the sound again. A child's cry.

Cracks and pops from metal expanding or contracting sounded like gunfire and made him jump. A fire on the opposite side simmered. There were dull hisses from water hitting the conflagration. Intermittent words drifted his way from the firefighters, the noises forming a strange backdrop as he strained to locate the child's voice. Smoke and stench assaulted him. He drew close to the wreckage of a railcar split open like a clam. It was worse than any battlefield he could imagine. The bombs and fiery metal had done horrible things to human bodies: crushing, severing, burning. He averted his eyes and hoped they had died quickly. As he turned from the carnage, he again heard the whimper. He scrambled in the direction of the noise, pulled himself into the remains of the train and clambered through the grotesque interior. A wheel had somehow lodged inside and the sound came from behind it. He saw a body cleaved in two through the midsection. A youngster, perhaps five years old, sat next to the upper half of the body, behind the huge wheel, stroking long, loose hair framing a woman's untouched and serene face. Her eyes were closed. The boy cried for his mama, patting her cheek as if trying to awaken her. Pavel squatted down to comfort the child.

"What's your name? I'm Pavel."

"Alyosha," the child whispered.

"I'm going to help you," Pavel said.

The little boy looked at him with wet eyes like saucers. "Mama," he cried.

"I'm sorry, little buddy." Pavel shook his head and scooped Alyosha into his arms like an experienced older sibling. The youngster whimpered and clung to him.

Unsure what to do with the boy, Pavel headed for some helmeted and masked emergency workers. They were pulling remains out of the wreckage. Pavel shielded the boy's eyes.

"I'm from the Ladoga Front. Just came through the station. Found this *malysh*, little guy."

Pavel started to hand the boy over.

"Listen, we're handling recovery . . ." The rescue workers waved at the stack of charred, mutilated remains. "Not survivors. Better take him outside. There'll be an emergency vehicle to get him to Erismann Hospital. The injured have been transported there."

Pavel nodded and held the boy tight as he made his way again toward the front of the station. Glass crunched underfoot as he stepped through what was left of the doors. Water from the firefighting hoses had frozen, coating the area in ice. He moved gingerly, clutching the child tight. When he reached the street, he set the boy down and pulled his scarf aside to drink in the clean air, trying to clear his lungs.

There were firefighting vehicles, but no ambulances in front of the station. He couldn't just leave the little guy and the hospital wasn't much out of his way. From Erismann he could catch a tram to Vasilevsky Island.

"Come on, little buddy, we're going to go to the hospital and have you checked out. Are you hurt anywhere? Can you walk?" Little Alyosha looked up at Pavel with big, sad eyes. "Don't worry, it's going to be all right. I'm going to take care of you." He tied the child's hat tightly under his chin and took his hand.

At the hospital, a nurse registered the boy and when she asked his name, Pavel said, "Alyosha."

"Alyosha what?" she replied.

He didn't know the boy's last name, and instead of asking him, Pavel said "Chernov. Alyosha Chernov."

As the nurse took them to an examination cubicle, Pavel

wondered why he'd done that. He didn't have a brother. But he had some Chernov cousins. While the examining physician probed and prodded the boy, Pavel touched the nurse on the elbow to get her attention.

"His mother's dead. What will happen?" Pavel asked.

"But I thought he was your brother," the nurse said.

Pavel shook his head. "Cousin. And I'm at the Ladoga Front."

She looked downcast. "He can't go with you. It'll be an orphanage for him."

"Aren't there any families that could take him?"

"No such thing in Leningrad right now. Just institutions." She paused. "You know there's almost no food in those places, and few caregivers." Her next words were a horrifying whisper. "Would've been better if he'd been killed by the same bomb that took his mother."

Aghast, Pavel glared at her. How could she be so cold? Were conditions in the city that bad? Had things changed so much in just a few weeks?

"I can take him," Pavel said. "I've got family he can live with. I'm on my way to see them now." He hoped Sofya Nikolayevna and Lena could figure out a better solution than an orphanage. Maybe they could care for him.

The doctor pronounced Alyosha unhurt but suffering from early stage *dystrofia*, the official term for starvation. While they waited for the paperwork to be completed, Pavel distracted the youngster with a fairytale he used to tell his sister. "This is the tale of the Firebird and the Princess Vasilisa. There once was a powerful and greedy tsar who had an archer named Alyosha." The little boy's eyes brightened when Pavel changed the name of the hero to his own, and he listened to the story of the archer and his wise horse and how they finally outwit the demanding tsar.

By the time he finished the story, the nurse returned, carrying spare clothing. An orderly followed, wan and ashen, but carrying two bowls of thin soup from the canteen. Pavel hadn't eaten since the evening before and he and Alyosha made slurping noises and looked shyly at each other. The boy smiled at him and Pavel put his spoon down and poured his remaining soup into the child's bowl. Lastly, the nurse handed Pavel paperwork including an official authorization for a new ration card. The entire thing took less than two hours.

He turned to the child. "Come on *malchik*. Time to go."

Pavel and Aylosha turned for Vasilevsky to make Captain Lagunov's delivery. The tram ride was another eye-opening experience. Pavel knew how the ration system worked. Factory laborers received the largest rations, not as large as those in the army, but enough to survive. Next were office workers. Dependents and children were last. The laborers he saw looked tired and thin, but not starving. The *babushki* and children were a different story. Cheeks hollowed out, facial bones protruding, two months into the blockade and they were already emaciated. He watched an elderly couple get off the tram and inch their way down the sidewalk, faces all sharp edges, nothing like the chubby grandparents of his childhood. What would happen in another month or two? He looked down at Alyosha who had fallen asleep. Angular cheekbones and arms like sticks. Just as the doctor said, the boy was starving.

Pavel found his destination in a neighborhood of identical apartments and knocked. A thin, attractive woman opened the door, baby on her hip.

"Can I help you?" she asked and motioned them down the hall to a single room. It was a communal apartment and this space served as bedroom and living room for the entire family.

"Captain Lagunov sent this." Pavel explained, setting down his rucksack and pulling out the large, heavy package.

"Do you know my husband?" Her eyes and voice grew bright.

She set the baby on the floor and Alyosha went right over and began entertaining him with funny faces.

"He's my commanding officer," Pavel said.

Her face drained of color. "Is he all right?"

"Oh, yes, he's well." Pavel nodded and smiled.

She burst into tears and turned away, carrying the package to a small table. Alyosha's bottom lip started to quiver. "My mama cried a lot too," he said.

Pavel squatted next to him and the baby. "I know you miss your mama, but you're going to have a new home." Alyosha sniffed.

Pavel stood and cleared his throat.

"I'm so sorry, Comrade," the woman said. "Everything is very hard, so little food." She paused, gathering herself. "Please, can you stay a few minutes? I'd like to write him a note."

Pavel nodded. "Would it be possible to clean up?" He glanced at Alyosha who had resumed entertaining the baby.

"Please." She pointed down the hall. "There's a towel hanging on the door."

Pavel scrubbed his face and neck and ran wet fingers through his dark hair. Using a corner of the towel, he brushed the worst off his clothes. The captain's wife was finishing her letter when he came out. She folded it into a triangle, wrote the captain's name on one side and handed it to him. He put it away while she opened the package. Cans of meat and fish, chocolate, bags of macaroni, sugar and flour, and many other items tumbled out. She began to sob again, then picked up the baby and clutched the little one to her chest.

"I'll tell the captain his family is well, and that the package will make a big difference."

"Thank you, I'm grateful," she said through her tears. "Be safe, Comrade."

Pavel took Alyosha's hand as they walked toward the center of

Leningrad. He lowered the ear flaps on his hat and pulled his scarf up for protection. Whirls of snow lashed at them and soon Alyosha couldn't make any progress. Pavel moved his rucksack to his chest, squatted down and had the boy climb up on his back. The child weighed little more than the food he delivered.

"Hold tight, now. Rest your head on my shoulder." The boy tucked his head down and gripped Pavel. Soon they were across the Palace Bridge and caught a tram. Two stops before Moscow Station they got off and walked to the Karavayeva's. As they climbed the stairs, Pavel heard music and smiled. Sofya Nikolayevna was playing.

"Pavel!" exclaimed Sofya, still holding her bow. "My goodness, what a surprise. Come in, set your things down." She brushed his cheek with her own. "And who is this young man?"

Alyosha brightened. "I'm Alyosha," he said.

"Well, do come in Alyosha. I'm Sofya Nikolayevna. I'll make us some tea. And maybe a little something to go with it." The boy beamed at the suggestion.

She turned to Pavel. "I'm so sorry, Yelena is checking in with her brigade. She gets her cast off soon. We planned to meet at the State Library around four o'clock."

Nothing was going as he planned. He'd spent so much time getting here: all night on the train, Finland Station and the hospital, and delivering the package. Now he had only a few hours left and Lena wasn't here. "My return train is at six."

Sofya put water to boil. "Still, let's get you warmed up. Both of you." She smiled at Alyosha. "Then we'll head to the library. Yelena might be early."

While she made tea, Alyosha looked curiously at Sofya's violin and bow.

"What's that?" he asked.

She smiled brightly. "It's a violin. Do you like music?"

He nodded. "My mama sings sometimes." He looked at the floor and began to cry.

Pavel knelt down and hugged the boy. "Of course you miss your mama, Alyosha." He whispered to Sofya. "Little guy lost his mother last night. Finland Station was bombed."

Sofya turned to him. "You poor dear. Come with me. Let's get that snack."

Pavel took a bundle out of his rucksack. Before leaving Ladoga, he'd pleaded his case to the quarter-master, and made the rounds of the barracks trading cigarettes for food. Now, he set the package on an empty chair, and slid it under the table when Sofya wasn't looking.

While Alyosha ate, Pavel explained how he found him and impulsively decided to claim he was his cousin. "The nurse told me about the orphan homes. He's been through so much. Look at him. The doctor said he weighs only seventeen kilos. I just couldn't leave him. It's asking too much, but I didn't know what else to do."

"Don't be silly, Pavel. He can stay with us." She whispered, "We've got food. I admire what you did. It was the right thing."

When they entered the library, the soft murmuring comforted Pavel. It was no wonder Lena and her grandmother came here often. So different from the cold, dark silence outside. Something of normal academic life—reading, writing, researching—percolated at the tables.

Lena looked up as Pavel approached. Her mouth fell open and she leapt from the table and ran into his arms, cast and all.

Ninety minutes had never been so short. Pavel and Lena leaned against each other, whispering and sneaking short kisses, library be damned. Pavel explained about Alyosha and the project to bring food into the city. She confided how deeply she missed Tanya. She touched the still fresh scar on his cheek, while he brushed it off as nothing more than an accident. Sofya sat near the front of the library with Alyosha, reading him story after story.

Pavel began checking his watch every few minutes, and finally stood and led Lena to the front of the library. He hugged Alyosha goodbye, explaining that Baba Sofya and Lena would take good care of him and that he'd see him as soon as he could get leave again. Alyosha nodded, his face blank.

Then Pavel turned to say farewell to Sofya and she placed a strong kiss on his cheek. It reminded him of his mother and his throat burned.

"Don't think you've escaped that duet you promised me," she whispered and smiled. "Seeing you has really raised our spirits. Be brave, young man, be safe."

Pavel nodded, pressing his lips together. He and Lena went outside to say their goodbyes in the privacy of the deserted streets.

THE AIRMAN

November 1941

SOFYA SAT AT the kitchen table by weak candlelight, her mind on the struggling orchestra. Fewer than twenty musicians showed up that afternoon for rehearsal. For a number of her colleagues, it was too far to walk. Several had moved into the Radio House. Their wives and children had evacuated and it was easier to sleep on a cot than to go back and forth from their apartments. Plus, they wouldn't be alone.

All of a sudden, the door opened and slammed shut, rattling the windows.

"You'll never believe it!" Yelena called. Sofya heard the thunk of boots being dropped in the entry and in a moment her granddaughter was in the kitchen, eyes bright. "I got assigned to our firefighting unit. I start as soon as I get my cast off and I turn sixteen." Her birthday was in five weeks and she'd be eligible for the job she'd coveted all along: rooftop firefighting.

Alyosha stood to one side. The little boy never complained, rarely cried, but hardly ever spoke either. Suddenly, he piped up. "Can I be a firefighter too?" It was the first time he'd expressed interest in anything.

"You are a brave boy, wanting to help," Yelena said. "You can't be a firefighter just now—you're not old enough. But I'm sure you can help. Maybe it can be your job to check that the sand bucket is always full."

A smile lit the boy's face and he came and stood close to Yelena.

Sofya sighed. Now the two of them were set on doing something dangerous. "Are you sure you want to be in the freezing cold on the roof? At least with the Komsomol you'd be moving, easier to stay warm."

"It won't be too bad," Yelena said. "I like the idea of being close to home. And I'm the only firefighter for our building. I'm supposed to work two or three shifts every day, a couple hours each, depending on the weather. Bombing raids are less likely in the extreme cold."

"That's one good thing about this bitter weather." Sofya mumbled.

"You don't seem very glad," Yelena said.

"It's dangerous. I'd rather you were in a shelter during air raids."

There were hundreds of civilians in the city sitting on rooftops, watching for incendiaries. The Germans dropped the small bombs by the thousands, starting fires everywhere. Ready with buckets of sand and water, the rooftop firefighters were responsible for burying the little fire bombs in sand or plucking them with special tongs and dropping them in buckets of water.

"I could get hit by artillery walking to work or standing in line." Yelena's voice was soft and earnest. "Being on the roof isn't riskier than anything else."

Sofya looked down, staring at the wood planks of the floor, dark and smooth with wear. Why couldn't her granddaughter do something less dangerous? Youth brigades were headed north of the city to gather wood, the perfect assignment to keep her out of harm's way. Or was it? She sighed audibly. Yelena was right. Nothing and no one was safe anymore.

She turned back to the teen and relented. "Promise you'll be extra careful up there."

The next day, Sofya watched her granddaughter climb the narrow stairwell that led to the U-shaped roof. Later, excited about her upcoming assignment even if tired from clearing the snow, Yelena described how she'd found a protected area next to the stairwell housing. Sheltered from the wind, it provided a clear view of the sky to the southwest, the direction of most attacks.

"I can see the Admiralty and St Isaac's and lots of other buildings. It's encouraging."

Every evening the three of them ate their largest daily meal. On this particular night it included a few ounces of hard, woody bread which they soaked in hot water, eating the mushy mass like cereal. Sofya added a substantial dollop of jam to their bowls. Alyosha greedily scooped the jam straight into his mouth. Yelena pushed hers off to one side, saving it for last. Sofya stirred hers throughout, little streaks of purple in the gray mush. They each had several slivers of ham and three pickled green beans on a plate. They cut their food into tiny pieces to make it last longer. After licking their plates, relishing the last drops of sour pickle juice, they sat in front of the barrel-shaped stove. Residents across Leningrad put in the small wood-burning contraptions after bombs damaged the main power stations. Sofya had taken Yelena's old sled and gone to the Haymarket to find one. Together they wrestled it up the stairs and set it on some bricks they'd scavenged.

After putting Alyosha to bed, Yelena brought two kitchen chairs close. This hour before they let the fire die out was precious. Sofya checked that the blackout curtains were in place. They removed their coats to enjoy the stove's heat when a thud vibrated from the roof.

"It might be an incendiary. I'd better go check," Yelena said before Sofya could react. The teen was weeks away from her start as a firefighter, but she went up to the roof once or twice a day anyway.

Yelena jumped into her boots and slipped on her coat. She grabbed the flashlight and rushed down the hall to the stairs. Sofya snatched her own coat off the hook and followed. She'd never seen an incendiary and was curious about the white light that came from the magnesium—or was it phosphorus?—that frothed out of the deadly fire bombs before they started to burn.

Moonlight reflected off the snow, casting ghostly shadows. Sofya stood by the stairwell door while Yelena crept in the direction of the thud. As her granddaughter moved stealthily, Sofya heard a familiar sound—clothes snapping in the wind. She could almost see the sheets fluttering on the clothesline at her grandparent's cottage and she sniffed at the air, remembering their fresh, crisp scent. Yelena's flashlight played over a body and illuminated a parachute flapping in the wind. A German airman lay motionless, eyes closed.

Yelena scrambled back, grabbing Sofya. "A Nazi," she whispered, eyes wide.

"Downstairs, quick," Sofya said. They hurried into the apartment. "Was he dead?"

"I think so," Yelena nodded. "His eyes were closed, but I couldn't tell if he was breathing. What should we do?"

"We need help. A soldier, the police," said Sofya.

"I'll go to the Nevsky," Yelena said.

"Not alone. It's not safe. Stop and ask Vladik." The Radchenkos were on the first floor.

Her granddaughter flew out of the apartment. Sofya hung her coat and pulled off her boots. She hated Yelena to be out at night, even with a neighbor. She should have gone herself.

Sofya picked up the lantern and went into the dark bedroom. She opened the night table drawer and pulled out Vasili's pistol, checked that it was loaded, and slipped it into her pocket.

Listening for anything out of the ordinary, all Sofya could hear was the soft, but mind-numbing tick-tock of the metronome coming from the radio receiver. Regular news broadcasts, literary and musical programs, had filled the airwaves during the summer and early fall.

Exhortations to defeat the fascists, support the troops, even programs highlighting letters from the front distracted and inspired the people. In the last weeks, regular broadcasts dropped off and the empty airwaves filled with the infernal noise meant to signal what? The city's heartbeat? Coming out of the bedroom, Sofya stopped. A current of colder, outside air brushed her and the apartment door clicked shut. She stared at the intruder leaning heavily against the door. He spoke. Was it German? Or a kind of broken Russian? She didn't know much German. She gripped the gun in her pocket. He limped forward a couple of steps and she ordered him to stop. Eyes fixed on him, she set the lantern down. From the floor it cast a strange glow. She took a step back, and then another.

The Nazi took off his bulky gloves, dropping them to the floor. She watched him unzip the neck of his jumpsuit and pull off his tight-fitting head-covering. Stumbling from the effort, he leaned against the wall, favoring one leg. His strange words seemed an unintelligible mix of German and Russian. Whatever language it was, Sofya couldn't focus. The tick-tock of the incessant metronome became a roar in her head.

Heart hammering, she pulled out the pistol and pointed it at him. In a shrill, unnatural voice, she ordered him to the floor. "*Na polye!*" He fumbled to get a hand inside his jumpsuit. When she screamed at him a final time, "Stop, or I'll shoot," he looked at her with a wry expression and said something that sounded strangely like "Yes, please." Then, unsteady but purposeful, he came at her.

She fired and he dropped to the floor.

Suddenly heavy in her hand, Sofya laid the gun next to the lantern and clutched at her chest. Oh, God, was she having a heart attack? Andrei died of a heart attack.

Yelena burst in, followed closely by Vladik, their neighbor.

"Are you hurt? Did he hurt you?"

Sofya shook her head. Sleepy Alyosha stumbled out of the

hallway. Yelena rushed to scoop him up and took him back to the bedroom. Vladik checked that the Nazi was dead.

Sofya shuffled forward. There was a hole precisely in the middle of his forehead.

"Quite a shot," Vladik said.

"I was aiming for his chest."

"So, beginner's luck," he added. "Still, you kept your wits."

Sofya lurched for the wall. The two teens grabbed her before she hit the floor. Yelena guided her to a kitchen chair, put some sugar in a glass of tea and helped her drink.

"The blood," Yelena said.

"Old undershirts in the back bedroom," Sofya replied, but then looked up. "The police are coming. Maybe we shouldn't touch anything." Yelena nodded her agreement.

"There's going to be trouble," Sofya said. "I shot him, with a gun, a gun I'm not supposed to have. They'll have questions. They'll take me away."

Yelena bit her bottom lip and Vladik studied the floor.

"I could say I shot him with his own gun," Sofya said.

Vladik winced. "No disrespect, but you against him? They won't believe you took his gun."

Sofya stared, contemplating her fate—the *Bolshoi Dom*. What would happen to Yelena?

"They would believe I shot him," Vladik said. "Sofya Nikolayevna, hide your pistol. I'll find his gun. We'll say Lena and I surprised him. He and I wrestled. I got the gun. Simple story."

Sofya moved toward the gun on the floor while Vladik locked the apartment door. He and Yelena unzipped the jumpsuit further and found his pistol.

"We need to fire it," he said.

Led by the two women, he carried it into the bedroom and pulled the bed away from the wall. The exterior brick would absorb the bullet. Directing Yelena to wrap a blanket around his hand holding the gun, and using a pillow to muffle the sound further, he aimed at the seam between the wall and the floor and fired. They moved the bed back into place. Sofya hid Vasili's pistol and Vladik set the Luger on the kitchen table.

"He was trying to tell me something, or ask me for something," Sofya explained. "He kept coming toward me. When I told him I'd shoot, he didn't seem to care."

"If you hadn't shot him," Yelena said, "we might all be dead. You were really brave."

As they went into the living room to review their story, a thunder of boots rumbled down the hall. Wide-eyed, all three of them stared at the door. Vladik stepped forward to open it.

"Take a deep breath," Yelena said. "It's going to be fine. We're heroes."

But Sofya didn't feel heroic. She felt guilty and scared.

Four security officers filled the apartment. Three congregated over the body, chattering excitedly about the precision of the shot. The more senior agent addressed her, oozing authority and condescension.

"Comrade Karavayeva, you did the right thing in getting us."

What a strange comment. What else would she do? Cart the body out to bury it in a snowbank? Maybe that's what they should have done, but it happened so fast, and who knew the airman would rise like Lazarus and tumble into their apartment.

"Thank you, Comrade. I'm grateful you came so quickly." Just stay calm. Reinforce his superiority. Remind him you're no threat. Sofya gripped her hands together, trying to hide her fear, as she recounted the story. "My granddaughter went to investigate after we heard a noise from the roof. She found the Nazi. He appeared dead."

The agent looked at Yelena.

"He lay on the roof, completely still." Yelena explained. "His parachute was flapping in the wind. I crept close to shine my flashlight in his face. His eyes were closed and he didn't move. I came back downstairs to get help."

He nodded as Yelena recounted the discovery.

Sofya's hands grew clammy as her granddaughter continued. "I asked our neighbor, Comrade Radchenko, to come with me. While we were gone, the Nazi came into the apartment."

Yelena looked at her grandmother. "He threatened me," Sofya said. "My granddaughter and Comrade Radchenko arrived a moment later, catching him by surprise."

"I tackled him before he could shoot," Vladik added.

The officer's eyes narrowed as they recited the story.

"So, Comrade," the agent addressed Vladik. "What exactly happened when you arrived?"

"The Nazi seemed to be advancing on Comrade Karavayeva. We startled him and then I rushed at him. We fought and I wrenched the gun away. I shot immediately."

"Did he say anything?"

"No." Vladik glanced at Sofya.

"Before Vladik and Yelena returned," she said, "the Nazi mumbled something I couldn't understand."

The agent turned to Yelena. "Comrade, the roof. Show me where you found him."

"Of course." She grabbed her coat and the two went out the door.

Sofya sat, patting her face with a handkerchief. She struggled for air, taking deep breaths. Her hand drifted to her throat, the necklace, until she remembered she'd given it to Vasili.

Vladik watched the agents inspect the soldier. They emptied his pockets, placing items on the floor. One of them grinned at the teen. "Some shot." Sofya glared at the floor, not wanting to look too closely. Couldn't they just take the body and go?

Yelena and the senior agent returned. He set the parachute and harness by the door.

"You were lucky," he said, nodding at the body.

The agents finished with the Nazi, setting another handgun, as well as a knife, on the floor with the other things they'd found: some food, a compass, a map, a photograph.

"Get him out of here." The agent in charge nodded to his colleagues, two of whom lifted the body. The third gathered the items on the floor and put them in a bag.

As they lugged the body out the door, the senior agent came back toward Sofya. Protectively, Yelena stepped close.

"You understand this never happened." His intimidating glare and heavy brow added to the threat.

Confused, Sofya wondered what event he was referring to: the German's appearance or the secret police standing in her apartment. Sofya expected him to order them down the stairs and into a Black Maria, trundling them off to prison. The agent's words buzzed in her head, "Cannot demoralize the population . . . destabilizing rumors . . . duty to keep the people calm."

"Comrade," she began, "we are simple citizens devoted to our great leader, Comrade Stalin, and to our glorious nation. We did what any loyal citizen would have done." She would give him the silence he demanded. "We understand what is needed at this difficult time. None of us will ever speak of the night's events." Yelena and Vladik nodded their agreement.

"I'm glad you realize the gravity of maintaining silence." He looked at each of them in turn. "The consequences of spreading panic—" he paused, "—are exceedingly severe."

After the door swung shut, Sofya clutched her chest and gasped for air. Once again, Yelena guided her into the kitchen. Vladik stood there as Sofya thanked him over and over, but even when she finished, he made no move to go. His eyes darted around, settling on their cupboards. Yelena blocked his path.

"It's late, Vladik. Thanks for everything," she said, glancing at Sofya. "We so appreciate your help, but shouldn't you be getting back to your family?"

He licked his lips. "I thought maybe . . . you know . . . some food for my trouble."

"We don't have extra food," Sofya said. "No one does."

He sneered. "Look at you. You're not as weak and thin as the rest of us. You must have some to spare." He stepped toward them, his gaze again flashing about the room.

Sofya moved toward Yelena, the two of them forming a barrier between Vladik and the cupboards full of food. "Of course, I'm grateful for your help." Sofya took him by the arm, leading him out of the kitchen. "Tomorrow I'll share our bread ration, but you understand, just this once, to show my gratitude. I'll bring it to your apartment."

His eyes gleamed. "I'll be waiting."

SCHOOL NUMBER 98

November 1941

"**P**OOR VLADIK," whispered Yelena after she locked the door. "I wish we could help."

"Of course you do, but even sharing tomorrow's ration . . ." Sofya shook her head. Beyond a bit of bread, they couldn't help the Radchenkos. They couldn't help her colleagues either.

Gennadi, the RadioCom's oboist, looked terrible, although he said he had a bit put away. Eliasberg was struggling. The only ones they'd really helped were the Petrov children after Mrs. Petrov died. They even gave them food for the trip across Ladoga. Sofya didn't want to think about what would have happened if Tanya and her siblings had stayed in Leningrad. Would she have let them go hungry to save Yelena and Alyosha and herself? Would she have forced Yelena to watch her best friend starve? She couldn't bear to think of it.

In public, you weren't allowed to use the words *starve* or *starvation*. The Soviet government used the clinical term, *dystrofia,* as if it somehow made the reality less horrible. Most of the civilians in Leningrad were starving, and some going a bit mad in the process. Sofya, Yelena, and Alyosha were better off than many. They ate twice a day: their bread ration plus 300 grams or so of their supplies. Divided three ways, it was still just a fraction of what they normally ate.

"After I get our bread tomorrow, I'll stop at the Radchenkos," said Sofya. "Better I give it to her. Vladik might eat it all." She looked around the kitchen. "Right now though, we need to move our food to a safer place. I've got the perfect spot. Something your grandpa built."

The next morning, after carefully watching the clerk take her coupons and weigh the bread—250 grams for herself and 125 grams each for Yelena and Alyosha—Sofya tucked the ration inside her coat. It had become too risky to carry the bread in a bag. Just the other day she'd seen a woman step out of the store with her ration and a teenage boy attack her in an instant, grabbing her bread and knocking her down. The startling thing was that he didn't run away. He curled on the ground and ate the entire portion, stuffing the bread in his mouth as fast as he could, despite the fact that passersby were yelling and beating him.

Sofya knocked on the Radchenko's door.

"Hello, Comrade," Sofya said to Vladik's mother, who stared blankly. "It's Sofya Nikolayevna, your upstairs neighbor."

A spark of recognition flashed in Mrs. Radchenko's eyes.

"Are you all right?" Sofya asked.

The woman nodded.

"Well, perhaps Vladik mentioned that he helped us last night. I told him I'd share our bread ration today as a way of showing my thanks."

The woman's eyes grew large.

"May I come in?" Sofya's neighbor stepped aside. "Where's your little boy? I haven't seen him for a while."

Finally, she spoke. "He's at school as always."

"School?" Sofya said. "I didn't realize schools were still open."

"Some of them. Yuri attends School Number 98, where Vladik used to go."

"I see," Sofya said. The same school Yelena attended as a child.

"Best thing," the woman's eyes gleamed, "is they give them a warm broth for lunch."

"Really? They feed them?"

"It's not much, just a teaspoon of yeast in hot water, sometimes a few cabbage leaves thrown in, but better than nothing."

Thinking about the possibility of Alyosha attending school, Sofya carefully took the largest portion of bread from inside her coat—nearly half their ration—and handed it to Mrs. Radchenko. "Thanks for allowing Vladik to help us last night. And you'll be sure to tell him I came by with this, won't you?"

She had turned away, greedily gnawing on the dense chunk of bread.

Sofya climbed the stairs, the image of Mrs. Radchenko pushed aside by the possibility of school for Alyosha. With rehearsals and performances, Yelena's upcoming firefighting duties, and all the time they spent in lines, school would be a huge help. Besides, the boy's quiet nature worried her. Being around other children might be good for him.

When Pavel brought Alyosha to them, she didn't check if schools were open. All summer, trainloads of evacuees—especially children—left Leningrad. Older teens like Yelena were working in the war effort. She'd assumed educational institutions were closed.

A few days later, Sofya and Alyosha entered School Number 98. She felt uneasy about enrolling him. He wasn't her grandchild and she might have to lie. Maybe they would be so sympathetic or so overwhelmed that it wouldn't matter who Alyosha was or where he came from.

The little boy looked neither happy nor unhappy when told he was going to school. Sofya explained in her best upbeat voice that it was a short walk and there would be a nice teacher and a classroom where he'd learn and play with other children.

They made their way to Yelena's old school, holding hands, boots squeaking on the snow. The hallway smelled of sour disinfectant, a scent Sofya recognized. Schools always smelled like that. Alyosha had been scrubbed clean too. His blond hair was slicked back. He needed a haircut.

At the main office, Sofya encountered a haggard administrator. "Fill this out and return it tomorrow." The woman then directed them to the correct classroom. Alyosha frowned slightly as he glanced in the rooms they passed, a serious, concerned look darkening his brow. Sofya wondered why there were no sounds. This wasn't the school she remembered—a serious place, but not a silent one. A place where children called out to each other and roughhoused in the halls when teachers weren't looking.

"*Zdravstvuyte.* Hello, my name is Sofya Nikolayevna and this is Alyosha."

"*Ochen priyatno.* Nice to meet you. I'm Irina Maksimovna. The previous teacher was . . . well . . . I've taken this class. Actually, we've combined a couple of classes as many children have been evacuated, or . . . you understand."

Sofya nodded. It must be hard to be a teacher now, every few days another child gone.

"Yes, Alyosha himself was supposed to be evacuated, but things didn't go according to plan. I'm grateful you're open."

"Our director is determined to keep life as normal as possible," the teacher said. "A number of schools have already shut their doors, but not us." She stood straighter. "We'll never close." Looking from Sofya to Alyosha, she continued. "And you're his . . . grandmother?"

"Not quite. He's the son of my husband's sister's daughter." The lie rolled right off her tongue.

Alyosha gripped Sofya's skirt. She felt the youngster trembling and reached for his hand.

"Look. They have a play table over there." Sofya saw some building blocks that were identical to the ones they had at home. Yelena's old toys were getting plenty of use.

Alyosha's eyes widened. "Will you come?"

The teacher nodded at Sofya.

The two of them sat down, gathering the blocks. Other children drifted in, and Alyosha looked up as each one settled themselves at a table or in the book corner. After one little girl joined them, the bell signaling the start of the school day rang and Sofya saw the teacher motion that it was time for her to go.

When she stood, Alyosha jumped up and grabbed her hand. They walked together to the door, where Sofya knelt down and pulled the youngster into her arms. Like a helpless tiny bird, he quivered against her.

"I'll be back this afternoon." She squeezed him. "When school is done."

The little boy's eyes were wet. "What if the bombs come?"

"Your teacher will take you to a shelter. You'll be safe."

"But I like the shelter by us," he said, speaking softly and slowly as always.

"Don't worry." Sofya squeezed him again. "We'll go to our shelter in the evenings."

The teacher interjected. "We have a very big shelter with games in it."

Alyosha relaxed his grip. Sofya stood and inched toward the door. She caught a last glimpse of him at the play table and hurried down the hall.

THE BOMB SHELTER

December 1941

E VERY TIME THE frightful air raid sirens shrieked, Lena could see Alyosha's trauma reopen—the deep wound of his mama's death rubbed raw over and over. Gripping her hand, he seemed to hold his breath until they tumbled into the shelter. She assured him the bombs couldn't reach them there. What horror he must have felt at Finland Station. First, excitedly boarding the train with his mother and settling into a seat. But then the fearsome wail, the sirens cranking up to a scream, the bombs.

There was a particular man at their shelter who always sat in the same spot. Even when he limped in after the space was crammed full, people made room. They left him to himself, but it was clear they respected him.

Alyosha wasn't put off by the sadness in the man's face, and he was fascinated by his wooden leg. He sidled up to Comrade Major Ivan, watching him play chess against himself. In no time, the Major taught Alyosha the basics and they became fast friends.

Lena and her grandmother knew how to play, and before Pavel brought the little boy to them, they sometimes passed the time in the shelter playing chess. But in their first weeks with Alyosha, they hadn't even thought to teach him. He was so young. Major Ivan looked at Alyosha differently. And now, thanks to him, the sirens frightened the little boy less and less. Soon he was glad to hurry to the shelter, even in the middle of the night, anxious to play chess with the melancholy veteran.

Early on, the second or third time they arranged the chessboard between them and Sofya and Lena nodded their thanks, Major Ivan asked Alyosha if Lena was his sister. The youngster's eyes grew bright with tears.

"My cousin."

Lena interjected, her voice low, "His mama died in the Finland Station bombing."

Major Ivan nodded knowingly. He reached over and brushed away Alyosha's tears.

"My family's gone too." Major Ivan sighed. "They died long ago."

"You miss them?" Alyosha asked. "I miss my mama."

"Of course you do. But you have Lena and Baba Sofya." He patted the boy.

The Major's sad expression compelled Lena to touch Alyosha too, and she tousled the boy's hair. Funny, it hadn't been a month and already Lena felt lucky to have the little guy. He made her think of the future. And somehow, she felt less anxious when the bombs fell. Focusing on him helped her.

Alyosha looked up at Major Ivan, his eyes big and bright. "We can be a family together," he said, pointing to each of them, one after the other. "Baba Sofya, Lena, and me and you."

Ivan's eyes crinkled. "I suppose we can."

The middle-aged veteran and the little boy took to each other in a way that made perfect sense to Lena. Shared sorrow forged a tight bond.

One late afternoon when the sounds of the air battle above the city were particularly loud, Major Ivan turned to Alyosha. "Do you hear that rumbling sound in the distance?"

The little boy nodded and scooted close.

"Those are German planes, bombers. They're called Stukas."

"Sounds like thunder," Alyosha said.

"Exactly," Major Ivan nodded. "Now, listen. Do you hear the fast, sharp, chattering sound from our anti-aircraft guns? They're trying to shoot down those bombers." He paused as sounds swirled above them.

The boy nodded, his head cocked at an angle. "Just like you did, right?"

To pass the time, the Major told them stories of air battles during the last war. He'd been a pilot with the Imperial Russian Air Service. Later, he flew for the Bolshevik Red Army.

Mesmerized, Alyosha never got enough of the Major's tales, asking him over and over about the time he shot an enemy pilot with his pistol in mid-air. The Major explained how he lost his leg: a crash-landing that ended his career. They were short two parachutes that day. The plane was hit and going down. Instead of bailing out to save himself, he guided it to a rough landing in a field and saved his crew. He lost his leg and couldn't fly again. "A good trade, don't you think?" Major Ivan's eyes smiled. "My leg for two men."

Every time he told one of his exciting stories, Alyosha slid closer and closer, finally leaning against him. Watching them, Lena smiled. The little guy was a snuggler. At home he always wanted to cuddle in the big chair, where every evening he'd ask the same thing. "Can we see Major Ivan tonight?"

Four or five days had passed since they'd last seen their friend. Bombing raids grew less frequent as the weather worsened, but artillery attacks, round-the-clock and without warning, took their place as a form of torment. One might have a few seconds to dive for cover after hearing the whistle of an incoming artillery shell. No time at all really.

One evening while her grandmother was performing, Lena sat in the big chair reading to Alyosha. Even before she heard anything, he started shaking her.

"*Davai, davai*. Let's go, let's go," Alyosha jumped down. "Hurry, Lena, they're coming."

The sirens wailed. The boy pulled on his boots and Lena did the same. He was at the door, impatient. "*Davai. Davai!*"

The usual neighbors crowded the shelter, but Major Ivan wasn't there. Alyosha tugged on Lena's sleeve as they looked for a spot to sit.

"Where's Major Ivan? He should be here. His chessboard," Alyosha said, pointing at the corner. Alyosha pulled her over and they sat by the board and pieces. Still waiting for his friend to appear, the little boy got sleepy and Lena cradled him in her lap.

An old *babushka* creaked to a standing position and tottered over. "You were friends with Major Ivan."

Lena nodded, glancing at Alyosha, checking to see that he was asleep.

"He was killed a few days ago. Struck by artillery in a bread line. So sad." The woman shook her head. "I knew you'd want to know. He really liked the little boy," she said nodding at Alyosha, sprawled across Lena, face unblemished and cherubic.

Lena looked up at the woman, eyes big. "Don't say anything. I'll tell him."

She leaned her head back against the wall and closed her eyes. Not Major Ivan.

After the all-clear, Lena and Alyosha held hands and walked back to their apartment.

"I have some sad news, *malysh*." Lena closed the door and looked down at Alyosha.

The little boy's bottom lip quivered and his eyes filled. "Major Ivan?"

Unable to speak, and unable to hold back her own tears, Lena nodded.

"Nooooo, nooooo." Alyosha shook his head, squeezing his eyes shut.

Lena clasped the youngster tight to her chest as they huddled in the big chair, sobbing for Major Ivan, for their mothers, for the losses piling up in Leningrad.

KRONSTADT

December 1941

V ASILI SWUNG HIS legs off the edge of the bunk when he heard the knock. His steward.

"Come in," he called, reaching in the near complete darkness for the flashlight he always placed inside his right boot.

"Good morning, Comrade Admiral." A few of the ship's lights illuminated the cabin interior as the young seaman entered. Cold air swept in and Vasili fumbled for his winter parka which did double duty as a blanket.

The steward set a small steaming pot on the desk filled with a bitter brew that tasted nothing like real coffee. A fist-sized piece of dark bread completed breakfast.

Before the seaman slipped out, Vasili spoke. "How are you, Comrade?" This steward had arrived a few weeks ago and seemed petrified of his commanding officer.

The young man stood ramrod straight. "Well, Comrade Admiral."

"*I vasha semya*? And your family?"

The seaman relaxed. "They're far from the front, Comrade Admiral. I'm from Irkutsk."

"Siberia's a good place to be these days," Vasili said.

"Yes, sir. They're lucky. Nothing like the poor people of Leningrad."

Vasili excused him with a nod. It was no surprise that news of the situation in the city reached his sailors. It was the kind of information that spread no matter what the authorities said or did. Sofya and Yelena and millions of others trapped without heat or sufficient food, winter now almost as great an enemy as the Germans.

He pulled off his gloves and wrapped his bare hands around the tin cup, relishing the heat. He dipped an edge of the semi-frozen bread into the steaming liquid. The heavy lumps and harsh brew challenged his stomach and he grimaced as he swallowed. Truth was, he found eating anything difficult. It seemed wrong somehow that he should eat when rations in the city were at critical levels. Sofya must be measuring every gram of food. What did she and Yelena have left? Even if they still had money, cash wouldn't help anymore. There was no food in Leningrad. How could he fix that?

He had never been so powerless. So close—an hour by boat—yet unable to protect her. It seemed the only thing he could do was fight, defeat the Nazis, break the blockade. Pouring himself a second cup of the vile liquid, he reached for the chain hanging from the brass lamp bolted to his desk. Sofya's necklace. He rubbed it between his fingers, remembering when he first saw her wear it—decades ago at her wedding celebration. There, he congratulated Andrei and Sofya, banishing the inappropriate thoughts of her he'd been having since they first met. Later, while enjoying the music and wine, his eyes caught hers from across the room. He raised his glass and nodded. Anna, ever attentive to the comfort of others, turned to him. "Vasili, the bride is alone. You must ask her to dance."

The waltz began and from the first note he was at ease. One hand fit perfectly in the curve of her back and he held her strong violinist's fingers in the other. Her dark hair was up, adorned with tiny pearls, and the gold chain with an ornate cross rested just below the hollow of her neck. The top sheer layer of her dress wrapped gently around his leg as they danced and her dark, sparkling eyes fixed on his. She anticipated his turns and changes in tempo and he relaxed with her skill, like long-time partners with an intimate understanding of each other. They moved so well together that it was easy to imagine their bodies doing far more intimate things.

As the music ended, he saw Andrei on the edge of the dance floor watching them, and deftly escorted Sofya back to her husband.

"Congratulations again, Andrei. Your bride is an exquisite partner."

"She is indeed," Andrei said, taking Sofya's arm. "I'm a lucky man."

Looking directly at Sofya with a slight grin, Vasili added, "Thank you for tolerating me. I hope my limited talent in no way diminished the experience for you."

She returned his smile, then glanced down. "It's kind of you to pay me such a compliment, but your skills on the dance floor are excellent."

"In that case, I shall look forward to another dance sometime in the future," he said, making his departure with a slight bow.

Restless now, and seeing his wife occupied with friends, Vasili crossed the room and stepped out on the veranda. The sun had dipped below the horizon but the remaining glow already held the promise of the next day. Neither light nor fully dark, the midsummer night sky was friendly and familiar, an old acquaintance he was happy to be around.

An expanse of rough lawn ran down to the river. Vasili found the main path, lanterns having been placed to guide the guests. At the riverbank the path descended to a small stone wall, built there as protection against the water. A hidden bench made it the perfect place to be alone. The tranquility of the spot soothed him. He sat, enjoying the gentle sound of the river, trying to dispel his agitation.

Vasili recognized the absurdity of his emotions. He hardly knew her. They were married to others. Still, there was something potent in his attraction. Her intellect challenged him. She was smart and liked being smart. That drew him to her.

His thoughts were interrupted by footsteps. Annoyed, he turned at the disturbance to see Sofya, gliding down the path, her white dress reflecting the moonlight so that she glowed, beautiful and otherworldly. Despite the social expectations for a bride, here she was, escaping the press of people. Alone. How could he not admire such a woman? A woman who knew herself. He stood as she drew near.

"Is that you, Vasili?" She addressed him informally. He tried not to read too much into it. As the bride, she could address anyone as she cared. Still, it made him feel close to her.

"I see you found the best spot for a respite," she added.

"Yes. I'm enjoying the view and the solitude."

"And I'm intruding."

"Not at all," he said. "I didn't mean to suggest your company is unwanted. Please, join me. You must be exhausted from the day."

He reached for her hand, helping her to the bench, and flushed at her touch.

"I'm grateful you lent me *The Count of Monte Cristo*. It's been a lovely distraction from all the preparations." She turned toward him. "You were right. A wonderful story, full of treachery and courage. I was surprised at how deeply it explores the boundaries of good and evil. The Count isn't a traditional hero. More like an anti-hero. He works years to exact his revenge."

"And it consumes him," Vasili said. "By the end he realizes the perils of playing God, and the limits of his morality. I think I gave the Count a long lead regarding some of his immoral choices, simply because of the evil and injustice that had been inflicted upon him."

"Exactly so." Sofya nodded and then narrowed her eyes a bit. "I'm curious what you thought about the ending."

"The one part I found disappointing. I wanted Edmond and Mercedes to be reunited, they suffered so much, I thought they deserved happiness."

"Me too," she said. Her eyes sparkled. "After all they'd been through, they loved each other, but it wasn't enough." Sofya shook her head. "Heartbreaking."

Her flash of emotion captivated him. "Did you think the story exaggerated the pain and suffering in life and minimized the love and happiness?"

"Maybe so." She looked up at him. "I like to believe that everyone gets both joy and sorrow, but sometimes the good receive little happiness in life. And Dumas is correct. It rains on both the just and the unjust."

Vasili was distracted by her mouth as she spoke. Her lips weren't large or full, but there was something sensual in her expressiveness. "You think deeply about things, don't you?"

She laughed. A rich, resonant sound. "Others haven't been as kind in their description. 'Serious' is the word most commonly applied. Even my parents describe me that way."

"It's not a flaw," he said. "Thinking deeply is important." Afraid of pointing out how attractive he found it, Vasili turned away and gazed at the deepening night sky. They sat for a minute or two in companionable silence.

"This is lovely, but I must get back. It's impolite to ignore my other guests," she said.

"I shouldn't have kept you." He stood with her, putting her hand through his arm.

"No, I'm glad we had a chance to visit. I enjoyed our discussion." She gazed at him, holding his arm just a bit tighter than he expected as they walked up the path.

Vasili's gaze lingered on her disappearing figure as she returned to the party. She glanced back and gave him a final half-smile, confounding him entirely. Could she be feeling the same attraction? She just got married for Christ's sake! He thought again of what he'd felt when they danced; her back under his hand, her lithe body brushing against his, her face tilted up at him.

❦

Vasili looped the chain back on the lamp, turning his focus to the day ahead. Several neat piles of paperwork covered his desk. A stack of condolences waited. Vasili wrote to the families of his dead sailors. Just a sentence or two of personal connection beyond the facts. Sacrifice demanded respect and to Vasili, communicating the nation's gratitude was important. Casualties were enormous, dozens from the *Kirov* alone. Across the nation, millions were already gone and soon every family would be touched by death. An entire nation grieving.

Still three hours before dawn, Vasili walked the deck in the bitter air. Wintertime attacks had grown less frequent because the Germans had technical trouble with the inhospitable temperatures. The *Kirov*'s crew bragged about their resistance to the weather. He gazed at the mass of silver pinpricks in the night sky. It might be a winter for Russians, but clear skies increased the chances that the Nazis would be in the air at first light.

Before heading to the bridge, Vasili checked the vessel. The men had gotten used to his appearances. His unpretentious, yet not overly friendly manner worked well with a wartime crew. They respected his authority, and ever since one September battle when he jumped in to help after several gunners were hit, they admired him too. He was an admiral, yes, but unafraid of getting his hands dirty, defending Mother Russia with the rest of them.

A quick look at the engineering and boiler rooms reassured him: the oily smells of diesel and grease were strong and the familiar odors meant everything was working well. Next, he checked the *Kirov*'s guns. Perhaps unimpressive in appearance—cramped and difficult to climb into and out of—they had a range of well over thirty kilometers. Vasili felt pride and a sense of peace from the formidable weapons, the kind of comfort other men got from vodka.

He'd served on plenty of ships, and felt security in the dozens of rituals and disciplines that united sailors, but with her firepower, speed, and mobility, he was particularly at home on the *Kirov*. Even the creaks and groans of the ice against the cruiser soothed him.

His second in command snapped to attention as he entered the ship's command center.

"Comrade Captain. Anything to report?" Vasili asked.

"A quiet night, Comrade Admiral, but the cloud cover moved off several hours ago. We've picked up radio activity. I've already cancelled the fishing rotation."

Ice-fishing was a popular diversion for the sailors. Many had grown up on the water and going out on the ice was a tiny bit of normalcy in the difficult landscape of war. Although the fishing was poor, the sailors insisted on informal competitions. Vasili himself enjoyed checking the list to see who'd caught the most or largest. And, of course, catching anything at all was cause for celebration. Once every few weeks, the cook took the frozen fish and pan-fried them with a little onions or potatoes. Nobody got very much, but even a few bites was a welcome change from the canned food they lived on that winter.

The relative safety of darkness slipped away and the black sky edged toward deep blue. The ship felt tense, poised, waiting. Vasili stared where he knew the *Marat* lay, half-sunk in the Gulf, some eight hundred meters to the east. The moment he could make out its main mast, the sirens started, screaming the approach of attacking planes.

Guns trained on enemy positions across the Gulf, the *Kirov* opened fire, releasing a barrage of thud-booms that shook the ship. A sizable battery had been established on the wreckage of the *Marat*. Vasili watched for the flashes from their guns. Dug into embankments of snow and ice, artillery positions, anti-aircraft and machine gun nests formed a protective, rough semi-circle around the harbor and the warships.

The deep throaty mutter of the bombers reverberated in his chest.

Vasili knew the sounds of battle: the sharp chatter of anti-aircraft playing their duet with the bass thunder of the incoming planes, the long, shrill whistles of falling bombs, the phlegmy rumble of impact. When close, the bombs had a distinct swishing sound. When very close—a colossal splintering scream.

The radio operator called out a hit. Smoke pouring from one side, the plane dipped lazily in the lavender sky. Through binoculars, Vasili could find no sign of a parachute, the pilot already dead perhaps, or staying at the controls in an effort to cause maximum damage on impact.

Eyes fixed on the falling plane, Vasili stepped out on the deck. It plunged toward them nose-first, off-kilter. Out-of-control, its wings spun big, uneven parabolas in the sky. An image from his childhood flashed: gathering dozens of winged maple seeds, then climbing a high tree to drop the whirligigs and watch them spin to the ground. The plane spun round and round, just like one of those seeds. It screamed closer and closer. The roar filled his head and his heart lurched. An instant later, the out-of-control Stuka slammed into the ice with a gigantic roar, extinguishing all other sounds. Flames shot into the air, and the *Kirov* rolled from the force of the exploding plane. The point of impact was just far enough. Vasili grabbed the railing as a wing skittered away across the ice. The remainder of the plane, and the flames, disappeared in the icy water.

Back on the bridge, attack over, he scanned the vessels as his radioman recited damage reports. A Soviet destroyer had been hit and there were casualties. Stretcher bearers clambered over the ice, pulling the wounded on sleds, a line of ants scrambling with their heavy loads. They scurried across the harbor and through the cratered and snow-filled streets to the hospital.

As calm descended once more on the *Kirov*, Vasili hurried to the wardroom for something to eat before heading across the harbor for the senior staff meeting. In between spoonfuls of kasha he tried to rub his neck where steel rods seemed to support his head. In his cabin, he retrieved some paperwork. Weak daylight filtered through the porthole and he glimpsed a bit of white, a letter. Relief washed over him, until he realized it wasn't from Sofi. The military markings made his stomach drop with recognition. Already late for his meeting, he slid the envelope into his breast pocket and bundled up for the icy crossing.

The last rays of the short day guided him to the staff building. The air was sharp and he took shallow, gentle breaths through his scarf. His hand drifted to the dark news in his breast pocket. Maksim was an idealist and served the Party since before he finished university. He idolized Lenin and Stalin after him. Vasili didn't share his son's commitment to the Party, but he accepted it. He agreed with lots of the objectives of the Bolsheviks, but didn't think the Party was going about it the right way. They just elevated a different class. But whatever distance had opened between him and Maksim didn't matter in war. Vasili had been proud when Maksim enlisted. Even prouder that he was fighting on the critical Moscow Front.

Sick at heart and filled with dread, knowing he carried a letter like the many he himself wrote as a commanding officer, Vasili shuffled into the conference room. Unable to concentrate, he half-listened to the series of reports outlining damage, casualty figures, and the limited ammunition supplies. By the time the meeting was over, his fear strangled him.

Vasili hadn't been to his quarters in the staff building for weeks. Blackout shades were drawn. He lit the kerosene lamp on his desk, took off his gloves and reached inside his coat pocket. He fingered the thin envelope. Could bad news weigh so little? He clutched it in his hand, standing at his desk, staring at nothing. He saw Maksim as he used to be: chubby, little boy legs, rod in hand, racing to the end of the pier for some early morning fishing.

He tore off an end of the envelope and opened the letter.

30 November 1941
Admiral Vasili Maksimovich Antonov,

I regret to inform you that on 18 November 1941, Lieutenant Maksim Vasilievich Antonov was killed in the line of duty . . .

He crumpled the letter in his fist and sank into the chair.

PATH OF DESPAIR

December 1941

"I HEARD COMRADE Shostakovich is composing a symphony for us." A woman standing in the bread line spoke to Sofya, nodding at her violin case. Carrying her instrument sometimes invited the occasional nod of the head or supportive comment. Sofya always left these exchanges feeling proud that the people's attachment to music hadn't been entirely destroyed.

"He started in July," Sofya said, "before he evacuated."

"Something to look forward to," the woman said.

Sofya looked at her sharp cheekbones and big eyes, her skin like ancient paper, and turned away to mask her fear that neither of them would live to hear Shostakovich again.

Even as audiences grew smaller and more wretched, music's unique power to make the war disappear remained. Music distracted people. It gave them something other than food to think about. Sometimes that was all they needed to face the next day. Time had become the period from one meal to the next. Music made those intervals easier to bear. At a concert, people stopped thinking about boiling a leather belt to make it edible, or stripping the wallpaper and scraping off the old potato flour glue to eat. For a few precious moments, they could bury thoughts of trapping a stray cat or rodent, forging an illegal ration card, or finding an old, forgotten chocolate bar hidden in the back of a cupboard.

As audiences dwindled, so too the Radio Orchestra itself wound down. By mid-December, it no longer had enough musicians to remain open. Standing in the vestibule of the Radio House, Sofya read the announcement of the orchestra's closure on the notice board and cried. She told herself it would just be a month or two.

Sofya's old company, the Leningrad Philharmonic Orchestra, was still performing. They evacuated to Tashkent early in the war. If Aleksandr hadn't been arrested, she would be there too, thousands of kilometers away. And so would Yelena. But, if they'd left in July, her granddaughter wouldn't have been on the children's evacuation in August. And if she hadn't been on that train, well, those sixteen youngsters probably wouldn't have survived. And what about Alyosha? He'd have died in an orphanage by now. Life could be curious, the paths that opened or closed.

Before stepping out of the Radio House, Sofya carefully raised the collar of her coat, tied the earflaps of her *ushanka* into place, and wound her scarf around both, covering her face twice then tying it tightly behind her neck. She put on gloves, and then mittens, her hands now so bulky that she couldn't hold her violin case by the handle, so instead clutched it to her chest. Threading damaged streets and scattered wreckage in the deepening winter afternoon darkness, she tilted her head down to protect her eyes against the wind-whipped snow and dust.

She caught distorted snatches of a female voice. Her friend and colleague, Olga Berggolts, lived in the Radio House with a small cadre of journalists. She was a beloved Radio Leningrad personality. They'd met when Sofya joined the Radio Committee just before the war. She liked the younger woman from the start, sympathetic to her struggles as a writer and her personal tragedy. Olga understood the people's experience: oppression, random arrests, and now the degradation of life in besieged Leningrad. She spoke for everyone. It was her voice that Sofya hurried to now.

By the time Sofya crossed the Fontanka Olga had finished. Another figure huddled under the loudspeaker, gathering strength from dear Olga, and now she turned away, hobbling around the corner. Sofya stopped and leaned against the building, wishing for more inspiration. She fought her freezing tears, cupping her hands over her face and blowing warm air, blinking rapidly. Something fluttered along the ground, catching Sofya's eye as she adjusted her scarf. The scrap of something took shape as it rustled against the snow. The shape of bread. A ration card. She pulled off her outer mitten and bent over, pinching the paper and bringing it close. Her heart quickened and she rummaged in a pocket for her glasses. The markings on the shoddy paper didn't lie, no matter how many times or how carefully she examined it. It was a nearly new dependent's card, worth 125 grams of bread every day for twelve more days.

A darkness rose in her then, keeping her from going after the woman, even though she knew it must be hers. A self-seeking voice told Sofya that no one would lose their ration card on the street. Cards were more valuable than gold, the difference between life and death.

Sofya edged around the corner. The woman was still in sight, moving at a glacial pace. She could call out. But the selfish voice drowned out the truth and smothered her compassion. What if it's not her card? She'll claim it is anyway. It must have been lying on the ground the entire time, dropped by someone earlier in the day, blown against the building and then caught there by the snow. Still holding the valuable scrap of paper, Sofya pulled her mitten back on, trapping the little treasure inside, and slunk toward home.

Sofya woke in the middle of the night. She flicked on the flashlight, slipped her feet into the boots at the end of the mattress and fumbled for a match. The smell of sulfur filled her nostrils as she lit the candle. Her head pounded and she shuffled to the kitchen, breaking the thin layer of ice on their drinking water and pouring a small glass. She wanted to believe her head throbbed from dehydration, but it wasn't so easy to explain away. Her body was rebelling against her inner torment. She'd stolen that woman's ration card. She might as well have shot her.

Cradling the candle, she edged into the dark, frozen bedroom, and opened the wall behind the bookcase. She did this often now. Examining their food soothed her.

Two pieces of paper were pinned to the inside. On one sheet, she'd listed each type of food with corresponding amounts: pickled cucumbers—two jars, kasha rectangles—eighteen, potatoes—fifty-six, bars of chocolate—five, one pork hindquarter, etc. It was a long list in September; more than twenty-five different food items of varying quantities. As the food diminished, Sofya penciled in the new amounts. When they ate the last of an item, she crossed it off. The growing number of dark lines on the list filled her with anxiety.

The second sheet was a consumption schedule. The paper had thirty lines, each representing a week, starting with the second week of October and ending with the first week of May. Of course, Sofya had no more idea than anyone how long the siege would last or when food supplies would return to normal. She'd set up the schedule based on thirty weeks because that's what fit on the page, and also because it seemed realistic. According to the plan, if she and Yelena each ate about 100 grams per day, their food would last until mid-May. With Alyosha, that would be several weeks earlier. And if the government hadn't found a way to break the blockade or to supply the city with sufficient food by then, well, they were all doomed.

Every Sunday she and Yelena would huddle together at the bookcase. Hovering over the precious supplies, worshipping at their altar of food, they'd discuss what they should eat in the coming days: several ounces of ham or a tin of beef, kasha, a chunk of cabbage, pickled vegetables or preserves. It was their favorite part of every week.

Now though, she hadn't opened the bookcase to look at their food supply. She'd come to make sense of her own actions, she'd come for penance. She steadied the candle on a pile of books on the floor, its weak, flickering light casting only the slightest of shadows.

Oh, God, what have I done? Sofya hung her head. Please help that woman.

No stranger to prayer, Sofya never worshipped in public for fear of retribution. Her unwillingness to renounce her beliefs had kept her from wholeheartedly embracing the Communist Party. She'd believed in God growing up, and just because the Party said there was no god did not make it true. Besides, her entire family had been Bolsheviks long before it was either fashionable or necessary, and that qualified her as a true believer. Or did it?

She put the bookcase back in order. There was one place she could go no matter the time of day or night. She crept out of the bedroom and pulled back the blanket hanging over the opening to the living room.

"Lenochka." Sofya knelt down and patted her granddaughter, buried in blankets on the mattress. "It's still early. I'm going to the Haymarket."

Yelena mumbled, then fell quiet. Sofya thought she'd gone back to sleep.

"The Haymarket? You shouldn't." Yelena struggled awake.

"Where else can I find winter boots?" Sofya replied. "If you don't get some soon you won't even be able to go outside."

It was true. Yelena's boots had several large cracks and didn't even keep out the snow. Her feet were always wet and cold. "Let me. I'll go between shifts." Propped up on an elbow now, the candle flame reflected in Yelena's eyes, strange flashes of life.

"You don't have time. You have to get Alyosha to school and then find wood," said Sofya. "Besides, I'm awake."

They usually divided chores this way, Yelena taking the harder, riskier tasks like getting fuel and water while Sofya spent more time waiting in lines.

"It's dangerous," Yelena said. "Alone in the dark. Someone could attack you, steal your money, worse."

"Well, it's unlikely those types are out and about this early. The stores aren't open yet. And I'll take the gun."

She pecked her granddaughter on the cheek and pushed herself up, joints complaining. "I'll be fine. See you when I get back. And if you're not here, I know you're looking for wood."

She dug her husband's old army boots from the back of the closet, hoping to trade them for some that would fit Yelena, and brushed aside the twinge of guilt at not telling her what she'd done and where she was really going.

Sofya kept to the main streets for a long while. Shuffling along in the darkness, using her flashlight now and then to check her way, she'd take nine or ten steps and then stop to catch her breath. Walking was so difficult, so exhausting. Everything required energy she no longer had. But she had to do this and she could take as long as necessary.

She entered a run-down area of town. Narrow streets, small bridges, and grim courtyards dotted this quarter—Dostoevsky's old neighborhood. Snow and ice had built up along the winding streets and covered the sidewalks. There wasn't fuel or manpower to clear snow and ice and she stepped gingerly, using her flashlight to keep from falling. That was the real risk here, not being attacked. If she slipped and couldn't get back up, she'd freeze to death. Sofya fell into a rhythm, moving forward a bit and then pausing to catch her breath and listen to the mostly silent city. Moving along the middle of the streets in the dark, Sofya imagined Raskolnikov, the murderer in *Crime and Punishment,* gazing from a tiny apartment window then creeping outside, following his prey. Sofya inched along those very same streets obsessing over what she'd done. Bundled up against the threat of frostbite and burdened by her own cruelty it was a wonder she could move at all.

The Nikolsky Cathedral was the only church in the city that the Soviets hadn't shuttered. Its main door creaked and groaned as she struggled to pull it open. She inched her way down the main aisle by the scant light of a lone prayer candle next to the altar. The last time she was here the many gold-framed icons adorning the walls flickered in the light of dozens of trembling flames. Now, she could barely make out the ornate gold and silver altar.

Huddled there, first kneeling, then sitting, she lost track of time. There'd been one other moment in her life she'd begged for forgiveness like this—when she betrayed Andrei. Perhaps God would forgive her this as well.

The creaking of the main door startled her and she quickly reached into her pocket for the ration card and the precious rectangle of kasha she'd taken from behind the bookcase. She set both on the altar rail and turned to make her way back down the nave, patting her other pocket, feeling for the gun. As she neared the door, she drew alongside a woman with a small child.

"You'll want to go to the altar rail," Sofya said.

The figure responded with an almost imperceptible nod, then shuffled toward the transept with the youngster tottering behind, both of them hardly more than skeletons.

Outside the church, dawn illuminated the corpses scattered around the cathedral grounds. The woman whose card she'd stolen would soon be one of those. Sofya lifted her head heavenward and breathed the icy air deeply, trying to cleanse her spirit. Turning for the Haymarket, she fumbled inside her bag for the nugget of bread she'd packed, then sucked on it like a piece of hard candy.

Exhausted, she wandered the stalls, glancing at the desperate, shriveled people, clutching the bag with Andrei's old boots and looking for a vendor selling winter things. Ahead there was a small crowd. As she drew close, stacks of meat patties tantalized behind the glass, beckoning like an oasis in the desert. People pulled out their rubles.

She looked at the pale meat, unlike anything she'd ever eaten. It had almost no color. She watched the man behind the counter. Large and well-fed, with wild, black hair, he towered above his merchandise. She stared at him. Why wasn't he in the army?

Sofya shivered at his dark expression, the emptiness behind his eyes. As she stood to one side, unsure what to do, an agitated elderly man approached. His eyes flashed about the scene, darting from the meat to the man behind the counter and back. A bit of spittle dripped down the corner of his mouth, where it would freeze if he didn't wipe it away.

"Someone get the authorities!" The old man waved his arms and looked around for help. He banged on the glass of the stall. The meat seller stepped around the side with a yell and reached for the agitator who slid beyond his grasp.

"You disgusting . . . you cannibal . . ." The old man's spit hit the display case with surprising force. "Vile, scum. Death is too good for you."

The big man roared and lunged around the stall a second time, but wouldn't leave his goods. Backing into the now protective and supportive crowd, the elderly man launched a final curse and hobbled away, his warnings echoing in the sudden quiet. A woman yelled. "What kind of meat is this? Get the police." As Sofya stumbled around a corner and out of the market, she heard another voice say, "Why bother? They already know."

She heaved and vomited a bit of yellow liquid and her undigested bread into the street.

Home. She had to get home.

Too stunned to cry, Sofya climbed the stairs. Before she even reached the top, she knew something was wrong and stopped, straining to hear. As she crept down the hall, she saw the open apartment door. She knew it wasn't Yelena. She'd never forget to close and lock the door. Silently, she placed her dead husband's army boots against the wall and pulled the gun out of her pocket, releasing the safety. Then she heard the scrapping of a chair, something shifting in the kitchen, someone coughing.

Vladik had his back to her. He'd ransacked the kitchen cupboards. Good thing they'd moved their supplies. The only thing he'd found were the three oversize glass containers from the *dacha* that didn't fit in the bedroom hiding place. Each contained perhaps 200 grams of flour, oats and sugar. He had an arm wrapped around the jars. Two were open and on their sides and he scooped the contents into his mouth so fast he choked. He wasn't even using a spoon.

"Vladik!" She snapped. "What are you doing?"

"Get away," he said, mumbling, his mouth full. "My food." He didn't even look up at her, just grabbed another handful.

"You broke into our apartment. You're stealing our food. You need to leave." She held the gun tight, but hadn't raised it at him.

"You promised me food."

"That was weeks ago. And I brought half of our bread ration to your apartment the very next day. Just as I promised. I gave it to your mother."

"My mother." He lifted his head and his yellow eyes flashed at her. "Mama ate it."

"I doubt that. I'm sure she shared it with Yuri and with you, you probably just don't remember." Sofya hated to imagine Mrs. Radchenko eating all the bread before her boys got home.

"No!" He yelled and slammed a fist on the table. A puff of flour rose. "You're lying. Mama ate it. Mama eats everything. There's never anything for me."

"Vladik, you need to leave. Do you understand?"

He wasn't big or tall for sixteen, but bigger than Sofya. She raised the gun. "If you don't leave now, I'm going to shoot you so you can't hurt me." Her voice quavered. "I'll try to shoot you in the leg. And then I'll go get the police."

He let out a tinny derisive laugh. "You're a terrible shot, remember? But don't worry, I'm going. And I'm taking the rest of my food with me."

"It's not yours, but you can take it. Share it with your brother."

He had a puzzled look on his face. "Yuri? He's dead." He walked past Sofya calmly. "I told you, Mama eats everything."

Horrified, Sofya keep the gun raised until she heard him going down the stairs. Little Yuri, dead? She hurried to the door, closed and locked it, then curled up on the sofa.

She wept. For Yuri, for Vladik and his mama. She wept for herself, that she couldn't help them. She wept for Vasili and Aleksandr, afraid they would never return, and for Yelena and the future she might not have. She wept because she'd stolen someone's ration card, and because the city had become a nightmare, a place where people ate each other to survive. Huddled in layers of clothing, in the dim, frozen apartment, she cried herself to sleep.

BURNING THE BOOKS

December 1941–January 1942

LENA DROPPED AN armload of broken boards as she kicked closed the apartment door. Her grandmother stirred on the sofa.

"Oh, you were sleeping. I'm sorry." She disappeared back out the door to get the sled and the rest of the wood she'd scavenged. Quieter this time, she placed the wood in a haphazard pile and returned the sled to its spot behind the door. She put the axe in a high kitchen cupboard and then caught sight of the boots. She pulled them on before her groggy *babushka* said anything.

"These are wonderful. Thank you." Lena lifted one leg in admiration. "They're nearly perfect, a bit big, but that doesn't matter. Such heavy felt. Where did you find them?"

Her grandmother burst into tears.

"*Babusya?*" Lena asked gently. "What's the matter?" She sat next to her.

"The boots are the ones I was going to trade," Sofya said sniffing. "I wasn't there long enough to find any. I should've realized these might fit; your grandpa had small feet."

"They're much better than my old ones. I love that they were *Dedka's.*" Lena again admired the *valenki*, the felt army boots.

"That's not why you're crying. Are you going to tell me what happened?" Lena prodded. "You aren't hurt, are you?"

"No, nothing like that." Her bottom lip trembled. "The Haymarket. Such a vile place."

"I've heard the rumors," Lena said.

"There was a stall, stacks of meat patties, an old man screaming accusations." She dropped her face into her gloved hands. "I can't get the sight out of my mind."

Lena put an arm around her. "I shouldn't have let you go alone."

"And then, when I got home, I found Vladik had broken in—picked the lock or stolen the manager's master key. He was eating the last of the flour and sugar and oats from those glass jars we couldn't fit behind the bookcase. He was wild-eyed and not making sense. Said I owed him food. But when I told him I gave it to his mother, he got angry. Said she eats everything. And his little brother is dead."

Lena gasped. "You don't think they hurt Yuri, do you?"

"I don't know what to think anymore."

๛ ๛

The next day, bundled up as always against the merciless elements, Sofya waited for her bread ration. It was not something she'd gotten used it, being surrounded by wretched, dying fellow citizens while waiting for a meager piece of bread. Nothing in her experience had prepared her for this. Not the terrible shortages after the Revolution nor even those long, fruitless days waiting at the *Bolshoi Dom* for news of Aleksandr.

Her gaze landed on a solitary figure and she began making up details about the woman. It was a game she played to help with the strain of spending so many hours waiting in the cold. The woman looked ordinary except for her extravagant fur *ushanka*. Many wore the traditional hat with flaps in winter, but this one was luxurious, a long white-tipped gray fur, something only someone of a certain class or position would own. Sofya pondered the striking hat. Rabbit, perhaps. The woman had a regal bearing and a roman nose. She could be descended from nobility, although more likely she simply had access to Party stores. While Sofya stared, constructing bits and pieces of her life, the woman crumpled with no warning, sprawling across the icy sidewalk in slow motion.

Sofya expected someone in the line to step forward, but the blank faces around her pretended that nothing out of the ordinary had happened. Some looked away. Worse yet, others looked straight through the fallen stranger. It was as if they were so accustomed to suffering that they couldn't imagine the woman being saved, certainly not by their effort anyway.

"Hold my place," Sofya demanded of the person behind her. She knelt by the woman and patted her cheeks in an effort to revive her. Next, she removed a glove and pressed icy fingers to the woman's still warm neck. No pulse. Nothing. Sofya hovered there. Would anyone come looking for her? Someone down the line muttered, "Phhh. That expensive hat couldn't save her."

Sofya cast a withering look down the queue. In case the perpetrator didn't catch the first evidence of her disdain, she sneered. "What's the matter with you? Have a little compassion. It could be you." She eyed the line of broken people, wondering how they could be so unfeeling. "We're in this together you know," she said, then shuffled back into the line, already snaking around the woman's body.

The same voice spoke up again, sharp and scornful. "Doesn't seem like that to me, more like every man for himself. Who do you think you are anyway? We're barely hanging on. Don't you think we know we could be next?"

Sofya stared at her feet, unable to meet the woman's icy glare and harsh words.

"Looks to me like you're in better shape than the rest of us—just like her," the stranger continued. "You aren't suffering like we are. You probably know people."

Sofya took half a step out of line to face the woman. "You know nothing about me. *Zakroy rot!* Shut your mouth!"

The woman laughed, a sick, hateful sound. "*Trakni sebya!* Fuck yourself!"

Stunned and ashamed at the exchange, Sofya slunk back into

line. In her entire life, no one had ever spoken to her that way. For that matter, she couldn't remember ever losing her temper like that. Especially in public.

Finally in the store, still indignant and upset, she told the clerk about the dead customer outside. The attendant shrugged, then snipped the squares off Sofya's cards and measured her ration. Business as usual.

Bread tucked away, Sofya moved swiftly down the sidewalk to avoid the person who said such shameful things, just in time to see someone bending over the body. "What are you doing?" Sofya said. The thief's age was impossible to guess, but her face had the tell-tale yellow hue of *dystrofia*. Starvation had a way of making everyone look ancient, turning skin to old parchment. The figure pulled her hand out of the dead woman's pocket, snatched the gorgeous *ushanka* off her head and dashed away. Someone in the line murmured, "Looking for her card." Sofya stood there for several minutes, guarding the body. When she finally turned for home an image of her long-dead mother flashed, dressed for a night at the opera, proudly wearing an expensive hat of long white-tipped gray fur.

Being inside was only marginally better than being on Leningrad's miserable, frozen streets. Indoors, Sofya still had to wear most of an entire wardrobe to keep from freezing, but at least she could escape the bitter wind.

Many weeks earlier, she and Yelena had dragged their mattress into the living room. Without heat, the only place to sleep was by the little stove. They hung a blanket over the opening to the living room to concentrate the warmth and closed the doors to the unused bedrooms to conserve heat. Sofya bunched rags along the crack at the bottom of the apartment door.

The ruthless, tyrannical winter made every day a desperate hunt for something to burn. Yelena looked for wood in half-destroyed buildings, clambering through dangerous piles of rubble to find broken pieces of furniture. Sometimes firewood could be found in the market. Sofya always carried cash so she could buy whatever bundles of sticks she found for sale. Soon, fuel became almost as important as food. In December they began breaking apart their own furnishings. Then they let themselves into the Petrov's apartment and took their furniture too, hoping their good friends would forgive them.

As she set out the next morning, Sofya prayed the corpse would be gone.

She grew more and more agitated as the line wound closer to the entrance, not wanting to see the body, recalling the stranger's words. It was true. She and Yelena had more food than most. Vasili had given them time to prepare, time to hoard supplies before the announcement came and shelves were stripped bare. Why did that make her feel so guilty?

The now frozen body was still sprawled across half the sidewalk. Cheeks and nose an unnatural bluish-white, the dead woman's ghostly visage shown through tiny ice crystals. Her boots and coat were missing. No doubt her ration card too.

Although corpses were commonplace, this was something else. Seeing the body every day missing another piece of clothing until stripped and abandoned was personal somehow. Couldn't the woman's relatives pull her body to a cemetery? It comforted Sofya to think that if she died, Yelena would have the strength to drag her body away, even if there was no way to be buried. Months of intense cold had turned the earth to steel.

When the city froze, the already half-destroyed water and sewage systems failed completely. Sofya and Yelena sat on their haunches over a dresser drawer which they put in a far corner of the second bedroom. The rest of the dresser fed the little stove. Initially, they used a pot in place of the toilet, emptying it in the nearby public bath. Everyone else had the same idea and the bath became unusable and impassable, slick with frozen urine and feces. Now, they still peed in the pot, which they poured out in a corner of the courtyard, but they kept their shit to themselves, a solidly frozen mound of excrement in a drawer. The only benefit to the extreme cold was that nothing smelled. And the only benefit to eating so little was that they didn't use it often.

As Sofya squatted one bitter January morning, trying to empty her rock-hard intestines, she wondered if things would ever improve. Life had been reduced to endless frozen days of grubbing and scraping for survival and now she was forced to relieve herself in a drawer.

Not long ago, if Sofya had been faced with the upsetting events in the queue she simply would have gone elsewhere to get her bread. But when the authorities assigned everyone to specific stores, she had no choice. She was stuck seeing the frozen, abandoned corpse.

Sofya shuffled along the line. Eyes down, she looked at no one, said nothing, and turned away when she glimpsed the dead woman, now stripped to her thin undergarments, arms and legs at strange angles, but mercifully covered with a dusting of fresh snow.

At home the following day, Sofya took Yelena's hand and pulled her into the bedroom where the solution to their fuel problem filled the wall.

"We can burn the books," Sofya said.

"No." Yelena shook her head. "We can't do that."

"What choice is there? We won't burn the important ones, and the truth is, I've meant to go through these shelves for years, ever since my parents passed and I stashed their books wherever I had space. Lots of these aren't worth keeping. Party leaflets, your grandfather's military books, out-of-date history volumes. Better used to keep us warm." There. She'd said it.

"Well, I guess that makes sense," Yelena said. "Then I can burn my old workbooks and that ridiculous biology text we used last year." She paused and leaned close to her grandmother. "But no touching your favorites."

Examining her library, Sofya separated the volumes by monetary and sentimental value. Many were ordinary, with cheap paper covers bound by a Soviet book concern. Others shone with ornate leather binding and gold lettering. Some brought back sublime memories of holidays and birthdays growing up. Her parents indulged her passion from a young age, and by the time she was a university student, she had over a hundred volumes. All through adulthood, her collection grew.

Sofya picked up Lenin's *What Is To Be Done?* For years it sat, self-important, on the secretary shelf in the living room. Heartbroken, her parents gave it to her after her brother's death in the late days of the civil war. It reminded them of what they'd lost. Opening the cover, she ran her fingers over the inscription: *To Aleksandr, True revolutionary, true believer, my comrade. V.I. Lenin.* Lenin was right. Her brother's belief in a socialist future had been powerful and unflagging. World revolution was coming, he liked to say. She could still hear his voice lecturing her. "Get your head out of that book, little one. The real world is waiting."

As much as she missed him, a part of her was glad her brother hadn't lived to see what became of his hopes and dreams. Devoted to changing the country, it would have crushed him to see Stalin rise to power: a leader more ruthless and unpredictable than any tsar. Sofya brushed a couple of tears from her face and put the volume that meant so much to him on the uppermost shelf in the bedroom with the other books of sentimental value.

That afternoon while Alyosha was at school, Yelena dragged several boxes into the living room. They opened the blackout curtains and weak sunlight filtered through the ice crystals on the windows.

She made quick work of her school papers, saving little, pronouncing most as 'burnable.' How wonderful to be young and unattached to the past.

"Look." Yelena hunched over a disorganized stack of papers spilling out of another box. She waved her papa's certificate from the Academy.

Sofya smiled and reached for a folder. "This has lots of things we want to keep." She paged through documents. "My diploma from the Conservatory." The gold-embossed script still gleamed. "And look at these ancient school reports my mother saved."

"Oh, let me see those." Yelena pulled them out of her hands and began reading. "You were quite the student. And here . . ." She lifted a simple form. "Mama and Papa's marriage record." She touched their names with a gloved finger and her voice became wistful. "Where do you think they are?"

"Perhaps your papa's still fighting around Moscow." It'd been months since they'd gotten a letter from Aleksandr. Mail into Leningrad stopped after the Germans surrounded the city. It made sense. They couldn't get food into the city, so why would there be mail? Letters leaving Leningrad were a different matter. It was important that soldiers hear from their loved ones. Mail went out of the city, but little came in. Morbid though it was, the only letters entering Leningrad were official death notices.

"And your mama? I know you're worried . . ." She went quiet, not wanting to say what they were both thinking, especially since they learned that Dimitri and Kolya had died when Luga was attacked. "But as long as we don't receive notification, there's reason to hope. No news is good news. And your mama is resourceful. Remember, there's no way she could get home, not with miles of Germans between her and us, not with the blockade." She hugged Yelena. "All we can do is fight the war from here, and hope that she escaped. Remember what Vasili told us."

Misty-eyed, her granddaughter sighed.

Boxes finished, they divided the papers into three groups: important records to keep, a large burn pile, and some loose blank pages they could use for writing letters.

"Nice to accomplish something," Sofya said, putting an arm around Yelena.

"You've always liked having projects, keeping things in order," Yelena said. "Remember when I was little, and you would wake me for school? Mama and Papa already gone to work, and you'd sit on the edge of the bed, talking and patting me so I couldn't go back to sleep. Even then, you kept us all organized."

"Just my nature. It's important to have a purpose, even a little one. And besides, as my mother used to say, *the devil finds work for idle hands to do.*"

That evening they began burning the books.

Sofya picked an old military volume that first night. Something she'd never looked at and wouldn't notice if it was gone. In front of the little stove—a fat, dwarfish sentinel crouching on its altar of bricks—she hesitated nonetheless, her heart fluttering within her chest, trying to escape fate and necessity.

"Let me," Yelena said. Her granddaughter took the book, cut off the covers and tore it apart, then opened the stove and placed balled-up pages with the covers balanced at strange angles so they'd catch when she struck the match.

Some evenings, they'd burn a bit of wood along with several books. As the coals turned red, they'd open the stove and slide a potato or two into the fire. Fishing it out later with a spoon, they'd share the delicious charred vegetable with Alyosha, crispy and burnt on the outside, but soft and warm inside.

Sofya tried to be brave, reminding herself they were only books. But that was like saying the scraps of nourishment they ate were only food. Books sustained her. They were much more than a distraction from the terrible situation. Books had seen her through dozens of difficult times. To Sofya, the written word was one of the last bits of beauty in the crumbling city.

As the days passed and winter gave no ground, the piles of books in the living room grew smaller and the bedroom shelves lightened. They burned some of the dangerous, hidden books too. Sofya tried to convince herself they wouldn't have to burn them all, that the city would restore power, or they would stumble across a cache of wood. Yet none of those things happened, and her heart broke, book by book.

❧ ❧

After her grandmother confided about the woman collapsing and the harsh comments from the stranger, Lena decided she should get rations for a while. She wasn't on the roof much. It was too cold for air attacks. Her grandma chuckled at the gossip that the Nazis couldn't cope. "One thing we're good at. Winter." Artillery attacks continued however, killing without warning; shrieking howls from the sky that ripped people apart. Dead before they knew what happened.

But then Lena woke with a bit of a cough one morning. If she had known, really known, how the woman's death affected her grandmother, she never would have let her go get bread that day. After her *babushka* and Alyosha departed, Lena dozed. When she checked the time, it was only ten. Her grandmother wouldn't be back yet, but still, she was uneasy. She didn't want her grandmother to be alone.

The store wasn't far. As Lena hurried, a keening filled the otherwise silent street. It reminded her of the return from Lychkovo, when Moscow Station reverberated with grief. Only this time it was just one voice. Running now, Lena found her grandmother next to the snow-covered body. Rocking back and forth, her *babushka* moaned, calling for her own mother, "Mamochka, Mamochka," pulling off her coat and placing it on the corpse.

Lena grabbed her by the shoulders and pulled her to her feet. She snatched the coat up and forced her grandmother's arms back in.

"Mama needs to stay warm," her grandmother said, her eyes dull.

Lena shook her. "*Babusya*! No! This isn't your mama."

Breathing heavily, Lena stood face-to-face with her disoriented grandmother. "It's me. Your Lenochka. You have to come home now." Lena saw a flicker of recognition in her eyes, and then her grandmother began to cry.

"Lenochka, my Lenochka."

Lena hugged her tight, nearly lifting her off the ground. "Shhhh. It's going to be okay. Someone died in the bread line. Remember? Someone that reminded you of Mamochka. Your mind is playing tricks, everything is so horrible."

Her grandmother wept while Lena propelled her home.

Later that afternoon, after she'd warmed her grandmother in front of a steady fire, fed her a substantial meal, lit the kerosene lamp and settled her with a book, Lena took the sled back to the bread line and moved the corpse. After dumping the body in front of Vladimirsky Cathedral, she turned for School Number 98.

Children were coming and going, a few adults and older siblings too. Lena went to Alyosha's classroom.

"*Dobry dyen*, good afternoon, Irina Maksimovna," said Lena.

The teacher looked at her strangely.

"Hello, Yelena. I wasn't expecting to see you. Is anything the matter?"

Lena was confused. She often collected Alyosha after school.

"Your neighbor came by and took Alyosha. Mrs. Radchenko. She said you'd asked her to come. Poor woman, losing Yuri and then her older son."

Lena ran out of the school and grabbed the sled. It bounced and bumped as she raced down the middle of the streets. She prayed she wasn't too late. She saw nothing on the way home, heard nothing but her own ragged breath. She dropped the sled and climbed the icy steps, banging on the Radchenko's door as she gasped for air.

"Mrs. Radchenko? Are you home? Please open the door." She heard stirring inside, and the door opened.

"Oh, hello, Yelena. What's the matter with you, dear? You look a fright."

Lena pushed her way in. "Where's Alyosha? You took him from school."

"Oh my, you're mistaken. I wouldn't take Alyosha. I have my dear Yuri to attend to."

Alyosha sat at the kitchen table. He was eating a tiny morsel of bread.

Lena scooped him up and he hugged her.

"What are you doing with my Yuri?" the woman cried. "Put him down at once."

"Comrade, you're confused. This isn't Yuri. This is Alyosha." She set the boy down and looked him in the face. "Alyosha, please tell Mrs. Radchenko your name."

"I'm Alyosha," he whispered.

"No, no, you've taken my boy and brainwashed him. Yuri, tell her the truth."

The boy froze. "Go upstairs," said Lena. "Here's the key. Be quiet because Baba Sofya might be resting. I'll be right up."

As the boy scurried out of the apartment and up the stairs, Mrs. Radchenko lunged past Lena and scrambled after him.

Lena screamed, "No! Leave him alone."

At the next landing, she caught the crazed woman while Alyosha scampered away. She heard their apartment door close as she held the woman's arm in a death grip. "Comrade, I know you're upset, but you can't take Alyosha. I'm sorry about Yuri and Vladik."

The devastated woman stopped struggling. Lena let go. Mrs. Radchenko turned and her foot hit an icy spot. She lost her balance, tumbling backwards down the stairs, her head hitting the landing with a sickening hollow thud, like a melon hitting pavement.

Lena cried out and rushed to help her neighbor, but she was already dead. After pulling her body into the apartment, Lena looked through the sad rooms for evidence of Yuri and Vladik. Wallpaper hung in tatters where the desperate family had pulled it from the walls to eat the glue. She found the boys, dead but untouched in the back bedroom. She hunted around for keys and locked the apartment, afraid someone might steal their things, or worse yet, their bodies.

SASHA

January 1942

THERE WAS NO food in Leningrad. At least none that Sofya and Lena could find. Pavel had told Lena that supplies were coming across the Ice Road, and it was broadcast on Radio Leningrad. So why were stores empty?

Most days they got their bread ration, but they were supposed to get allotments of meat, grains, fats and sugar three times a month. They hadn't seen anything like that for weeks. Lena could tell her grandma was worried. They tried to stick to their original plan— eating only small amounts of their hidden food every day. But it was getting harder and harder. They weren't dying, not yet anyway, but they were weak.

As a last resort, Lena decided they should hunt in old Petrograd, the neighborhood behind the Peter and Paul Fortress. They'd heard rumors that there was food in other areas of the city, and her grandma wanted to check on Admiral Vasili's apartment. "There are still some valuables, and maybe a few things in the pantry," her *babushka* said. "If it's not been ransacked already."

The idea of finding treasure in the Antonov's apartment took shape: stacks of canned goods, sacks of flour and oats and macaroni, maybe some chocolate. Lena usually tried hard not to think of food, but now, with this possibility, she couldn't help herself. Her mouth watered. Fresh crunchy cucumbers sprinkled with vinegar, the grilled fish they used to have when her papa returned from fishing, a simple sweet carrot. She loved carrots.

Suddenly her grandmother interrupted her reverie. "You're thinking about food again."

"What else is there to think about?" Lena said. "Either I think about food or I worry."

Her grandmother's expression grew pained and she changed the subject. "Come on. It's time to take Alyosha to school. Then we'll make our expedition across the Neva."

It took them two hours to reach their destination, taking tiny steps on the ice and snow. There'd been no streetcars since December when the Nazis bombed the city's main electrical plant. Buses had stopped back in October because there was no fuel. If you wanted to get anywhere in Leningrad, you walked.

Admiral Vasili's apartment was their first stop. Lena had been there once the previous spring when Admiral Vasili had them all for dinner. It had been a curious and somewhat awkward evening. Lena felt almost as if he was seeking their approval to court her grandmother. The Antonov's apartment was lovely, with a separate dining room and a parlor. It had a library as large as any other room, with a comfortable reading chair and polished mahogany desk at one end and shelves all the way to the ceiling. She'd never seen so many books outside of a real library. No wonder her grandmother had fallen for him. Even her mother, who didn't care for books, agreed it was a stately home. Of course, her mother being such a committed Communist meant she looked down on the Antonovs and their bourgeois trappings. But she'd been polite enough that evening.

They turned the corner to the Antonov's street and her grandmother stopped. Directly in front of them, the entire end of the street was unrecognizable, the buildings reduced to piles of snow-covered rubble. Lena sighed. It wasn't so much a surprise as it was a disappointment.

Her grandmother picked her way around the chunks of granite and burned remains of furniture that had been the Antonov's building. She nudged a few things with her boot and then sat and stared. Lena sat next to her, broken buildings all around them. It was a scene repeated all over the city. When Lena took her grandmother's arm and they stood to go, some debris fell free.

"Look," she said, pointing at something bright blue. She squatted down to brush the snow and gray ash away, revealing a blue velvet box.

"It's Vasili's," her *babushka* said, her eyebrows raised and eyes wide.

Lena lifted it and held it out to her grandmother who undid the clasp. Resting in an immaculate satin lining were two ornate crystal glasses etched in gold with the double-headed eagle of the Romanovs. They shimmered when she turned the box to the light.

"My," Lena said. "Those are gorgeous."

"And dangerous." Her grandmother closed the box quickly, casting a glance to check that they were alone and unobserved. Possession of anything sympathetic to the monarchy could still be a death sentence.

"Should we just leave it here?" Lena asked.

"For someone else to find?" her *babushka* replied. "They might trace it back to Vasili. Or falsely blame someone else in the same building. Better to take it with us and hide it." She put it in the huge pocket she'd sewed inside her coat. For a moment, her grandmother looked as if she wanted to sift through the rubble, but Lena pulled her away. "It's a bit dangerous, don't you think? Let's go," she said.

They headed further into the Petrograd district, first waiting in a long queue at a store that ran out of whatever they were selling before Lena and her grandmother reached the front of the line. Disheartened and unsure where to go next, they turned a corner. Lena glimpsed a small crowd up the block, raised voices echoing along the otherwise empty street. Unbalanced by its load or run into something, a bread cart had tipped to one side. Three or four women threatened the young female driver who stood between them and several dozen loaves scattered on the ground. Lena hurried to intervene.

"Comrades, comrades, what's going on here?" she said.

"None of your business," one of the would-be thieves yelled.

"I waited hours this morning and got nothing," said another. "My children are starving."

Lena raised her hands, her voice beseeching. "Let's not attack each other. This woman is trying to do her job. You know what will happen if she doesn't deliver this bread. She'll lose her position and her rations will be docked. Maybe worse."

She and her grandmother stood in the midst of the small, angry crowd. Lena turned to the woman who hadn't gotten her ration. "Comrade, I'm sure if you go and get in line now, you'll get your share." The cart driver nodded. With authority, Lena began stacking the bread on the cart, while her tiny grandmother tried to look imposing. The remaining people drifted away.

"Thank you so much." The cart girl's eyes were wide with gratitude. "I don't know what I would've done without your help. They'd say I stole the bread and then I'd be arrested."

"People are crazed with hunger," Lena said. "All sorts of horrible things happening." As they finished stacking the loaves, she continued. "You wouldn't happen to know of any stores with protein rations?"

"Hmmm. Maybe I can do something for you," the cart girl replied. Her eyebrows knit together. "We have some tinned beef, reserved for employees. If you ask, they'll deny it. Follow and let me do the talking. It's only two blocks."

In the shop, she whispered to the woman in charge, explaining how Lena and her grandmother rescued her from the unruly crowd and that they needed protein rations. Without a word, the woman motioned them to a back room where she produced a stack of cans that gleamed like treasure.

"She's my mother," the girl said under her breath. "Don't tell anyone, but it's the least we can do."

The surprisingly still hefty matron glared at Lena. "That was a good thing you did. Nice to know there's some civilization left in the city. But if I ever hear you told anyone about this, I promise I'll come after you and make your life a living hell."

"Mama! Really. Is that necessary? They won't say anything."

"Nothing to tell," Lena said. "We got protein rations on Furmanov Street. End of story."

Lena nodded at the cart girl and rushed out, afraid she and her stern mother might change their minds. Her grandmother was waiting in the street, beaming, having somehow gotten their bread ration even though this certainly wasn't their designated store.

Their hopes for the Antonov's had been dashed, but getting their entire protein ration was extraordinary. Buoyed by their luck, they linked arms and headed back to central Leningrad.

Once across the river, they disappeared into the Summer Garden, snow swirling in every direction. The park, like the city, was empty. Lena kept thinking about the matron at the store and her daughter. They were obviously eating plenty. The system infuriated her. Most in the city starved while those in power or those who worked in food distribution were well fed.

She and her grandmother didn't talk. It was too cold and took too much energy. They walked with their heads down and almost missed the older couple on the bench. A fine layer of snow had turned them white. Drawing close, Lena saw ice sprinkled on their eyelashes like silvery mascara. The woman's head rested on the man's shoulder. Their peaceful death masks made Lena shudder and she saw her *babushka* blink back tears.

They cut through a neighborhood bordered by the Mikhailovsky Gardens, the Nevsky, and the Fontanka. The squeak of their boots on snow made a mournful sound as they crossed courtyards lined with discarded corpses. The snow-covered mounds were unavoidable. As they passed an open entryway, a high-pitched voice, agitated and complaining, floated down amidst the snowflakes. Lena caught a few words and looked up. "Mama needs me," the voice squealed. Lena and her grandmother slowed, concerned and curious. As they exited the courtyard, the voice piped again, unhappy and urgent.

"Something's not right," her grandmother said.

Lena nodded and they returned to the courtyard just in time to glimpse a giant of a man exiting the opposite direction with a small child under one arm. The tyke struggled and cried.

"That's him," her grandmother exclaimed. "The man from the Haymarket. We have to stop him!"

Lena chased them up the street, yelling at the man to let the child go. It was difficult to move quickly—her boots heavy, the cans jouncing in her big pocket. Her lungs began to burn after just a dozen steps and her heart pounded so hard it seemed about to burst from her chest. Somehow she kept shouting, "Stop! Let her go!"

For a second, she wondered what she would do if she caught up with them. She looked around and grabbed a fist-sized piece of concrete. Maybe her grandmother had the gun. She'd taken to carrying it everywhere.

They were just a couple of turns from the Nevsky. Surely someone would be on the main boulevard to help. Lungs searing, she sucked in enough air to yell again. "Stop!"

The giant dropped the child, then accelerated and disappeared around a corner as the little girl bounced and rolled.

Lena ran to the youngster, trying to speak and catch her breath at the same time.

Doubled over, she panted. "You hurt?"

"Owwww," the little girl cried. "B-b-b-bad man," punctuated her sobs. She was bundled up in a heavy coat and snow pants. Her hat had fallen off in the melee.

"Yes, that was a very bad man, but he's gone now. Does it hurt anywhere? Can you stand up?" Lena took several deep breaths. She brushed snow off the child and put her hat back on, tying it under her chin with care. "I can walk you home." The girl was not much more than a toddler. Lena took her hand and they turned back the way they'd come when her grandmother finally caught up, moving at a brisk shuffle and waving the gun.

"Where is he?" she demanded. "I'll use this again."

Lena smiled. Her grandmother looked almost as wild as the giant. Her hat hung loose around her neck and strands of her hair flew wildly about her face. Her eyes flashed with anger and determination.

"He's gone. I never would have caught him, but I yelled loud enough that he must have been scared someone would hear and come investigate." She smiled at her grandmother. "You know, *Babusya*, if I ever went into battle you're the only one I'd need with me."

Her grandmother smiled shyly, slipped the gun into her pocket and took the child's other hand. "I'm Sofya Nikolayevna and this is Yelena. What's your name?"

"I'm Sasha," the little girl said brightly.

"Well, little Sasha, don't you worry. We'll take you home."

Together they made their way back to the apartment building.

"Which apartment is yours?" Lena bent down as they stood in the entryway.

"Up," the little girl said. She struggled to climb the stairs, too high for her little legs stuffed into snow pants. Lena put both arms out and the child stepped into them without hesitation.

At the second landing there was an open apartment door. Lena set her down and she toddled down a hall, calling for her mama. They followed the child into a room. There were two bodies on a mattress: the child's mother and an older sibling. Her grandmother arranged a blanket over them. The little girl sat next to the mattress and picked up a filthy rag doll, cradling it in her lap. Lena looked down, sadness and anger burning. Their father was probably fighting and what did he get in return? His loved ones starved to death. Ordinary citizens like these didn't have a chance, yet there were plenty of Party members taking care of themselves.

"Is there anyone else here?" Sofya asked, watching the girl's big brown eyes look toward a curtained section of the room.

"Baba and Dedka."

Lena and Sofya found the two corpses in the corner. Swaddled in sheets, the little girl's grandparents were ready for burial.

Lena sat down so she could look at the youngster.

"Your mama, your family, they've gone to heaven."

The child narrowed her eyes, an expression that made her seem older.

"What's heaven?"

"I'm not really sure, but it's a good place. People go there when they die. No one is cold and no one is hungry in heaven."

"Ooooh," she said, nodding her head gravely. "Are we going to heaven too?"

"Not now, little one."

Her bottom lip quivered in a pitiable way, and her sharp-edged cheekbones made her dark eyes enormous. She looked like a tiny, old woman with owl eyes. "Will Mama come back?"

Lena held her on her lap. Such a sweet girl. There was only one thing to do. She looked at her grandmother who whispered in agreement. "There's no other choice for now."

"You can't stay here alone, *malenka*. You'll come with us. We'll take care of you. The bad man can't get you where we live."

She nodded and sniffed, but pursed her little lips. Lena set her on her feet as her grandmother gathered some clothes, making a small bundle. In the mother's handbag Lena found ration cards and slipped all three into her pocket. At the same time her grandmother took the mother's identification papers.

The little girl looked at Lena with a grave expression. "I'm hungry."

"Well," a smile flashed across Sofya's face. "It just so happens I have a little something." She reached inside her coat and broke off a small corner of bread. The child popped it into her mouth and backed away, eyes darting around. They finished organizing her things while she sucked and chewed.

"How old are you?" Lena asked.

"I'm four. And Misha's seven," she said, pointing at her dead brother lying with her mother. "Will Misha come too?"

"No, Misha can't come. He's in heaven with your mama and your grandparents."

"But I want to go with Mama and Misha." She wiped her mitten across her nose, sniffing and crying. "Why does Misha get to go? I'm a good and helpful girl, Mama says so."

Lena knelt and searched for words. "Of course you are, Sasha. I don't know why Misha and your mama have gone to heaven and you're here. *Tolko Bog znayet.* Only God knows."

"Is God in heaven too?"

Lena nodded. "You know, when you're old like your *babushka*, your time will come to go to heaven. Then you'll get to see Misha and your mama and your grandparents again." She paused and stood. "My baby brother," her voice cracked, "is also in heaven."

Lena was seven when he was born and had memories of him—good memories. But he died before his first birthday and her parents never spoke about him. Lena understood there was a dreadful pain there.

Sasha considered this for a few moments.

"Is he happy?"

Lena sniffed and turned away. Little Shura they called him. He used to shriek with glee when she played peek-a-boo with him. "Yes," she said. "I'm sure he is."

She took a deep breath and squeezed Sasha's mittened hand. "*Davai*. Let's go. It's almost time to collect our cousin from school. His name is Alyosha. He's six."

"Can I come?" Her voice jingled with excitement.

"Of course, *malenka*."

She hugged her doll tight and gave a little jump.

Lena grinned at her grandmother as the impish youngster talked all the way down the stairs.

THE ORPHANAGE

January 1942

NOT LONG AFTER they brought Sasha home, Sofya and Yelena spent an evening considering their list of supplies and doing calculations.

"With another child, and if we continue eating at this rate, we'll be out of food in March, instead of May," said Sofya. "There's enough for eight or nine more weeks." The grim reality of another mouth to feed weighed on them both.

"Even if you and I eat less," she said, "there still won't be enough. And we have no idea when the blockade will be broken and food will start to arrive." She studied Yelena's face, looking for a clue as to her thoughts. Instead Sofya saw that the curves of her cheeks had faded. "I don't see how we can keep both children. I know it's terrible, but we need to think about taking Sasha to a home, before she gets settled and attached." She glanced at the corner where the two children slept curled on a mattress under a thick layer of clothes and blankets. "Soon we won't be able to send her away. She'll be family."

Yelena's gaze grew intense. "An orphanage? Remember what Pavel told us the nurse said. And that was two months ago. We can't send her someplace where all she gets is two pieces of bread a day and a bowl of warm water."

"I remember, but the Party must be caring for children who've lost their parents. I'm going to check with the District Committee."

❧

At the government office, Sofya sat. The reception area was empty, so why did she have to wait forty-five minutes to see the clerk? She tried to suppress her irritation.

"My name is Karavayeva, Sofya Nikolayevna." She handed her residence permit to the woman. "A distant relative, a child, has been orphaned, and she's with me now. We don't have enough food and I wanted to inquire about possible arrangements."

"You mean an orphanage?"

"I suppose so, unless there is some policy for increased rations."

The woman sneered. "Increased rations? For dependents? You must be joking. If we did that, everyone would claim extra dependents. The only choices are to keep her or put her in a home. Some have ended up on the street, but I hope you aren't so hard-hearted as to do that. So many street urchins now." Under her breath she added, "Plus, it's a punishable offense."

Stunned at the idea of abandoning the little girl, Sofya stepped back and raised her voice. "I am not suggesting the child be turned out. That's not only against the laws of the Soviet state, it's against the laws of nature. But taking in an additional mouth to feed is risky. We need help."

The administrator shrugged.

"Can you at least give me the address of the closest facility so I can take a look. Make sure the children get enough food."

The woman muttered. "Enough food? Orphans are as poorly off as the rest of us."

Frustrated and disappointed, she glared at the woman, her fleshy neck showing above her collar. Sofya fought the urge to say something rude, to vent her anger at this well-fed apparatchik. Instead, she held her tongue, took the slip of paper with the address, and slammed the door on her way out.

The orphanage was close to Alyosha's school, and Sofya made her way before the last of the afternoon light disappeared. She avoided the Nevsky and other main boulevards where incoming artillery attacks concentrated. Instead, she cut across the Griboyedov canal on the Bankovski Bridge, a beautiful small pedestrian crossing complete with stone griffins at each end. She stood next to one for a couple of minutes, feeling completely alone. There was hardly another soul on the streets. How could she take Sasha to a home? Such a spirited, lively child. They had saved her. That must be for a reason.

As she neared the building, she tried imagining that it would be a really nice orphanage. Cheery decorations on the walls, matrons with happy children gathered round for story time, a cafeteria with child-sized tables and chairs and food bubbling in the kitchen. They could leave Sasha just until things improved, and go back for her in couple of months. Maybe then they would even adopt the little charmer.

The orphanage resembled a school. Cement block construction and smallish windows. She peeked around the side before entering the main doors. The surrounding buildings increased the penitentiary feel of the place, but it had a sizable enclosed yard in the back. A nice outdoor play space, except the deep, untouched snow meant no one had played outside in a long while.

Up the stairs and through the main doors, the typical paintings of Lenin and Stalin greeted her. Every Soviet institution displayed them prominently. Sofya didn't waste a second glance. It was cold, perhaps just a few degrees warmer than outside. Didn't they have heat? Even Alyosha's school had sporadic heat—not enough to stay warm, but enough to make a difference. The main hallway was quiet. There was an office. "Reception" was painted in big letters above the door. She thought about going in, but decided instead to poke around on her own. She snuck past and started down another hall. Still no sounds.

The sign over the next room said "Nursery." Sasha would not be in a nursery, but Sofya opened the door anyway. In a corner to her left sat the *dezhurnaya,* the room attendant, sound asleep. Sofya crept along the rows of cribs, peeking at the babies. Many slept, and the ones that were awake lay listless, enormous eyes open, staring at nothing. Their bodies were shriveled, their skin yellow. Sofya leaned over to coo at one baby. Why on earth didn't the staff hold these poor things, play with them? The infant didn't respond to Sofya's smiles and whispers, so she pulled off a glove and touched its cheek. She drew her hand back sharply and gasped. The baby was ice cold.

Neither her gasp nor her hurried footsteps woke the *dezhurnaya*. Maybe she was dead too. Sofya rushed down the hall. Sasha couldn't be in a place like this. It didn't matter if they had enough food to last until May or not. This was not the answer.

As she turned down the main steps, a door opened behind her and a voice called out, "Can I help you?"

Sofya turned to see a woman approach, her steps so tiny she hardly appeared to be moving. "Can you help me? No, I think not, but you could help the babies dying in your nursery."

The exhausted matron sighed and sat heavily on the top step. "We have no milk, we have no food." Her voice quavered. "We cannot save them."

The woman herself looked weak and ill.

Sofya snapped. "I understand what a dismal and desperate time it is for everyone in the city, but don't the most helpless of orphans deserve to be fed and cared for? And, if there is no way to provide that, don't they still deserve to be held and played with and loved for their short lives?" Sofya heard her own fury and judgment. "Can't your staff at least hold them as they die, and offer them love in their brief existence?"

The woman did not look away. Her yellow skin announced her own grim future. "Most certainly they deserve that, and much more. But it is beyond us now. My staff are dying. There is no energy and little compassion left. We are doing all we can." The matron struggled to her feet. "Sometimes our best is not good enough."

Sofya stepped for the door, but then turned back. She stood in the bright hot light of shame. "Forgive my harsh words, Comrade. You deserve better. And I have no right. It is indeed a terrible struggle for all of us."

When Sofya got home, Yelena was making dinner: four small pancakes with tiny bits of minced ham sprinkled into the flour and water batter. There was no oil, or butter, or salt, but everyone was well past the point of caring about taste. They each had the other half of their daily bread ration too. The last pancake was a bit bigger than the others. To avoid any arguments, Sofya said, "I'll take that one." Both children whined. "I want the big one." "I'm so hungry, can't I have it?" Sofya cut her pancake in half and then one of the halves into two equal pieces. She slid those quarters, one onto each of the children's plates, and both youngsters lit up. "Thank you, Baba Sofya, thank you."

After dinner, Yelena pulled her aside. "You can't give your food to the children."

"I know what I'm doing," she said.

"No. We all struggle together," Yelena said. "So, tell me about the home."

Sofya shook her head. "It's not an option. The place was like a tomb, deserted, freezing cold. No one caring for the babies. I reached into a crib to touch an infant and it was dead." Her eyes filled. "It doesn't matter if we have enough food or not. She can't go there."

"I've been thinking," Yelena leaned into her grandmother. "I'll write Pavel and ask for help. He brought us food before. He'd want to know about Sasha and how bad things are. After all, he's the one who gave us Alyosha in the first place and started us down this path."

"You can't do that," Sofya said. "The censors."

"Don't worry. I'll be smart. Pavel and I use lots of code words."

"Still, it seems risky," she sighed. "We'll all end up in prison. Pavel could be shot. It would be safer if I gave half my portion to the children."

"That would be your death sentence." Yelena's voice rose. "You can't give up. You aren't making sense."

Yelena was right. She was not making sense. It was a risk worth taking and Pavel had done it before. A few kilos of food would make all the difference.

THE ROAD OF LIFE
February 1942

PAVEL LEFT HIS truck in the first loading bay at Kobona station. Several of the big metal doors were already open, revealing pallets of supplies, but his crew was nowhere in sight. He loved this first solitary run of the day—the Nazis still asleep and the lake dark as pitch with only his headlights to show the way.

Except for his very first crossing in late November—which wasn't a truck crossing at all, but a team of horse-drawn sledges—Pavel always tried to be out before his comrades. That first trip by horse had been something. Three hundred-fifty men and beasts trudging thirty-five kilometers across the newly frozen lake in a blizzard. It had taken ten hours, and after loading the sledges with the first food for Leningrad they'd turned around for the equally numbing return.

Then, almost overnight, the ice thickened and they switched to trucks. The first few of those trips were brutal too. Bumping and bouncing along the rough terrain. The Nazis shelling and strafing, sending trucks to the bottom of the lake. But now, conditions had improved. There were repair depots, bridge layers, and first aid stations out on the ice. The only thing that hadn't changed was how Pavel thrived in his work: the constant race against the clock, bringing more loads across than anyone else, the thrill he got from helping save Leningrad.

Pavel went into the mess hall and found his loading crew finishing breakfast. They grumbled good-naturedly about him always being so early, but Pavel knew they liked him. He had a reputation as first out and last in, something they respected and admired. He filled his tin cup with hot coffee as the men dribbled out to load his truck. As he approached the loading bay, lights on the lake from the first convoy of the day shone faintly through the darkness.

"Come on, boys," Pavel said. "Can't you put your backs into it? Even my *babushka* works faster than this."

"Fuck your *babushka*," said one.

"No, actually, I have someone else in mind." Pavel laughed.

"Oh, yeah? What's her name, Pavlik?"

"Who cares about her name?" said another with a lewd laugh.

"Probably doesn't matter. His dick will freeze off before . . ."

The men fell silent as an officer approached.

"Good morning, Comrade Major," Pavel said, saluting as he walked past.

"As I was saying," the first soldier continued as the officer moved out of earshot, "your *babushka* is probably living the high life east of the Volga by now, warm and well-fed."

"True enough," Pavel said. "Lucky to get out of this hell-hole. Still, can't you get me loaded quicker? I want to be gone before they arrive." He gestured toward the line of lights growing brighter. "You know I get antsy when there's too much company."

"*Nu ladno.* Okay. We're almost there." The soldier gestured at the nearly empty pallets as the crew scrambled to finish. "Gunning for a new record today?"

"Crossed my mind," Pavel said, running a gloved hand over the pockmarked passenger side door, proud of the bullet holes he'd gotten the week before. He hadn't heard the Stuka, his truck rattled so loudly it drowned out the attacking plane until it was nearly on top of him. At the first ping of bullets striking metal he stepped on the gas instead of pulling over and scrambling away from his truck. He'd prepared for the moment in his mind and decided it was harder to hit a moving target than a stationary one. Racing for the shore and the protection of the anti-aircraft guns, he didn't slow until he finally glimpsed the lighthouse. Damned if he was going to lose a full load of supplies without a fight.

As the last bags were loaded, Pavel jumped into the driver's seat and signaled his thanks to the loading crew. With no surprises, he'd make the crossing in forty-five minutes. A round trip could be three hours with loading and unloading—more if there were problems. Everyday his personal goal was to complete three trips. Once in a while the stars would align and he'd do four, but more often than not he'd be ambushed by trouble in the way of new craters from German artillery, an unexpected fissure, or something as simple as a flat tire. Today though, he was focused on something else besides being the first out in the morning and last in at night. He had to get food for Lena.

Partway across the lake, he stopped his truck and jumped out. It would be at least thirty minutes before the other vehicles caught up to him. He climbed into the truck bed with his flashlight and began looking for open boxes or anything damaged. He moved a few things around and found just what he was looking for: a box with one of the top flaps ripped off. He pulled the other flap up. Butter. A whole box of it. Underneath, he saw another identical one, but sealed tight. The bricks of butter were wrapped and stamped. He took one, and then a second, and closed the box. What else? Flour. He'd seen them loading open crates of two kilo bags. He found them in the far corner and pulled out two bags, shuffling the others around so the empty spaces wouldn't be visible. He decided that was enough for this trip and dropped everything in his rucksack, set it on the seat next to him, and put the truck into gear. There weren't even any headlights behind him.

Arriving at Osinovets, nervous and sweating, he grabbed the rucksack and tossed his keys to one of the loading crew. "Can you gas it up too? I'm starving."

"Sure, Comrade. We'll have it unloaded and ready to go in forty minutes."

Pavel gave a two-fingered salute as acknowledgment and rushed to the barracks. The other drivers were either out on the lake or in the mess hall, so he slipped the rucksack under his bed. He felt sick to his stomach. Stealing. Even though lots of drivers and loaders did it, he could be shot. He pulled out Lena's last letter. She never wrote about their struggles. She hadn't even told him when she broke her arm. But this time her tone was different. Pessimistic and dark. Along with diminishing supplies, they'd taken in another orphan. He had to get them food as soon as possible. He couldn't let anything happen to her.

In the mess hall, he looked for some of the small group of talented, aggressively committed drivers he'd befriended. They often ate together and compared notes. At the end of the day they'd sometimes stay long after supper, drinking lukewarm coffee, sharing information and encouraging each other, always looking for ways to bring more supplies across. They were still out on the lake so he ate breakfast alone.

Pavel sipped coffee and ate his kasha. He already tried to deliver the most kilos every day, thinking it might earn him a short leave into Leningrad. Now there was extra urgency. He finished eating and hurried out to make another trip across the lake.

The pass came—not as a result of his hard work though, but because of a broken axle. While his truck was under repair Pavel and several other drivers received orders to pick up new vehicles at one of Leningrad's factories and drive them to Osinovets. If he took an early train from Ladoga Station, he'd have the entire day—and the entire night—to spend with Yelena before joining the convoy of new trucks the following morning.

Hustling back to the barracks, Pavel pulled out his rucksack and looked through the food items. In addition to the flour, butter, kasha and canned meat he'd stolen, he'd collected a nice little stack of chocolate bars and a couple of mealy apples from his own rations. He set aside today's bread, almost one and a half pounds, and he'd add tomorrow's ration before leaving, but he wanted to bring Yelena more than that. At dinner he went looking for his friends.

Entering the mess hall, Pavel scanned for familiar faces. On his way over to the far corner where the older guys sat, he glanced at the group who'd been continually harassing him.

"Still trying to make us look bad, eh, Chernov?"

"There goes Mr. 'I'm the best fucking driver on the Ice Road,'" said another.

Pavel clenched his teeth. He'd like nothing better than to get back at them, especially Mazarov, the ringleader who'd been after him since October when they'd worked on the rail line. He touched the scar on his cheek. This wasn't the time. The bastards weren't worth jeopardizing his trip into Leningrad.

Making his way over to Bogdan and Anatoli, the guys who'd mentored him all summer, he grabbed their shoulders.

"Pavlik," said Bogdan. "How goes it? Still hot-shotting across the ice?"

Pavel smiled. "Yeah, well, someone's got to do it."

Bogdan shook his head. "Sure, but someone doesn't have to break records and shit. You make the rest of us look bad," he said with a smile.

Pavel shrugged. Bogdan and Anatoli liked him even though they ribbed him sometimes. They just didn't want him to get a big head.

"Well, you won't catch me out there," said Anatoli, one of the mechanics. "I want to make it through this war in one piece. Get home to the wife and kids when it's over."

"Speaking of family," said Pavel. "I'm picking up a new truck in the city tomorrow."

"What'd you do to the old one? Drive off a cliff?" Laughter spilled across the table.

"Very funny," he said, but then winced. "I was a bit rough with it. Broke an axle."

"Shit, Pavlik," said Anatoli. "That's what? The fourth or fifth truck you've fucked?"

"It's only the third," Pavel shook his head. "Now, getting back to my point—family. Got any food? I've got cigarettes and vodka to trade." Bogdan and Anatoli's families had long since evacuated, so they weren't saving food to send home.

"Maybe. Who's it for?"

"Lena, of course." Pavel leaned down so others couldn't hear. "She and her grandmother are in a bad way. And, I'm going to ask her to marry me."

"Seriously? Shit. That's a cause I can get behind."

"I've got a few things if the price is right," said Bogdan.

"I'll make it worth your while," Pavel said. "Come by later?"

"We're finished," said Anatoli. "Let's go now." He elbowed Bogdan. "A cigarette sure sounds good."

Asking Lena to marry him was a big step. He figured she'd be surprised, but would she say yes? She was only sixteen. Were they too young? He felt so much older than eighteen. Their lives before the war—such trivial, simple lives—seemed like ancient history.

Late that night, surrounded by grunts and snores, the creaking of bunks and the occasional groan, Pavel lay awake with his desire for company. He tried not to think about being with Lena—though he'd showered just in case—but kissing and touching her were impossible to get out of his mind.

Hours after the train departed Ladoga, it inched through Leningrad's suburbs to Moscow Station. Pavel exited the cavernous, near-empty building and turned up Vladimirsky Prospekt. Along the fence by the cathedral, he saw the first corpses, a massive pile—some neatly wrapped in sheets, but others looked like they'd been tossed without a second thought, arms and legs at odd angles. He shuddered and stepped into the broad boulevard to avoid the bodies, then caught sight of two people pulling a sled down the middle of the street. It was the same kind he'd used as a child, the type of sled he and his little sister had ridden just last winter. Only it had a swaddled corpse tied to it. Pavel shrank away, embarrassed by his relative health and shocked at the evidence of death all around. He'd been so sure the supplies coming across the Ice Road were making a difference.

Dread swept over him. He hadn't seen Lena for three months and her last letter was a plaintive plea for help. It was the only time she'd hinted at how difficult the situation was, how hard the struggle. Why hadn't he'd known before now? What if it was too late? By November she'd already lost weight. Yes, the Karavayevas had hoarded supplies, but then he'd brought them another mouth to feed. And now, they had another. What if they'd died? Panic delivered a jolt of adrenalin and he began to run.

At the building's back entrance, Pavel pushed the outer door, now permanently wedged open by snow and ice, and sped through the courtyard. Keys often didn't work in the intense cold, so he wasn't surprised that their entryway door was also ajar. He flew up the three flights of the tomb-like building and was knocking before the sound of his footsteps faded.

"Lena. Lena. Are you home?" He called out, rapping again on the door. "Sofya Nikolayevna?" Their names echoed in the emptiness.

All at once, Lena herself opened the door, her face half-hidden behind layers of winter clothing.

He pulled her to him and whispered, "Lena, you're all right."

Pavel held her tightly against his chest as she whimpered into his neck. His thudding heart calmed. He carried her into the apartment, kicking the door closed with one foot and setting her on the sofa. He knelt next to her and pressed his lips to hers.

She smiled and touched the red star on his *ushanka*. He'd enlisted on his birthday.

A tiny voice nagged for attention. "What's wrong with Lena?"

Lena reached out a mittened hand to pull the child close. "Don't worry, Sasha. Everything's all right. This is Pavel, my Pasha. I'm crying because I'm so happy to see him."

"Pavel, this is Sasha," Lena said. "She's part of our family now." Then she whispered, "I'll explain later." She turned back to the child. "Sasha, say hello to Pavel Ivanovich. He's a brave soldier."

"Hello, Pavel Ivanovich," Sasha said in a bright, sing-song voice.

He smiled at the sunny, articulate child. "Pleased to meet you, Sasha."

"Are you going to stay, Pavel Ivanovich?" the little sprite continued. "Did you bring your ration card? We can get bread with your card."

"Thank you, Sasha. I brought my own food. But yes, I'd like to stay tonight if that's okay with Lena and Baba Sofya." He whispered to Lena, "I got your letter. My rucksack is full."

Lena smiled. "Oh, Pavel, thank you. Of course you can stay. How did you manage to get a pass?" She threw her arms around him. "I'm so happy to see you. I can't believe you're here."

Sitting next to her, he explained about picking up a new truck the next day.

"Let's boil some water for tea," he said. "I have some surprises for you."

"We would love that." Lena cast a glance downward. "But we ran out of tea weeks ago. There's nothing besides bread in the stores, and hardly any of that. Even if we had tea, boiling water is difficult. There's nothing to burn so we can't make a fire whenever we want. We're out of water too. Sasha and I were about to go fill our buckets at the Fontanka."

"There's no fuel or water?" Pavel tensed, his eyes wide and dark.

Lena nodded. "It's been weeks since the heat and electricity gave out. Then the pipes froze, so there's no water, no toilet, no bath. It's all become extremely primitive. My grandma and I sleep together here." She pointed at a mattress near the little stove. "And Sasha and Alyosha on that other mattress. In the evenings we use the stove for heat, and since we're almost out of fuel, it's the only time we can boil water. We've had to start burning my grandmother's books."

"Well, first things first," Pavel said. "I'll go get water right now."

"We'll come too," Lena said, energized. "Sasha and I can show you the way."

There was a hardness to the air. Frigid, arctic winds bore down on the city, and every inch of skin had to be covered to prevent frostbite. The three bundled up so that only their eyes showed. Pavel's long, wool military coat hung below his knees and he wore the *valenki*, felt boots, of the military. Lena wore *valenki* too, her grandfather's. All three had *ushankas* with flaps pulled down tight, and scarves across their faces. Pavel held Sasha's hand while she bounced about, talking despite the scarf covering her mouth. Her muffled, unintelligible words accompanied them the entire way. Lena walked on his other side, carrying the empty buckets. Anyone watching them would see a family: two young parents with their child. Pavel glanced at Lena over and over again. There was so much he wanted to tell her. At one point, he paused and pulled her close while Sasha tugged at his other arm.

A small crowd had gathered out on the frozen canal having already slid down the short but steep embankment. Lena pointed out the rough steps worn into the packed snow by steady foot traffic. The path had turned to solid ice where people sloshed their buckets and spilled water as they struggled to climb back up.

Pavel rested the buckets on the frozen surface and turned to the small crowd.

"Comrades, if three of you will help me," he began, pulling his scarf down and securing it around his neck. "I'll draw the water. One of you can stand here, and another there and there," he said, pointing to a position close to the ramp, with another a few steps up, and the third a few steps beyond that. "We'll pass the buckets up. Working together we'll finish in no time."

A few in the crowd snickered at his optimism. Pavel ignored the doubters and began filling buckets. Several older women stepped forward to help and took their places at appropriate intervals. One woman was exhausted after only a few buckets and Yelena took her place at the bottom of the icy steps. Pavel smiled and as he handed her the first bucket he leaned in to kiss her cheek. The crowd tittered. An older female voice rang out, "Can I get a kiss too?" Pavel and Lena both laughed, and a few minutes later when the woman took a spot, Pavel welcomed her with a kiss. The crowd roared its approval. And when the next volunteer stepped forward, an elderly man, Pavel didn't miss a beat and kissed him on the cheek as well.

Soon no one cared how long it took. Voices lighter, eyes brighter, the crowd laughed and teased with Lena and Pavel. For a few minutes their burdens lifted and it was just another winter day on the Fontanka Canal.

ONE NIGHT IN LENINGRAD
February 1942

ON THE WAY home, Sasha bounced ahead while Lena eyed Pavel. He carried the water buckets, insisting it was easier for him to carry both for balance. She knew he'd do a better job of not spilling on the stairs to their apartment anyway. It was always a trick to bring enough water in one trip without filling the buckets so full that some splashed out. There were already lots of icy spots where water had spilled and frozen. Ever since Mrs. Radchenko's terrible fall, she worried about her grandmother slipping.

Pavel navigated the streets with ease. Although thin, he was strong and radiated confidence. The difference between him and the shivering skeletons out on the ice was striking. Lena felt a fullness in her heart that was new and powerful. Pavel was compassionate and self-assured. He took charge on the ice, kissing those strangers, no shyness, just sharing a light moment. In her mind she replayed how he'd charmed the crowd. The scar on his cheek made him look older, experienced, and he acted that way too.

The feelings she had last year were a childish crush compared to what she felt now. A warmth settled over her, and with it the certainty that she belonged with him. No other man would have been so kind to those strangers, distracting them from their burdens. Her eyes filled and she looked away while he called to Sasha to slow down.

Once in the apartment, Pavel replenished the kettle and pulled a small packet out of his duffel—tea. Lena filled the tin canister.

Over the last weeks, she and her grandmother sometimes opened the empty container to sniff the still pungent scent and imagine they were drinking tea instead of foul-smelling water.

"Let's warm things up in here," Pavel said.

Embarrassed by what her life had become, Lena murmured. "It never really gets warm, just less cold. We have to stay bundled up all the time. Nighttime is the worst. No matter how many clothes we wear, we're never warm."

She so wanted to feel his arms around her and now he came up from behind, holding her and breathing on her neck. She shivered from the closeness of his lips.

"I'm sorry things are so awful," he said. "We're bringing food across."

"But the stores are still empty." She didn't say it unkindly, just matter-of-factly. The crestfallen look on Pavel's face told her he believed they were saving the city. "I'm sorry. I know how hard you're working."

She didn't want to think about the food situation. She wanted to kiss him. When he finally leaned down, his lips were rougher than she remembered, but after a few seconds they felt soft and still fit perfectly on hers. She opened her mouth slightly and touched his lips with her tongue. He pressed harder, then pulled aside her scarf to kiss her neck. Pleasure radiated through her body, her arousal growing with Pavel's every touch. Sasha tugged at her coat and called her name, but Lena ignored her and kept kissing Pavel, wanting to feel more of what felt so good. The little girl's pestering grew louder and more insistent until Pavel gave in to the distraction.

"Okay, Sasha, shall we start a fire?"

"Yes, YES." Sasha jumped up and down, dark curls escaping her hat.

He took most of the last scraps of wood and got the pot-bellied stove snapping and crackling while Sasha hung on him, offering an exhausting commentary. Lena looked at Pavel and mouthed the words, *she's always like this.*

"Can I take your sled?" he asked. "I passed several ruined build-ings. I think there'll be wood." The red wooden sled was propped against the wall by the door.

Lena nodded. "There's a small axe too. We've started on the furniture."

"I hate to leave you, but I want to help in every way I can before tomorrow. And it'll be dark in a few hours. I should go now."

"Can I come?" Sasha pleaded. "I'm a good helper. I can put wood on the sled."

Lena rolled her eyes and Pavel stopped Sasha before she got up a head of steam.

"Now, Sasha, you know I can't take you with me. It's danger-ous, and it's my job to keep you safe. Stay here with Lena and when I return you can help me stack the wood."

Pavel disappeared and Lena smiled at Sasha as the little girl squealed. "I can't wait to tell Baba Sofya and Alyosha about Pavel and the water buckets, and everything."

He returned later with a huge load of wood, which he and Sasha stacked carefully, adding some to the *burzhuika*, the wood-burning stove. "How did you get this?" he asked.

"My grandma took the sled to the Haymarket when she first heard about them. It was a while ago—must've been right after you were here in November. She paid extra so they'd help her lash it to the sled. Then she pulled it all the way home and together we got it up the stairs."

"And you scavenged the bricks and you got the exhaust pipe out the window and sealed up the hole. I'm so impressed. You and your grandmother."

As Pavel tended the fire and Sasha handed him bits of broken furniture, the apartment door opened, and her grandmother entered.

When she came into the living room, holding their tiny bread ration, her face shone with shock and delight. "Pavel, is it really you?"

He stepped right up to her, smile big and genuine, and kissed her on both cheeks. "I have a short leave—until tomorrow morning."

"Wonderful." Her grandmother hesitated. "You'll stay with us."

The tension on her *babushka's* face could only be because they couldn't feed him a proper home-cooked meal. Pavel wouldn't care, but her grandma had been raised to feed guests. You always offered food. But they didn't even have a pot of *shchi,* cabbage soup, a dish so cheap that anyone could afford to make it. What would really be delicious would be her grandma's chicken cutlets, fried crispy with mushroom gravy. Lena pressed on her stomach. Thoughts of food caused a physical pain. Oh, for a thick slice of fresh bread, not the adulterated stuff they ate now, but real bread, slathered with butter. Or a plain boiled egg with a few grains of salt. She hadn't had an egg since June.

"Before we do anything else, I want to give you this." He smiled, looking at Lena and then back to Sofya, before picking up his bulging rucksack. He opened it on the table, carefully stacking the contents. Lena stared wide-eyed at the assortment of food and threw her arms around him. Her grandmother's hand flew to her mouth.

"I wish I'd brought more," he said. "But getting food is tricky."

Sofya looked up at him. "I don't have the words to tell you what this means. With extra mouths, we weren't sure how to manage." She sat at the kitchen table gazing at the pile of food, brushing away happy tears.

"Baba Sofya, don't cry," Sasha piped. "Look at all the food. We won't be hungry anymore."

"Oh, you sweet thing," she pulled the child onto her lap. "Now, Sasha, this doesn't mean we can eat as much as we want. This has to last until rations increase."

"Pavel," she continued. "I'd love to write to your mother and tell her how well you're looking after us. Do you have an address?"

His cheeks colored. "Yes, I have their address, but I haven't heard anything in a while."

"Well, don't worry. No one in Leningrad is getting mail. But the outgoing is still moving, or so I've heard. Anyway, be sure to give me the address. She'll eventually get the letter."

"Thank you" he said. "She'll be happy to get some news. I'm not the best at writing."

Lena began sorting the package contents. Tins of beef, another packet of tea, a small bag of sugar, bricks of butter, two big sacks of flour, bars of chocolate, a large bag of kasha, and a smaller one of oatmeal, a box of powdered milk, a half-dozen cans of vegetables, two loaves of bread, three apples, a sizable chunk of cheese, and a single can of sweetened condensed milk. Even with her grandmother's hoarding, it was a shock to see so many precious items.

"Look!" Lena held up the sweetened milk, an impossible treasure. "And butter, too." Her grandmother turned away, her emotions raw and exposed. She was doing better since the terrible experience in the bread line, but Lena still worried. Her *babushka* seemed to have lost her center, her purpose. There was no word from Papa or Admiral Vasili and each night they burned more of her precious books. The Radio Orchestra was shut. Weeks had passed since she'd played or practiced. The violin had been one of the pillars of her grandmother's life. *The* pillar maybe. Perhaps Pavel could get her to play.

Grabbing his hands, Lena pulled him close. "You've saved us, you know, in so many ways." She kissed him right in front of her grandmother.

It was half-past three and getting dark by the time they had their tea and Pavel shared a few tales of the Ice Road. Lena didn't expect her grandmother to go to the library as she often did after collecting Alyosha from school. The apartment was warmer than it had been in weeks and the library would be dismal by comparison. Like the rest of the city, the library had lost electricity and power. The reading rooms were shuttered and patrons now gathered in the small, dimly lit director's office. Elbow to elbow at a single table, bombarded by the sniffing of one person, the muttering of another, reading was a struggle. Writing a private letter—impossible.

Lena grew quiet, wondering if she and Pavel would ever get to be alone.

Several minutes later her grandmother announced. "Well, I'm off to collect Alyosha, and then we'll stop by the library. He's been pleading for a new book. We'll be home around five-thirty. Come along Sasha."

"Baba Sofya," the little girl whined. "I want to stay with Pavel."

"Not now, Sashenka. I need your help at the library."

The youngster reluctantly pulled on her boots.

Lena expected her grandmother to whisper something about 'behaving properly.' She'd given a full-blown lecture back in July when she and Pavel went to the movies. Now, her grandma was leaving them without a chaperone or any mention of rules.

Locking the door behind her grandmother—they always locked the door—Lena felt suddenly awkward. She glanced at Pavel, wondering what he was thinking. Perhaps she'd given him the wrong idea. Would he think she wanted to have sex? Did she?

Pavel was her first boyfriend and Lena was inexperienced. She'd seen men naked, of course, out in the countryside, swimming in streams, sweating in the *banya*, but she'd never touched a man intimately, and although she knew what intercourse was and generally what it entailed, she still wasn't really sure she wanted to do it. Nor was she sure it would feel good. After Tanya's older cousin got married, she told Tanya all about how much it hurt the first time. But Tanya also told Lena she'd overheard her parents, moaning in a pleasurable way and it didn't sound like anything was hurting.

Lena sat on the sofa and took Pavel's hand. At first, they just kissed. Then they started exploring each other, feeling through the layers. Pulling their coats and gloves away, Pavel took her hand and guided her to the mattress next to the stove. His hands were icy, and he rubbed them together and blew on them. Then he traced the skin of her neck and undid her blouse. His lips moved down and when he kissed her breasts, she melted with pleasure, warmth rising between her legs. Pavel moved to undo the buttons of her pants and she didn't stop him. In a moment, his fingers found her. Wet and aroused, she scooted her pants off, wanting him to keep touching her. Pavel pulled something out of a pocket. He said he got the small, cylindrical-shaped protection from one of the men in his unit. It was wrapped in brightly colored plastic and Lena thought it looked like a strangely shaped piece of candy.

He struggled to unroll the condom and get it on, but finally climbed on top of her. He was sweet and gentle, asking if she was okay, if it hurt. It didn't hurt much at all, just some tightness and a small, sharp pain when he pushed all the way in. After that, Lena thought it felt wonderful. Funny how all the parts just seemed to fit together.

Afterwards, his weight rested on her like a heavy blanket. One hand inside his shirt, Lena traced his spine with her fingertips.

"I love you," he whispered. "You mean everything to me."

"I love you too."

They lay together, half-naked, keeping each other warm and Lena drifted into a pleasurable sleep.

"Lena." Pavel's urgent voice woke her. "Your grandmother will be home soon."

She struggled up, pulling at her clothes. They straightened the blankets and unlocked the apartment door, then sat rigidly on the sofa, trying not to look guilty. She was certain her grandmother would be able to tell right away that something was up.

Suddenly Pavel took her hands. She gazed at him, aged in the dim candlelight.

"Right now, the war is everything," he said. "We have to defeat the Germans. But I think about you all the time, about us, about a future together."

Her heart jumped. He felt the same as she did.

"I want to spend my life with you. I know we're young, but I don't feel young, and I know my own heart. I love you, and that's not going to change, except that it will get stronger and deeper." He took a breath. "Will you marry me?"

Eyes filling with happy tears, she nodded and squeaked out a "Yes" as he held her. Some of the struggle and fear of the war disappeared in that moment, trampled by the power of love. The war wouldn't last forever. A happy future would come, even if not now, not yet.

Lena began preparing dinner, trying to act as if everything was normal. She told Pavel about her grandmother: the books, the corpse, her breakdown. "She's doing better since we got Sasha, but do you think you could play with her this evening? She teased you months ago about a duet, but really, it would help."

When her grandmother walked through the door with Alyosha and Sasha, the youngsters attached themselves to Pavel. Lena sliced some canned meat and focused on frying it in a small pan on the little stove, the crackling of the oil and the smell making them all stop talking and gather round to watch and sniff.

The young lovers waited until they were eating—the delicious, crispy fried meat, plus a generous piece of bread, an apple divided five ways, and some chocolate waiting in the center of the table for dessert—to tell Sofya that Pavel had proposed. Lena studied her grandmother's calm, unfazed face. She asked if they weren't a bit young.

Lena took Pavel's hand. "We are young, but love doesn't necessarily come at a specific age." She wanted to point to her *babushka* and Admiral Vasili finding love so late in life, but thought better of it. "Pavel is a wonderful man, the right man for me." She squeezed his hand. "I wish you could have seen him today, helping the people draw water down at the Fontanka. You would have been proud. We're at war, our old life is gone, and planning our future will help."

Sasha jumped in, eyes all big, trying to understand the conversation. "You're getting married?" Alyosha got a serious and disturbed look on his face. "That means you have to kiss."

The adults smiled and Lena excused the children to go play a game in a corner of the room. Pavel returned to their conversation. "Sofya Nikolayevna, I'm confident that when the war is over, Lena and I will continue our education. I plan to study engineering, and I'll be able to care for her." He looked at Lena, smiled and squeezed her hand. "I realize it seems to have happened quickly, but we were drawn to each other even before the war. I feel much older than eighteen, and I know Lena feels the same. I hope you'll support us with your blessing. We can't imagine marrying without you behind us, you're the most important thing in the world to Lena and we both need you very much."

"Of course, you have my blessing. If I had a grandson, I would want him to be just like you. You're a good man, Pavel."

Lena's chest hurt, as if her heart was suddenly too big for its cage of flesh and bones. Hugging her grandmother, a happy future took shape through her tears. Her grandma turned to her and whispered, "Your papa would like Pavel." They cried some more.

"Look at us! My, it feels good to cry for happiness, doesn't it?" Her grandmother stood. "I need to get something." She returned carrying a simple platinum ring set with a single perfect sapphire.

Lena inhaled sharply. "That was your mama's."

"Yes. Many years ago, my parents and I lived in Paris for several months for my violin studies. Papa bought this at a quaint jewelry shop in Montparnasse, and it was Mama's favorite piece of jewelry." Sofya paused and took a breath. "They had a good marriage, and a strong love, and were devoted to each other. My wish is that you share that kind of love." She placed the ring in Pavel's hand. "Now, Pavel, I know that someday you'll want to give Lena something of your own choosing, but for now, I hope you'll accept this as a substitute."

Pavel's eyes brimmed. Lena loved him even more for it.

"I don't know what to say, Sofya Nikolayevna. It's perfect. I'm honored." He slid the ring on Lena's finger and kissed her gently. Then he stood to kiss Sofya's cheek and embrace her as well. "Now, to celebrate, how about we play that duet you teased me about?"

Her grandmother went silent and looked down. For a moment, Lena thought she was going to refuse. Then her *babushka* returned Pavel's expectant gaze and nodded. "Something simple. I haven't played for weeks."

He laughed, bright and warm. "Well, I haven't picked up my violin since June."

A tiny light shone on her grandmother's face. "How about the Mozart you were practicing before this all started? Duet number two."

He smiled. "As long as I can be second violin."

Lena pulled three chairs in a semi-circle while Pavel and her grandmother tuned their instruments. The children's eyes flashed with excitement. Alyosha sat with his hands tightly folded in his lap, but he turned to Lena. "Maybe I'll be able to play a duet with Baba Sofya someday."

"Of course you will," Lena said and put her arm around his shoulder.

Sofya dug through her music and found a copy of the piece which she placed on the music stand between the two of them. She could have just as well put the stand in front of Pavel since she knew the piece by heart. But it was just like her grandma to put Pavel at ease.

The two musicians began, Sofya playing the more complex part. Pavel faltered a few times with the fingering, but the short piece

wasn't difficult and they finished smoothly to a chorus of "*bravos*"
and "*urrahs*" from their enthusiastic audience.

When Lena woke the next morning, her grandmother wasn't on the
mattress. She heard a few faint sounds from the kitchen. Propping
herself on an elbow in the dark, she saw Pavel asleep on the mattress
they had dragged into the living room so he wouldn't freeze during
the night. The two smaller lumps on the other side were the children.
She lay back down for a moment, hugging herself, and then took off
her glove to check for the ring. Crawling over, she reached for her
fiancé under his blankets. "Hello, Private Pasha." She could barely see
his face in the darkness, but when he spoke she knew he was smiling.
"My beautiful love," he said, in a deep, rough voice, and pulled her to
him. She lay against him for a few brief minutes, tracing the scar on
his cheek and savoring the sensation of his body next to hers, even
through the layers.

Pavel had to be at the factory by eight, which meant he'd be leaving soon. Lena's stomach began to hurt and she could barely swallow
her water. Pavel's departure filled her with dread. She fidgeted, wanting him to have something substantial for breakfast.

"You need all of this, Lena. I get fed well enough. I can go one day
without much food." She burst into tears at his words, at the sound of
his steady voice. How would she manage without him now?

He held her and whispered soothingly into her hair. "Don't cry,
everything will be fine. We'll defeat the Germans soon, I'm sure of it.
You and I will be together before you know it."

She nodded into his chest, steeling herself to be without him.

THE REFUGEE ROAD

February 1942

THE OSINOVETSKOYE LIGHTHOUSE materialized on the grey horizon. Arriving with the small convoy of new trucks, Pavel hardly noticed the energy of the bustling lakeside. The astounding reality that Lena loved him and wanted to marry him was the only thing on his mind. That and the fact that sex most definitely wasn't a disappointment. He turned his truck into the parking area—a vast frozen field draped with camouflage—where it rocked along icy ruts until he guided it to a halt. Striding from his vehicle, heart full of swagger, Pavel dropped his bag in the barracks before heading for the mess hall where Captain Lagunov corralled the unit.

"Comrades, we have new orders," he said, ever to the point.

A collective groan rippled through the men. Pavel put his head in his hands. Oh, God. They were going to the front. He loved working on the Ice Road.

"Quiet down, we're not leaving Osinovets." He shook his head and waited until the men fell silent. "The Ice Road has changed. Our objectives change with it. Trucks will no longer cross empty. Evacuees from Leningrad will fill the vehicles. You'll take them to Kobona. From there, they'll be transported to safety. After the evacuees are unloaded, you'll pick up supplies as usual for the return trip. A true Road of Life."

Pavel heard some grumbling as the captain spoke. Handling human cargo would be more difficult, riskier too, than the driving they were used to.

"This will reduce the number of crossings each driver can make on any given day," the captain continued. "Evacuees will be loaded directly from Ladoga Station. Most of you will do both a morning and afternoon run. As the days get longer, we may add a third trip. No one," he said, looking directly at Pavel, "will make more than three crossings a day. The added time to transport civilians will make that impossible."

"Too bad for you, Chernov," came a mocking voice from the crowd.

Lagunov scowled in the heckler's direction, but continued. "So be ready, any day now. That's it. Dismissed." Finished, the captain turned away and started for the exit.

"No more showing off. Guess you won't be so fucking special anymore," said Mazarov, who'd given Pavel the scar on his cheek.

"Fuck you, you bunch of ignorant, lazy sons-of-bitches," Pavel challenged, unable to let it go. He was tired of taking shit from them.

His friend, Bogdan, a well-respected soldier, stood and spoke loud enough for everyone to hear. "Ignore them, Pavlik. If they weren't so busy putting their dicks up each other's asses they might be half the driver you are." The unit roared.

Mazarov and one of his lackeys were up and rushing toward him and Bogdan in an instant. Eyes fixed, the strong, stocky ringleader of the group barreled down the aisle like a freight train. Pavel had the advantage of height, but he wouldn't have more than one shot to use his longer reach. He'd lose if Mazarov got a hold of him.

Pavel timed his attack with two steps forward and threw the first serious punch of his life. Despite all the noise, guys yelling and shuffling about, he heard something crunch when his fist connected with Mazarov's face. He wasn't sure if it was the guy's nose or his own hand, which hurt like hell. Blood streamed as his tormentor went down. Bogdan had intercepted the second thug and now all four were being restrained by other men. The fight was over.

"That's enough," the captain yelled. The security detail materialized out of nowhere, looming behind Lagunov. "Stop acting like fucking idiots or I'll send the whole lot of you to the front." He put a hand up to stop the security detail from hauling them to the lockup. "You two," he said, pointing at Bogdan and the second thug. "Get your heads out of your asses. If I see any more of this you'll be in Schlisselberg so fast you won't have time to load your weapons before the fascists shoot. Understood?" The two men apologized and slunk away, happy to have escaped serious punishment.

Turning to the security detail, Lagunov continued. "Get Mazarov to the infirmary, and escort Chernov to my office."

Shit. Pavel was in deep trouble. Funny, even walking toward his punishment, he felt so good. He'd finally given Mazarov some of his own medicine.

"What the fuck is wrong with you, Chernov? Three thousand drivers here and my best one gets into a brawl. What were you thinking?"

"I wasn't thinking, sir." Pavel hung his head. "May I explain?"

Lagunov cut him off. "What the hell for? You think I don't know that Mazarov has been tormenting you—that he gave you that," the captain said, pointing at Pavel's cheek. "He's an asshole, so what? The world's full of assholes, now you're an asshole just like him."

"I had to defend myself, he was coming at me," Pavel said with just a bit of energy.

"Enough! What a load of shit. There are all kinds of idiots in the army, Chernov, and you need to find a better way to deal with them."

"Yes, sir." Pavel shoulders slumped. He waited for his punishment. Solitary? Reduced rations? His truck? Oh, shit. The captain wouldn't take away his truck, would he?

"Twenty-four hours solitary. When you get out, I expect a model, intelligent Soviet soldier to appear. The one I know is in there," he said, poking Pavel hard on the chest.

"Yes, sir. Absolutely. It won't happen again, sir."

"It better not. Next time I'll take your truck. Now get out."

Transporting the emaciated and dying residents of Leningrad was draining, emotional work. On the one hand, he was saving lives. But the evacuees represented the magnitude of the city's distress, and he couldn't help but feel sick at heart. The fragile, skeletal citizens climbed into the truck and found a place to sit. He warned them of the extreme cold and rough ride across. Still, they screamed when the truck bounced hard along the ice. His mother and grandmother and sister had been lucky. They'd gotten out while they still had some strength.

On one of his very first trips with evacuees, Pavel blew a tire part way across. Leaving his freezing human cargo, he set off for the next repair station, a half-kilometer or so ahead. Along the way, he stumbled across a frozen bundle—a dead baby. Unheated, open trucks, bouncing over rough terrain. Weak, starving passengers, barely able to hold on, much less grasp anything securely. The baby had probably flown out of the arms of its mother when their truck hit a bad spot. Pavel carried the bundle to the station.

When he returned that evening, he knocked on the captain's door.

"Comrade Captain, may I speak with you for a moment?"

The captain set down his pen and looked up. "I'm listening."

"Sir, I'm sure this will sound like an odd suggestion coming from someone who loves to drive as fast as possible across the lake, but the evacuees are extremely weak. They can barely hang on. When I stopped to get a tire repaired today, I found a frozen baby that must have flown out of the arms of its mother."

Lagunov let out a sigh, but otherwise remained silent.

"I think if we drove slower," Pavel continued, "we'd save some lives."

He looked at his commanding officer, bloodshot, glassy eyes, face haggard and drawn.

"Private Chernov, I appreciate the facts you're bringing to my attention, but what will happen if each truck slows by twenty or thirty minutes per crossing?"

"Well," Pavel paused. "I suppose that would mean fewer trips."

"And fewer trips would mean?"

"Yes, sir, I see. Fewer trips would mean fewer evacuees transported to safety."

"Exactly so. And which is better? The occasional death along the Road of Life, or more citizens starving in Leningrad?" He didn't wait for Pavel to answer. "You see, Private, innocents are going to die, are already dying. Our objective is that it's the fewest number possible."

MUSIC RESTORED
March 1942

THREE MONTHS HAD passed since Sofya last stood in the Radio House. It felt like three years. Faint light strained to illuminate the granite-floored lobby, like sun filtering through a dense forest. The expansive stone entry radiated cold, but she edged her stiff, icy scarf down and hurried to the notice board to scan the postings. Nothing new. Had she imagined the Radio Leningrad announcement?

The stairwell door creaked and Karl Eliasberg unfolded from behind it.

"Comrade Director. It's you." Sofya took several steps in his direction.

Squinting, the conductor of the Radio Orchestra removed his glasses, gazed at her, and then put them back on. "Comrade Karavayeva?" It sounded like half question, half answer to prayer.

He inched across the lobby, hunched like a strange, thin bird, his nose a beak and the skin on his face yellowed. As he got closer, his appearance shocked her. He'd obviously had little in the way of extra rations these last months. She thought of Mravinsky and the Leningrad Philharmonic, warm and well-fed in Tashkent, and felt strangely proud of Eliasberg. He hadn't abandoned them.

She nodded and smiled in response, instinctively thinking to kiss cheeks as one did with old friends, but as she moved close, a sharp, sour smell filled her nostrils. She stopped and stayed out of reach. The stink of his unwashed body and greasy hair was unmistakable, even bundled up in layers of clothing. He smelled of decay. Reflexively, she reached under her *ushanka* to touch the edge of the headscarf that covered her hair. She must stink too.

"Thank goodness you're here," he said. "I was beginning to fear almost none of the orchestra would return."

Normally reserved and distant, his warmth surprised her. "And you look well," he added.

"Well enough to play. Eager to play, in fact. Is it true? We're going to start rehearsals? I just heard the announcement and came to see for myself."

"Yes, it's true," he said, shuffling toward the notice board. "What a relief, eh? Help me with this. You can be the first to register."

Together they posted the announcement and Sofya penned her name at the top of the new list of available musicians.

"Do you know how our colleagues are doing?" There were some musicians living at the Radio House with Olga and the other journalists.

"I just came from telling them. Only seven. But I hope there are others like you, Sofya Nikolayevna. Of course, some have succumbed, a number evacuated. I'll be delighted if there are fifteen of the old guard at the first rehearsal."

Fifteen. Not enough to play much of anything.

"We'll find others to fill our ranks," he continued. "Perhaps some students. And the Party has made noises about Red Army musicians. In fact, I'm to plead my case at military headquarters. It'll be an interesting process, rebuilding the orchestra."

"No matter," Sofya enthused. "If anyone can do this, you can."

"About time, isn't it?" he said. "After all, what is Leningrad without music?"

He had begun creeping toward the door.

"Are you headed home, Comrade Director?" The conductor lived halfway to the Smolny. How would he make it that far? The streetcars still weren't operating.

"Yes, yes. And I must get going." He clucked his tongue. "Such a distance."

"Let me walk out with you." Sofya took his arm. All winter she'd waited for this news. Enthusiasm fluttered inside her, like a baby bird trying to launch itself out of its nest.

They chatted about other musicians as they held on to each other. Taking tiny steps, they minced carefully down the Nevsky and across the Fontanka where Sofya turned for home.

Alone, her steps quickened. Music was returning. She was going to play again. At home, she went straight for her violin. Joy rushed over her and she cradled the instrument in her lap like a baby, admiring it, touching it, seeing it as she had decades earlier when her parents first presented her with the expensive, glorious piece of magic.

The small, soft cloth still cushioned the scroll, and Sofya took it now. Her hands weren't the same strong musician's hands of several months ago. They objected as she cleaned the instrument, but she rubbed and wiped until all the bits of dirty white rosin yielded. After loosening the strings, she slid the cloth back and forth under the bridge. When the violin shone, all traces of dirt, smudges, and rosin gone, she tightened the strings, then tuned it by ear.

Standing, Sofya wedged it awkwardly at her chin. Her bulky, black coat with its substantial collar made for a strange, uncomfortable angle. Still, she drew the bow across the strings, her left hand struggling to keep up and find the correct positions, long fingernails getting in the way. She played a few simple scales and then the first notes of Vivaldi's Concerto for Violin in E Major. Her heart quivered at the forgotten beauty. Captured by the gorgeous strains, she closed her eyes as she played. This piece was part of her, its artistry as familiar as her name and address. After a few minutes, her heart flying with the birds of Vivaldi's spring, she became lightheaded. She stopped playing, sat, and listened to the rest of the piece in her head.

Her thoughts returned to Director Eliasberg. He looked so poorly.

Of course, no one was bathing. The *blokadniki*, the citizens inside the city, were fighting for survival—no one cared about appearances or if they smelled. Sofya rarely glanced at her own reflection, and hadn't taken a proper bath since November. The last month or two she couldn't even be bothered with the occasional sponge bath where'd she'd wipe her underarms and between her legs. It was a harsh punishment to take off one's clothes in such frigid temperatures.

Now she went down the hall. In the bathroom, she stared in the mirror. Her eyes were still bright and dark, but larger than she remembered. Harsh, sharp ridges rose above her sunken cheeks instead of smooth cheekbones. She hardly recognized the austere reflection.

Afraid to examine her hair, she told herself it couldn't be that bad. She and Yelena had celebrated the new year by building a large fire, warming plenty of water and washing each other's hair as they knelt over the empty bathtub. They combed and dried their locks sitting close to the stove, drinking vodka, toasting and talking about Pavel, Vasili, Aleksandr, and the Petrovs. They raised a glass to Katya too, imagining her behind German lines attacking the enemy from the rear, giving the Nazis hell. How long ago was that? Two months?

Sofya untied the scarf knotted at the nape of her neck, half-expecting her dark, wavy hair, salted with gray, to cascade out. Instead, she gasped as she unveiled an oily, matted skullcap of dull silver. She hurriedly put her scarf back on and then looked at her hands. Her fingernails were discolored, long and broken. Filth was embedded in the cuticles and under the nails. They looked like the hands of a beggar, not those of a violinist. She considered removing her clothes, but couldn't bear to see the horror that lay underneath—her shriveled flesh, bones protruding, dirt, dead skin, and sores on her body. Oh God, what she wouldn't give for a bath.

A RUSH TO THE GRAVE
March 1942

T HE CITY LIMPED toward spring. Sofya saw snow turning to slush as she walked Alyosha to school. It finally stayed light into the late afternoon. Soon there'd be buds on the trees. How astounding that the city's trees were still there. They hadn't been hacked apart by the desperate, freezing citizens. Peculiar too. People didn't cut down the city's gorgeous arbors to stay warm, but, in some cases at least, they ate each other to survive.

Sofya welcomed the energy of longer days. She was excited to be practicing again. But her granddaughter seemed not to notice the approaching end of winter. She struggled with everything. A trip for water would send her straight to bed. She ignored her firefighting duties. Sofya fed her extra food from their shrinking supply, but Yelena could not get enough sleep. To Sofya, activity was a key to survival—to move was to live. Yelena's crushing exhaustion meant *dystrofia* and death.

Sofya and Sasha walked Alyosha to school and when they returned, Yelena was still curled on the mattress in the living room. Sofya sat next to her.

"It's not normal to sleep so much, Lenochka. You need to see a doctor."

Yelena grunted. "There's nothing wrong. I'm just tired. Doctors are overwhelmed. I know you're worried, but really, I'm not giving up." Yelena rolled over and pulled the layer of blankets tighter.

"You've been there for twelve hours." Sofya waited for her to move.

"Okay, I'm getting up." She peeled off the blankets and peed in the back bedroom. Then she sat at the table, washing down a chunk of bread with cold water while Sasha chattered.

They dropped the child with a family they'd gotten to know back in September when they'd practically lived in the bomb shelter and continued toward the hospital. In the low winter light, discarded corpses along the Vladimirsky Cathedral made the sidewalk a deranged, grisly landscape. Sofya and Yelena moved to the empty street, averting their eyes. As they approached the hospital entrance, the two women stepped carefully, keeping clear as best they could, afraid of brushing against the dead. Entering the courtyard, they froze. Corpses stacked like so much cordwood rose as fortress walls on both sides. To enter the hospital, one had to use a narrow walkway in the shadow of those frightful fortifications.

"Oh, God." Sofya whispered. She pulled Yelena, eyes wide and frightened, guiding her back into the street where they could breathe. "I'm sorry. I never should have suggested this."

Yelena shook her head and stared at the ground.

Sofya looked around to see that they were alone. "The authorities better do something."

"And soon," Yelena said. "Spring is coming."

Not long after the aborted hospital trip, the first rumors of typhus spread. Worried about the risk of disease, Sofya gave up on getting her granddaughter to a doctor. She seemed to have more energy although Sofya imagined Yelena was pretending to feel better so she wouldn't worry.

This is Radio Leningrad, began the announcer one evening. Yelena moved toward the radio receiver, on the floor in a corner amidst broken boards and chunks of wood waiting to feed the stove. Sofya hurried to listen.

Citizens of Leningrad. Thanks to our heroic leadership and the efforts of those working the Road of Life, rations will increase again effective immediately. Yet we still face many difficulties. Spring will arrive in a matter of weeks and sanitary conditions must be restored. We are calling upon the citizens of Leningrad to do their part by cleaning the city of refuse. The ice and snow, waste and garbage, all must be removed.

Sofya and Yelena looked at each other, sharing the dark meaning of "waste and garbage."

The women of Leningrad will be at the vanguard of this effort, starting on the eighth of March, as a way of marking International Women's Day. Our glorious leader, Comrade Stalin, expects everyone in the city to help achieve our objectives.

Nothing is too difficult if we put our hearts and minds to the task. As a reward, everyone who participates will be granted entrance to the newly opened public baths.

As the announcer droned on, praising the Party and Stalin, admonishing and intimidating the population, Sofya turned to Yelena with a wry smile. "Not exactly what I was hoping for when I said the government needed to do something."

Yelena smirked. "Just like them to demand that the women clean the city on International Women's Day," she said. "Who's strong enough for that kind of work? We're in better shape than most and I'm not sure we can do it."

"Is there a choice?" Sofya said. "Besides, what about the *banya*? I'm willing to go out and shovel for that."

Yelena sighed. "You don't believe they're actually going to open the baths?"

"Maybe not, but if we don't clean the city, we might not survive."

❧

Leningrad was a carcass even the rats had quit. Courtyards and side-walks were filled with shattered buildings, frozen excrement and human bodies. Months of snow and ice covered the city. Small bands of women appeared that first day, working in slow motion. No one had much strength, but they did what they could: a few shovelfuls of snow and debris, chopping for a short time at a frozen pile with nothing more than a stick. A stream of lorries loaded the refuse and trundled off to dump the loads.

Sofya and Yelena set to work on a pile near their building. They removed layer after layer like an archeological dig: first snow and ice on top, then waste mixed with snow, then debris from a bombed building. When they uncovered a rigid, naked body with a thigh and buttocks hacked off, Yelena refused to touch it. Sofya got the driver of the truck, a woman not much younger than herself, and together they put the disfigured corpse in a wheelbarrow and moved it down the street to a designated collection spot for the dead. Special trucks loaded the corpses. Sofya always knew when one was passing by from the sharp smell of the disinfectant used to douse the bodies. It burned her nostrils and stung her eyes. Almost as soon as one truck left for the new cemetery at Piskaryovka, the next appeared.

Sofya watched Yelena carefully as they worked that first day, worried she was too weak for physical labor. Instead, after an hour or so, when Sofya had just about run out of energy, she noticed her granddaughter's rosy cheeks.

At home that evening, exhausted and distraught over the destruction and lack of humanity visible in the refuse, neither one could imagine doing it again.

"Let someone else," Yelena pressed. "It's too, too . . ."

"I know." Sofya took her granddaughter's hand, squeezing it in support.

Yet, the next morning, as they sat glumly and silently at the kitchen table, the rumble of trucks beginning the day's work spurred them. Yelena looked at her grandmother, who nodded and stood. "We should," she said.

The repetitive work made them sore and tired but every day they shoveled and chopped a bit longer than the day before. It became easier and easier to join the legion of emaciated women. By late March, tens of thousands attacked the city's frozen and filthy shroud before the weather warmed and finished what Hitler had started.

On their assigned day and time, Sofya and Yelena giggled like school-girls as they hurried to the *banya*. They'd discussed how they would stand in the big communal shower for an eternity, or as long as they were allowed anyway. Handing their vouchers to the attendant, they padded into the changing area. Sofya kept an eye on Yelena as they removed their clothes. First, her granddaughter's skinny legs and knobby knees appeared. Then, her sharp hipbones and flat stomach popped out. Her ribs looked like a shelf of sticks, although her breasts were still smooth and round. At least she hasn't lost everything, Sofya thought, looking down at her own flat chest. Yelena led the way to the shower and Sofya was ever so grateful there were no mirrors.

Relishing the warm water, a silken lover caressing her skin, Sofya couldn't recollect anything that had ever felt so wonderful. When she washed her hair though, small clumps rinsed away with the soap. She cried, silently, under the warm water, but then glanced at the drain and saw that everyone was losing hair. Other women were in much worse shape. Once pendulous breasts now hung like empty wineskins. Scurvy's purple splotches discolored most of the women. Sofya had a few spots on her legs and torso, but Yelena didn't have any. Thank goodness for all those jars of pickled vegetables.

After every inch had been scrubbed and soaped, crusts and dirt and scabs washed away, they sat in the sauna. The women smiled shyly at each other, taking stock of everyone's damage, but also simply glad and grateful finally to be clean.

The heat felt glorious. Closing her eyes, Sofya began to doze when the attendant pounded on the door urging the entire group to finish up. "There are others waiting for their turn, ladies." Basking in the pleasure of warmth and cleanliness, they tumbled out the door, naked, laughing, a gaggle of hollow-eyed, wasted women, not a Rubenesque shape among them.

THE SEVENTH SYMPHONY
March–April 1942

A S SOFYA FOUND her chair in the concert hall, the familiar energy of the orchestra ignited in her. They were going to play. She scanned the rows of chairs as other musicians took their places at that first rehearsal, nodding shyly at those she recognized. Skull-like faces peeked out under hats and behind layers of clothing. The scene was both wonderful and macabre.

A number of musicians were new, of course. The brass section—one trumpet, one trombone, one bass trombone, and one tuba—was entirely Red Army. The military musicians were in better shape than the *blokadniki,* but still thin and haggard. Sofya did a quick count: twenty-two. It was a start.

That first rehearsal of the reconstituted Radio Committee Orchestra lasted forty minutes, although they didn't play for more than ten. She smiled at Eliasberg when he dismissed them, thinking how strange it must be for him. More like conducting a secondary school band or a factory group instead of the only orchestra remaining in the greatest cultural center in the nation.

Afterwards, Gennadi, one of her closest colleagues, pecked her cheek. She felt him steady himself by holding her shoulders.

"It's good to see you," she said. "Isn't it wonderful to play again?"

Gennadi shrugged. "I can barely carry my oboe, much less play it. I'm sure Eliasberg meant me when he complained that none of the winds were playing. Truth is, I have no breath."

"But you will," Sofya said. "Just a few notes at a time. Now that we have more to eat, the canteen starting up again too, you'll feel better soon."

Rations had increased since the heart of that horrible winter and for the first time since September, Sofya found food in her neighborhood store. A few things, cooking oil, sugar, and grains, began to appear regularly. Their food supply was almost gone, but they would survive.

"I hope." He nodded. "At least I was able to walk here. At home I've been playing a few minutes every day, but today I couldn't manage a single note."

The orchestra's first performance came soon after that rehearsal. Like the other musicians, Sofya wore layers of clothing under her concert attire for warmth. Nothing fit, so she fastened pins to prevent an inopportune slip. They played Tchaikovsky—the polonaise from Eugene Onegin and other familiar pieces—to a packed hall. The enthusiastic clapping at the curtain, though muffled by the audience's gloves and mittens, still bathed her in a warm wave.

She soon learned that the revival of music in blockaded Leningrad was not just a springtime coincidence. News of the Kuibyshev premiere of Dimitri Shostakovich's Seventh Symphony, the Leningrad Symphony, reached the ragtag orchestra.

The first Moscow performance took place soon after, getting rave reviews. Word of the tribute to Leningrad spread. Sofya devoured the newspaper report about the concert. A quote from Shostakovich himself made her heart swell. "*To our fight against fascism. To our coming victory over the enemy. To my native city Leningrad. To these I dedicate my Seventh Symphony.*"

A copy of the score was smuggled out of the Soviet Union by plane via Tehran, setting up performances in London and New York—Carnegie Hall, no less. Audiences loved the Leningrad Symphony.

Sofya wondered if Shostakovich was surprised by the worldwide reaction. Not all that long ago, at least within the artistic community, it was believed he might disappear. Stalin had leveled such harsh criticism at him and his 1936 opera, *Lady Macbeth of Mtensk*, that everyone expected his arrest. It was a bit shocking that he was still around and still composing. How had he found a way to maintain an artistic existence in the new Soviet world? And instead of languishing in prison, or worse, here he was, having composed the Leningrad Symphony, now the toast of the entire nation, the toast of the world.

It was all the RadioCom musicians could talk about. The symphony was famous. The whole world knew about Leningrad, about Shostakovich, their own Dimitri. Leningrad's native son. After rehearsal one day, Sofya turned to Gennadi and said what they were all thinking. "Maybe the Leningrad Symphony will return to us, to Philharmonia Hall."

ROAD OF DEATH

April 1942

PAVEL COULDN'T BELIEVE his luck. He'd gotten another pass into Leningrad. Actually, it wasn't just him. Most drivers were getting a forty-eight-hour leave, divided into groups of several hundred at a time. The Ice Road was melting, and they'd be sitting on their heels for a while, waiting until the barges could get across. In fact, today was Pavel's last trip across the lake. In two days, he'd be with his sweetheart.

The day began like dozens of others on the Ice Road: breakfast in the mess hall at six, a quick conversation over the day's assignments, and a check that his truck was fueled and ready. The Road of Life was trying to save what was left of Leningrad. What had begun as a few hundred members of a construction battalion was now a massive undertaking of over thirty thousand workers and drivers. The initial barely visible single track in December became six lines of traffic, three in each direction—long, continuous columns of trucks. The Road of Life provided thousands of starving civilians a route of escape and enough food to save those who remained in the city.

In the last two months, Pavel's days of racing across the lake, dodging German bullets and making more trips than anyone else, had evaporated. Everyone worked in convoys now—some large and some, like today, just a few vehicles. Pavel's convoy was assigned the outside lane, the one most open and exposed. Most drivers preferred traveling on the other routes, hemmed in by huge icy berms created by the plows scrapping paths through the snow. Pavel guessed those walls of white made them feel secure. But he liked the freedom of this one last open route. How else could he dodge the Luftwaffe or avoid other trouble? It reminded him of the first month when routes were barely marked and drivers had to make lots of split-second decisions.

After loading the evacuees at Ladoga Station, the trucks headed out together. Pavel was third of four vehicles. Behind him was Mazarov, his nemesis. Since their fist fight, Pavel avoided him as much as possible. He knew Mazarov still had it in for him.

Although he warned the evacuees in the open truck bed that he would accelerate dramatically when they got onto the ice, Pavel still heard loud shrieks as he took the truck close to fifty kilometers per hour. The first eight kilometers were flat and fast. After that there were some rough sections.

The convoy slowed to a crawl navigating a crevasse, bumping and rocking over the logs lashed together as a bridge, then sped up again on the opposite side when all seemed clear. Suddenly, the lead truck veered off abruptly, while the second one lost control in water that had seeped up onto the ice. It spun around and back toward Pavel.

Taking his foot off the accelerator and turning to the right to avoid colliding with the second truck, Pavel shut out the chorus of screams as his wheels spit plumes of water. The fourth truck, following too close, either by accident or on purpose only Mazarov would ever know, clipped Pavel from behind, sending him spinning further out into the water field. Amidst the alarm and frenzy, the truck slid backwards on the water and weak ice underneath. Pavel fought to slow his vehicle and stop it from sliding further into danger. When it finally came to a halt, he drew a deep breath. Then he heard the gunfire-like retorts of ice giving way.

Cries of panic and hysteria rose from the back of the truck as it broke through. Thrown out of his seat, Pavel scrambled to find the door handle. He wrenched it open as the truck submerged, took a deep breath as the cab filled with icy water, and pushed himself free.

A heart-stopping, paralyzing cold gripped him as he kicked away. His truck and its flailing passengers disappeared below him into the black, icy depths. His head hit something. Realizing it was the frozen surface of the lake, he fought hard to stay up against the ice—boots and heavy coat weighing him down as he turned this way and that, groping for the opening. With only a few moments to escape the frigid water, he searched frantically, the intense cold tightening its grip, immobilizing and numbing him as he spun around. He reached for the icy surface a last time, but his hand found nothing to grasp.

THE ATTACKS INTENSIFY
April 1942

A DMIRAL VASILI ANTONOV came to consciousness. Blurry flecks of light floated through his field of vision. He closed his eyes, then opened them again, hoping he'd be able to see something. Slowly, he made out several windows, a large room. A shadowy figure moved closer, grew larger, leaned over him. He struggled to say something, but couldn't seem to make anything intelligible come out.

"Admiral, you're awake. Don't try to move," said the silhouette. "I'll get the doctor."

He must be in the naval hospital. He'd been here numerous times to check on his men, especially after the September attacks. One entire side of the square building had been destroyed.

What happened? How long had he been here? He began an inventory, starting with his legs and feet, arms and hands, but even the tiniest motion let loose waves of crippling pain. His left arm was immobilized. There were tubes on his face, attached to his right arm, on his chest. Everything hurt. Especially his head and his chest. Was he even breathing? The pain was an anvil, crushing him, refusing to let air in or out. He turned his head, then grunted from the searing flashes. *Bozhe moi.*

He lay still to stop the torment and took in his surroundings as best he could without moving. He saw rows of cots, but not much else. A sharp scent assaulted him—disinfectant? Something faintly fetid too. He sniffed. Perhaps it was just his own sour, damaged body.

He listened to the struggles around him, the ragged breaths

of the dying and seriously injured. A few scattered words rose up. A whimper or two of pain or distress. Then, a sudden cry for help, *pomogite mnye,* rang out from the far end of the room.

Wondering about his ship, the casualties, he closed his eyes and let himself drift. The next time he opened them, two figures stood at the foot of his bed.

"Comrade Admiral. It's good to see you awake," said a male voice.

The figures buzzed about, taking his vitals, poking, prodding. He winced at every touch.

"Do you know where you are?" The voice wore a white jacket.

"Kronstadt," Vasili said slowly. "The *Kirov.*"

"Yes, you were on the *Kirov.* Now you're in the naval hospital."

"Your name, Comrade Admiral?"

"Antonov, Vasili Maksimovich."

"And do you remember what month it is?"

He closed his eyes from the effort of remembering. "April," he said. "April 1942."

"Very good. What's the last thing you remember, sir?"

Vasili closed his eyes. Flashes of images came and went. The sounds of the ice, cracks and booms. Standing on the deck of the *Kirov* under swarms of fire-breathing birds. The sailors handling the guns, focused, almost serene as they performed their duties. The *Kirov* rocking.

"Under attack. The *Kirov,*" Vasili said.

"Yes. Excellent that you can recall. The *Kirov* was hit. You were injured in the attack."

"And my men?"

"I don't have much information, Admiral, no casualty lists by ship yet. Every bed is full, and then some."

Vasili wanted to respond, but rasps and wheezes came out instead.

"Nurse, let's give him some water."

A woman tilted a cup to his lips and he swallowed.

"Thank you," Vasili said, his words less hoarse. "My ship?"

"Still standing, sir," the doctor said. "I'll arrange for you to be briefed, perhaps in a couple of days. I'm certain your staff will be grateful to learn you're on the mend. You've been unconscious since the fourth of April. Today's the eighth. Your left side took the worst of it. Collarbone and five ribs broken, which required surgery. Your lung is healing well and your breathing has been gratifyingly clear." The doctor put on his stethoscope.

Unconscious for four days? Shit. His entire body felt broken. He could barely move, barely breathe, and everything hurt.

"Why don't I listen?" The doctor pulled back the sheet. Vasili looked down. Discoloration spread across his bandaged, battered chest, distorted from swelling. No wonder it hurt.

"Can you take a slightly bigger breath than normal? Not too deep." Vasili tried to breath in. Pain exploded in his chest and head. He grimaced, gripping the bed rails.

"Perfect. I don't hear much fluid. There's good air flow. It's going to be painful for a long while though."

Pain? This wasn't like any pain he'd ever felt. Hurts like a motherfucker.

As if reading his mind, the doctor said to the nurse. "Give him an additional dose of morphine when we've finished."

"We're most concerned about the head trauma," the doctor said, holding Vasili's eyes open and flashing a tiny light into them. "Regaining consciousness is the first major step in recovery. The brain is a tricky thing, it is hard to say if there will be any lasting effects. Now that you're awake, there's reason for optimism. Chances are good the damage isn't permanent. We often see a complete return to the pre-injury state, but not always. We'll know more in a week or so, but in any case, prepare for months of recovery."

Months? He had a ship to command. Responsibilities.

"You can see your left arm is immobilized." The doctor continued his examination. "Good news there, a straightforward compound fracture, about eight weeks to heal."

Good news? How could any of this be good news? And why was this white-coated youngster so damned cheery? Looking at him, Vasili suddenly understood the doctor thought he was lucky to be alive, to have regained consciousness at all, to have a future and his wits.

"Now that you're conscious, Comrade Admiral, our plan is for you to remain here a few weeks until we're certain of no complications or recurrence. As soon as you're able, we'll move you elsewhere to rest and recuperate long-term."

"Another hospital?"

"Well, sir, the hospitals in Leningrad have less space than we do, and probably more disease. I was thinking more along the lines of sending you home."

PAVEL
April 1942

B Y APRIL, THE melting snow and ice could not be denied. Sofya smelled the familiar mineral scent of spring. It wasn't just the soggy snow that told her things were improving. After dropping Alyosha at school one morning, she and irrepressible Sasha heard a surprising Radio Leningrad announcement—repairs to the water system were completed. Excited, holding hands, they rushed home to find Yelena and see if it was true.

"Lenochka. Have you heard?" Sofya stood in the slush on the roof, out of breath, but holding Sasha tight so she wouldn't wander near the edge. "They're saying water is restored. You know what that means?"

Yelena smiled. "Is that a trick question? It means we'll have water."

"Yes, yes, but it also means the toilet will work."

"Oh, my, that is news," Yelena said, getting to her feet.

The trio trooped down the stairs, thrilled at the prospect of no longer having to carry their waste out of the third-floor apartment. Sasha raced ahead into the tiny bathroom squealing, "Let me, Baba Sofya, let me."

"Ready?" Sofya said, smiling at the excited four-year-old. The toilet hesitated, then bubbled and the water drained.

Yelena reached for the sink faucet and carefully turned it. At first nothing, then a gurgle from deep in the pipes and it sputtered and spewed filthy brown water.

"Disgusting," she said. "Maybe we'll get water from the Fontanka for a while yet."

"Could just be sediment from the pipes," Sofya said. "I'll run the kitchen faucet too."

She put an arm around Yelena, brushing her cheek. Perhaps the worst was over. They had each other and these two children. They had survived the unimaginable winter and rations were increasing.

"Come on, Sasha, it's not raining," Yelena said. "Let's go get water now."

As the two girls went to the canal, Sofya turned on the kitchen faucet and retrieved a bar of soap that had been mostly unused all winter. Under the icy, discolored stream, she rubbed the soap between her palms, rinsing and lathering so many times that she felt like Lady Macbeth.

A short time later, on their way back into the building, Yelena checked to see if there was any mail. A brown package wrapped with twine lay against the wall. She set the bucket down and picked up the package. It was addressed to her.

"Ooooo. What's that?" Sasha grabbed at the package in Yelena's hands.

"Maybe it's from Pavel." Yelena's eyes lit up. "How about you carry it upstairs for me?"

Sasha snatched it with glee and skipped up the stairs. Yelena brought the buckets.

"Baba Sofya," Sasha called. "Look. Lena got a package from Pavel."

Sofya came over, examined the parcel, then quickly set it down, backing away.

"I wonder what it is," said Yelena, fingering the twine. "Handwriting looks different."

Yelena got scissors while Sofya gazed upwards, hoping, praying that goodies would come tumbling out and that the strange handwriting was simply someone in the postal service being helpful to a soldier.

"Sasha, come here." Sofya pulled the youngster away and put a finger to her lips.

Yelena cut the twine and pulled back the brown paper. A stack of letters revealed themselves. Her love letters to Pavel, neatly tied in a bundle. Eyebrows drawn together, she picked them up. A solitary letter, folded into a triangle with her name on it, fell off the top. No envelope because they were hard to come by, it looked like the letters Pavel always sent except for the unfamiliar handwriting. The soft plunk it made against the wood floor was loud and out-of-place in the suddenly quiet room. Sofya's sharp intake of air added a fearful whisper. Yelena stared down at the letter on the floor for a long moment, then picked it up and slowly unfolded it.

Dear Comrade Karavayeva,

It is with a heavy heart that I write to inform you of the death of your fiancé, Pavel Ivanovich Chernov, on the 5th of April. He drowned when his truck broke through the ice on Ladoga. Please accept my heartfelt condolences.

Private Chernov was a brilliant driver. The very best of thousands on the Road of Life. He was also an exemplary soldier and a man who, despite his youth, we all looked up to. He served our great leader, Comrade Stalin, and fought for our great nation and the people of Leningrad in the best of ways. I have been honored to have him in my unit.

I fear words will be of little comfort under the weight of this loss. Know that his sacrifice was not in vain. Private Chernov has sped us on the path of victory.

With deepest sympathy,
Captain Mikhail Grigorovich Lagunov

Slipping from Yelena's fingers, the letter fell to the floor a second time. Expressionless, she shuffled to the bedroom. After Sofya read the message herself, she followed and sat on the edge of the bed. Stroking her granddaughter's hair, she whispered, "Lenochka, oh Lenochka."

Not wanting to compound or complicate Yelena's anguish with her own sorrow, she tip-toed back to the kitchen. Sasha was sitting on the floor amidst the letters.

"Look, Baba Sofya. So many."

"Shhh, shhh, Sasha." She looked away to hide her tears while gathering the correspondence. "We need to keep our voices low. Yelena isn't well. Go get a book."

They settled on the sofa. Heartbroken for Yelena, Sofya could only read the same paragraph over and over. Couldn't she be spared this? Wasn't her darling Lenochka suffering enough? Her mother missing. No word from her papa. Pavel had brought her such light, such love and hope. Did Yelena have to lose everyone except her old *babushka*?

She strained to hear any sounds from her granddaughter. Eventually, she poked her head in the bedroom. "Lenochka?" No answer. Sofya moved to the bed. "We're headed for rations, and then we'll collect Alyosha from school. We'll be home after that."

That evening Sofya left Yelena alone. She offered her dinner, checked on her once or twice, then sat with the children to explain what had happened to Pavel. Sofya and Sasha slept together in the small bedroom with Alyosha on the sofa to give Yelena some privacy. She still hadn't spoken a word, but at least Sofya heard her flush the toilet that night.

The next day, when Sofya returned with Sasha after taking Alyosha to school, she found Yelena still curled in bed.

"*Malenka*, have you had anything to eat or drink?"

Yelena didn't respond. Sofya returned to the living room, settled Sasha with a snack, then brought tea and bread to Yelena, placing both on the night stand. She sat next to her granddaughter and leaned down, hugging her as best she could with her own small, frail body.

"You must eat something. You're already weak and dehydrated. Sit up, Lenochka."

Yelena lifted her gray face out of the pillow. Her eyelids were puffy; her eyes red and dull. "My life is over. I can't live without him. He's everything, my future, my hopes. Just leave me." She dropped back onto the pillow. "It hurts too much. I just want my Pasha."

Overcome with her granddaughter's pain, Sofya wept. After a minute or two, she collected herself and took a deep breath.

"Oh, my love. Do you think that's what Pavel would want? For his generous, loving fiancée to give up?" She paused, letting her words sink in. "Don't you think that maybe, just maybe, he would rather you live life for him, as well as yourself?"

Yelena's body trembled then. It convulsed as wave after wave of sobs rose from someplace deep. Loud, grief-soaked cries and desperate wails filled the apartment. Pleas and entreaties came out with the anger and pain and despair. She pounded her fists into the mattress until she collapsed, exhausted. Sofya held her as the howls became cries and the cries became whimpers. Then she got a warm cloth to wipe Yelena's face and helped her drink the cool tea.

"I would give anything to change what happened or to make this easier, but wishing for impossible things is futile. You'll never get over losing Pavel. Your life will be different, but as time passes it will hurt less. I can promise you that. You'll find reasons to carry on and you'll learn how to keep living. It's terrible that Pavel won't have a full, long life, a life filled with years of love and joy." Sofya paused. "But you can have that kind of life, in fact, you really must live that kind of life. By doing so, by valuing your life, you'll honor him and his sacrifice."

Sasha had crept into the room. As Sofya stood up, the youngster tip-toed to the other side of the bed and clambered in. She cuddled Lena, stroking her hair and patting her, repeating over and over, "Shhh, *malenka*. I'm here. It will be all right."

INTERLUDE
May–June 1942

ONE CALM MAY morning with two orderlies as medical escorts, Vasili rode a fast Tupelov torpedo boat for home. They raced across the Gulf for the relative safety of Leningrad's barrage balloons and anti-aircraft artillery. Drawing close to the city he spotted the sad shipbuilding facilities. One pier tipped into the water at a precarious angle, a half-submerged wreckage of concrete. Pieces of a steel crane stuck out of the depths like an enormous, exotic water bird. Grimy ruins of facilities and factories ran along the edge of the port, encircling it like a black eye.

The boat slowed entering the Neva River and Vasili felt a strange sense of relief as they cruised past the damaged buildings on Vasilevsky Island. Gray, broken, and forlorn, yet the city was still there. He had imagined the bombings, the struggle for food. Now he would actually see what had become of his home.

St Isaac's grey dome appeared on his right, hulking over the city. The Bronze Horseman, still buried under scaffolding and sand bags, stood next to the Admiralty. He thought wistfully of his teaching days, the endless, tedious classes he'd been all too anxious to escape. He could see the cadets in his mind, those rows of young, brave lads who'd died last August, giving the Soviet Baltic Fleet time enough to escape Tallinn.

They passed the Winter Palace, battered but still elegant along the right embankment of the river. Opposite, the stone Peter and Paul Fortress lay low and graceful. They docked by the Summer Garden where the orderlies half-carried him off the boat. They held him strongly, and the three moved carefully to catch a streetcar. Vasili felt another glimmer of relief that the city had electricity sufficient to power transportation.

"Why not disembark at the Winter Palace and take a *tramvai* down the Nevsky?" he asked.

"Orders, Comrade Admiral. Nevsky's dangerous. Artillery attacks on the rise. Streetcar stops are vulnerable."

Vasili nodded. Of course, the Germans targeted places where people gathered. His stomach tightened. Sofya spent most of her working hours along the Nevsky: rehearsals, performances, walking back and forth to her apartment.

At Fontanka Embankment 54, Vasili climbed the stairs in slow motion, the powerful aides helping him up every step. As he stopped to catch his breath, Sofya materialized at the top of the stairs. Tiny and thin, her face was all sharp angles and edges. She'd mentioned in a letter that Yelena cut her hair short after it turned silver, but still, it was a striking change. It had been eight months since he'd seen her and it seemed she'd changed more than in all their earlier decades of separation. His dear sweet love. How she must have suffered. He tightened his clumsy grip on the railing and then saw her eyes flash with warmth. The same dark pools. He managed a faint grin.

"Oh, Vasya. You're home."

A lovely hitch of emotion in her voice drew him up the last few steps. "I'm sorry it took so long," he said, pulling her into a one-armed embrace while the orderlies looked away. He had sent a telegram weeks earlier, saying he'd be home soon to recuperate, but the ice took forever to melt and he was stranded at the naval hospital on Kronstadt for longer than expected.

"Many things outside your control," she smiled and kissed him. "You aren't too shocked? My hair?"

"It's, it's . . ." He searched for the right words. "Actually, it's kind of cute." He ran his fingers through the elfin haircut.

Sofya smiled. "You're a terrible liar."

"No, no. I mean it, Sofi. It suits you. Fashionable in a revolutionary sort of way." He winked to convey the inside joke. No-nonsense hairstyles had been popular with the Bolsheviks.

Glancing at the aides, she reached for his bag while they helped him down the hall and into the apartment. He thanked and dismissed them, then rested along the wall and pressed his good hand against his head.

"Admiral Vasili," Yelena said, coming to greet him. "Welcome home."

"Yelena. Words aren't sufficient." He pulled her close with his good arm, feeling her bones through her clothing. She was nearly as thin as Sofya. Now that he was here, they could use his access to special stores.

She rested her head on his shoulder and shook with quiet sobs. He didn't know what to say, so simply held her and whispered "Shhhh," over and over into her hair.

"And this must be Sasha," Vasili said.

The little ball of energy bounced close, brushing his leg, and Yelena grabbed Sasha's hand, pulling her back a couple of steps. "Be careful, Sasha," Yelena snapped. "Admiral Vasili has been in the hospital."

"I'm not hurting him," said Sasha. "He's a brave soldier. Like Pavel."

She dropped the child's hand with a whimper and hurried to the bedroom. Sasha's eyes filled and her chin trembled.

"It's okay, Sasha," Vasili patted the little girl. "Yelena's just worried about Pavel."

She blubbered.

"Oh, Vasya, there's terrible news," Sofya whispered. "Pavel died last month." She wiped the youngster's tears. "Go get one of your books, Sashenka. I'll meet you in the kitchen."

Sasha sniffed and obeyed, disappearing down the hall.

Vasili sat on the sofa, cradling his head as Sofya gathered pillows. Another good, brave young man gone.

"His truck broke through," she said. "Yelena's devastated."

Vasili moved to stand again. "Can you help me, Darling?"

They shuffled to the bedroom and he tapped on the door. "Lenochka? Can I come in?"

Curled in bed, Yelena unfolded and sat up.

"I didn't know," he said. "I'm so sorry. I know you loved each other, and I know he was a good man."

He glanced at Sofya. She was clenching her jaw and a single tear rolled down her cheek. Watching a grandchild suffer was a cruel pain. It made him think of his fatherless grandchildren.

Yelena dabbed at her eyes. "Well, it seems there's pain enough for everyone these days. You've had your own terrible loss. Grandma told me. I'm sorry about your son."

It was the only time he'd used the military pouch to get a letter to Sofya. Back in January, he had no idea how long it would be before they'd see each other. He couldn't keep the news to himself.

Yelena sniffed. "Sasha didn't mean anything by mentioning Pavel. It's just so hard." Her eyes filled again. "The life I wanted, the one I thought I'd have."

Vasili gripped the bedpost for support.

"You're exhausted from the trip, Vasya," Sofya said. "You must rest. Doctor's orders."

He nodded and squeezed Yelena's arm before leaving the room. Sofya helped him to the sofa. One corner of his mouth turned up and then he was asleep.

After several days of rest when he did little more than read to the children, Vasili felt some strength returning. Soon, he began helping

Alyosha with his lessons, sitting at the kitchen table with the youngster. They played chess too. Alyosha, whose voracious appetite for
the game had stunted the entire family's enthusiasm, was energized
by fresh competition. The boy went straight for the chessboard the
moment he got home from school.

"Grandpa, Grandpa, are you ready to play?" He'd call out,
coming through the door.

"I never get to play," whined Sasha.

"Now, now, Sashenka," cooed Yelena. "You'll get a turn."

"But when Alyosha's finished, it'll be dinner, and after dinner,
Baba Sofya likes to read with Dedka. Then it's bed."

"Come here, *malenka*." Vasili pulled her into a half-hug. "I've
been thinking about something for you and I to do, just the two of
us."

Her eyes brightened.

"I need help with my daily walks. You would be the very best
helper."

She was grinning. "Tomorrow?"

"Yes, tomorrow." He kissed the top of her head as she wriggled
away.

"I'm Grandpa's special helper," she sang out, bouncing from
room to room.

Sasha's sunny nature helped him process what he saw around
Leningrad. Everywhere he walked, buildings had been leveled. Many
of those still standing had windows blown out, some boarded up with
plywood and others open to the elements. And he hadn't even been
along the Stachek or near Badayev where entire blocks were flattened.
When the wind blew, which was more often than not, dirt and dust
from destroyed buildings swirled up and filled his nostrils with the
smell of pulverized brick and concrete. Sometimes the dust collected
in the back of his throat and he choked on the harsh taste. Even so,
he wandered the city.

Gostiny Dvor, Leningrad's main shopping center, was a blackened ruin. A gigantic hole in the Kirov Theater gaped. While Sasha threw pebbles into the canal, he thought of the opera and ballet performances he'd attended there. How he'd dragged Maksim even though the boy hated opera. Oh, my son.

Several times a week he and Sasha stopped at one of the special government stores. The little girl squealed with joy, eyes wide at the selection. His access meant Sofya, Yelena, and the children had enough to eat. Food seemed miraculous to them and their delight in the most ordinary things weighed on his spirit rather than lifted him. They had suffered so much.

This was what he'd been fighting for: his family, these streets, this city. He wondered about the deaths in Leningrad. The city felt small and deserted. Reports from around the Soviet Union were grim. The military was hemorrhaging, casualties already in the millions. It made his stack of condolence letters seem insignificant.

"Writing these doesn't feel like enough, Sofi." He sat at the kitchen table one afternoon, fulfilling his duty as the commander of the *Kirov*. Giving families the dreadful news that they'd lost a loved one. "I need to pay my respects."

"I understand," Sofya agreed. "It's important to express our gratitude for the sacrifices. The army's burying the dead near Piskaryovka Station."

All they had to do was follow the parade of corpse-filled trucks.

"Are you sure you don't want to wait at the station for me?" Vasili asked. "You've already seen so many terrible things."

"I don't want you going alone," Sofya said. "And I'd like to know where everyone's being laid to rest."

Mostly walled-off from the street, it wasn't even an official cemetery yet. They walked through the broad opening, wide enough to handle truck traffic as well as heavier earth-moving equipment.

Guards approached, but backed away when they saw the gold braid. Vasili removed his hat and nodded at them.

On either side of a wide dirt path stood rows of raised rectangular mounds. None were marked, but the ones nearest the entrance had been leveled and groomed. Sofya could imagine the emerald grass, bright and full of life, which would someday sprout on their flat brown surfaces. A strange contrast to the decaying bodies entombed underneath, forever lost in an uneasy sleep. They stood together at several of the mass graves, offering silent entreaties.

Vasili counted the mounds as they walked up and down the rows. The sharp smells of turpentine and decay filled the air as trucks rumbled past, kicking up dust. Sofya pulled out a scarf and pressed it against her nose and mouth. They followed the vehicles down one side where the graves were not yet groomed, but simple brown hills of dirt. A bit further on, open rectangular trenches gaped, waiting to receive the city's offerings. They stood silent, while trucks pulled up one after the other, and the corpses—some naked, some clothed, some swaddled—were laid in rows in the deep pits. The putrescence of rotting flesh filled their nostrils, along with whiffs of spoiled cabbage, feces, and sulfer. Those handling the bodies wore gas masks, making an already surreal landscape even more so. Vasili found himself trying not to breathe.

"Wait over there a moment," he said. "I want to ask that officer something."

Sofya stepped away from the trenches while Vasili approached the officer in charge. After a short conversation, he returned and took her arm and they retreated to the entrance, away from the stench of death.

"The officer said the corpses are separated by military and civilian, and generally organized by when they died. Eventually, every mound will be marked, but no names. Each one has thousands of bodies. There are already almost a hundred trenches. Hundreds of thousands of dead. And this isn't the only place in the city where victims are buried." The wind swirled grime around them as they stood, heads bowed.

Wordlessly, they returned to the station and huddled on the platform. They rode the slow-moving train through Leningrad's suburbs together but alone. Sofya wept silently. Vasili pulled her close, knowing her heart was breaking for the nameless thousands, entire families starved to death. So many lives lost: Leningrad's innocent civilians, men on the *Kirov*, his naval cadets in Tallinn, Maksim.

The war began a year ago. He shuddered at the thought of another year, or more.

They did regular things during his convalescence—waited in lines, read books, walked, ate meals together. He and Sofya shared the large bedroom, while Lena and Sasha slept on the single beds in the smaller one. Alyosha announced he was too old to sleep with girls, so he slept on a pile of blankets in a corner of the living room. It was Vasili's first taste of family life in many years. To hear children laughing worked a special kind of magic and he felt himself slip into the role of family patriarch.

Spending time with Yelena was a special source of joy. He and Sofya worried that having him around, alive and well, would make her grieve all the more. At first, evenings seemed particularly difficult. The natural melancholy of day's end, the sun starting to dip, the light growing dim, often sent Yelena escaping to the bedroom or the rooftop to be alone. Sometimes they heard her crying.

More and more though, there were evenings when Yelena and Vasili sat together on the sofa. They'd lean close, talking in low tones, watching the city's rooftops out the window in silence, enjoying the glow of the long evening sky. A bit at a time, her hard shell of sadness began to soften. Her energy and appetite improved too, and pretty soon Vasili and Sofya joked how she was eating them out of house and home, just like Aleksandr and Maksim had done at her age. They thought nothing of it until Sofya accidentally walked in on Yelena in the bathroom, catching sight of her newly rounded belly.

The news didn't much surprise Vasili. When Sofya mentioned Pavel had used protection, he laughed. "Those old condoms the army hands out? I'd imagine they're not terribly reliable. Besides, inexperienced young men with a powerful sense of urgency? Fair to presume the failure rate is high."

ᴖ ᴖ

They lay in bed cuddled against each other. Sofya's secret burned. It was past time to tell Vasili.

"It's wonderful how close you and Yelena have become," Sofya said. She kept hoping he would figure it out himself. "She's drawn to you. You're a big part of the reason she's doing so well. She's not as depressed. Crying less, too. Having a father figure around has given her something to hang onto. You're an anchor for her."

"Being around her has been wonderful for me. I miss . . . ."

She squeezed his hand.

"It doesn't seem real," he said. "Feels like once the war is over, Maksim will be back. I never got to say goodbye. And my grandchildren. They must be suffering. Yulia too."

She'd planned their conversation, but now it again seemed like the wrong time. Maksim's death complicated things. Finding out Aleksandr was his son would not help Vasili with his grief.

They lay together in silence. A few minutes later he kissed her head. "You know I'd do anything for Yelena."

He pulled her against him, tucking his good arm around her. She buried her face in his chest and let the moment pass. She couldn't bring herself to tell him while Maksim's death was so fresh in his mind.

He lifted her chin and kissed her. Gently at first, and then deeper, with desire and gravity. He tried to pull off her nightdress, but she resisted.

"I know how thin you've become, Darling." His fingers traced her ribcage. "You mustn't think it matters. I love *you*, and besides, you may be skinny, but you're still beautiful."

She snuggled tighter against him. "I hardly recognize myself."

"We can put out the light if that will help." He chuckled and pulled back, looking at her slyly. "I can even promise not to look."

She laughed out loud. "Can I trust you? What'll happen if I catch you peeking?"

"Well, I don't know, perhaps I'll let you have your way with me." They both laughed. "Besides, I'm busy trying to figure out how to manage with only one good arm."

She pulled her nightdress over her head and lay on top of him. Light as a bird, she nestled into his scarred chest, careful not to put pressure on his left side. He ran his good hand over her back, bumping along her spine, stroking every inch of her diminished frame, the body he knew and loved, more than any other, more than his own. They made love gently, carefully, fearful of hurting each other. Afterwards, they curled together, grateful and content.

Some minutes passed before Sofya spoke. "Are you tired?"

"Did I seem tired to you?"

"You're such a tease." She slipped out of bed. "We should have a toast."

She pulled the empty shelves out and pressed the hinge to the hiding place. Reaching inside, she removed a box with a royal blue velvet exterior. Vasili inhaled. Decades earlier they'd toasted each other with the gorgeous glasses inside. When the Revolution came, he should have destroyed them. It was risky to keep the stunning, gold-etched crystal.

"I never could get rid of them," he said. "They reminded me of you."

She retrieved a bottle of vodka from the kitchen. Sitting on the bed she reached into the box's satin lining.

"How did you find them?" he asked.

"I know I told you there was nothing left of your apartment. Really there was nothing but rubble and this box near the surface."

The Romanov medallions glittered in the lamplight.

ODE TO LENINGRAD

Summer 1942

NOT LONG AFTER Vasili returned to Kronstadt, Shostakovich's Seventh Symphony—now known as the Leningrad Symphony—was smuggled by plane into the still-blockaded city. Sofya and the rest of the orchestra settled into their seats for an ordinary rehearsal and Eliasberg rapped his baton. The director gleamed with excitement.

"Comrades," he said. "After inspiring audiences all over the world, Shostakovich's tribute to our valiant city has come home." A low murmur spread through the musicians. Eliasberg raised a thick folder, hands trembling, eyes glistening. "I hold in my hands the first movement of Shostakovich's Leningrad Symphony," he said, lifting it toward the orchestra.

Cheers rose from the stage, the musicians yelling their own enthusiastic battle cries. Emotion rising in her throat, Sofya held her bow aloft, waving it and croaking "*Urrah! Urrah!*" along with the rest of them.

No ordinary forty-member orchestra would do for Shostakovich's masterpiece. Director Eliasberg demanded long, frequent rehearsals with little small talk or socializing. He led by example, never using his weakened state as an excuse for offering anything but his best. His devotion was compelling and contagious. The new musicians brought in from military bands or recruited off the streets of Leningrad were led by the small, ravaged old guard. Novices and masters, young and old, together they formed Eliasberg's private army.

In addition to rehearsals, the score had to be reproduced.

Eliasberg had but a single copy and every musician needed his or her part. Within a couple of days, the director arranged for them to use the empty canteen after rehearsals. They took turns, spread out at the long narrow tables, heads bowed in concentration as they painstakingly copied their parts, the occasional question or explanation by Eliasberg the only accompaniment to the scratching of their pens.

The intense focus suited Sofya. It gave her less time for worry. Despite evidence that Leningrad had pulled out of its death spiral, life in the city remained dangerous. Rations climbed and civilians died more slowly, yet for every life saved from starvation, another fell victim to the Nazi's vicious onslaught of air and artillery attacks. Commonplace things that were a little risky early in the war—standing in line for bread, waiting for a streetcar—became serious opportunities for death. The whistling of incoming shells sent the scarecrow civilians scurrying for cover. Sofya feared for Yelena, less agile as her belly grew.

The day of the concert dawned grey and overcast. Sofya paced the apartment, agitated and on edge. When her nerves refused to calm, she left for the concert hall. Yelena and the children stood by the door as Sofya hugged them, a little choir of well-wishers. She pecked her granddaughter's cheek. "I'll see you after the concert. Be sure to come backstage."

Strolling toward central Leningrad, concert attire in one hand, violin case in the other, Sofya sensed an energy long missing from the city. The once grand Nevsky, pockmarked and war-torn, radiated some of its old hum. The House of Books in the Singer Building had reopened and it seemed other businesses were following suit. People came and went in a way they hadn't since the siege began.

Nearing the main entrance, she found an enormous throng of shriveled citizens clamoring for tickets to the one and only performance of the Leningrad Symphony. People had converged as if train tickets to Tashkent or Irkutsk were for sale. Even for Leningrad, it was a shocking crowd. Sofya watched the citizens from a distance, proud, but nervous too.

Many of her colleagues also arrived far ahead of the four o'clock call-time. Spirits were high as they congregated in the canteen. After the late lunch, Sofya took her violin to a small rehearsal room. She played a few sections of the symphony to calm herself. The performance would be a trial. There were challenging sections for the novices to be sure, but Sofya's main fear was that none of them had the strength to play for as long as the symphony required. After a short review, she made her way to the women's wardrobe room. The only other woman in the orchestra was a young clarinetist, dressing when Sofya entered.

"Hello, Galya. Ready?"

"Not exactly, but what choice is there?" The young woman chuckled. "It would be weeks before I'd feel prepared." Her eyes flashed with humor and anxiety. "I don't want to let anyone down."

"No possibility of that," Sofya said. "You've helped make the performance possible."

Galya looked down. "That's kind of you. Playing with musicians like yourself, is—"

"Instructive?" Sofya smiled.

"Intimidating would be more accurate. Or maybe inspirational. I never imagined I'd be performing such a symphony, at such an important moment when I answered the call for musicians." Galya sighed again. "I'm not experienced enough."

"Now, hold on. You may not have much experience, but you play very well. You should be proud. You're quite talented."

"Thank you. It means a lot coming from you." She motioned to the dress she was struggling into. "Could you do this for me?"

As Sofya zipped the simple black fabric, she couldn't help but notice the young woman's shoulder blades sticking out like the beginnings of angel wings.

At five-thirty, the musicians made their way onto the stage. Sofya watched her cadaverous colleagues hobble to their seats. Loose, sack-like clothes covered the most obvious damage. Still hidden from the audience, she listened to the hum of people finding their seats behind the heavy, gold-fringed curtains. She made her final adjustments, moving her music stand a fraction, thumbing through the pages to check that they were in order, then placing a cushion on the hard chair. The natural padding of her behind had been one of the first things to go.

At fifteen minutes before six, the curtain rose. Sofya rarely looked at the audience, but this time she did, unsuccessfully search-ing for Yelena. She glimpsed the boxes filled with government offi-cials. Then Gennadi played an A, and the rest of the orchestra tuned their instruments in that lovely hodgepodge of sound that always calmed her before a concert. As the notes died away, she heard the thud-boom of artillery fire and froze, ears straining for the whine of incoming shells and air raid sirens.

Philharmonia Hall was lit like a midsummer party. Eliasberg had told them that the authorities wanted the concert hall to shine like a beacon. In the next moment, swamped by his ill-fitting coat and tails, the conductor shuffled out to a generous applause and deci-sively ignored the artillery fire. Sofya realized the guns must be their own and she felt a rush of pride.

The audience fell silent as Eliasberg looked out over the impres-sive bank of microphones, ready to broadcast the symphony to the war-weary world. "Comrades, in a few minutes you will hear, for the first time, the Seventh Symphony of Dimitri Shostakovich, our out-standing fellow citizen. Europe believed that the days of Leningrad were over, but this performance is witness to our spirit and cour-age. Listen!" As he turned to the orchestra, Sofya cast a glance heavenward. It was a holy moment, and she felt God with her. God finally with Leningrad.

Throughout the city people stopped what they were doing and gathered around loudspeakers in apartment buildings, factories, and on the streets. Soldiers defending the city huddled around radio receivers specially organized for the event. Speakers had even been set up along the front lines, to broadcast the music toward the enemy, so the Germans would know Leningrad could not be vanquished.

The city's experience was laid bare in the music: the enemy hurtling toward Leningrad and the people's resistance. The German attack, the lyrical history and hope of Russia, unbearable sadness, and finally, the bitter victory.

Towards the end, Sofya felt nothing but her hands on the violin and bow, saw nothing but Eliasberg directing, the notes long memorized. She played with complete absorption, as if not for a typical audience, but for the ears of God. The music was in her, and she was in the music. They raced toward the end, toward survival, toward victory, and there it was, the last strains fading.

Sofya watched Eliasberg bow his head and grip the rostrum with both hands, steadying himself. A few colleagues seemed near collapse, their exhaustion adding to the emotion. Seconds of silence, punctuated by sniffing, settled over the auditorium. And then, the audience—no longer weak, no longer dispirited—rose to its feet. A thunderous applause filled with cheers and cries rose, over and over, to its own magnificent crescendo.

THE PROPOSAL

August 1942

T HE AUDIENCE REACTED as if they'd never heard anything so brilliant and so moving. Sofya knew better, but that didn't change the fact that the applause and cheers went on forever, everyone crying and hugging like the war was over.

Afterwards, the musicians congregated backstage for their own celebration. In the midst of the rich food and vodka, the congratulations and misty eyes, Sofya realized she didn't want it to end. It felt so good to get a bit drunk, to laugh with her colleagues. When had she last known the freedom that came with success, laughter, and vodka? When had there last been something to celebrate?

Deep in her pillow the next morning, the first few knocks were shadows in her dreams. She stumbled out of bed and grabbed her dressing gown, then leaned against the wall, stomach and head pitching every which way. The apartment was silent, save for another round of gentle but persistent tapping.

Relaxed in his combat uniform, fatigues tucked into black boots, Vasili beamed at her when she opened the door. His eyes flashed that bright blue and he opened his arms.

"I'm sorry, Sofi. I've surprised you."

"This early in the morning, I thought, well, you know." She pursed her lips.

"No need to worry," he said. "I forgot my key is all. My trip was very last minute."

She pulled him into the kitchen. "Sit, Sweetheart, I'll make coffee. We can have breakfast." The thought of food made her queasy. She hurried to the bathroom and rubbed cold water on her face in an attempt to wash away the puffiness, headache, and nausea. After combing her hair and brushing her teeth, she rejoined Vasili.

"I'm hungry, Baba Sofya." "Me too!" The children sped down the hall to the kitchen. When they saw Vasili at the table, Sasha jumped into his lap and Alyosha gripped his arm. "Grandpa Vasili! Where have you been? Can we play chess?" Sasha turned to Sofya and exclaimed, "Look Baba Sofya, it's your Vasili!"

Hugging both children, he explained. "I'm only here for a few hours, *detki*. No time for fun, I'm afraid. Just a hug and a kiss, some breakfast, and then I have to go." He turned to Sofya. "I have a noon meeting at the Smolny, then back to the *Kirov*. Let's eat and walk. The next few hours are yours. I want to hear about last night."

Hand in hand, they strolled along the Fontanka. The summer sun was bright in the near cloudless sky and the river glistened like it was sprinkled with jewels. With plenty of black coffee and fresh air, Sofya's hangover subsided.

"Did you hear the concert?" she asked. "Not that our playing was remarkable, but I so wish you'd been there. I wanted to share it with you."

"Well, you did, in a way," he said with a mischievous grin. "Who do you think was protecting you last night?"

"The artillery?" she said. "That was the *Kirov*?"

"Anything for you, my love. Turns out a lot was riding on the performance, orders from the top. We pounded the Germans so they couldn't fire a shot. Our protection was so successful that I was called to a briefing this afternoon. Finally, they're pleased with the Baltic Fleet."

"When it suits their purposes. Now I understand why they gave the orchestra bigger rations too. The higher-ups and their political objectives." She wrinkled her nose like something smelled bad. "Well,

I'm not going to let that diminish our success. Whatever the Party's purposes, I'm proud of the orchestra."

"As you should be." He leaned down and kissed her.

She rested her head against him for a moment. "Of course, it wasn't polished like before the war, but it was more emotional, more meaningful somehow because it was performed by those who've suffered. It may have lacked precision, yet I think Shostakovich himself would have been pleased."

He had an arm around her as they walked. "Everyone's saying it was brilliant, I can't wait to hear it. It was broadcast all over the lines. What a boost for morale."

"I hope so. It sure seemed that way." She leaned into him. "Thanks for the protection."

As they wandered the Tauride Gardens and then the grounds between the Smolny Cathedral and the Smolny Institute housing Leningrad's Military Command, Sofya grew uneasy. She was so happy to see Vasili, to share the previous night's victory, yet her secret rose inside her like disgusting bile.

Alone, they sat on a bench overlooking the Neva. Normally, Vasili wasn't very affectionate in public. He had the cool, stern exterior of a naval officer. Today he was different though, holding her hand, his arm around her, unafraid of showing his attachment.

"Is everything all right?" she said, knowing she was the one who was out of sorts.

"Absolutely, Darling. I'm so grateful to see you. These last weeks have been difficult. I've been worried. Even more than last winter, if that's possible." He gazed at her, touching her cheek. "I love you."

"I love you too," she said. "More than I ever have." She glanced down, summoning the courage to tell him, when he interrupted her.

"You know, there's only one thing that could make me happier than I am at this very moment." His eyes gleamed and he took her hands. "Marry me."

"Marry you?"

One side of his mouth turned up and his eyes twinkled. "Is it really a surprise?"

"No," she shook her head. "Of course I've thought of it, dreamt of it, many times. Thinking of you and our future got me through the worst. I . . . I just didn't think it would happen."

"And yet, here we are," he said. "Perhaps it'll be a long time before the war is over, still, I feel a change for the better. It's time to do more than dream."

She smiled shyly. "Of course I'll marry you. I've always wanted to marry you, my whole life it seems, but there's something important we need to talk about." She pulled her hands away.

"We can talk about anything you want," he said. "As long as you mark October on your calendar. Admiral Tributs has granted me an extended leave. Our marriage and Yelena's baby. Two things to look forward to."

Sofya looked at him as he beamed. She gave a half-hearted smile. "It would be wonderful if you could be here for the baby. I'm already concerned about getting to the hospital." She gripped her hands tightly in her lap. "But first, Vasya, please, we have to talk. It's a serious matter." She scooted a few inches away so she could look him in the eye. "I've kept something from you. Something you had a right to know. For decades I couldn't take the chance that anyone would find out. I wanted to explain this spring while you were recuperating, but everything happened so fast, you were grieving Maksim, and then you were back in the Gulf. I should have told you even before that—right after Anna died. That night two Aprils ago when you came to see me at Philharmonia Hall and we sat at the kitchen table falling in love again. But I was afraid the truth would destroy our second chance."

"What are you talking about?" Vasili said. His face was open, questioning. He really had no idea about Aleksandr.

"Aleksandr is your son." She blurted out the words and watched his eyes move from bewilderment to shock. "When you and I ended our relationship, when Anna announced her pregnancy, I was pregnant too, but I didn't know it yet. I found out a few weeks later and I knew he was yours, but we'd already made a crushing decision. If I had told you, it wouldn't have changed things, but it would have made you even more miserable. And really, what choice did I have?"

Vasili cradled his head in his hands.

"So, I never told a soul. Andrei didn't know. Aleksandr doesn't know. It's been a horrible burden. I've been so alone. It's one of the reasons I don't have any close friends. I've always been afraid of what would happen if someone found out."

Sofya stopped talking. Vasili was hunched over, gazing down the slope to the river. They sat like that for a long time. Sofya waiting, Vasili silent and stone-faced.

"I have to go," he finally said and stood.

"Vasya, please. Tell me what you're thinking. Can't we talk?" She said quietly. "I'm so ashamed that I didn't tell you sooner. All these years I thought silence was best for you, to protect your marriage and your career, to save you from pain. Please, forgive me."

"Did you really keep the secret for me? Seems like you did it for yourself." His voice started soft and understanding, but soon became angry. "Didn't I deserve to know? Shouldn't I have had a say? I have a son I don't even know."

The pain on his face made her hurt. What could she say? How could she explain? But Vasili hardly paused. "Right now, I don't know if it was right or wrong or reasonable or not. I need to think, to sort out my feelings. And I don't want to say something I'll regret. I have loved you so deeply for so long, and now I feel . . . betrayed. It may be understandable that you kept it to yourself all these years. I could certainly imagine that as Aleksandr grew, it would have become harder and harder to disrupt his life, to disrupt all our lives. But Sofi." His voice accused her, although his eyes were filled with sadness. "We've been together for a year and a half now, loving each other, planning a future, and you said nothing. All this time."

Sofya sat on the bench long after he left, paralyzed by the mess her life had become. She had felt this pain before: the long-ago moment their relationship ended the first time. Sick to her stomach and despair spreading to her very bones when he told her Anna was pregnant. He spoke of duty and explained that the church wouldn't grant an annulment with a child involved. He said he loved her desperately, but even she wouldn't love him if he became the kind of man that could leave his pregnant wife and unborn child—a self-centered man. In that moment, her heart had shattered like a piece of glass, a thousand tiny shards skittering across the floor, disappearing into cracks and under doors so she'd never be able to put herself back together. Now, she pressed on her chest, where the jagged pain was, where her heart had shattered a second time.

TRUTH-TELLING

September 1942

L ENA HAD BEEN tiptoeing around her grandmother for weeks. All she knew was that her *babushka* and Vasili had some kind of falling out. She'd asked about him a few times, circling the unhappiness that filled the apartment, but her grandmother refused to talk about it.

Until one afternoon when she shooed the children into the bedroom and sat heavily at the kitchen table, wringing a hanky in her hands and telling Lena to come sit. The last time they had a serious talk was when Papa was sent to a labor camp. Lena felt a wave of fear-induced nausea.

"*Babusya*, please, what is it?"

Her grandmother must have seen the fear on her face and in her voice. "Oh, Sweetheart, it's not about Papa."

Lena's relief came out in a little hiccup of a cry, and she put her face in her hands. She'd expected something terrible. Since Pavel died, she thought she'd eventually lose everyone that mattered to her. The war was going badly. The blockade showed no signs of ending. Her days were still filled with the whine of aircraft, the frightful whistling of incoming shells, explosions, and the cries of the wounded. Just last week, tending her patch of vegetables in the Mikhailovsky Gardens, she'd mistaken the buzz of a bee for the drone of attacking aircraft, and started to waddle for shelter.

Food still consumed her. She dreamt of making dumplings with the Petrovs and woke crying, seeing Mrs. Petrov's face so clearly it seemed she must still be alive. She missed Tanya and worried about her and her siblings. Was she eating steaming bowls of borscht with large dollops of sour cream floating on the surface? Obsessed with oranges, Lena wondered if she'd ever taste one again. She used to pull the segments apart and examine the tiny juice-filled membranes as she ate them. If she closed her eyes, she could smell them, bright and sweet.

Lena looked up and wiped her eyes. "Sorry. I guess it's just the baby."

"No need to apologize. I'm sorry I frightened you."

And then her grandmother told her how she and Vasili had fallen in love decades earlier and had a secret relationship. She talked about how they'd bonded over books and music and shared an intense interest in the world. They really were meant to be together, she explained, but were already married to others. Just when they formulated a plan to annul their marriages, his wife announced she was pregnant. So, they sacrificed happiness and love for loyalty and duty and agreed never to see each other again.

Her grandmother held her gaze. "I didn't know it yet, but I was pregnant too. That baby was your papa." She looked down. "Vasili is his father. Your grandfather."

For a long moment, Lena absorbed the news. Having a love affair seemed out of character for her grandmother, who'd never been frivolous or self-centered. She always put others first. But she did have an emotional streak—Lena had seen her perform enough times to know how music moved her. Perhaps she and Admiral Vasili shared that. Or perhaps she didn't know her *babushka* as well as she thought.

"I'm sorry I kept this from you," her grandmother continued. "I didn't trust anyone. A lifetime of worry. For years I was certain someone would be hurt if I told the truth: your grandpa Andrei, your papa, Vasili, Anna. So I kept it to myself."

She gazed at her grandmother. So earnest, so generous, so devoted to her family and her music. Of course she would lie to protect family. Somehow, after all they'd been through, this secret didn't seem all that important. The trials and deprivations of the last year were so much bigger. The siege had distilled life down to food, but also love and family. Nothing else mattered. Certainly not some secret her grandmother had kept to protect herself and her unborn child.

"Why would I judge you? I mean, look at me," Lena said, holding her tummy. "Pregnant, unmarried. Who am I to be disappointed in something you did decades ago? Besides, maybe it's a bit strange, but I'm happy he's my grandfather."

Her grandma turned to her. "You really did like him from the start, didn't you?"

Lena nodded. "I don't feel upset, I feel . . . lucky." Her grandmother squeezed her hand. Swallowing hard, Lena continued. "It's one of the few times since April that I've felt glad. And there's something special about you two, when I see you together it makes me happy. Hopeful."

"Lenochka, I love you very much. You're the heart of my heart. Thank you for forgiving me. But it seems that we're not going to be together, Vasili and I. We talked about getting married in a couple of weeks, around your due date, but I've gotten no word. Nothing since the day after the concert when he proposed and I told him about your papa. I've written three times. He hasn't answered."

"He's hurt," Lena said.

Her *babushka* nodded. "I think it's more than that. I think I've lost him." She started to cry. "I'm trying to be strong. I love him so much. For my entire life it seems."

"He loves you too. He just needs time. He'll come around."

Her grandmother sniffed and wiped at her eyes. Lena got her a glass of water, catching sight of the dusky sky, a palette of pinks and reds that gave Leningrad a bit of its former beauty. Lena visualized her grandmother as a young woman. In love with a man other than her husband. Then pregnant by him. She didn't know whether to admire her grandmother for trying to follow her heart, or to be critical of her cheating. Life could certainly be odd. Besides, did anyone tell the truth? Silence was its own kind of protection in a place where the truth meant little and could easily be used against you. It was no wonder her grandmother lied.

"You know I almost told him many times. I decided to wait until we'd been together a few months, but then the war came and I couldn't bear to part from him with such news. And then in the spring when he was recuperating, I wanted to tell him but he was grieving Maksim and it seemed cruel to tell him he had another son." She sighed. "Plus, I didn't want to spoil those weeks together. It was such a special time. When I finally told him last month, he was angry and disappointed. He seemed so cold. He didn't care how broken-hearted or how trapped I was all those years."

Lena put her arms around her grandmother and pulled her tight. "Give him time. He loves you very much. That kind of love doesn't just disappear." Her voice trailed off. Both women knew how beautiful and terrible love could be. Lena took her hand and squeezed it hard. They were quiet for a few moments until she said, "So, Papa doesn't know."

"Someday," her grandmother said.

A weighty word. Lena had thought she and Pavel would have their someday. What about Papa? Would someday come for him? People were whispering that Stalingrad was the last chance to defeat the Germans. He was there.

"There's just one more thing I want to tell you." Her grandmother paused. "I loved your grandfather Andrei very much. In spite of what I did, in spite of loving Vasili, with time we had a good marriage."

Lena patted her grandmother's arm. "I know."

ALEKSANDR PAVELOVICH ANTONOV

October 1942

WHEN THE TIME came, they dropped the youngsters with a family from school and started for the tram. Sofya was certain Yelena would be in labor many hours. First babies always took their time. The hospital was far, all the way across central Leningrad near the shipyards—a good military hospital, more reliable and better equipped than others closer to home. Vasili had made the arrangements long before they had fallen out but now wasn't around to get a car. Yelena had bravely agreed to take a tram part of the way, but they still faced a walk that for a woman in labor seemed a ridiculous distance.

They slowly made their way from the last tram stop, Sofya holding her granddaughter's arm, halting for every contraction. Yelena settled into a four-bed room in a wing filled with recovering soldiers. The other beds would remain empty unless female patients arrived or the hospital was over capacity. Sofya relaxed.

Her granddaughter labored steadily through the night, the contractions coming harder and faster in the early morning. A nurse checked on her now and then. They hadn't yet seen a doctor.

Yelena called out. "It feels different somehow. I think I have to push."

Sofya jumped up and stuck her head into the hall calling for the nurse. Then she checked between Yelena's legs. "Oh, yes, there's the head. Baby's almost here." She glanced at the door. Where was that damn nurse? When she checked again, the baby's head had fully crowned. Only a couple more contractions now. She fixed her eyes on her granddaughter. "When you have a contraction, push with it. Bear down and relax between."

The infant came into the world without any help from nurses or doctors or Sofya for that matter. All she did was take the only clean towel she could find and grab him as he slid out. She wiped him off while he cried good and loud.

Sofya held the baby and looked at her granddaughter. "He's perfect," she said.

"A boy," Yelena said. "Pavel's boy." She smiled though her cheeks were covered with tears. "Let me," she said, reaching.

"I've got to cut the cord first." Sofya looked around for the tray of equipment and recognized the clamps. She could do this. She knew the clamps should be attached close to the baby, and the cord cut in between. Her hands shook as she put the first clamp just above where the cord entered the infant. Finally, a nurse strolled through the door.

"Well, well, look at this. That was quick." She turned to Sofya. "I'll do that." In a moment she attached the second clamp and cut the cord, finished cleaning the baby and then, unable to put her hands on another clean towel, pulled a tan cotton hospital gown out of a cupboard and expertly wrapped him. Sofya thought the nurse was curiously adept since they were in a military hospital without a proper maternity ward. When the nurse handed the warm bundle to Yelena, the baby stopped crying and gazed at his mother. The nurse turned for the afterbirth. After waiting several minutes, she pulled gently on the umbilical cord. "The placenta hasn't delivered, but I'm certain it will soon. Just keep an eye out." She pulled again on the umbilical cord trying to encourage the placenta to detach and motioned to a small metal pan with which Sofya understood she should catch the placenta.

Patting Yelena, the nurse said. "The doctor is on his way, but we've had several emergencies. I'll take your blood pressure and then I'm needed elsewhere."

She took Sofya aside. "Her blood pressure is lower than it should be. Watch her closely. The doctor will be here in a few minutes."

Moments after the nurse left, the placenta slid out. Relieved, she turned to her granddaughter, trying to show her how to get the baby to latch onto the breast. Several minutes later, Yelena complained that she was wet. "Could I be peeing?" she said. "Maybe I need to go to the bathroom."

"Let's wait for the doctor to check you."

Sofya lifted her granddaughter's hospital gown and pulled the old towel from underneath. It was heavy with bright red blood. She took her cue from the nurse and slid a folded hospital gown in its place.

"There's some blood here," she said as casually as possible, while Yelena remained focused on the baby. "Let me get the doctor. I'll be right back." She swallowed hard, trying not to panic although she knew something was gravely wrong. The nurse was at the station.

"My granddaughter's bleeding," Sofya said.

"Well, she just had a baby."

"No, no. This is something different. There's a lot of blood. A steady flow."

The nurse moved quickly to check on Yelena and then disappeared to get the doctor. In her swift movements and silence, Sofya saw fear. The doctor came right away, a youngish man. He nodded at Sofya as he entered Yelena's room.

"I'm Doctor Kiprensky." he said and pulled a stool to the end of the bed. He examined the afterbirth in the pan. He palpitated Yelena's abdomen, and examined between her legs. Sofya could see the steady trickle already darkening the cotton fabric.

The doctor pulled Sofya outside. "I suspect a piece of the placenta is still attached. See here," he pointed to a ragged spot along one edge of the placenta in the pan. "Her body is continuing to support it, hence the blood. We'll need to remove the remaining tissue. And quickly too. Are there healthy family members nearby? We need blood."

"I don't understand," Sofya said. "This is a hospital. Don't you have blood?"

"Not much since the siege began. Some plasma through the Red Cross now and then, but even our supplies of normal saline are critically low. We can't keep up with our soldiers' needs."

"She can have mine."

"My dear woman, look at you, tiny and frail. You don't have blood to spare. We can't take more than one unit from you. Even that isn't a good idea. Is there no one else?"

Sofya hesitated. Vasili. "Yes, her grandfather, but he's on Kronstadt."

"What's his physical condition?"

"Good. He's tall, big, fairly healthy. He's an Admiral."

"You must send a telegram immediately. The situation is grave. We only have a few hours." He turned to the nurse. "Escort her to the communication center. After she sends the telegram, bring her back and take her blood. One unit only. Bring it to operating theater two. Quick now, both of you."

Yelena hemorrhaging in childbirth. Needs your blood. Not much time.

In a daze, Sofya listened to the doctor explain that the surgery was successful. They stopped the bleeding. Then he took her arm and led her to a chair.

"I'm sorry, Comrade. She's already lost four or five units of blood, almost half her total volume. We found one last bag of frozen Red Cross plasma which will reduce the strain on her heart. It will give her some extra time. But her body is diminished from a year under siege. Without sufficient blood, the demand on her weakened organs is too much. Her blood pressure is too low. Her body is already shutting down. I am so very sorry. You need to prepare yourself."

Prepare herself? Nothing could prepare her. Nothing could help her with this. Nothing else mattered. Yelena was everything. Oh, God, if only she'd told Vasili earlier. He'd have sorted through his feelings and he'd be in Leningrad. On leave. They'd have gotten married. They'd both be here, helping Yelena, watching their great-grandchild come into the world. Instead, she'd lost Vasili, and now Lenochka was dying before her very eyes.

Sofya jumped up and grabbed the doctor's shoulders. "No. She cannot die. She's all I have. Please, please, I beg of you. Take another unit from me. My life's nothing without her."

Dr. Kiprensky sighed and Sofya saw the sadness and defeat on his face. Dark circles under his eyes, his skin sallow. He'd aged a decade in a few hours.

"Comrade Karavayeva, if I take more from you, then you both may die. One unit is not enough to ensure your granddaughter's recovery. But, if you promise to rest now, drink plenty of fluids, I will reconsider taking another unit tomorrow should she hold on." He touched her shoulder and then hurried to the next crisis.

Perhaps the telegram—marked urgent and all—hadn't reached Vasili. He would come if he'd received it. Maybe he was in the middle of a battle, or worse. There were always worse possibilities. Vasili dead. Sasha, now in the death grip that was Stalingrad, probably dead too. Yelena slipping away. Her entire family gone.

When Yelena first woke from the surgery, she was lucid which surprised Sofya. "This is the way it's supposed to be. I'm going to be with Pavel," she said, clear-eyed and focused. "I'm not afraid. He's waiting for me. I'm so tired."

The minutes ticked past as her Lenochka faded. There were no more prayers to say. She'd begged and pleaded for God to save her granddaughter, offered Him her life instead, but Yelena's blood pressure refused to improve. Her chest hardly rose with brief, shallow breaths. Sofya could see her let go of the struggle, unable to fight any more. Her eyes fluttered open again. "My baby," Yelena whispered. "Aleksandr Pavelovich Antonov. It's what I want. Teach him about his papa." When she closed her eyes, Sofya knew it was for the last time.

She held her granddaughter's hand, her tears spilling. "Hang on, Sweetheart, please. Don't leave me. Don't leave your beautiful baby," she whispered. "Help is on the way."

The room was still. She could feel the rhythmic pulse in Yelena's wrist, so very slow. She watched her every breath, willing her to find some strength. Yelena couldn't have survived the last year only to die now.

Sofya lost all sense of time, urging Yelena to fight, thankful for every breath she took. Her despair grew until the door unexpectedly swung open and the doctor strode in, the nurse behind him carrying a miracle—a bag of dark crimson blood. Sofya struggled with her disbelief as they attached it to the intravenous drip in Yelena's arm.

"We'll get this first bag into her quickly," the doctor said, turning the drip as high as it would go, a drop nearly every second. "It should stabilize her. You understand she's still not out of the woods, but there's hope." Some of the strain seemed gone from his face. "Admiral Antonov is donating a second unit right now. We may take a third from him late tomorrow or the day after, so he's confined to bed and drinking plenty of fluids. He's just down the hall, and anxious to see his family. Those were his words." The doctor hesitated. "Also, he asked me to beg your forgiveness on his behalf. Something about being a damn foolish idiot."

Sofya started down the hall, then paused as her vision blurred, flashes appearing. She put a hand against the wall to steady herself and bent over, slipping to the floor, trying to stop the blackness now edging her vision. She'd forgotten they'd taken her blood. They warned her not to stand or move quickly. She sat there, waiting to return to normal, taking long, slow, deep breaths. After a minute or two she stood and continued to Vasili's room. A nurse had the second unit of blood on a tray and nodded as she left.

"Vasya." Her voice cracked.

"Oh, Sofi, I am so sorry," he started.

She sat on the bed and placed two fingers on his lips. "Shhh. If I had trusted you, this wouldn't have happened. It was my fear and stupidity that put Yelena's life in danger. You were right, I should have told you before the war started, the moment it became clear we still cared for each other. Instead, I kept it from you all this time. I am so sorry and ashamed. I've become untrusting and fearful. It's no way to live."

He kissed her fingers and took them off his mouth. "My turn?"

She nodded.

"That's all true, Sofi. But, if I hadn't been so pig-headed, if I had done the right thing and forgiven you the moment you told me, instead of focusing on my hurt, Yelena would have had both of us here, and her life wouldn't be in danger." A small version of his slightly crooked grin broke some of the tension. "Plus, we would have had a great wedding story."

Relief surged in her, and she couldn't help but encourage him. "The marriage registration bureau is just down the street."

"I hope that means you forgive me." He sighed.

Lena's nurse entered with a calm, almost beatific look on her face. "I wanted you to know right away. Your granddaughter's blood pressure has already risen eight points. She's responding very well."

Sofya couldn't speak. If she did, the relief would overwhelm her. She nodded at the nurse who was already out the door and turned back to Vasili.

She gazed into his eyes, his own emotions visible there, then leaned down to place a brief kiss on his lips. Saying nothing, she rested her head on his chest and drew a deep breath, letting go of some of her fear and loneliness, drawing strength from him, calmed by the soothing thump, swish of his heart.

EPILOGUE
Summer 1945

BERLIN REMINDED MAJOR Karavayev of Stalingrad. The German capital was larger, but the amount of destruction took him back to the elbow of the Volga. Both cities had been leveled, although more civilians remained in Berlin. Destitute, homeless, former citizens of the Reich hid in the rubble, scrabbling in the debris, searching for food, trying to escape the wrath of their occupiers.

Awash with relief and revenge, many Red Army soldiers inflicted their rage on the city's inhabitants, especially the women. But for Aleksandr, exacting retribution was not the way to end the war. He and his closest comrades drank instead. They toasted Stalin (reluctantly) and General Zhukov (wholeheartedly). They raised glasses over and over again to Mother Russia, her noble citizens and their military comrades—those who'd fallen as well as those who survived. Lastly, but with genuine longing, they drank to their families. Aleksandr soon realized that permanent inebriation wasn't the answer either. He needed to see his family. He needed to go home.

Weeks later, he traversed the scarred and blackened landscape of the Soviet Union in a caravan of tanks and trucks snaking eastward out of Germany that had started out well enough. Rail lines west of Moscow needed repair and petrol supplies were unpredictable. Many soldiers struggled to find transportation home. Seniority meant Aleksandr had a truck to ride in, but when he fell ill somewhere south of Minsk, he ordered the driver to carry as many as possible and go on without him. They dropped him in a town hoping for a hospital, but, like everything else of value, it had been destroyed. They left him, feverish and incoherent, with an old *babushka* who nursed him back to health with her wild mushroom soup, porridge and even her few precious eggs. Sometimes she called him Vanya, her eldest son's name. She wept when he left.

As he drew close to Moscow, he learned bits and pieces about the years of struggle in his hometown. How Hitler starved the city. The evacuations, the Road of Life, the bombings, the horror of that first winter. In public, no one talked about numbers. The total dead in Leningrad was a whisper in the wind. Hundreds of thousands of civilians had perished. A monstrous kind of battlefield.

All he knew for certain was that his daughter and mother had survived. Shortly after the surrender, one of Yelena's letters had caught up with him. Katya was alive too, but in Moscow. He was glad she'd made it, but also glad he wouldn't have to face her right away. His reaction to the news about Katya told him more about himself than he wanted to admit. He hadn't gotten a single letter from her in four and a half years and yet deep inside he felt it. A tiny flame still burned.

Now he was on the overnight train to Leningrad, the last leg of his journey. All night long, the steady clack-clack of the train wheels soothed him as he slumbered. After four years of sleeping in trenches, tanks, fields, peasant huts and destroyed buildings, the train was heaven. Now, full from a breakfast of tea and fresh buttered bread, he stood on the swaying platform between cars, braced against the railing, smoking a cigarette as the world crept past, slower and slower as they entered Leningrad's suburbs.

When he recognized the central district, he tossed what was left of his cigarette and returned to his seat. Energy and excitement filled the car. Passengers, mostly soldiers, but also some displaced civilians, gathered their belongings and lined up for the exit.

Aleksandr remained in his seat until the last soldier dragged an enormous duffel out of the carriage. Shouts of homecoming filtered into the empty car and he drank in the scene out his window. Embraces everywhere: wives kissing their husbands, mothers hugging their sons, children shyly greeting the fathers they barely remembered.

A trainman inspecting the now empty cars stopped beside him. "Comrade? Are you all right?"

"*Konechno.* Of course. I'm alive, aren't I," Aleksandr said, one corner of his mouth turning up in a sardonic grin. "Just lost in my thoughts." He didn't mention that he was afraid. Afraid no one would be on the platform waiting for him. Afraid he might not recognize his daughter, or even his mother, should they be there. Afraid he would be a stranger to them. It had been that long and he had changed that much.

≈ ≈

Sofya and Lena had been meeting the early morning train from Moscow for several weeks, ever since receiving the telegram that their beloved son and father was returning home. Arm in arm they walked to the station first thing every day, leaving Vasili to watch the children for an hour or so. They could be a handful, but he never seemed to mind. And it only made sense that the two women would go together. That they were close showed in every look and word, every gesture and touch. They were bonded in a way which only other survivors of the siege could understand—their very souls welded together during the terrible struggle.

They did the same thing every day. Took a position near the end of the platform closest to the station so they could examine each person that disembarked. After the initial rush, the crowd thinned and the hum of voices faded. In their disappointment, Lena would put a supportive arm around her grandmother.

❧ ❧

Aleks remained in the train until the platform cleared. Rucksack over one shoulder, he stepped down, adjusting his simple khaki cloth *pilotka*, a lightweight hat that provided little protection against the summer sun. He looked around. Just a few stragglers. Toward the end of the platform, a woman had her arm around a petite, silver-haired lady, comforting her. The older woman's head was bowed, like she'd received bad news, and as he drew near, he looked closer. The younger woman's face was turned away from him, focused on the old woman. Her hair was pulled into a tight bun, so unlike the way his Lenochka used to wear hers. And the elderly *babushka* looked much smaller and older than his mother, who had black, not grey hair. He watched for a gesture, a smile, a voice he might recognize. But they hardly noticed him as he passed by. The younger woman was gently wiping the old woman's tears.

At the end of the platform, something made him stop. When he turned, the two women were shuffling toward him, still intent upon each other. The younger one spoke. "Don't worry, he'll be here. One day soon."

He stared at them. The voice was hers. She returned his gaze, surprise and recognition and joy in her expression. Her blue eyes so like his own. The three of them hesitated for a few seconds, weighed down by unbelief, until Aleksandr whispered their names like a final reverential entreaty.

ACKNOWLEDGEMENTS

WITHOUT THE WORK of talented scholars and novelists that went before me, this book would not be possible. They paved the way for my story. A detailed bibliography can be found on my website: www.suzanneparrywrites.com.

Numerous individuals aided me in this project. Chief among those is Laurie Davis. I benefited in a multitude of ways from her early careful readings and detailed comments. It's no exaggeration to say Laurie helped me learn how to write and I'm deeply grateful. Thanks also to Natalie Hirt who read many, many chapters and provided startling spot-on feedback, always with a kind word of support or encouragement. And to author, developmental editor, and teacher extraordinaire, Suzy Vitello, who advised and challenged, always knowing what would work or what was needed. Without a doubt this novel is better for her efforts.

My deep gratitude:

To Roman, my guide in St. Petersburg, Russia, who graciously shared his extensive knowledge of Kronstadt, St. Petersburg, and the Siege of Leningrad. His grandmother was a siege survivor and through him I was exposed to the unique perspective of a local.

To my early readers—Natina Gilbert, Alex Berg, and Bonnie Mae Ward—whose feedback improved the novel and kept me moving forward.

To daughter Julia, whose suggestions enhanced the story in many small and several not so small ways. And to son Brad, for his advice on medical matters.

To copy editor and graphic artist, Sophie Hale-Brown, who helped polish the novel and did the fantastic map as well.

To publisher Brooke Warner, project manager Samantha Strom, and cover design guru Julie Metz, who together shepherded my novel to publication. And also to my outstanding publicists, Crystal Patriarche, Tabitha Bailey, and Hanna Lindsley.

Some dear friends gave me the priceless gift of their enthusiasm over the years of this endeavor. Love and thanks to Melissa, Laura, Charmine, Joanne, Kathy, Sallie, Erin, and Cindy. Thanks also to the wonderful women in my book group and countless other friends who shared their support by simply asking, "How's the book coming?" You all helped get me to the finish line.

When I embarked on this project, my stepfather, E. R. Baxter III, environmentalist, author, poet, and retired creative writing professor, provided me the sage advice to "write a page a day; in a year you'll have a first draft." For that suggestion, and many, many other bits of wisdom and unflagging encouragement, I am deeply grateful.

Lastly, in addition to their love, my children, Lindsey, Brad, Stephen, Julia, and son-in-law, David, provided support, interest, and zeal through all phases of this project. Every writer needs that. I'm thankful for you every day.

ABOUT THE AUTHOR

© Julia Eckelmann

Aformer European security specialist, Suzanne Parry now writes historical fiction about the Soviet Union. She studied Russian in Moscow and worked at the Pentagon where she helped negotiate the first security agreement of the Gorbachev era—the Conference on Disarmament in Europe. To learn more visit: www.suzanneparrywrites.com.

SELECTED TITLES FROM SHE WRITES PRESS

She Writes Press is an independent publishing company founded to serve women writers everywhere. Visit us at www.shewritespress.com.

Tasa's Song by Linda Kass. $16.95, 978-1-63152-064-8
Caught in the gathering storm of World War II, aspiring Jewish violinist Tasa Rosinski finds herself swept away from her peaceful, rural village in eastern Poland. As her secure world unravels, she relies upon her music and memories to keep her spirit alive.

This Is How It Begins by Joan Dempsey. $16.95, 978-1-63152-308-3
When eighty-five-year-old art professor Ludka Zeilonka's gay grandson, Tommy, is fired over concerns that he's silencing Christian kids in the classroom, she is drawn into the political firestorm—and as both sides battle to preserve their respective rights to free speech, the hatred on display raises the specter of her WWII past.

All the Light There Was by Nancy Kricorian. $16.95, 978-1-63152-905-4
A lyrical, finely wrought tale of loyalty, love, and the many faces of resistance, told from the perspective of an Armenian girl living in Paris during the Nazi occupation of the 1940s.

An Address in Amsterdam by Mary Dingee Fillmore
$16.95, 978-1-63152-133-1
After facing relentless danger and escalating raids for 18 months, Rachel Klein—a well-behaved young Jewish woman who transformed herself into a courier for the underground when the Nazis invaded her country—persuades her parents to hide with her in a dank basement, where much is revealed.

Portrait of a Woman in White by Susan Winkler. $16.95, 978-1-93831-483-4
When the Nazis steal a Matisse portrait from the eccentric, art-loving Rosenswigs, the Parisian family is thrust into the tumult of war and separation, their fates intertwined with that of their beloved portrait.

The Sweetness by Sande Boritz Berger. $16.95, 978-1-63152-907-8
A compelling and powerful story of two girls—cousins living on separate continents—whose strikingly different lives are forever changed when the Nazis invade Vilna, Lithuania.